The Green-Eyed Doll
By
Jerrie Alexander

The Green-Eyed Doll

This is a work of fiction. Names, characters, places, and incidents are either the product of the author's imagination or are used fictitiously, and the resemblance to actual persons living or dead, business establishments, events, or locales is entirely coincidental and not intended by the author.

This novel was previously published in 2012 through The Wild Rose Press. However, the rights reverted to me, allowing me to update the storyline.

Chapter One

Leave it to Mama to die in the middle of the hottest Texas summer on record. He kicked the dust off his boots and stepped inside the stifling, cramped trailer for the first time in eleven years. He'd drop off a dress and some flowers at the funeral home. Then he was done. The state could kiss his ass if they thought he'd spend a dime to bury her.

He glanced around the familiar hellhole, and fourteen years of beatings and abuse boiled up from his belly. One of his earliest memories was cowering inside her closet, trying to be quiet. She used to whip his bare back with a straightened wire hanger if he so much as grunted while she entertained a guest.

"Guest my ass." His voice broke the eerie silence. "Mama fucked anybody with a dick and a dollar."

He'd learned to mind real good. He used to crawl in that dark closet, hunker down, and peer through a small crack between the doorframe and the wall. There, up on the top shelf, the green-eyed doll. She was the only clean, pure thing in the trailer. He'd lock his gaze on her porcelain face and pretend she was real. Because if she were real, she'd never let anybody whip him again. If she were real, she'd love him. If she were real, he wouldn't hear Mama's headboard banging against the wall.

Nobody messed with Mama's stuff without paying one hell of a penalty. Once, he'd taken the doll down to hold her. Mama caught him—and called him a pervert. She'd left long, painful welts across his bare back and legs with that hanger. What'd she think he was gonna do, fuck the damn thing?

Mama taught him to take what he wanted, and prison taught him how to do it. He walked down the hall to the bedroom. Well, the doll belonged to him now.

Sweat broke and ran down his face while he stared at the empty shelf. Rage released the hornets. The buzzing in his head grew louder and louder. He clamped both hands over his ears. The one shred of innocence in this dump was gone.

A straightened-out wire hanger hung from a nail next to the shelf. A cruel message from the dead.

Get your own doll.

****

Catherine McCoy's old Ford sputtered up to the red light and shuddered to a stop. She stabbed her hand through her hair while scanning the small town in front of her. How had she let herself run short of money? One-hundred-sixty-nine dollars and one lonely credit card—for emergency use only—kept her from being stone-cold broke.

She had to find work. Fast. The light turned green, and Catherine drove into Butte Crest, Texas. Population 19,016. The trip through town took less than ten minutes. At that time, her hopes of finding a job fell. She circled the quaint square with its antique shops and boutiques, then drove past a couple of gas stations, a few cafés, lots of churches with tall steeples pointing toward heaven, and one dance hall on the outskirts named Saddleback Inn. No help wanted signs beckoned. She made a U-turn at a traffic light to circle around for a second look.

The scream of a siren and the sight of colored lights flashing behind her sent tremors through her chest. The last thing she needed was a cop getting near her. She pulled over in front of a funeral home, loosened her white-knuckled grip on the steering wheel, and fished out her wallet.

She dropped her gaze to the outside mirror and waited. The cruiser's door opened, and a pair of dark brown western boots hit the gravel. They belonged to a set of long legs wearing khaki uniform pants. A matching shirt covered broad shoulders. He adjusted his aviator sunglasses, retrieved a white western hat, and settled it over jet-black hair.

Catherine's heart rate quickened while she rolled down the window. She reminded herself she had nothing to fear and greeted him with her best fake smile.

"Hello, officer. Is there a problem?" She passed him her license and proof of insurance without waiting for him to ask. She leaned back in the seat, proud her hand hadn't trembled.

"Sheriff Ballard." He cocked his head slightly and tipped his hat.

She waited silently while he studied her identification. She'd legally changed her name back to McCoy before leaving Oklahoma and starting her trek across Texas. Catherine had started life over, and getting rid of Andrew Randall's name had been a big step.

"Ma'am. Did you hear me?"

Catherine turned her attention to the man standing beside her car. The sheriff's whiskey-toned drawl reverberated with impatience. He leaned down, removed his sunglasses, and squinted in the bright sunlight. Eyes as blue as the Texas sky and cold as Antarctica bore down on her. Catherine tightened her grip on her composure. She'd learned her lesson when dealing with the law. The less you say, the better.

"Sorry. Wha...What did you say?" Had she stuttered? Her tongue and brain refused to coordinate. She struggled against overreacting.

"For starters, you made an illegal U-turn. Not to mention, the emission control system on your vehicle needs attention. I almost choked walking up behind you."

"I didn't see a sign." No need to debate his choking comment.

"It's hanging from the light, in plain sight." He slid his sunglasses back on, moved away a few steps, and pulled a ticket book from his hip pocket.

She'd be broke if she had to pay a traffic fine. Maybe, if she looked him in the eye, he'd listen to reason. Armed with a plan and full of determination, she got out. A gust of wind jerked the car door out of her grasp. It swung out fast and clipped the sheriff, knocking him off balance.

"What the hell?" His sunglasses went flying when he staggered backward a step before regaining his footing. "Are you trying to get arrested?"

One word slammed into her brain...arrested? Not again. Never again. "Oh, my God. I'm sorry. I only wanted to talk to you."

"Ma'am, get back inside your vehicle. Please." Great, she'd made matters worse by trying to reason with him. She settled in her seat and sighed. The sheriff wore a white hat, but he was no John Wayne.

"No, ma'am." His eyes narrowed to slits. "I'm not John Wayne."

Crap. Had she said that out loud? Catherine closed her mouth. His stormy eyes grew darker. In the middle of a heat wave, she shivered from the chill.

The sheriff retrieved his broken sunglasses. One black eyebrow twitched when the earpiece came off in his hand. She was sure to get that ticket.

"Your car's packed." He tilted his head toward the backseat. "You moving to town?"

"Moving isn't against the law, is it?"

"No, ma'am. Not that I'm aware of."

Did he almost grin? "Here's the truth. I hadn't planned on staying, but I'm running short on cash. I need to find a job. When I've saved enough money, I'll move on."

She swallowed hard, waiting as he stared at her. He closed the citation book, then handed her identification back.

"No ticket?" She relaxed and smiled for the first time.

"Not today. Look, if you're serious about finding a job, I know of one here in town." He paused. "Make that two." A frown crossed his face. "The second one's not a good choice."

"What are they?"

"The funeral home you're parked in front of needs office help, and the local bar—which in my opinion is not a good idea—needs a waitress. As far as I've heard, Butte Crest has nothing else to offer."

The tension in her neck eased. "I appreciate your help."

"No problem. Drive safely."

Catherine checked her rearview mirror before easing her car onto the road. The handsome sheriff had walked off the pavement and now stood in the ditch. Sheesh. Did he think she would run over him?

****

Matt checked his messages and then radioed his dispatcher that he was back in service.

"Took you long enough," Sue grumbled. "I received a call from Tanya Perry over in Curry. Her best friend, Julia Drummond, is missing. They'd agreed to meet for supper last night. Julia never showed."

"Go on." His gut clenched. He never ignored his gut.

"Julia owns a flower shop on Main. Didn't open this morning. You want to wait twenty-four hours?"

"No need to wait. We'll check it out. Tell Jake I'll meet him at the florist shop. Run a background on her and start a file. Toss the info on my desk if I'm not back before you leave."

"There's no room on your desk." Her surly tone held a hint of laughter.

"Oh. When you finish with the Drummond woman, run this license num...." He stopped. Besides personal curiosity, he had no reason to use the system to check out the new woman in town. That kind of unethical behavior sounded like something his Dad would've done. Matt wanted none of it.

"You gonna give me a number?"

"No. Never mind." Matt pulled onto the highway and headed toward the small town of Curry.

His mind drifted to the newcomer in town. Her driver's license picture hadn't done her justice. He would've used something more definitive than the word red to describe her hair. Shoulder length, her curly locks brought to mind a wildfire out of control. Bright green eyes had looked directly into his. Judging from the sparks shooting from her gaze, the lady had a temper to go with the hair. His cop's instinct had perked up when she broke contact with his gaze.

Yep. A redheaded puzzle had arrived in his town. She piqued his curiosity. He kicked the cruiser up a notch and set the air conditioner on high, pushing the image of those bright green eyes from his mind.

Concentrate on the missing woman.

****

Catherine's hands still shook from her visit with the sheriff when she parked in front of the Saddleback bar. She ran a brush through her hair while convincing herself that any job would be better than the funeral home.

The outside of the bar wasn't much to look at—a huge, square, sheet metal building with few windows. Three pickups, all with oversized tires, and one car sat on a large gravel lot. A giant neon saddle complete with rider topped the sign out front advertising a weekly pool tournament and a band on the weekends. The absence of a help wanted sign worried her. This had to be the right place. Catherine got out, straightened her shoulders, and went inside. The odor of stale beer and cigarettes slammed into her senses. The door closed and plunged her into darkness.

"Welcome. Come on in here." The raspy voice sounded like it might be female. "Walk straight ahead a few steps. Your eyes will adjust."

Catherine made her way toward the voice, and her vision became acclimated within seconds. The place wasn't as dark as her first impression. Along the back wall hung dozens of beer signs, illuminating a long, shiny, wooden bar lined with chrome stools. Tables and chairs were tucked around a small stage. A square dance floor barely left room for four pool tables.

"What'll you have?" The sandpaper voice belonged to the woman behind the bar.

"Coke, please." Catherine sat on a barstool. "The sheriff mentioned a job opening. Who do I see about applying?"

"That would be me. Name's Marty Carlton. I own the place." She popped the top and then pushed the canned drink to Catherine. "So you met our hotter-n-hell new sheriff?"

"He's new?" She wiped her sweaty palm on her pants and extended her hand.

Marty reached across the bar, her grip was strong and firm. Hard to guess her age in the dim lights, but Catherine estimated Marty to be in her mid-forties.

"New to us. Couldn't be much more than a year." Marty chuckled to herself. "He caused a mighty stir with the women when he first hit town."

"I'm sure." Catherine shifted on the barstool. "I'm Catherine McCoy. About the job?"

One of the men playing pool interrupted when he yelled out an order.

"Hang on a second." Marty pulled a couple of beers from the cooler and delivered them, taking a few minutes to chat. Her long, blonde ponytail tied with a pink ribbon swung from side to side, keeping time with the sway of her hips. Her skintight jeans and a two-sizes-too-small, pink tank top revealed way more cleavage than Catherine would be comfortable showing.

One of the customers followed Marty back to the counter.

"Be right back with you, Catherine. Gotta make change for the pool table." Marty opened the register, put a bill in the tray, and counted out a handful of coins.

The man took his money, winked at Catherine, then sauntered away.

"I think he was flirting."

"He's a guy ain't he?" Marty laughed. "The tighter a waitress wears her jeans, the bigger her tips."

Catherine understood the concept. "About the job?"

"You got experience?"

"No. But I learn fast."

The woman's eyes narrowed. "You're not local. Where are you from?"

"Born and raised in Oklahoma." Chills skittered across Catherine's skin. She'd perfected the art of measuring her words without appearing to be evasive. Prevented her from answering too many personal questions.

"Hmm." Marty's head moved back slightly. "What brought you to town?"

"I'm just passing through and need to work a few months."

Marty came around the bar and sat next to Catherine. Closer and in better light, Marty's heavy makeup and long, false eyelashes didn't hide the lines around her mouth and the crow's feet at the corner of her eyes. Catherine's estimate of Marty's age rose to at least fifty. Her pale blue eyes told a story of their own. Underneath the paint and powder, she had an air of sadness about her.

"Honey." Marty's voice grew louder when the jukebox blared with an old Trace Atkins song. "If you're running from something or somebody, here may not be a good place for you. I don't need the trouble."

"I'm not wanted if that's what you mean. There's no crazy husband or boyfriend stalking me." She pushed bad memories away. "I'm a hard worker and need a job. Truthfully, I need the money."

"Can't say I've ever met a woman who's 'just' passing through." Marty pursed her lips and sucked air through the narrow space between her front teeth. "There's more you ain't telling."

Piercing blue eyes made Catherine squirm.

"You've met one now. It's the same sad story you've probably been told a million times."

"Cheating husband?"

"Dead husband." The shock on Marty's face quickly morphed to pity, which was the last thing Catherine wanted.

She should've lied. Damn, she was sick of untruths.

"Well, I don't rightly know what to say."

"Sorry. I shouldn't have blurted that out."

"Couldn't have been a happy marriage. I've been a bartender long enough to know sorrow when I see it. Or the absence of."

The air in the room thinned. Panic tightened her chest. This job couldn't get away from her. "Long story short, we fell in love in college. I dropped out and worked while he finished law school. A few years after he passed the bar and signed on at his family's high-profile law firm, he decided I was beneath him. I didn't measure up to his intellectual level and lifestyle."

Marty sat quietly.

Catherine gripped the can, hoping Marty wouldn't pry and ask how Catherine's husband had died. The bar was her only hope. The Final Touch Funeral Home was out. She'd just now added working around dead people to her *Never* list.

"You own a pair of boots?"

"Sure do," Catherine answered, flashing her best smile.

"Well, I'll try and forget you're not a Texan. Let's give it a go."

"Thank you." The tight coil in her belly relaxed a smidge.

"Here's the deal. I pay thirty dollars a shift. You keep your tips. I need you Friday and Saturday nights, Sunday afternoon. Start tonight if you want."

Catherine's heart sank. The place was empty, except for the three men gathered around one of the pool tables. "That's not much to live on."

"That's 'cause you're here in the afternoon. The Saddleback sets on the edge of a dry county. Come the weekend, everybody gets thirsty. We pack 'em in. You can easily make a hundred bucks a night. Sometimes more. What you report to Uncle Sam, is your business."

"Then I'd love to give it a try. I'll check around for some part-time work during the week."

"I'm gonna like you, Catherine McCoy. I can already tell."

For the second time today, Catherine breathed a sigh of relief. "Now all I need is a place to stay."

"Don't look at me. My place is barely big enough for one. We've got a couple of motels that aren't too expensive." Marty drummed her long pink fingernails on the bar. "The Williamsons' little house is empty and about five miles south of town. It's furnished, and you might be exactly what Emma needs. I can give her a call. Ask if she's interested in renting."

"I can't tell you how much I appreciate your help." This day was getting better by the minute. "That'd be really nice of you."

"Nice?" Marty looked both ways and then wagged her finger. "Don't you dare start that rumor. You'll see a different me when this joint gets busy and the guys get rowdy." She stood. "Sit tight. I'll call Emma." She put her hand on Catherine's shoulder and squeezed lightly. "I'm being nice to you, because you're running. Maybe you'll figure out whether it's away from something—or to something—while you're in Butte Crest."

****

"Crap," he yelped. Daydreaming had cost him a little skin. He wiped off the blood and finished shaving. Keeping his mind off his new doll was as hard as his dick.

She'd been difficult at first, fought some when he'd made her strip. The doll didn't like mama's lipstick or makeup. After a few whacks across her bare ass with a wire hanger, she'd painted her lips without arguing. Then he'd tied a red ribbon around her neck into a bow.

Both Mama and the prison guards had used the punishment and reward system. It worked for him, too. When his doll hadn't behaved, he'd whipped her good. What a powerful feeling. A rush of blood had flooded his cock with every down stroke.

For a man who didn't put much stock in fate, he had to admit destiny had smiled on him. When he'd stopped by a florist to pick up some carnations for Mama, he'd found his doll. Her green eyes looked right into his, and her red lips smiled. Oh, yeah. He'd found a live doll to replace the one he'd lost. He'd gotten flustered, tongue-tied to the point he'd left without buying flowers.

He'd immediately decided not to sell Mama's trailer. It was the perfect box for his new doll. He couldn't have handpicked a better spot to keep her. Isolated, out in the country and sitting at the end of a long dirt driveway, nobody would hear a thing.

All the storeowners on the square parked in the back alley, leaving the prime parking for their customers. He'd waited until nearly six, drove around back of her flower shop and waited until she closed.

His heart had jumped clear up to the back of his throat when she came strolling out alone. With no one around, he'd grabbed her and forced her into his pickup. Amazing how exciting it had been to feel her struggle against him. He'd wanted to rip off her clothes right there in the alley.

He'd hated to leave her tied up and alone, but they'd have lots of time together—just the two of them. She was all his and he'd play with her.

Mama had been right all along. He did want to fuck the doll.

Chapter Two

Matt hadn't slept Friday night. He'd rest when he found Julia. Fatigue numbed his brain, but he pushed on. He entered his notes on Julia Kaye Drummond into the computer then reread every word. He'd located her car in the alley behind her building with her purse and cell in the front seat. How the hell did a twenty-four-year-old woman close her florist shop and vanish? A thorough search of her place of business, her home, and the surrounding area had netted zero clues.

Crest County was normally quiet and peaceful. Ms. Drummond's disappearance ate at Matt's gut. He rubbed the heel of his hand over his eyes, pressing at a headache the likes of which he hadn't had in over a year. In the morning, he'd pull a second deputy, Rey Santos, in to help. Between Matt, Jake, and Rey they'd break this case.

"I'm going home." Sue leaned against the doorframe to Matt's office. "It's after five."

"You were a big help today." He pretended to straighten the files on his desk. If his hunch was right, another lengthy chat about his personal life was about to take place.

"No problem. You got plans for the rest of the weekend?"

"Tomorrow, Jake and I are canvassing Julia Drummond's neighborhood."

"You've done that once. What do you expect to find?"

"Won't know until we look." He grinned at her...waiting...waiting.

Sue stepped inside his office. "This is a sparsely populated county with nothing but rattlesnakes, underbrush, and mesquite trees. Gonna be hard for you to find a missus."

Matt leaned back in his chair. Marrying him off was one of Sue's favorite subjects. "Still not looking. Keep feeding me apple pie and I might propose to you."

"Thirty-four's a mite young for me. Besides, I buried one husband. Don't want to go through that again." Her face sobered. "You have your messages, right?"

"Got 'em right here. See you Monday." After his gentle hint of picking up a file and glancing at the front page, the tap-tap of her shoes faded, indicating she'd left his office.

Sue Conner was one of Matt's favorite people. Prim and proper, he couldn't remember her wearing anything other than dark-colored dresses to the office. Somewhere between sixty and seventy years old, her sea blue eyes could cut a man in half or freeze him in his tracks. Her knowledge of the county's past and present business boggled the mind. She'd successfully guided three sheriffs before him through their terms and not by using kid gloves. She ran a good bluff but didn't fool Matt for a minute. A sweetheart lived under her crusty exterior.

He pulled the messages off the post. Three calls from Ash Hunter, Matt's first partner when he'd made homicide detective. After his transfer to the narcotics task force, they'd remained good friends. When Matt had been shot, Ash parked his butt next to Matt's bed and refused to budge. His friend pushed harder than the physical therapist during Matt's recovery. Ash probably wanted to talk about subjects better left alone. Matt lived in the present. Didn't need to relive the past. He lived. Elena died. End of story.

He pushed away from his desk, stretched out the kinks, and then reached for his hat. His stomach growled as he headed for the exit.

The night dispatcher glanced up and smiled. "Calling it a night?"

"Yeah. Have a good evening." Matt stopped at the exit and glanced over his shoulder. "Donnie, call with any updates on Julia Drummond."

"Will do, Sheriff."

Matt stepped out into the evening air. The sun going down hadn't offered much relief to the sweltering temperatures.

Curry had little traffic this time of day, and within minutes, he pulled onto the highway. He'd bought a place last month, a white frame house with a hundred acres. Located on the outskirts of Butte Crest, he was home in twenty minutes.

The stray who'd adopted him waited on the porch. "Come on, dog." He patted his leg, and the brindle mutt tagged along into the kitchen. Matt poured food in a bowl on the floor and watched it disappear in seconds. He reached for the empty dish, sending the dog scurrying out of reach. "Still don't trust me. Somebody beat the hell out of you, didn't they?" The animal twisted his head sideways watching Matt. "It's okay. I won't pet you until you're ready."

He changed out of his uniform and slid on a pair of jeans and a T-shirt. Barefoot, he headed to the refrigerator where he grabbed the makings for a ham sandwich.

The second he kicked back in his easy chair, his cell buzzed. The display indicated his dispatcher was calling. Had the missing woman turned up? "What's up, Donnie?"

"I hate to bother you, but Carl's an hour away, and there's been a fight at the Saddleback."

"I'm on my way." Matt disconnected, hurried to his bedroom, and jerked on his socks and boots. He glanced at his bed, shaking his head in resignation. The price of being sheriff in a large county with a small budget—too many miles to cover and not enough men.

He put the dog outside, gulped down a couple of big bites of his sandwich, tossed the rest to the always-hungry mutt, and then headed to Butte Crest.

****

The bar opened and closed, but she refused to turn and look. Marty calling the cops was the last thing Catherine needed.

"Well, how 'bout that," Marty called out. "The man himself. Come on in."

"Marty."

Catherine recognized the deep baritone even though they had only met once. First, he spoke to the bartender, JC Harper, and if she were any judge, he was headed straight for her.

"You have trouble tonight?"

"Hell," Marty exclaimed, waving him to a chair. "Fight's over. Almost everybody went home."

"What happened? You keep your customers under control—most of the time."

His gaze met Catherine's and held for a long second. There was that almost grin again.

"Let me guess, you were in the middle of things. Right?"

Sitting at a table with an icepack on her jaw, she gave him her best "who me?" look.

"I forgot," Marty commented. "You two know each other."

"We've met." He tipped the brim of his hat with one finger. "One of you ladies care to tell me what happened?"

"Wasn't a big deal." Marty waved him off. "Catherine took a punch from a jealous wife."

"I'd like to hear her side."

His broad shoulders turned, and suddenly Catherine was face-to-face with him. She succinctly described the incident. His face was a blank slate, making it hard to get a good read. For some stupid reason, she wanted him to understand.

"It's the truth," she ground out. "I didn't flirt with Jessie Bradley's husband."

"Whoa." He held his hands up in the sign of surrender. "I believe you. You want to press assault charges?"

"No." The idea brought back images of bickering lawyers. She'd had enough of those vultures to last a lifetime.

Marty put her hand on Catherine's shoulder. "I'm sorry I called for help. Jessie is jealous as hell, and when Vince started fawning over Catherine, Jessie went a tad crazy. She did smack Catherine a good one."

"And I didn't touch her." She could've broken Jessie's nose, but martial arts training had taught Catherine self-control along with self-defense.

The sheriff leaned forward and pulled the icepack away. He ran his finger across her skin, inspecting her injury. His touch left a trail of heat on her skin. Surprised, she pulled away.

"You're looking at me like I'm a virus under a microscope."

The corners of his mouth lifted when he pushed the icepack back in place. "Skin's not broken. I see a small bruise forming. I did warn you against working here. This wasn't a good choice. There's trouble at this bar most every weekend."

"I'm not afraid of a little trouble." Catherine blinked back the tears edging toward the surface. She refused to cry. No more tears ranked in the top ten of her *Never* list. She didn't care if he approved. Like it or not, she needed this job.

"That's the God's honest truth," Marty said. "She showed amazing restraint. I should've known a looker like Catherine was gonna cause trouble, especially her being an outsider. Hell, I love it. Tomorrow night, this place will be packed."

"I might as well put a deputy in the parking lot," the sheriff grumbled.

"Listen, Catherine," Marty said. "This night's done. Why don't you head on home?"

"Thanks. I think I will."

Catherine went behind the bar for her purse and removed the cash from the tip jar Marty had given her. Considering she hadn't worked the full shift, the stack of bills in her hand gave her a rush.

"You heading out?" JC asked.

"Yes. I appreciate your help—you know— earlier." When Marty introduced the two of them, she'd said JC kept a close eye on the floor. Sure enough, he'd put a stop to the dispute before it got out of hand. Broad shoulders, at least six feet tall, and an easygoing personality made him perfect for the job. He calmed everybody down without losing his temper.

"Not a problem. Want me to walk you to your car?"

"No thanks. I'll be fine." She shoved the bills into her purse and then waved to Marty and the sheriff.

She crossed the parking lot and got into her old Ford. It felt good to have cash in her purse. Based on Marty's recommendation, Emma Williamson had allowed Catherine move into the tiny house with only a fifty-dollar deposit. A couple of nights like tonight and she'd pay her new landlady the full month's rent.

Catherine's engine groaned. Turned over once, then nothing. She tried again. Again, nothing. She rested her head on the steering wheel to indulge in a minute of self-pity. Her car door opened, scaring the crap out of her.

"Something wrong?" The sheriff crouched and put his hand on her arm.

"No. Everything's fine." His touch was surprisingly gentle for a man with such a large hand. Warmth rolled under her skin and across her chest. Confused, she pulled away from him.

His head tilted as if to get a better view. "You were collapsed across the steering wheel."

"It's nothing." Damn, she wasn't weak or needy. Yet every time he showed up, she needed help. "Sheriff, I'm fine."

He removed his hat and rubbed his forehead. "Think you could call me Matt?"

"Matt," she said his name softly, letting it rest on her tongue for a second. "I'm Catherine."

The tension in the air eased when both their stomachs growled in harmony.

"Look, we got off to a rocky start. How about I buy you a late supper?"

She hesitated. Making friends with the sheriff went against her good judgment.

"You'll be safe with me. Off duty or on, I'm one of the good guys. I promise."

His full smile transformed his handsome face to beautiful. Catherine couldn't remember the last time she'd eaten a meal sitting across from a member of the opposite sex. His offer made her want to forget the crisis of the hour. A car that wouldn't start.

He stood and extended his hand. "We'll grab a bite, and I'll bring you right back."

Defying all logic, she laid her palm against his. "I haven't eaten since morning." His grip was strong and warm. Before she had time to rethink her decision, he'd tucked her in his car and was buckling up his seat belt.

"Nothing's open this time of night except the truck stop, but the food is good."

"Truck drivers always know where to eat." She looked around inside the cruiser and remembered a past and unpleasant ride in one. "What happens if you get a call, and I'm in the car with you?"

"If there's a shootout at the OK Corral, I'll leave you somewhere safe and come back later." He tossed her a smile. "The chances of that happening are slim."

So he had a sense of humor. How would he handle a more serious question? "Marty and some of the customers were talking about a missing woman. That sort of thing doesn't happen a lot, does it?"

"No. And we're doing everything we can to find her."

His words sounded thick with concern, and his sharp jaw was set with determination. For some reason, she believed the statement came from his heart.

"Is that why you're out late?"

"No. I live close by, and none of my deputies were in the area."

"I get it. You can't talk about the case."

"I can tell you every available resource is working the case. And she's never far from my mind. Will that do?"

"Now you sound like you're reading a press release."

He laughed a hollow sound. "That did sound rehearsed. But it's the truth."

His mood had shifted. The tone of his voice was solid yet warm with worry when he spoke of the missing woman.

A slight musky, woodsy scent filled the car and her senses. Her stomach fluttered. Not butterfly wings, Mallard ducks. She couldn't remember the last time a man had made her nervous.

"Hello?" His voice pulled her attention back. "You drifted off. Keep that up, and you'll give me an inferiority complex."

"Sorry." Her cheeks heated, making her grateful for the darkness. She'd forgotten how to make small talk with a man.

Matt drove around a half dozen big rigs and found a parking spot. He brought out feelings she didn't want to remember, sensations she thought were long forgotten. She was more than uncomfortable at the revelation.

"Doesn't look like they're too busy."

He got out and waited for her at the front of his cruiser. She accepted his extended hand as she stepped up on the walk. His nearness slammed home the absence of human contact in her life.

Seconds after they slid into a booth, the waitress laid menus in front of them.

"What can I get you?"

"Whatever the lady wants, works for me. If you'll excuse me, I'll wash up."

Catherine ordered while Matt made a trip to the men's room. He stopped to visit with a couple of people on the way back. She averted her gaze when he glanced across the room and caught her watching him. He broke off his conversation and rejoined her when the waitress delivered their food.

"Sorry. I didn't plan on being gone long. Hard to walk away when people are concerned about the missing woman. The locals are getting jumpy."

"I could see the worry on their faces." She pushed the basket of fries over to him. "These are for you. I hope you wanted a combo."

"Works for me." He ripped open a pouch of ketchup for his fries. "Eat up."

"So what's your story?" She unwrapped her burger. "You don't have the typical Texas twang. I'm guessing you're not a country boy. Yet you're working out here in the mesquite trees and underbrush."

"You're wrong. I was raised one county over. After I graduated from The University of Houston, I stayed in town. Spent the better part of ten years on their police force."

"You've been home over a year or so."

"Wait a minute." One dark eyebrow lifted. "Have I been the topic of conversation at the bar?"

The booth seemed to shrink in size. Heat rushed up her cheeks, and she stared at her food. "Marty might've mentioned you once or twice."

"Believe only the good things. What about you? I've met a few vagabonds in my life. None of them looked like you."

"Born and raised in Oklahoma. I was married. Now I'm not. One day my life fell apart. And here I am. Alone, on my own, and loving it." She laughed, trying to keep it light. She'd kept her sentences short and to the point, intentionally not sharing much information about herself.

"May I ask...are you divorced?"

"Widowed." She swallowed a couple of times. "I hung around wondering what to do for a year, until I figured out I didn't belong. I decided to see the country, working my way across each state. Every three or four months, I leave again." Her chin lifted, and her gaze locked with his. "I always leave." Catherine was positive he got the message that had no interest in a permanent relationship.

His eyes narrowed as he studied her over the top of his drink. "Aren't you too old to run away from home?"

She straightened her shoulders to let him know he'd hit a nerve. "Apparently not. I'm enjoying a freedom at thirty other people had in their twenties." She was through sharing information. "You ready to head back? I need all the rest I can get for tomorrow night at the bar."

On the ride back, she felt his eyes on her occasionally, heating her skin from the inside out, making her super uncomfortable. The interior of the car warmed in spite of the air conditioner being on high.

"Thank you for supper. It was nice," she said when he reached the bar's parking lot.

"You're welcome. We'll find someplace nicer next time."

"I'd like that."

Him asking and her accepting shocked the hell out of her. She remained seated in the cruiser when he parked, and for some unexplainable reason, she hated to get out. Their bodies almost touched when she stepped out. Heat rolled off him and slammed her in the belly.

"You saw worry on people's faces at the café. What do you see now?"

She looked into his eyes. "John Wayne."

Catherine's insides trembled. The sheriff's laser blue eyes had delivered his message loud and clear. It was a message she didn't know how to handle. She'd had no interest in sex for a long time. Besides, Andy had assured her many times, she was a lousy lay.

Matt walked her to her car and returned to his cruiser. She took a deep breath, put the keys in the ignition and turned the key. Nothing happened. The door to the bar opened, JC stepped outside, and lit a cigarette. Like it or not, she had to ask if he or Matt would give her a hand. Damn, she hated to ask for help.

She got out and spoke loudly. "Can I get a jump? My battery seems to be down."

Matt made an about face and both men headed her direction immediately.

"I've got cables," JC said. "Let me pull around beside you. Won't take a second."

Catherine stood out of the way while Matt hooked up the two batteries. After a couple of tries, they quit. JC, with his shaggy brown hair and kind hazel eyes, turned his truck's engine off. He got out and shook his head.

"I can pick you up a new battery tomorrow. Cheap one is around fifty bucks."

Catherine dug out her tips, handed over the money, and thanked him profusely. Her heart grew heavier. Getting ahead would take time.

Matt lowered the hood. "I'll take you home and bring you back tomorrow."

"I don't know what to say. Thanks, both of you." Being obligated to anyone didn't appeal to her, but she was in a bind.

Matt held the door to his cruiser for her, walked around, and climbed in. "Why didn't you tell me your car wouldn't start?"

"I don't like asking for help. I prefer to take care of myself." Leaning on other people would make her vulnerable, something she never wanted to be again.

"What if Marty and JC had been gone?" He drove out of the parking lot, then quickly pulled to the shoulder, and stopped.

"I would've figured something out. Why did we stop?"

"Because I don't know where we're going."

"Oh. Sorry." Catherine hid her embarrassment. "I've forgotten the name of the road, county something. I'll show you."

She directed him to the highway and off at the County Road 617 sign. Darkness swallowed them the minute they left the main drag. No streetlights, no housing additions. Dead quiet except for the gravel roadbed crunching under the tires.

She broke the silence. "Take a left at the next turn."

"Looks like we're neighbors. My house is not far from here."

"Turn right at the next place then follow the driveway around back." The cruiser's headlights swept across the lawn and came to rest on the small white frame cottage.

"Hang on." Matt killed the engine, reached across her, and pulled a flashlight from the dash compartment. "I can at least get you inside safely. Might be a good idea to leave the porch light on tomorrow when you leave."

She stiffened. "Are you always this bossy?"

Matt got out and waited for her. "It's hard to turn off being a cop." He shined the beam in front of her feet and took the key from her to unlock the door.

Catherine flipped the switch, and flooded the toy-sized living room with light. "I can imagine." She stood back and let him enter.

The white lace curtains and hand crocheted doilies on the furniture made Catherine feel like she was playing dress up. A love seat and small rocking chair filled the room to capacity. Hardwood floors covered with tattered throw rugs added to the ambience.

"I think this is what you call shabby chic. Mrs. Williamson and her late husband built the little house for their handicapped daughter who lived in it all her adult life. They cared for her until she died at the early age of forty. Mrs. Williamson seemed happy to have someone rent the place. "

"I live right behind you. My office is about twenty miles away in Curry. Guess I need to do a better job of getting to know my neighbors."

"Can I see your place from here?" She followed Matt into the kitchen.

"There." He pointed out the backdoor window.

He stepped back, allowing her to stand between him and the door. Matt didn't touch her. He moved up and stood directly behind her.

"See the light in the distance? In the dark, I can't tell exactly how far, but I'm fairly close."

His warm breath brushed across the top of her head. A rapid heartbeat reverberated in her ears. Did the pounding come from her chest or his? She couldn't tell. Fear snaked through her veins, slithering under her skin. He'd trapped her between his body and the door.

She bit back a cry of relief when his boot heels hit the hardwood floor as he walked away. Damning herself for lack of control, she braced her hands on the doorframe, rested her cheek on the glass, and collected herself. She prayed her reaction to being cornered had gone unnoticed.

"Thank you for supper and the ride home." Catherine hoped she appeared poised and self- assured.

"You're welcome. What time tomorrow?"

"Marty wants me at the bar by one."

"I can manage that." He moved toward the door. "See you then."

Catherine leaned against the wall and listened to the gravel crunch under the cruiser's tires when Matt backed out of the drive.

Marty had said women drooled when they talked about him. Catherine could see why. His blue eyes sent her stomach churning. At first, she thought him to be distant, expected him to be bad-tempered, wanted him to stay away. Now, she hoped he'd settle for being a friend.

She'd flipped the living room light off and moved to pull the curtain closed when her skin came alive as every hair stood on end, electrified. A familiar sensation crawled up from her stomach, sending goose bumps racing up her arms. Familiar, because she'd been watched from the shadows in the past. She shook her head, tamped down foolish memories. No one was out there. She was safe.

Chapter Three

Catherine's sheets lay on the floor and sweat soaked through her sleep-shirt. She smoothed her hands over her neck. Swallowed. Breathed. Touched her ribs. Her back and kidneys. Felt no bruising. Another nightmare.

The feather bed, hand embroidered pillowcases, and butter yellow bedroom reminded her she was safe. Dropping her head in her hands, she used her breathing technique to slow her racing heart.

A male laughed, and Catherine bolted up in bed. Was Matt already here? She dressed, made a mad dash through the bathroom, and then went in search of the voice. A brown pickup sat beside the main house. With no sheriff's cruiser in sight, she sighed in relief, her heart rate slowing.

"Good morning, Mrs. Williamson," Catherine called out.

"We're in the garden."

When Catherine reached the tool shed, she froze. A sizzle of fear stood the hair up on her arms. The man who caused the ruckus last night stood next to her landlady. Even though he wore a ball cap today, Catherine recognized Vince immediately. "Sorry, I didn't mean to interrupt." She turned to leave.

"Don't go on my account," he said.

"Please stay, and call me Emma." Mrs. Williamson beamed at her. "We're talking about some handyman work." Emma introduced Catherine to Vince Bradley and told him Catherine had rented the cottage.

"Mr. Bradley and I met last night at the bar." Catherine shook his extended hand. His palm was sweaty, and he held on to her a second too long. His smile made her fear antennae rise and vibrate.

"Yes, we did." He paused. "It's nice to see you again."

He was tall like Matt but proportioned differently. Proof of Vince's appetite for beer hung over the top of his jeans and pushed outward on the snaps of his western shirt. His gaze trailed over her body, setting her temper right on the edge.

The sun beat down on her head and within minutes sweat trickled down between her shoulder blades. After a minimum of small talk, Catherine used the heat to excuse herself and retreated to the air conditioning in the cottage.

She made her bed and laid out the night's work clothes. Matt would arrive soon, and the excitement building spooked her a little, confused her. A light tap on the door put an end to her mind wandering. She swung the door wide to find Vince on her porch. The smile disappeared from her face.

She braced her feet apart. He wouldn't get inside. "What do you want? There's nothing we need to say to each other."

The heat had taken its toll on Vince. Last night's alcohol mingled with perspiration and drained profusely from his pores. Catherine instinctively recoiled. He smoothed a hand over his receding hairline and then wiped across his belly.

"Sorry about last night. Jessie acts pretty stupid when she's drunk."

Catherine's anger edged toward relief. "Fine. No real harm done. We can forget it as long as it doesn't happen again." If Vince wanted to put things right, she'd accept his apology. She stepped out on the porch when he offered his hand. He clasped his fingers around hers and squeezed, then leaned closer.

"I'm leaving her at home from now on. You and me, we can be good friends without her getting all bent out of shape."

Catherine jerked free, disappointed in herself for trusting. She glared at Vince, hoping to drive her message through his thick skull.

"Get this straight. We'll never be 'friends,' whether Jessie's with you or not."

She inched backwards. When she felt the knob under her hand, she stepped inside, slammed the door in his face, and then locked it. Fury churned through her body. Her knees went weak and brutal memories came crashing in, but she pulled herself together. Fear would not control her. She'd taken self-defense courses and learned how to fight if she had to. Nobody would mistreat her again. No more being bullied and no more accepting the blame for someone else's behavior.

Getting showered and dressed for work took precedence over fretting about a foolish drunk. She fixed her face and hair, then slipped on the yellow western-cut blouse to go with her jeans. Catherine studied herself in the mirror. Nope. No outward signs she was a killer. The Tulsa newspapers and reporters told a different story. As had Andy's family. In her mind, she knew the truth, but her heart never let her forget she'd taken another human being's life.

Considering the treatment she'd received from the cops in Tulsa, being drawn to the sheriff seemed odd to Catherine. Matt made her warm inside, and the feeling u n n e r v e d her. She'd shared her bed with only one man...her husband. He'd repeatedly pointed out her sexual performance was stiff and inept. Something was missing in her. The subject was moot. No way would the sexy sheriff want her.

The knock on her door startled her. She hurried to the front window and peeked out, careful not to open the door without checking. A shiny black pickup was parked in the driveway. Matt stood on her porch, and the sudden lift to her mood made her smile.

"Hey," she said while her brain searched for something clever to say. "Nice truck." The sheriff had a quiet, self-assured manner, and Catherine thought it might be nice to have a friend. At least until the time came for her to move on. She hated that she didn't know how to make casual conversation.

"Hey, yourself." He handed her a cup of coffee. "It's black and from the Stop' N Go. You won't find a Starbucks for miles. I don't know your cell number or I would've called."

"It's perfect. And appreciated." She backed out of the way, commanding herself to relax. He'd only asked for her number, yet her heart sputtered as if he'd asked for a date. "Come in. I'll write it down for you."

He stood quietly looking at her.

Her cheeks heated under his scrutiny while she jotted down the information. She slid the cheap throwaway phone into her purse and handed him the scrap of paper. His hand closed over hers when he traded her slip of paper for his business card. An open flame wouldn't have sizzled more than his touch. A shock of heat ran through her, straight to unfamiliar places.

"Mine's on the back."

"Are you stopping by the bar?"

He cleared his throat. "I can't. I'm interviewing friends of Julia Drummond today. My free time will be limited until I get her home, safe and sound."

"I understand and appreciate you driving me to work."

"I wanted to see you again." He waited while she locked up, followed her to the passenger side of his pickup, then opened the door for her.

Catherine didn't know how to respond. She remained quiet until he backed out of the driveway. "Why?"

"Why...what?"

"Why would you want to see me again?"

He chuckled at her with an I-can't-believe-you- said-that expression. "That's an odd question coming from such a beautiful woman."

"Now you're just being kind."

"Not hardly." He slowed his pickup then turned to look at her. "Whoever screwed up your self- confidence was either stupid or blind."

"Suffice it to say, I haven't been told I was beautiful a lot in my lifetime."

"Then he was a damn fool."

Catherine didn't want to continue along that line of conversation. "Any news on the missing woman?"

"Nothing, yet."

JC pulled in the bar's parking lot right behind them, making their timing perfect. He took her keys and shooed her inside, telling her how he and Matt would handle the men's work. An hour later JC came through the door. He'd paid a heavy price for installing the battery in the sweltering heat. His brown hair was damp, and his shirt clung to his body. Guilt hit Catherine hard when sweat dripped from his chin.

Marty handed him a bar towel. "God, you look like you're gonna stroke out on us."

"I brought a clean shirt." He tossed Catherine her keys. "Here you go. She started right up."

"I don't know what to say." She moved her tip jar to the front of the bar. "By the end of the shift, I'll have enough money to pay you for your labor."

"No way." JC waved her off. "Ain't no big thing."

"It was huge to me." Catherine stared at the front entry. Matt hadn't come through the door with JC. She understood why. Still, a moment of unreasonable disappointment washed over her, which she tamped down. Keeping her distance from the sheriff was a good thing.

****

He hadn't intended to kill her, but the bitch had kicked him. The hornets had exploded, and he'd choked her. Funny, but it was the biggest rush of his life.

Next time, he'd plan better. Next time, he'd find a doll who wanted him. *Next time?* He rubbed his bulging crotch. No way was finding her a coincidence. He was meant to have his own doll.

He blew out a disappointed sigh and carefully applied a fresh layer of Mama's powder and red lipstick to the doll's ashen face. After retying the red bow around her neck, he sat back and studied her. A touch of glue on her eyelids and she stared straight ahead. Now she looked more like the green-eyed doll.

She'd have to wait here until he got off work tomorrow. He chuckled when he locked the trailer door. It wasn't like she had anywhere to go, and he'd lowered the temp on the air conditioner for her. He'd figure out a good spot to leave her. Pick a place she'd be easily found. She was too beautiful to let the varmints get at her.

Something hadn't been quite right about her. She wouldn't cooperate, and he'd whipped her more than once. He adjusted his cock. It sure jacked him up. In fact, he'd had fun with his plaything after each punishment. He'd considered having her one last time, but she was too cold. The idea intrigued him. Maybe, he'd be inside the next doll when she died.

****

Butte Crest, its quaint architecture and beautiful old homes coupled with the nicest people, had made Catherine feel welcome, like perhaps she'd found a place to build a new life. A flash of panic hit her, reminding her of why she never stayed put too long. All it would take is one person to dig into her past. What would Matt think of her? Would he understand she'd done everything she could to get away from Andy?

Pushing the past from her thoughts, she counted her cash. She'd earned one-hundred-twenty-five dollars plus the sixty dollars for two shifts from Marty. Not enough to pay the rest of the rent and way short of what she needed to get the emissions on her car fixed. She'd drive to the town square and ask around, maybe someone needed help during the week, other than the funeral parlor.

A potted plant of African Violets sat on her porch. She didn't find a card. Shivers hit her arms. Surely, that ass Vince hadn't dropped them off. Matt? No, that was wishful thinking. Emma had probably left a welcome gift. Catherine stopped at the main house on her way to town.

Emma opened the door wearing a cotton housedress complete with apron. The blue flowered print matched the color of her eyes and complimented her curly silver hair. Catherine instinctively reached one arm out and hugged the older woman. "Thank you."

Emma's eyes widened with surprise. "For what?"

"The flowers. Didn't you leave them for me?"

Emma looked at the pot and shook her head. "I didn't."

"There's no card. Wonder who brought them."

Emma stepped outside on the porch. Her brows dipped. Her hand fluttered to her chest. "I should've noticed if someone was on the property. My George would've been plenty upset with me for talking to your friend, Mr. Bradley."

"Vince Bradley isn't my friend. In fact, he scares me."

"Then I'll find someone else to do the work." Her tiny frame straightened.

"Your husband would be proud of you. There's one other person who might've dropped them off. He drove me home and to work when I had car trouble."

Emma beamed at Catherine. "A secret admirer.."

"Could be." She marveled at the flutter in her stomach. "I'm going in to town. Can I bring you anything?"

"Nope, can't think of a thing."

"Okay, I'm off to hunt for a day job." She handed the plant to Emma. "Will you take care of my flowers? With my brown thumb, plants don't survive long."

Catherine ran back to her car and waved as she pulled out of the driveway. She understood the loneliness Emma must feel, not having anyone to care for. Not having anyone who cared about her.

****

Catherine had walked the square and checked with every shop owner or boutique clerk. Nobody needed help. She'd found a particularly beautiful green and yellow silk scarf she wanted to buy, but good sense had prevailed, and she'd hung onto her money. Her brain was fried, and her feet were killing her by the time she got back to her car. She turned the air conditioner to high before driving away.

The further she drove, the hotter the air coming from the vents on her dash became. Had she run over a black cat? Broken a mirror she didn't remember? What had she done to bring about this run of bad luck? Could somebody please move this elephant sitting on her chest? Accepting that a pity-party wouldn't fix the air conditioner, she drove out to the Final Touch Funeral Home. Catherine killed the engine and prepared to scratch a recently added item off her *Never* list...working around dead people.

Stepping from the blistering heat outside to the ice cold air in the waiting room of the funeral home made her light headed. No, the abrupt change in temperature wasn't it. She'd stopped breathing. In and out, she commanded her lungs.

A young girl sat behind the desk with a Teen magazine in front of her. "Can I be of service?"

"I'd like to apply for the job if the position's still open." She'd passed the first hurdle and was stronger for it.

"Great. Take a seat. I'll see if Mom has time to talk."

The cut-off jeans and Dallas Cowboy jersey the girl wore made Catherine hope the owner might be desperate for a receptionist. The teenager strolled down the hall, opened a door, and yelled for her mother. Catherine listened to the slap-slap of rubber flip-flops as the girl returned.

"I'd hire you myself if I could. School starts mid-August, and I've been stuck in here all summer." She flipped her long blond hair over one shoulder before returning to her magazine.

Catherine cleared her throat. "What happened to the previous employee?"

The young girl looked up and pain radiated from her face. "This was Mom's job. She's had to help in the back ever since Dad died."

"I'm sorry for your loss." Catherine's insides crunched.

"Say it like that every time, and you'll do fine." An older version of the girl working the desk came toward Catherine. Her dark slacks and gray blouse took on the somber tone of the funeral home. "Susan King," she said. "And I'm joking. I'd expect you to do more than that. Are you the woman the sheriff mentioned?"

"Catherine McCoy." She clasped the woman's extended hand. "If he said nice things, I am."

"Come on back. Judy, take a message if anyone calls."

Catherine followed the woman down the hall into a small, neat office where they chatted briefly. The job amounted to simple filing and a three-day workweek. Mrs. King's staff consisted of her daughter and the mortician, Steve Abbott. Her laid-back personality was endearing, and Catherine surprised herself in trying hard to get the job.

"Then I'll leave you to fill out the application. Give it to Judy on your way out." Mrs. King handed Catherine some paperwork. "I'll let you know something by tomorrow evening."

Catherine thanked her and dug out the necessary information. An hour later, she walked out into the heat. The sign on the bank across the street read one-hundred-four degrees.

Waves of heat came up from the pavement and made breathing difficult. When she opened the car door, hot air billowed up, scorching her face as if she'd opened an oven. In her grandmother's day, they rolled down the windows. Catherine could do the same.

Chapter Four

Catherine's door opened, and the smile on her face convinced Matt he'd made the right decision by calling her. He hadn't planned to ask her for a date. It was just going to be a courtesy call. The minute he'd heard her voice, things took off in a different direction.

"Is that look for me?" he asked.

She laughed. The sound was magical, pulling him into her good mood. Being around her helped him forget how alone he was, except for the dog he couldn't pet.

"Come in. Susan King called right after you did. I start tomorrow. I'll work Tuesdays, Wednesdays, and Thursdays."

Matt entered her house and stepped into her scent. He breathed in the faint whisper of vanilla. "Congratulations."

"It's filing and working the front desk, but that's fine with me. I'm never going in the back."

A fleeting look of sorrow darkened her face. She'd told him over burgers she was a widow. Did the funeral home bring back painful memories of her dead husband?

"The King family has a reputation for being the best. It takes a special calling to run a funeral home."

She tucked a red curl behind her ear and frowned for a second. "A special calling. I hadn't thought of it that way."

"You ready?"

"I am. Let me get my purse."

He followed her outside and opened the door to his pickup. She stepped up and in with ease. He feasted his eyes on her long legs. Good Lord, they ran on and on. His groin tightened, followed by a deep ache. She'd think he was some kind of perv if he didn't get his libido under control.

"Will you back out slowly? Emma likes to know when people come and go."

"Sure thing." After she buckled up, Matt forced his attention away from her extremities, slid behind the wheel, and started the engine. "How about I cook a couple of steaks at my place? I haven't been home more than a few hours in the past couple of days."

"I'd love it. Someone else waiting on me will be a nice change after the weekend."

"Sorry I haven't had time to check on you. Everything going all right at the bar?"

"The job's okay. I had a few dust-ups with a couple of drunks. Thankfully, JC keeps a close eye on the waitresses and Marty."

Matt wasn't about to analyze why the idea of some guy hassling her, or JC looking out for her, sizzled a nerve. "Good. Make sure he walks you to your car or at least watches until you drive away." He frowned at her raised eyebrows. "Don't go all I-can-take-care-of-myself on me."

"The news reported you haven't found the missing woman. Not a good sign, huh?"

"No, it's not." Matt parked in his driveway and turned toward her. "Look. I'm not trying to scare you or boss you around. Just want you to be aware."

He opened her door and wrapped his hands around her waist when she started out of the pickup. He lifted her and helped her to the ground. "Pay attention to your surroundings, okay?"

"Okay."

She'd never know how close he came to kissing her. Damn, he couldn't take his eyes off her mouth. Her full lips drew him to her.

Pulled with the strength of a magnet. Her hands pushed against his chest.

"Turn me loose." Her tone dropped an octave with each word, sending him back a step.

"Of course. I don't know where my mind went." Crap, he hadn't acted this foolish since junior high. Vulnerability hid under that layer of tough-girl independence, and he found her captivating.

Red flags of color hit her cheeks. "I do."

"Come in." The dog approaching from the barn provided him an excuse to change the subject. "I'd better feed him first. He's always hungry." Matt grabbed a sack of groceries from the bed of his pickup and carried it inside. "I wouldn't try to pet him," he cautioned as he put the bag on the counter.

"What's his name?"

"He doesn't have one, he..." Matt's jaw dropped, and he stared in amazement. Catherine had squatted down, and the big lummox of a dog had his head buried in her hands. "I don't believe it. Ungrateful mutt eats my food but won't let me near him."

"He's a sweetheart. You can't own a pet and not name him."

"He doesn't belong to me."

"Obviously he does. He lives here with you."

"We sort of share space. We do talk. For some reason, he hasn't told me his name."

"Tell me what I can do to help with supper." She walked to the sink to wash her hands.

"You can scrub those two potatoes, wrap them in plastic wrap, and stick them in the microwave. I'm going out back to start the fire."

Catherine was standing in his living room when he stepped back inside. She smiled and her beauty hit him in the gut. She'd called him John Wayne the other night. Shit, his attraction to her was far from heroic. It was old-fashioned lust. He couldn't keep her out of his thoughts. She was not only beautiful...she had a secret. And secrets made him curious.

"Want the grand tour?"

"Please."

"Not much to see."

His living room furniture consisted of one leather recliner and a big screen TV. He had no pictures of family to show her, but then there were no tables to set them on. They passed by a couple of rooms with unpacked boxes setting around. He paused in the hallway before allowing her to venture into his bedroom.

"I'm not much of a housekeeper," he said looking at his unmade king-size bed. Until now, he hadn't noticed that it looked like a small army had marched over it. The closer she got to the bed, the closer he got to her.

She turned and bounced off his chest. Instantly her cheeks turned pink.

"I've seen enough. Thanks."

"You're welcome to look around anytime."

He inched closer, raised his hand to her cheek, and drew a line down her jaw with the tips of his fingers. He tipped her chin up and brushed his thumb across her bottom lip. Somebody moaned. Thank God, it was her. In a quick move, Catherine stiffened and pushed him away.

"Don't."

Her eyes darkened to hunter green, like an angry ocean right before a storm. No. Not anger. Fear. Her gaze bounced between him and the door.

Shit. Was she going to bolt?

She stepped around him and started out of the room. "Maybe we should get the steaks on the grill."

"Hey." He touched her arm carefully, gently. "Was that too forward of me?"

"I think so. I'm not sure."

His mind spun as he followed her to the kitchen. She checked the potatoes while he stacked silverware, plates, and raw steaks on a tray and carried them outside. His backyard had a couple of huge oak trees. One shaded an old wooden picnic table. Catherine wandered over, sat, and then stretched out her legs. The mutt jogged past him, walked over to her, made a couple of circles, and then plopped down, resting his chin on her feet. Matt considered growling.

"If it's too hot out here for you...."

"No. I wish I had these trees in my backyard."

He tossed the T-bones on the hot grill. "How do you like your steak?"

"Medium well, please."

Supper with her was a good idea. Sex would've been better. The visceral reaction he had whenever she got close sure screwed with his mind. Her low moan and then rapid pull-back stumped him. Hell. The more he thought about it, the surer he was...he'd scared the crap out of her. She'd sent a message before when she said she always left. Always moved on. She'd warned him not to get serious. He didn't want serious. He'd done permanent and made a mess of two lives. But scared? Jesus. He'd never forget that look in her eyes.

"Matt?"

"Yeah?"

"Want me to bring out the potatoes?"

He blinked a couple of times. "Not yet." She'd caught him drifting, just like he'd caught her a few nights ago. "Sorry. My mind wandered."

"I understand. You look bone tired."

He walked over and squatted in front of her. She smiled but leaned away from him. Damned if he didn't see a hint of fear. Again.

"Catherine, I've never touched a woman and seen raw fear in her eyes. Until today. I'm sorry if I came on too strong. Understand this, no means no to me. I'll never expect more from you than you're willing to give. Nothing will happen without your expressed consent."

She held his gaze for only a second before looking away. "We need to talk."

"Talking's good. We can do that while we eat." Matt rose and stepped over to the grill to flip the steaks. His cell vibrated on his hip. He answered without looking. "Ballard."

Anger surged through his veins while he listened. Harness it, channel it, and find justice. It was the least he could do for Julia Drummond. He disconnected and turned to Catherine.

"The missing woman's been found. Dead. I have to go." His brain raced. How would he get Catherine home? She damn sure couldn't come with him.

"Of course you do. I'll take care of the steaks and wait here."

She'd given him the answer to his problem. His heart popped him in the ribs. "You sure? I may be gone a while."

"I'm sure. Go."

Matt hit the house in a dead run. He grabbed his gun, hat, and keys, and then raced back to the yard where she was taking the steaks off the grill. "I'll be back as soon as I can."

She hurried to him, compassion written on her face. He leaned down, rested his forehead on hers for a moment before he jogging to his pickup. He glanced back at her standing in his driveway, and it hit him. She hadn't pulled away from him.

"Be safe," she called out.

He flipped on the siren, hit the lights, and raced down the highway. He'd left homicide years ago but remembered every case. The faces of innocent victims who'd been murdered on his watch still haunted him. Don't take it personal, his boss had preached. The hell with that. Murder was personal. This was more personal than ever. The people in Crest County looked to him to keep them safe. And he'd failed Julia Drummond.

He punched in Jake Foley's home number. His wife answered. "Rose Ann, Matt Ballard. Sorry, but I have to speak to Jake."

"I'll get him," she said.

Jake's familiar voice came on the line a few seconds later.

"This can't be good." Jake blew out a sigh. "Somebody found the Drummond woman."

"Yeah. Truck driver spotted her propped up in front of the old Culver cutoff sign on Highway 283."

"Damn," Jake whispered. "I'm on my way."

Jake Foley had been a deputy in Crest County for eighteen years. In his late forties, with two teenage boys, Jake's fair-mindedness had earned a lot of people's respect, including Matt's. Jake had been clear from the git-go, he didn't want the sheriff's job. Honorable and trustworthy, Matt respected Jake the way a son respected his father. Well, not his father. He'd spent his life lying to Matt's mother.

****

En route, Matt called the Medical Examiner. Dr. Reinhardt's reputation ranked with the best, and Julia Drummond deserved the best. Matt and his team would take pictures and secure the crime scene while waiting for the Doctor and his team to arrive from San Antonio.

Onlookers lined the stretch of well-traveled interstate. Murder in a small county brought people out of the woodwork. Rey had already established crowd control to prevent them from trampling evidence into oblivion. Matt insisted the two reporters who ran to meet him stay back with the spectators. Then he pissed off the local TV reporter and her cameraman by refusing to stop and talk.

Matt adjusted the badge clipped to his belt and then pushed his way through. "Where is she?"

Rey led the way around the eighteen-wheeler to the body. Matt stopped at the yellow tape and slowly scanned the area. The intersection had a speed limit sign mounted on a steel post on the south corner. At the base was a body with a green plastic sheet over her. Only bare feet were visible.

"Who covered her?"

"I did," Rey said, looking older than his twenty- six years. "I've worked shootings and bloody wrecks, seen about everything, but this is sick. This is twisted."

Rey slipped shoe covers over his boots. He signed the cross before he dipped under the tape. Then he carefully stepped over and uncovered Julia's body. Matt sucked in a breath. Rey had called it. This was sick.

Propped into a sitting position, arms hanging limp at her sides with legs crossed at the ankles, Julia was naked except for a red ribbon tied around her neck in a bow. Some kind of pale makeup covered her face, and her lips were bright red. Her raw wrists and ankles showed signs of restraint. Matt squatted and sat back on his boot heels. He looked toward the heavens before returning his gaze to her. She stared back at him, a blank nothingness behind wide-open emerald green eyes.

"Something's odd about her eyelids," he said to himself more than anyone. He stood and turned to Rey. "Cover her back up."

"You ever see anything like this?" Rey laid the sheet over the body, taking great pains not to disturb evidence.

"No. And I'll be sitting across the glass when the state puts a needle in this bastard's arm." Matt waited for Rey to back away, noting he was careful not to disturb the surroundings. "She couldn't have been out here long, not in this heat."

"Forensic team's finally here." Rey nodded his head toward the road.

"Good. Doesn't mean we stop taking pictures. We'll give them copies." Matt pushed a finger to his temple trying to ward off a headache. "Where the hell did all these people come from? Half the county is here. Vultures stretching their necks to get a look."

Rey glanced at the crowd and at the horizon. "Sun will set soon. Maybe then the morbid bastards will go home."

"Where's the guy who found her?"

"Sitting in my cruiser. Carl's with him."

"I'll talk to him. We need to know more about him."

"He's already radioed his dispatcher, told them he'd be late with his load."

The ambulance arrived, followed by the medical examiner's county car. "Let's get Ms. Drummond out of here with a little dignity. Rey, stay with the body. Make sure none of the onlookers sneak across the road."

"Consider it done."

Jake wrote furiously in his notebook, none of those modern gadgets for him. His hand raced across the paper then stopped abruptly. He adjusted his hat. "How do you tell her parents?"

"There's no easy way. The collateral damage to everyone involved changes people forever." Matt understood Jake's reaction. He'd probably never seen anything like Julia Drummond. "I'll stop by and tell them when I leave here."

"I don't envy you." Jake straightened his shoulders, his hazel eyes clouded with concern.

"Talk to the folks across the street. See if any of them knew Julia? If anybody says yes, get their name." Matt shook his head in disgust. "Then chase every damn one of them away."

Matt introduced himself to William—Willie, the truck driver—Phelps. He made this run from the manufacturing plant in Michigan to the warehouse where he delivered washers and dryers once a month. Matt jotted down his information, and then passed it to Sue for a background check. Matt followed protocol but didn't make the truck driver for the killer.

Doctor Kurt Reinhardt stood by the gurney. He looked up over the top of his glasses when Matt joined him.

"Occasionally, I think I've seen the worst of the human race and the things people do to each other." The ME sighed before he continued. "Someone always proves me wrong."

Matt refrained from sharing his thoughts. His gut coiled into a knot. "What else are you thinking?"

"Best guess, COD was strangulation. She also has irregular welts on her back and legs plus bruising around her neck." The ME moved a step closer and lowered his voice. "Her eyelids have been glued open."

Matt scrubbed his hand over his face. "I suspected as much."

"This woman went missing this past Thursday?"

Matt's stomach rolled over. "Yes, around six in the evening."

"At first blush, I'd say she's been dead over twenty-four hours."

"In this heat, she's been somewhere out of the elements. Where the hell has she been all this time?" Matt removed his hat and mopped the sweat off his forehead.

"Good question. I'm sure you'll find the answer, my boy. I'll rearrange my schedule and perform the autopsy myself tomorrow morning at nine. Will you attend?"

"I'll be there." The temperature had to be over a hundred in the shade, but a chill settled in Matt's bones. He had a vicious son-of-a-bitch loose in his county. One he had to stop. Soon.

He finished up with the truck driver and sent him on his way. Julia's body was whisked away. The crowd became disinterested and slunk off into the night. Jake and Rey would stay with the county forensic investigators while they searched for clues. Matt made the drive back to Curry. To Julia's parents.

****

Matt stayed until Mr. and Mrs. Drummond had calmed down enough to face their heartbreak alone. To look a mother and father in the eye and tell them their only daughter wouldn't be coming home was something no cop wanted to do. Mrs. Drummond, her eyes already swollen and rimmed in red, had broken down and sobbed. Matt left them clinging to each other and headed home.

For the first time since driving away from his house, he remembered he'd stranded Catherine. A picture of her and the traitorous dog curled up asleep on his couch flashed through his mind. The brief vision was a relief. He'd seen his share of ugly today.

The weight of the murder set his temples to pounding. A vice squeezed his skull. Stress induced, the shrink had said. Try death induced. Turmoil, danger, and murder did the trick every time. Trouble had followed him to the country, and trouble was exactly why he'd left Houston.

Trouble had followed Ms. Drummond, too. Trouble had murdered and painted her up like a doll. Recognition hit him. Son-of-a-bitch. Julia looked like a doll.

This nightmare was only beginning.

His house was dark, and the dog was asleep on the porch. Matt tried the door and the knob turned easily. Why hadn't she locked up after he left to go to the crime scene? He flipped on the kitchen stove light and walked lightly through the house. His heart jumped to the back of his throat and blood sped through his veins. Where was Catherine? A note on the counter next to the coffee pot explained. She'd called Marty. A wave of relief washed over him while he read. His steak was in the fridge, the potato had been delicious, and Catherine was sorry she couldn't wait. She started her new job tomorrow and didn't want to be late.

"She's sorry. I forget, and she apologizes." Matt was starving, but his head hurt too damn bad to eat. He collapsed in his easy chair and waited for the pain to ease.

****

The closet was smaller than he remembered, and his little corner of it was full of musty old boxes. He tossed them out onto the bedroom floor and crawled inside, pulling the door closed behind him. If he scrunched down, could he see the shelf through the narrow crack? Yes! A strange shot of excitement surged through his system. The sensation confused him because he'd hated being hemmed in. How many times had he hunkered down, staring out at the doll? Her green eyes had been a beacon, an anchor, proof he wasn't alone.

He shoved the closet door open and got out. He'd better stop wasting time. Today was his day to lock up at work, and once everybody had gone home, he'd weld the hasp onto the chain he'd bought. Thanks to the size of the small trailer house, he could bolt it to the frame of the bed. His next doll would wear a tether, one that allowed her to move from the bedroom to the bathroom. There'd be no more messes to clean up.

Hell, he'd dumped the old doll yesterday. Already, he ached for a new one. He whacked his leg with the hanger. An old familiar pain zinged straight to his groin. He stretched out across the bed, unzipped his jeans, and freed himself. The cool air sent his cock throbbing. His eyes closed. He was rock hard. The hanger came down with more force, again and again. He relived every minute he'd spent with his doll while his hand moved faster and faster. Too soon, he spent himself.

He'd look around somewhere other than Curry tonight. His heart pounded as he laid out his next moves. The new doll would fulfill his every desire. Maybe this one would cooperate.

Chapter Five

The smell of coffee pulled Matt out of a sound sleep. Still dressed and in his easy chair, he roused himself to investigate. His nose led him to the kitchen, where he found a beautiful redhead cooking eggs.

"Good morning. Did I die and go to heaven?" Her smile wiped away some of his exhaustion.

"You may wish for death before this is over. The local TV ran a story about the murdered woman. I figured you had a rough night and could use a helping of kindness this morning." She handed him a cup of coffee.

"Thanks." He held the mug under his nose and breathed deeply. "If I make it to heaven, I hope all angels look like you."

"You probably don't have time to die, but you might work in a shower before breakfast's ready."

"I'm gone." He hurried through his daily ritual and made it back seconds before Catherine set his loaded plate on the table. He pulled her into his arms and kissed her lightly. A simple thank you for being understanding. God, her soft lips were warm, and he struggled against the desire to crush her against his body. He'd forgotten the gentle feel and sweet taste of a woman's lips. He slid his hand around the back of her neck, cupping her head. Her back stiffened, and her hands pressed against his chest. He quickly moved away.

Her cheeks flushed red, then she smacked her lips. "Minty."

"It's not okay to kiss?" Matt found nothing humorous in her attempt to joke. Any hint of intimacy made her uncomfortable. He scared the crap out of her and wanted to know why. "We should talk about this."

"You need to eat." She sidestepped him, pointing to his plate. "Sit down. Besides, the real reason I came over this morning is to thank you for the flowers. I'm embarrassed to admit I forgot to tell you sooner."

"What flowers?" He slid into his chair and stuffed a bite of bacon in his mouth.

"Didn't you leave me a pot of African Violets the first weekend I was at Emma's?"

"You're not taking away my breakfast if I say no, are you? I'll bet they came from your landlady."

"There's not much left to take." She sat across from him and slid a slice of her bacon onto his plate. "They weren't from Emma or Marty."

Matt stopped chewing. "No card?" His curiosity about her fear of intimacy went to the back burner.

"No. I opened my door, and there they sat. Emma, being a romantic at heart, said I had a secret admirer." She shifted her gaze away. "I thought maybe you'd left them."

His freshly eaten breakfast backed up on him. "Did you find a florist tag?"

"No. Why?"

"It's the cop in me coming out. You'd only met a couple of people that first weekend?" Julia Drummond's blank green eyes flashed through his mind. The need to protect swelled in his chest.

"Let me think. Three." The color slid from Catherine's face. "You're scaring me."

"That's okay. I'm scaring me too. You need to be extra careful, be aware of your surroundings, and call me if you get any more gifts."

"I will."

"Promise me." Matt's mind raced with questions. No one had mentioned Julia having a secret admirer. Had the killer go into Julia's shop to buy flowers for Catherine and taken Julia instead?

"I promise."

"I'm sorry you had to call Marty last night. I couldn't leave the Drummond family. They knew the minute they opened the door."

"Don't apologize. I'd have been disappointed if you hadn't stayed." She paused and studied his face. "I was right. You do have a John Wayne soul."

"Not even close. Besides, that's too heavy a burden to put on a guy. What happens when I disappoint you?" Allowing her to build unreachable fantasies around him would be a mistake.

"What makes you think you will?"

"John Wayne always played a hero. That's not me."

"Whatever you say."

"Just don't expect me to be something I'll never be." He fidgeted. The chair shrunk. The room shrunk. The air thinned.

"That brings me to what I wanted to talk to you about last night." Her gaze was steady and unflinching.

"I feel a brush-off coming." He'd spooked her more than he realized.

She wagged a finger at him as if he were a child. "Not at all. I want to be honest with you. I'm not looking for a forever relationship. However, I think you'll need a friend before the murder investigation is over."

He liked her, enjoyed her company, and respected her honesty. She didn't want things to get serious. Neither did he, so using his best Colgate smile, he said, "I understand and accept your offer of friendship." He hoped she'd change her mind and want more.

"My independence is important to me. I went straight from my parent's house to my husband's." She paused again, appearing to be deep in thought. "Making the decision to throw caution to the wind and hit the road wasn't easy. But it was the right one. After eleven months, I've discovered if I put my mind to it, I can do anything."

"Which is why instead of feeling stranded last night, you managed to get home on your own."

"Right. I'll figure out a way to pay Marty back."

"I'm proud of you." He rose and put his plate in the sink, hating to end their conversation.

"You are?"

"I am. And I never lie." Her eyes widened and then quickly dropped to a skeptical frown. He believed somebody had lied to her more than once. "Leave the dishes, I'll wash up later."

"I should get to work."

"You can always come back and wash them tonight." He was serious, but she laughed.

I cooked. You clean," she said pointedly.

"He extended his hand. " I'll walk you out." Matt could've told her then and there, he'd never lock the door again if it meant she might be waiting for him. He put out fresh water for the ungrateful, unnamed dog lying under the mesquite tree, and headed to the county morgue while analyzing the tingle in his fingers. Damned if it didn't happen every time he touched her.

****

The long stretch of interstate surrounded by dry, parched land numbed Matt's brain. He radioed Sue before he reached the morgue in San Antonio. "I'll be out of pocket until after the autopsy."

"Let me know when you're back on call."

"You got it." He always checked in with Sue, yet she never failed to remind him to call.

"Is there anything I can do from this end?"

"Mr. and Mrs. Drummond insisted on making a visual identification this morning, so Doc's going to try to close her eyes." Matt's chest ached for Julia. "After they get back to Curry, you might check on them. See if they need anything."

"Hmmph." Sue huffed out a sound of disbelief. "A sheriff with a heart. That's a new concept in this county. Anything else?"

"Yeah. Can you call the florist shops in Curry and Butte Crest. Get me the name and address of anyone who bought African Violets in the past two weeks. Ask Jake to find out if Julia Drummond mentioned having a secret admirer to anyone."

"Have you learned something?"

"Too soon to say. I need to know if Julia had a stalker."

"I'm on it. Stay in touch."

"You got it."

Though he wasn't required to attend, the autopsy was important to Matt. He wasn't taking any chances with this case. Each individual scrap of evidence would be vital for the prosecution of Julia's killer.

He signed in and was escorted deep into the building where Mr. and Mrs. Drummond waited with an ME's assistant. The curtain slid back and revealed her daughter's face. Dr. Reinhardt had worked a miracle, because through the glass, Julia's eyes appeared to be closed. Julia's mother collapsed into her husband's arms. Matt swallowed a couple of times to control the ache in his chest.

After helping the Drummonds to their car, Matt joined the ME and his team to observe the autopsy. Matt's shirt clung to him, damp from the heat and humidity. Cold air and a musty, dank smell slammed into him when he entered.

"Sheriff. Have a seat on the stool, and we'll get started." Dr. Reinhardt's receding hairline, short legs and perpetual scowl reminded Matt of the detective who'd trained him. One he'd liked and respected. The ME passed him a smock and latex gloves. Even though he wouldn't touch the body, there were strict protocols to follow.

The doc's back had a permanent stoop. Matt wondered if years of bending over the autopsy table had caused it.

Today was about the business of death. There'd be no small talk, no chitchat. The ME turned on the recorder before he read the deceased's identification and case number out loud. Thus, the forensic investigation into what lead up to and ended Julia Drummond's life began.

Matt blocked out his anger and focused on the sound of Reinhardt's voice. The killer had washed the body, making the search for biological evidence such as hair, saliva, and semen difficult. A Y-STR analysis would target male DNA, in case some small clue remained.

Finally, Reinhardt backed away from the table and directed his assistants to complete the last few details. He and Matt stripped off their gear and walked in silence to the ME's office.

"I was right in my initial assumption." Dr. Reinhardt closed the door and sat behind his desk. "TOD was last Sunday between ten and midnight. The young woman died..."

"Julia. She had a name. It was Julia Drummond." Anger heated, boiled, and scorched his insides. Matt wanted, needed to punch something.

Dr. Reinhardt paused. "Sit down, Matt. I know her name. You have your method of coping, and I have mine."

Matt rubbed his hand across his eyes and sat with a sigh. "I'm sorry, Doc. Go ahead."

"COD was asphyxiation by choking, her hyoid bone was crushed. From the purple bruises on her throat, which were evident when we removed the two-inch wide ribbon from her neck, I'd say your killer has strong hands. As you know, contrary to the way TV portrays it choking is not an easy way to kill a person. Based on the different stages of healing, she'd been beaten across her back, buttocks, and legs at different intervals. The welts indicate a long thin object. I'll let you know if we identify what made the marks."

"Any idea what caused the abrasions on her wrists and ankles?"

"My guess is a form of tape. I took scrapings to send to the lab." The ME pinched the bridge of his nose. "One last thing and it's most disturbing."

"Are you saying she was raped? I'd assumed as much."

The doc waved his hand in the air, dismissing the observation. "Based on the bruising on her inner thighs and vaginal tearing, I'd say numerous times. No semen. What troubles me the most—" Dr.

Reinhardt hesitated. "The layers of makeup had been applied both pre and post-mortem. Her eyelids were glued open after death."

Dr. Reinhardt might as well been speaking in a foreign tongue. A tornado must've sucked Matt into its vortex and spit him out into an alien world.

"Matt?"

Lost in a void, it took him a second to respond. He repeated Reinhardt's words. "Julia Drummond was kidnapped, had her face made up, was beaten, and sexually assaulted a number of times. The bastard strangled her to death, which by itself was no easy feat. Then he washed her body, glued her eyes open, and applied more makeup?"

The ME nodded. "Correct. This behavior is deeply disturbing. My office will be at your disposal, for anything...anytime. You'll get toxicology and DNA reports. With the backlog at the county lab," he shrugged, "these tests take time."

The air left Matt's lungs. For a few seconds, he didn't seem to be able to refill them. "The sick son-of- a-bitch."

"I would say so."

Matt leveled his gaze on the ME. "I'd like to keep the information about the postmortem glue and makeup from the public."

"I'll brief my staff." Reinhardt escorted Matt to the exit and shook his hand. "And I'll personally track each piece of forensic evidence. Nothing will be compromised."

"I'll tell Julia's family she was treated with dignity and respect by you and your team."

Outside, Matt sat in his cruiser lost in thought. The sweltering August heat, the kind that filled his lungs with hot air, soaking his body in sweat, went completely ignored.

A press conference could make things worse if the killer wanted recognition, but how could he not warn the public, especially women? He radioed Sue to let her know he'd headed back. He wanted to meet with his deputies before he spoke with the local news people. If he handled it right, he could use the media's eyes and ears to his advantage.

Catherine had rehashed the morning a dozen times by the end of the day. Matt's early morning kiss warned her. He wanted her. That had been surprise enough, but the fire he'd ignited in her belly scared the crap out of her. She wanted him. She rubbed her hands up and down her arms. Something way past want stirred. Her body needed him. Needed with a passion that was painful. Needed his hands to touch her. Needed his body joined with hers. That knowledge was exhilarating and terrifying at the same time.

She'd grown to dread having sex with Andy. A word, a bad day, cold mashed potatoes—it didn't take much to make him angry. The first two years of their marriage, his abuse had been verbal. Everything changed after he joined his father's law firm. He'd become physical. Violent. Afterwards, he'd explain to her how the whole thing was her fault. Without fail, he'd demanded make-up sex. Like that made everything all right. Her hand slipped behind her and rubbed her right kidney, Andy's favorite place to hit her. A queasy sensation rolled into a knot in her belly. She shook off the fear. He'd never hurt her again.

Matt's hands were tender. His touch was gentle. He'd started a fire she thought burned out long ago. Her inner voice pulled her back to reality, reminding her that he was a cop and by nature a curious breed.

A noise from behind startled her. Instinctively, she raised her hands to defend herself, and whirled.

Susan King clapped a hand over her heart and squealed like she'd seen a rattlesnake. "I didn't mean to startle you. It's after five. You should've already headed home."

"No biggie." Catherine commanded her heart to slow. "I was deep into the letter G. I'll have these files in order in a day or two. There's more paperwork than I would've expected."

"Lots and lots of forms are associated with death and burials." Susan sat on the edge of the small desk. "You went all kung-fu when I surprised you. Have you taken classes?"

"It was a defensive stance. I've studied a couple of different martial arts." She'd told the truth before thinking. Damn. To avoid any questions she grabbed her purse and started out.

"Good for you. The murder of the Drummond girl makes me wish I knew more about self-defense." Susan tried a few karate stances out and then laughed at herself. "Go. Get out of here."

"See you tomorrow." The stiffness in Catherine's shoulders had reached the point of pain. Every muscle ached from bending over the file cabinet drawers.

A record hundred-and-six-degree day sent the heat outside rolling upward off the paved parking lot in waves. She stopped beside her car. The driver's side window was down, not cracked the way she'd left it. On the seat lay a small box. She reached in, lifted the top, and removed the beautiful green and yellow silk scarf she'd fallen in love with at the boutique on the square—over two weeks ago.

She dug out her cell and dialed Matt. Her insides trembled. The urge to run rushed through her.

"Hey. Catherine."

"I need to ask you something and tell me the truth."

"I don't lie. Remember?"

"Did you truly not send me the African Violets?"

"I did not. What's happened?" The pleased-she'd-called tone had left his voice, replaced by the gruff sheriff who'd threatened to arrest her when she'd made that illegal U-turn. "Did you get more flowers?"

"No. A silk scarf." She swallowed back the growing fear. If Matt hadn't given her these gifts...who had?

"Where are you?"

"In the parking lot at work."

"You have two choices. Go back inside and wait for me or come straight to my office."

"The funeral home is closing, and I'm not coming there. Can't I go home?" Alone, out in the open, she scanned the area, looking in all directions. Her instincts screamed run and hide.

"No." His sigh was audible. "My house is closer. If you won't come here, go straight there. Don't stop for anyone or anything."

She returned his huff of irritation. "Fine. I'll go to your place."

"I'm leaving right now. Stay in the car with the windows rolled up and doors locked."

She'd started to tell him she couldn't sit anywhere closed up inside her car. Not in this heat. Catherine wasted no time getting on the road. Within a few minutes, a sheriff's cruiser met her. He made a stop-on-a-dime U-turn and pulled up behind her. A glance in the mirror told her the driver wasn't Matt. He didn't engage his lights or siren, following until she drove into Matt's driveway. He stopped, waved as if they were old friends, and then sped away.

The no-named dog wandered out of the barn around to her side of the car. He plopped down on his butt and stared up at her. He turned his head sideways as if to ask why she didn't get out.

"You'll protect me, won't you, boy?" Like he understood, he jumped up and wagged his tail. She got out and scratched behind his ears. "I'll bet you'd like a cool drink, wouldn't you?" She dumped out his bowl and filled it with fresh water while keeping an eye out for Matt.

****

A face-to-face run-in with a mayor had kept Matt from leaving immediately, and Jake hadn't stayed with Catherine. Matt's gut tied in knots while he pushed the cruiser faster during the drive home. Here was another woman who needed him. No way would he let her down. Not this time.

He blew out a sigh of relief at the sight of her standing in his driveway. A gust of wind caught her hair and sent it billowing around her shoulders. She gathered the wildfire in one hand and held it off her face. She'd gotten out of the car and was wandering around with that useless mutt. His relief morphed to anger. Did she think the dog would protect her? Hell, he might lick an intruder to death. She had to be more careful. Matt slammed the cruiser door and stomped toward her. Fear for her safety seared his insides.

"Hey." She met him halfway.

"Dammit. I told you stay in the car."

Green fire flew from her eyes. "You 'told' me? Nobody tells me what to do. Never again." She pushed around him and headed for her car.

"Are you crazy?" Had she yelled "never again" at him? Somebody had been super controlling of her in the past, but he wasn't that person.

She spun on her heel, marched back to him, and jabbed him in the chest. "No, I'm not. And don't you dare insinuate I might be."

"Wait." He blew out a breath. "I may have overreacted. A little."

"Ya think?"

She'd slammed her hands on her hips, not giving an inch. He had to make her understand the gravity of the gifts. "Don't leave. Please." He looped his fingers around the back of her neck, leaned down, and laid his forehead to hers. "I think you may be in danger."

"Because if you didn't leave this stuff for me, who did? You think that didn't scare the crap out of me?"

"I hope it did. May I see the scarf?" Fear flickered in her eyes, and he fought the urge to jerk her into his arms. Why and how had this woman gotten under his skin?

He had to pull back, put some distance between the two of them. His paranoia and fear for Catherine couldn't control him. However, the nagging question about the flowers still plagued him. He tried to ignore the headache bubbling below the surface.

He reached in her car and retrieved the scarf and box. A picture of a man's bicep fluttered to the ground. Catherine's gasp and horrified expression confirmed she hadn't seen the picture earlier. "Come inside."

Matt pulled a pitcher of tea from the fridge while Catherine paced back and forth across his kitchen. Her reaction was typical. She was not only frightened, she was furious. He picked out a few muttered words when she stormed passed. He'd never been friends with a redhead, but she certainly lived up to the stereotype. Phrases like, "kick somebody's ass," and "I'm not afraid," tumbled out while she walked—no, stomped through his house. Had he not been pissed himself, her behavior would've been funny.

He sat a half-filled glass down on the kitchen counter and caught her hands with his to stop her. He led her to a chair and coaxed her down. "I was afraid of this when you told me about the flowers."

"You think I'm being stalked?"

"I don't make assumptions. I'm trying to find the florist who sold the African Violets." He had to be honest with her. "The fact Julia Drummond was a florist and you received flowers..."

"Shit." Her eyes flooded with panic. "Am I a target?"

"I don't know. We've found no evidence Julia received any gifts." Matt finished filling two glasses, handed one to Catherine, and joined her at the table. "There weren't any pictures of body parts found in her belongings, and I don't get the significance of the scarf."

"I found it at the 'All Bright Things' boutique the day I went job hunting, but didn't have the money. At the time, I thought it was beautiful. Now I can't look at it."

"Someone watched you. Do you remember seeing anyone from the bar?"

"No. I got into town on a Friday, and the following Monday I hit all the shops on the square looking for a part-time job." She stood, resumed pacing. "I need to go."

"Go where? You're safe here with me." Then her meaning struck him, she was talking about leaving town.

"I should move on. Pack my stuff and leave."

"Bull. We'll figure out who this is. I don't suppose in your travels you stopped long enough to take a class and have a license to carry a handgun?"

The color drained from her face. Catherine stared at him, blinking rapidly. For a second, Matt worried she'd faint.

"Hey. I didn't mean to upset you. Guns are safe if you're properly trained." Matt went to her and placed his hands on her shoulders. "Breathe. Let your heart rate slow a fraction."

"No guns. I can defend myself without a weapon."

"Defending yourself isn't as easy to do as you might think."

"I'm not scared. I don't want a gun."

Matt studied her face, trying to read something in her eyes. Anything he could use to understand what was going on in her head. She wouldn't hold his gaze.

"I'm going home."

"First, let's go to my office. You need to fill out a report."

"No report. I left my windows down too far. I'll be more careful."

"Your safety is important to me." He tried to tug her back to the table, but she resisted, so he relaxed his hold.

"Listen, it's getting late, and I have to get home. I'll exercise caution. I promise."

"It's a mistake not to get this on record."

"Mistake or not, I have no intention of setting foot in your office."

He heaved a sigh of aggravation. "Keep your phone close, and call me when you get home."

Matt kept the scarf, picture, and box. Concern for her and curiosity about her swirled in his head as he closed her car door and stepped back.

****

Catherine fluffed her pillow, rolled over onto her side, and did her best to fall asleep. She sat up when a sharp stab hit her in the chest. What a liar she'd become, telling Matt she could defend herself without a gun. She'd used one to protect herself from Andy, but the idea of ever holding another weapon in her hand repulsed her.

She'd driven away from Matt's house fully aware she'd missed her chance to tell him why she'd never hold a gun again. Or why she'd refused to go to the courthouse. No one ever looked at her the same after learning of her past. She'd taken another human being's life. She couldn't bear seeing Matt's beautiful, blue eyes turn dark and full of doubt. He was a cop for Christ's sake. The ones she'd dealt with in Tulsa had believed the worst. He'd be like everyone else and question her motives. Didn't she still? Didn't at least part of the blame lay with her?

Nausea stirred and her throat filled with bile. She'd opened her soul and relived her humiliating life with Andy to the police and the DA. Their eyes had been cold, full of disbelief. She might've been convicted of murder had she not permitted her doctor and the director of the women's shelter to come forward. Thanks to their records, she wouldn't spend the rest of her life in Oklahoma's Tutwiler State Prison for Women.

Why shouldn't she have this little bit of respite? Maybe spending time with a handsome man before she moved on would be okay. Maybe someday she'd tell him, and maybe he'd ask her to stay.

She wanted to run. She wanted to stay. She wanted to find peace.

She   could   dream,   couldn't   she?

Chapter Six

Regardless of the situation, Rey's appearance was immaculate. Black hair, black eyes, and a snow-white smile, women liked talking to him. Matt counted on Rey's familiarity with Tanya Perry to keep the questions relaxed. The plan had worked until he'd pushed her to dig deeper into her memory.

Rey plopped a box of tissues in front of Tanya. "Did Julia mention someone she'd met at the Saddleback making her uncomfortable?"

"No." She wiped tears from her cheeks. "I don't know what else to tell you. I'm sorry."

"Why didn't you tell us you two hung out at the bar the first time we talked?" Matt watched her expression closely. He couldn't understand why she'd kept their visits to the bar a secret.

"I didn't think it was important." Her eyes flashed wide. "You think she met the killer at the Saddleback?" Tanya fidgeted, opened and closed the snap on her purse.

"I don't know." Matt pushed a legal pad across to her and laid a pen on top. "Write down the names of any of the men she talked with, danced with, anyone at all. Deputy Santos will stay with you until you're finished."

Matt paused at the door. "You're sure Julia didn't mention having a secret admirer?"

"Yes."

"No surprise gifts from a secret pal?"

"No. Why?"

"She ever mention receiving unwanted pictures?"

"She would've told me."

"Thanks for coming down."

He believed her. A mixture of relief and disappointment swamped him. He wanted to believe the killer hadn't targeted Catherine. But if the gifts came from someone else, Matt was looking for two men. He wasn't ready to buy into that yet. He walked to Sue's desk. "Did you contact the newspapers and TV station?"

"You asked me to." Her raised eyebrows and tilted head indicated he'd asked a stupid question. "Just be sure you're here at two this afternoon. You don't want them quoting my opinion of the murdering bastard."

"Sue." He choked on a chuckle. "You surprise me. I'll have to keep an eye on you."

"I'm the least of your worries. Your message post is full." She narrowed her eyes and glared. "Half of them are from Harold Fletcher. Don't throw them in the trash this time."

Matt stood next to Sue's desk and presented her with his best smile. "Do I have to talk to him? Couldn't you put him off?"

"I've put him off for two days. He wants to know your plan to catch the killer." Her eyes lit up with mischief. "I could tell him you went fishing."

"I'll call him later." Matt went back to his desk and called Julia Drummond's parents. They deserved to know about the press conference before the interview aired. He pushed his way through the conversation, and then leaned back to sort through the stack of messages. Rey knocked on the doorjamb right before Matt picked up the phone to call Curry's mayor.

"Got a minute?" Rey waggled the legal pad in his hand. "I've got the list from Tanya. I can split it up. We'll work faster if we don't crisscross each other's paths."

"Good idea. Sit down, let's take a look." Matt recognized a few of the names. Most of them meant nothing to him. Of course, JC and

Vince, those names he recognized. "Are you friends or acquaintances with any of the guys?"

"Yeah. I know most of them, call a few of them friends. Why don't you let Jake and me look? We'll come back with the list prioritized and divided three ways."

"Do that. I need to call Mayor Fletcher and then make a run to the square."

Sue spoke from the doorway. "No need calling Harold. He's coming down the hall now. You've got thirty seconds."

Matt heaved a sigh. "Crap."

"I'm gone," Rey said with a chuckle.

"Coward," Matt muttered under his breath.

Harold Fletcher didn't wait to be announced. Rey stepped out of the way to allow the mayor's stubby body through the door. He nodded at Rey, then sat in the chair directly across from Matt.

"Harold. Nice to see you." Matt noted the sweat on the mayor's forehead. How anybody wore a suit and tie in a hundred-and-four degree temperature was beyond understanding.

"I don't appreciate you not returning my calls. My office is inundated with voters wanting to know what's being done to find this maniac." He threw his hands in the air. "What am I supposed to tell them?"

"You need to understand, this office has been busy too. I don't have time to drop everything and call you because you're getting pressure from your constituents." He raised one finger to stave off Harold's interruption. "I'm talking to the press at two if you'd like to attend. In fact, you backing me up might have a calming effect on the public."

Harold shifted his bulk to one side. "I don't know if that's a good idea. What will you tell them?"

"Very little. We haven't uncovered any clues at this point in time. If anyone has information that might be helpful, I need him or her to come forward. Plus, I'm cautioning the young women of Crest County to exercise good judgment, and to be careful about going out alone."

"But why? You'll add to the anxiety already growing. You should hear some of the complaints my clerks are getting. If this was the old west, you'd have a mob mentality building."

"Harold, we're doing everything we can to catch Julia's killer. It's up to all of us to calm the fears."

****

The boutique owner met Matt at the door. "Come in, Sheriff." The pretty brunette extended her hand. "Lynn Kerensky. Welcome to All Bright Things. Can I help you find anything in particular?"

He waited while she scanned him from head to toe. She stopped at his badge and offered him a smile. Matt pulled the scarf from his pocket. "Do you carry this brand and style?"

She inspected the brand tag and smiled up at him. "I do. I'm not the only one on the square who sells them."

The clerk led him to a shelf of various color- blended silk scarves. Matt's hopes dropped a notch. There were dozens like the one in his hand.

Ms. Kerensky stood too close. Matt stepped back out of her space.

"My guess is you'd be hard pressed to tell me who bought this particular one."

"I don't keep track of cash transactions, but I can get you credit card purchases. It'll take a while."

"I'd appreciate you checking. Don't go back further than July twenty-sixth."

Her brown eyes widened. "Does this have anything to do with the murder?"

Matt ignored her question. "When do you think you could have the names?"

Ms. Kerensky closed the distance between them. "Around six. Come back when I close, we can grab a bite to eat."

"I'll have to pass on supper. But I appreciate the offer." Matt made a quick escape, crossed to his cruiser, and headed back to his office. Ms. Kerensky's offer was flattering. Oddly enough, he had no interest in spending his free time with anyone other than Catherine. If he believed in reincarnation, he'd think they'd met before, in another life. The urge to see her again was powerful. He checked the time. He had to get back for the press conference. A phone call would have to do.

She answered on the second ring. "Hey. I was thinking about you."

"Good to know. Care to share?" His body instantly reacted.

"Sure. If you don't have plans, I'll cook supper for you tonight." She spoke quietly, in a whisper.

"What time and what can I bring?"

"How's seven? That will give me time to fix my famous spinach lasagna."

"Spinach? Uh...okay." The sound of Catherine's laugh, soft and low, rumbled through his cell. Hell, he'd eat anything she put on the table, including spinach.

"How about sausage lasagna."

"Much better. Can I bring the wine?"

"Sure. You choose. I'm not much on Chianti."

"Trust me. See you at seven." Matt parked and hurried inside.

Sue followed him into his office. "You're mighty pleased about something."

"I don't know what you're talking about?"

"You were grinning from ear to ear when you swaggered through the door. Look at you. You can't keep a straight face. I'm guessing it ain't the press conference."

"You're too smart for your own good." Matt leaned down to whisper in Sue's ear. "I've got a date with a beautiful woman tonight."

She stepped back and studied him intently. "I knew it. It's the new redhead." At his nod, she patted him on the cheek. "Good. Now go meet the press."

"Ask Rey and Jake to come in first." Matt had one more point to make. "And I don't swagger." He'd have sworn Sue muttered, "Do so," behind his back.

Matt wanted background checks run on every name Tanya Perry had provided. In the morning, they'd start interviewing, hoping to unearth something to bust open the case. After sharing his expectations with his deputies, they talked briefly about the flowers and if they had a possible connection. Then Matt collected his thoughts and went to the conference room.

He dreaded the press, remembered the hoards of unscrupulous newshounds he'd encountered in Houston. Here he faced the editors of two small town newspapers and one lone newscaster from local channel nine. Sue had settled them in with coffee and rolls from the Sweet Shop. The concern on their faces was real. Matt hoped the razor sharp ruthlessness he'd been used to in Houston was nonexistent. He accepted the cup Sue handed him and sat.

"Thanks for coming today. I don't do prepared statements. In fact, I prefer face-to-face, impromptu conversations. I'll tell you what I can. Feel free to ask questions. You've already run stories on Julia Drummond's assault and murder. I can tell you the killer did a good job of erasing all clues, and I need the public's help. I'm also asking the women of Crest County to be vigilant when they're out, especially at night."

Steve Evers from the County Record spoke first. "When exactly was Julia abducted?"

"We believe she was taken after she closed up her florist shop last Thursday. That doesn't mean caution shouldn't be exercised during the daytime. Everyone should be aware of their surroundings, keep their cell phones charged and close, and go in pairs when possible."

"So you think another woman will be killed?" Andrea Simpson of the Curry Weekly News spoke up.

"That isn't what I said. Please, don't misquote me. You can state my department should be contacted right away if a loved one goes missing."

"You're waving the waiting period?" Andrea's pen was posed over her notepad.

Matt put what he hoped was a reassuring smile on his face and nodded. "That's correct. Don't make a big deal out of it. The last thing I want to do is cause a panic."

"You've already got that," Steve grumbled. "The men-folk of this county are edgy and ready to turn on each other."

"The press can go a long way in helping the public control their emotions. You've all seen stories on the national news where an innocent victim's death is sensationalized. It only serves to make matters worse. I'm asking you to report the facts in a responsible manner. We want to hear anything your audience thinks might help us catch this guy."

Sylvia Horning from channel nine hadn't spoken a word. Sue had warned Matt that Sylvia wasn't to be trusted. She was on the hunt for one big break to catapult her to fame. Apparently, she thought her way to a larger market was through destroying people's reputations. Sylvia liked to spin scandal in with the story whenever possible. The two newspaper editors were dressed casually, but Sylvia wore a navy blue suit with a blue blouse underneath. Matt figured the camera loved her highlighted hair and creamy complexion. She batted her eyelashes and crossed her legs. Her skirt slid up another inch or so.

"No questions, Ms. Horning?"

"Oh, I have several. Are we to understand you have no clues at all?"

"I believe that's what I said."

"Hmm. Exactly what are you doing to ensure the safety of the women in this county?"

A loaded question. One he intended to avoid. "Ms. Horning, every available deputy is on the streets. As always, we are vigilant and watchful for our citizens."

Her eyes narrowed. "I'd like to film an interview with you for tonight's news."

"Sorry. The investigation takes precedence over me getting in front of a camera. If that's all, Sue will see you out."

"My viewers expect more of a story from me. I don't work well with 'no comment.'"

"I've told you as much as I can. I'm sorry if that's not enough." Matt excused himself. His part of Tanya's list needed his attention. He waited until the press was out of the building before asking Sue for help.

"Will you look at the names Tanya Perry provided? If you know any of these men, give me a brief history. I'd like your personal take on them."

"You want my opinion?" She covered her heart with her hand and blinked rapidly a couple of times. "Huh. You're the first man since my Bobby who's asked me what I think."

"I trust your read on people."

"Now you're flattering me. When will I meet this new woman in your life? I hear tell she's a looker." Sue picked up the list and pulled a chair around next to his.

"She's beautiful."

"I should meet her. You'll want my opinion of her. Right?" She tilted her head sideways and looked at him.

"No, ma'am. I've already made my mind up about her."

Sue grinned, then studied the page before speaking. "First on the list is James Claude Harper, better known as JC. Everybody around here knows him. In the neighborhood of forty, he's worked at the Saddleback for years. Don't know why he never made more of himself. Best I can remember he had no ambition."

"Him, I've met. If I leave the list with you, can I get a typed overview of each man?"

"Sure thing. Do I get investigator's pay?"

"If that's your price." He held his hands in the prayer position. "I'm willing to beg if you want."

Color flooded her neck and spread to her cheeks. "Not necessary. Go on and get out of here. Make yourself *purdy* for your new woman. And here I was worrying about you finding a missus."

"Don't start that." Matt fumbled for words. "I'm not looking for a wife." A rapid retreat seemed in order. He stopped at the door and added a request. "Rey and Jake have a list of names, too. I'll want you to do the same for them."

****

The sound of an engine rumbled up Catherine's driveway. She pulled the curtain back to see Matt climb out of his black pickup. She'd been unable to put him out of her mind since his phone call. She wiped her damp palms on her jeans and forced herself to wait for his knock.

"Hey." She swung the door wide and stared. Streaks of gold from the evening sun highlighted the side of his head, and his raven hair shimmered. Standing there in jeans, a blue pullover, and alligator boots, he could've been a magazine model.

"Hey, yourself. May I come in?" The corners of his mouth curved upward in a lopsided grin.

"Oh." Catherine moved out of the doorway. "How embarrassing. You're just so... I should check on the lasagna."

Using the kitchen for a safe haven, she made herself look busy. If he didn't think she was crazy before, he must now. She couldn't believe she'd stood there staring at him. How juvenile. She could hear him behind her, the rustle of the sack when he removed the wine, the soft pop of the cork. His mere presence undid her. His body heat surrounded her. She didn't know if she could manage a friendship with him. He'd need more than she knew how to give. She'd have to face him sometime.

"I hope you like this. I'm not exactly what you'd call a wine connoisseur." He opened and closed a cabinet door and then another.

"I'm sure it's wonderful." Grateful he'd ignored her behavior, she turned and accepted the juice glass he held. "Emma probably didn't let her daughter have wine."

"Probably not. These work fine." He sipped a taste as if to prove it. "Something I can do to help?"

"If you'll get the salad from the fridge, we're all set."

Catherine loved to cook for anyone who loved to eat. Matt rewarded her by enjoying her hard work to the last bite. Conversation with him came easy. She learned they shared political views and could talk sports as long as they stuck to football. He didn't push for personal information, but she found herself telling him about her childhood. The compassion in his eyes was real when she explained how her parents died in a six-car pile-up on an icy road when she was twenty.

"How about you? Are your parents still living?" She refilled his glass and handed it back. Their fingers touched and heat shot up her arm. His gaze darkened briefly.

"Lung cancer took my mother a couple of years ago. After Dad died from a massive heart attack, she wasted away. He was sheriff of the adjoining county for thirty years. No doubt his name and reputation helped me win the election."

"Were you and your father close?" She held back the urge to touch him. The change in his expression when he spoke about his father sent chills racing up her arms.

"Hell no," he snapped. "But he taught me plenty. When I was a kid, he used me for alibis and excuses. Never tried to hide his affairs from me. Put me in the position I had to lie to my mother to cover his sorry ass. She trusted me, and I couldn't break her heart." Matt blinked, coming back from a long time ago. "No siblings...how about you."

Her heart rolled into a ball and dropped to her stomach. Matt's pain had poured out of him and into the words, "she trusted me."

"A brother. Jack and his family live in Flint, Michigan." She didn't add they'd been estranged for years. Andy hated her to have contact with her family. To stop the argument, she'd finally severed ties with Jack altogether. Not that her action had helped their relationship. Later, at the women's shelter, she'd learned it was one more way she'd allowed him to control her.

Matt's hand on top of hers stopped her mind from wandering. The pressure of his thumb rubbing a circle over her skin made her smile. She twined her fingers through his.

"I'm glad you asked me over."

His palm was large, calloused, and warm. "Me, too."

She held his gaze when he pulled her to her feet and into his arms. His fingers ran down her jaw and back up where he looped them around the back of her neck. His lips descended and lightly touched her cheek, moved to her earlobe then on to her neck. She leaned her head back, enjoying the small nips and kisses. Her eyes fluttered closed, and she sank into the wonder of being gently touched. His mouth covered hers, and the tip of his tongue ran lightly across her bottom lip. The pressure increased, and she welcomed him inside. God, he tasted of wine and spices. His fingers buried in her hair and held her head in place.

The feeling of being trapped by his hands slammed into her. Catherine jerked away and stumbled a few steps backward. For a split second, she looked for a way around Matt. Looked for somewhere to run. Looked into kind, startled eyes. She caught herself and tried to smile. He advanced a step, holding his hands up in surrender.

"What just happened?"

Catherine's heart broke at the stunned look on his face.

He closed the distance with another step.

This time she stood her ground when he tucked a strand of hair behind her ear before cupping her cheek in his palm.

"That look of panic in your eyes, while fleeting, destroys me. Tell me what I'm doing to scare you. How do I prove you can trust me?"

Catherine pressed her face into his warm palm. She wouldn't let this slice of happiness get away from her.

She had to warn him.

She clasped his hand and led him to the couch.

Chapter Seven

Matt checked his raging curiosity, knowing if he pushed Catherine too hard she'd change the subject. He sat, doing his best to appear calm. Finally, he'd learn why she panicked at his touch. Her shoulders rose and her back stiffened. He scoured his brain for a way to make whatever she was about to tell him easier and drew a blank.

"I'm not scared of you."

"I'm glad." Matt was totally lost.

"I'm not a good lover. There's an excellent chance I'll disappoint you, and I hate to embarrass myself."

"We kissed." He refrained from commenting how sweet her lips felt under his. He worked at keeping his confusion from flashing across his face too. "I wasn't trying to pressure you into anything more."

"I know. The thing is... I'm sexually attracted to you. And in all honesty, I'm surprised."

She clamped her lips shut. Matt didn't push, because if her squirming meant anything, there was more.

"Sex hasn't been on my list of priorities in a long time. I've been assured I'm cold and inadequate."

"The person who 'assured' you was an idiot. He made excuses for his own incompetence." Matt ached for the chance to prove the guy wrong. "You have a list of priorities?"

"Yes, it's compiled of things I'll never do." She smiled, and her bunched shoulders relaxed a little. "The *Never* list."

"I see." Matt went to the kitchen and returned carrying their glasses of wine. He moved her to the love seat next to him. "Am I on this *Never* list?"

That sexy blush of hers crawled up her neck and settled on her cheeks again. On her, the high color was beautiful.

"You did threaten to arrest me the first time we met."

His mind ran back over previous conversations. He chuckled when their first encounter played back in his memory. Her hair had reminded him of wildfire. It still did.

"I can honestly say I'm glad I didn't. As far as being inadequate, no one who has such a powerful effect on me is lacking anything. Trust me, I don't lie." He paused to ensure she understood he was serious. "I don't know where we're going. I know I want to go there—with you." He sat back on the small love seat and let out a big breath.

She sipped her wine. "We'll see."

"We will?" He picked up the remote and turned on the TV. She didn't resist when he wrapped an arm around her shoulder and pulled her close. She rested her head against him. It was enough for now.

"Yeah. I think so."

Her tense body calmed, relaxing in to him. He wouldn't pressure her, but he'd be there when she was ready. Then he'd prove she was a beautiful and sensual woman.

Somewhere between shows, Matt felt her body relax. He readjusted his position, nestled her in his arms and watched her sleep. Was this her big secret? If so, he had to convince her whoever crushed her self-confidence was a dumb ass. He wanted to make love to her, but first she had to trust him. He'd gain that trust by letting things happen on her terms.

She had no idea how beautiful she was. The sprinkling of freckles across her nose, the dark russet lashes, and her soft, full lips made him ache all over.

Her body twitched, her brow furrowed, and a soulful whine came from deep inside. Matt cradled her closer, whispering. "Shh. You're okay. I've got you." He stroked her forehead and spoke softly.

On a gasp, her feet kicked, and she slapped at his hands. Her eyes flew open, wide and full of terror. Shit. There was more she hadn't told him. She calmed when her gaze landed on his face.

"Easy. You had a nightmare." He relaxed his hold, allowing her to come fully awake. She blinked a few times. Tension left her body as she relaxed, safe in his arms. "Want to tell me?"

"It was nothing." She laughed off the dream. "I can't believe I fell asleep."

"Stay." He tested the situation by placing his hand on her arm. "Do you have nightmares often?"

"Not anymore." Her lips thinned.

"Can you tell me?"

"Nothing to tell."

"I hope someday you'll trust me enough to confide in me. Until then, I won't pry." He saw no need to press her. She'd shut him out if he did. "You're incredibly beautiful when you sleep."

"Stop. I'm incredibly ordinary."

"Ordinary's not a word I'd use to describe you. Incredible? You bet. And I..."

"I know—you don't lie." Catherine pushed up and straightened her rumpled blouse.

"I intended to say, I'm an expert." The moment had passed and she'd retreated. "It's close to ten. I should head home. Let's clean up the dishes before I go." He cut off her protest. "Remember? You cooked. I clean."

****

Matt read the typed document and nodded his head at Sue in appreciation. "Thanks. You didn't have to work on this last night. How late did you stay?"

"It was nothing." She lifted one shoulder. "No one's waiting for me to come home."

Matt didn't consider himself sentimental, but Sue's statement kicked him right in the heart. He'd never asked how long she'd been a widow, nor had she mentioned having any children. Maybe her being alone explained why the sheriff's department and the community had become an important part of her life.

Matt looked up from his copy and caught her staring.

"How was your evening?" she asked. The corners of her mouth twitched.

He should've known better than to tell Sue about the date with Catherine. Sue questioning him was his own fault. He considered a flip answer; instead, he leaned back and waved her to a chair. "Okay, I guess. She's got problems. Something happened she can't get past."

"And she's not letting you fix them."

Damn. Sue cut right to the heart. "Can't fix anything if I don't know what's broke. She's not talking."

"Did you Google her? Want me to?"

"No to both." Guilt that he'd already considered the Internet shrunk him in stature a couple of inches. "Wouldn't feel right. She'll tell me when she's ready."

"You better be good to her. Rumor is more than one man has noticed her good looks."

"What rumor?" His thoughts went straight to Catherine's gift-giver.

"Ha. That perked your ears up. Didn't it?"

"Seriously, Sue. What're you talking about?"

"Word is out that Vince paid too much attention awhile back. Why Jessie thinks another woman would have him is a wonder." Her eyes sparkled. She was having a good time. "You wouldn't be jealous. Or would you?"

"No. Somebody anonymously left her flowers. A few days later, she found this inside her car." He opened a drawer and handed Sue the silk scarf. "The box had a picture of a man's bicep inside." He held the snapshot out for her to see.

Sue dumped the scarf on his desk and dusted her hands. "That's sick. She's coming in to fill out paperwork, right?"

"No. She refuses to file a complaint."

"Foolish girl."

"Nothing says I can't look into who left them. Tanya insists Julia hadn't received any gifts or pictures. I'm not convinced the killer and the stalker are two different men." Matt looked up and motioned Jake and Rey into his office. "When I catch up on last night's activities and lay out today's assignments with these guys, I'm starting at the top of my list. If you need me, give a shout."

****

Matt knocked on JC's front door. He'd done a decent job of keeping the house paint maintained. The shrubs and grass had withered and died under the blistering heat wave. A trellis with a few limp, brown remnants of a climbing rose bush offered no shade to the sprawling porch that ran the length of the house. Even though JC worked nights, his name was first on the list, and Matt was a right-down-the-page kind of guy. He knocked, waited a few minutes, and then repeated the process.

JC opened the door a crack, scowled, and rubbed his knuckles across his eyes. "What's up, Sheriff?"

"If you have a minute, I'd like to ask you a few questions."

"About?"

"Julia Drummond." Matt didn't offer further explanations. JC's reaction would speak volumes. His eyes shifted away from Matt for a second, then returned and held.

JC swung the door wide. "Might as well come in. I'm up. I gotta have caffeine."

Matt followed him through the living room into the kitchen and waited while he fixed two cups of instant coffee. Matt couldn't hide his surprise at the way the place was decorated. The burgundy leather couch and chair had seen better days. The widescreen TV made his mouth water. Damn thing dwarfed his. Dallas Cowboy memorabilia and posters were scattered around the room.

"Big football fan?"

"Yeah. Hard to miss." JC plunked two coffees on the table. "Sit. Drink. Ask away."

JC slumped down in a chair at the breakfast table, and Matt sat across from him. "Just conversationally, tell me about Julia. How often she came in, and who she talked to, that sort of stuff."

"She's...sorry, hard to think of her as gone. Her and Tanya been coming in for a year or so. Neither of them drank much, a few beers. With me stuck behind the bar, I can't tell you who she danced with or talked to. Marty probably could. She's on the floor with the customers."

"You ever see any of the men hit on Julia?"

"No. I told you. I don't see much from behind the bar."

"How about yourself? Was she your type?"

JC snapped to attention. "What the hell does that mean?" He shoved his hair off his face and glared at Matt.

"It's a question. I see no reason for you to get upset."

"Pissed is a better word. Did you roust me out of bed to ask about the dead girl or make accusations?"

"JC..." Matt hesitated for a second. "I'm looking for answers. You may have seen something you don't know is important. Since you brought up the subject, where were you Wednesday, July twenty-sixth?"

"Hell, I don't know." JC walked to the fridge, pulled off a magnetic calendar, and tossed it onto the table. "Feel free to check my appointment book. Best guess? Right here at home. Alone."

Matt finished his questions, thanked JC, and then headed to the next name on the list. Most of the men were at work. A tinge of regret for taking the list of names in Curry hit Matt. If he'd been in Butte Crest, he could've stopped by and asked Catherine to have lunch with him.

Hell, he'd strung more sentences together last night at her house than he remembered ever doing. Why'd he share that stuff about his dad? Matt jerked off his hat and shoved his fingers through his hair. People had trusted the unworthy bastard. Mama never questioned or doubted his word. Most of all, Mama had trusted Matt.

He hoped Catherine didn't think him too cynical. Truth was he could count on one hand the people he trusted. There used to be another, but she was dead.

****

Backtracking every step Julia Drummond had taken for the last few weeks of her life had netted zero clues. Matt reread the reports from the initial search of her house and store. A warrant for her phone records from the florist shop and home had produced nothing. The young woman apparently led a quiet, uneventful life right up to the day she disappeared.

Jake and Rey were working their section of the list Tanya had provided. A couple of the men from the bar had records. No violent offenders, but Matt wanted to finish his list today. He intended to double back and interview the ex-cons himself.

Matt had one name left. He pushed the doorbell at Vince Bradley's and waited.

Jessie Bradley opened the duplex door wearing a pink, satiny robe, holding a mascara wand in her hand. The makeup on her face and sky-high blonde hair indicated she was dressing for a night out. She propped one hand on her ample hip and ran her gaze from his toes back up to his eyes. He hadn't saved the easiest for last.

"If you've got a warrant for Vince's unpaid traffic tickets, you can wait in your car until he gets out of the shower." She closed the door before Matt uttered a word.

He pushed the doorbell again. "I'm not here to arrest Vince. I need to speak with you both."

The door opened s l o w l y. "What's there to talk about?"

"Julia Drummond."

Jessie huffed out a sigh and waved him inside. "Have a seat." Without another word, she walked back to what Matt assumed was the bedroom and closed the door.

Matt chose to stand. A lot of furniture had been crammed into the small duplex. Newspapers and magazines were strewn about, most of them weighted down by empty long neck beer bottles. One or both of the Bradley's smoked. The smell and number of butts in ashtrays staggered the senses. A few minutes later Jessie and Vince emerged, both pressed and polished in jeans and western boots. Vince offered a smile and a handshake, waved at a chair, and then seated himself in an oversized recliner.

"What'd you want to know about Julia?" Vince smoothed back his hair, accentuating a receding hairline.

"Anything that might help me apprehend her killer." Jessie flinched, but Vince's face muscles remained relaxed. Maybe too relaxed.

"She came in the Saddleback. We weren't friends," Vince said.

"Not that she didn't want to be 'friends.' With Vince—not me." Jessie's tone dripped venom, her green eyes fiery with hate.

"Shut that shit up, Jessie." Vince shot his wife a warning look. "I never messed with her, and she never hit on me."

"Yeah. Right. She and that friend hung out at the bar. Always came alone. I can tell you what they were looking for. Somebody else's man."

Matt held his hands up in the timeout sign. "Either of you notice her leaving with anyone? Dancing with any one individual?"

"Nope." Vince shook his head. "I don't remember her on the dance floor."

"Vince wouldn't have noticed her walking around naked. He ain't had eyes for anything or anybody but the mystery woman. He's too busy sniffing around that redhead." Jessie, unfazed by the dirty looks Vince fired her direction, kept right on going. "The killer could've hauled Julia out right in front of him."

She'd referred to Catherine, but Matt played dumb. "Mystery woman?"

"That fancy new waitress." Jessie spit the words. "I asked about her. Marty said she was passing through. Can't leave too soon."

"Stop your bitchin' about Catherine," Vince barked.

"Catherine? You're on a first name basis with her now?" Jessie's voice shot up an octave.

"About Julia..." Matt tried to get back to the reason for his visit. "Where were you folks Wednesday, July twenty-sixth?"

Both Vince and Jessie stood. They moved to stand next each other, their hands met and clasped together. "Why are you asking us?" Vince asked. "We had nothin' to do with her death."

"Standard procedure. If you'll give me that information, you folks can get started on your evening out."

Jessie stared at Matt as if he'd read their minds. "How'd you know we're going out?"

Matt suppressed the urge to shake his head in amazement. "Lucky   guess."

Chapter Eight

Stretched out on the couch, pictures of his last doll flashed slideshow-style through his memory. Tomorrow would make two weeks since the accident, and that's what it was... an accident. The anger at himself had passed. He hated to admit it, but eventually she had to die. He couldn't allow a doll to leave the trailer alive. He'd learned long ago all women were like Mama. Liars and whores, every one of them.

Thinking about Mama stirred up the hornets. They'd quieted down while he'd had a doll. They swirled, buzzing louder until his head roared. He needed another doll.

He had a plan. Was gonna do things right. The first time he'd been impulsive. Careless. He'd been too excited to think straight. Somebody could've seen him. Was he being too picky by taking his time? No. After all, this was a private matter between him and his doll. He'd recognize her. His new doll would treat him better than the old one had. She'd want him. The look in her eyes would be a sign. No matter how much she lied and denied it...he'd know. The new waitress offered great possibilities, but she'd take some planning. When he took her, he'd want to keep her for a long time.

****

Sweat ran down Matt's face, met at the tip of his chin, and fell to the hard, parched earth. Starving for any type of moisture, the thirsty ground greedily absorbed the liquid. He brushed his gloved hand up his neck to stem the flow and ignored the small rivulets, which rushed downward from his bare chest and back, drenching the waistband of his jeans. With one final blow of the hammer, he secured the new hinge, stepped back, and smiled while the gate on his corral swung back and forth. The renovation of the old barn behind his house was near completion. Soon he'd start a search for a couple of horses.

Hard labor, working with his hands in particular, usually brought him a small measure of satisfaction and peace. Nothing provided such luxury these days. Nothing would until Julia Drummond's killer sat on death row in Huntsville Prison.

At the sound of an engine, he walked to the driveway, chuckling when Catherine's old car wheezed and coughed a puff of smoke before shuddering to a stop. He hadn't had time for more than one quick lunch with her for the past week. He liked that she'd stopped by.

"Come out back," he called out. "I'm working in the barn."

She stopped all forward movement. Her gaze skittered across his bare chest. Bright pink shot up her cheeks into her hairline. Damn, he liked that she blushed easily.

"Sorry." Matt grabbed his shirt. His fingers and thumbs became unfamiliar with buttons. He struggled but finally succeeded. "I forgot I was half- dressed. The dog doesn't notice whether or not I've got clothes on."

"Uh...okay...not a problem." She tapped her chest with her fingers. "My fault for stopping by unannounced. I'm on my way to work, but I have a question."

Matt started toward her then stopped. "I'd better not come any closer. You can probably smell me from there, but it's good to see you. I've missed you." The traitorous dog rushed ahead, tongue lolling out to the side and fell at her feet.

"Oh. Thanks," she stammered.

Damn, he'd made her uncomfortable, which was the last thing he wanted to do. "You stopped by to ask me something?"

"Did you learn if Julia Drummond had a stalker before she went missing?"

Matt blew out a sigh. Worry behind her eyes made him want to wrap his arms around her, but the distance she kept between them sent him a *don't touch* message. "We questioned her friends and family. She never mentioned a secret admirer or gifts from an unknown person to any of them."

The frown on Catherine's face relaxed, but her eyes showed no relief. "That makes me feel better. No less creeped out, but better." She knelt down and scratched behind the mutt's floppy ears. "Have you picked a name?"

He glared at the slobbering animal, licking her hand. A name popped into Matt's brain. "Yeah. Benedict Arnold."

"That's not a name for a dog," she protested over a laugh.

"It fits him. If you can stand me, I'll show you what I'm working on."

"I can and I'd like to see." She patted Benedict one last time, rose, then headed toward Matt.

"In a week or two, I'll have the place ready to house a couple of horses." Matt noticed the slightest wrinkling of her nose. Undaunted, she continued without complaint.

She wandered through, nodded her approval, and then paused to inspect inside the two new stalls. Dressed for work at the bar, she could've been headed to a rodeo. A tucked-in blue western-cut blouse highlighted her tiny waist, but the tight jeans drew his attention to her unbelievably long legs.

"Do you ride?" He could see himself shopping. Not only for horses, but two sets of tack.

"Many years ago. I imagine I could still ride."

"Good. I need a roping partner."

"Sorry." She held her hands up in protest. "No way can I ride and throw a rope."

"I'll teach you."

"We'll see." She ran her hand over the stall door. "You've done a great job. The place looks like you hired a professional carpenter."

"I like working with my hands. It's good therapy."

She leaned back against a stall door and studied him in silence. "Why do you need therapy?"

He'd stuck his foot in his mouth and opened himself up for questions. Questions he didn't intend to answer. "I don't. Physical labor gets my mind off work."

Her eyed widened. "That was thoughtless of me. I'm sure you need something to take your mind off the murder. I don't know how you deal with death every day." She glanced toward the driveway. "I'd better go."

The dog ambled past him, avoiding the hand Matt extended. Wagging his tail, Benedict bumped her leg with his head as if aware she was leaving. "Take that mutt with you."

She laughed the kind of laugh only Catherine could. The kind that gave pleasure to anyone within earshot. The kind that drew you into her good mood without thought as to what was funny. The sound reverberated off the walls of the empty barn and slammed hard against his chest, hitting him like the sun poking its head up on the horizon dawning a new day—bright and full of hope. His heart rate quickened and blood thundered through his veins.

Brave soul that she was, she extended her hand and let him walk next to her all the way to her car. He theorized she might be holding her breath.

"There's a movie theater in Curry. Want to take in a show one night next week?" He held her door while she slid behind the wheel.

"I'd like that."

He plunged ahead before she drove away and he lost his nerve. "We could eat first. Curry has a couple of restaurants where a waitress comes to your table instead of you ordering at the counter. How's Monday night sound?"

"Monday's good."

Matt leaned down to the window. "Why's it hot in your car?"

"Duh." She gave him a wide-eyed grin. "Because it's over a hundred and three in the shade?"

A puff of smoke from her exhaust billowed up when she pushed the gas pedal. Matt shook his head. One of these days, her car would cough up a piston rod, roll over, and die.

****

He didn't need no high school diploma to read the message the doll at the Dairy Dream had sent him. Odd, he'd never noticed her before. Annie h a d openly flirted with him, delivered his food right to his table instead of hollering out his order number. She'd smiled and batted her eyelashes over those green eyes, then twisted her sexy ass all the way back to the cash register. He'd understood her true meaning when she'd told him to come back soon.

Not tonight, but soon. He'd wait for her to get off work, pick the right spot, and then take her. Mama's trailer was ready. He'd stocked the fridge and made sure the utilities were paid up. Anticipation sent chills up and down his arms while he cleaned the .380 pistol he'd found in Mama's nightstand. A sissy's gun and an old model at that, but purchased long before any of these bullshit laws about background checks went into effect.

He had a good feeling about this doll. They'd have fun together. She'd be nice to him, but if she wasn't, he'd learned how to bring her around.

****

The heat wave prevented her from jogging, forcing Catherine to stay indoors to exercise. Her martial arts instructor had stressed the importance of practice. She finished with twenty minutes of meditation, then rewarded herself with a leisurely soak in the antique, claw-foot tub before six o'clock.

Her small frame house shook against the brunt of a gust of wind. The windows rattled and dry tree branches scratched across the roof. She closed her eyes and blocked out all sound. Nothing would ruin her good mood. Let the wind blow hot air, sandblasting her skin. Let the sun dry the land and leave foot-wide cracks. Let the car air conditioner refuse to offer any respite from the punishing heat wave.

Matt would knock on her door soon. He'd said she was beautiful. In the few short weeks she'd lived in Butte Crest, she'd begun to feel he might be right.

She studied her sparsely filled closet. She'd made good tips the past three weekends but refused to buy anything new. The sense of accomplishment when she presented Emma with the rest of the rent was worth a lot more than a new outfit.

Finally satisfied with her appearance, she sat on the couch and read until Matt's black pickup rolled down the drive. A guilty pleasure, she watched him walk to the door. His long strides, the deliberate manner he planted each boot on the ground, his gaze set on his destination, all of his mannerisms screamed John Wayne swagger.

She mentally rehearsed answering the door. He'd ask, "Ready?" She'd answer, "Almost." And that would be a true statement. Her heartbeat increased the closer he came to her door. Blood raced and heated. Warmth settled in her lower stomach. Yep. Almost.

****

Matt picked Antonio's Italian Restaurant for his supper date with Catherine because of the ambiance its owners created. The candles, the grapevines, and the soft music in the background spoke of romance and sweethearts. The owners, Antonio and Maria to their patrons, greeted their customers as if they were family. Although short and robust, both were capable of lifting someone Matt's size off the floor with a hug. Catherine was embraced before he'd finished introductions.

"No. No," Maria admonished Matt when he slid into the booth. "You don't sit opposite the lady. Sit beside her. No wonder she's the first one you've brought in to meet us."

"Sorry," Matt whispered, sliding in beside Catherine.

"Catherine," Antonio said, her name rolling off his tongue. "Welcome. You sit back and relax. Maria and I gonna take good care of you."

"Thank you." Catherine smiled at the happy couple before they disappeared into the kitchen.

"Aren't they great?"

"They complement each other. Are they always like this?"

"I've never seen them act any different."

Maria returned with two salads and two glasses of wine. She winked at Matt. "Enjoy."

"Thanks." He silently blessed her for forcing him to Catherine's side of the booth. Her nearness made it hard to think about food. This pull she had on him, the desire to feel her under him, damn, it spooked him a little.

"Did you preorder?"

"No. When those two say they're going to take care of you, be ready. You'll see."

The stream of conversation and food kept pace with each other until Catherine pushed her plate away with a sigh. Talking with her came easy, and both shared stories of their childhoods. Matt found himself back on the subject of his father's infidelity and the years of lying. "Strange, talking about him makes me sound bitter." Matt paused and reflected. "I guess all the lies my father told molded me into the person I am today. Nothing I hate worse than a liar."

Catherine scooted away from him. The air between them chilled while she swirled the wine around in her glass. Had he said something that triggered a memory? He'd certainly revealed more about himself than she had.

"Tell me about your brother. Jack, isn't it?"

"Yes. We used to be close. Back when we were kids and lived in the country. He was my best friend. It broke my heart the day he started school and left me behind, so my mother would tell me a few minutes before the bus brought him home in the afternoon. I'd be sitting on the fence post at the front gate waiting for him."

She paused, had mentally gone to another time, somewhere in the past. The distant pain in her eyes forced him to ask. "What happened?"

"Marriage. Mine," she said on a whisper. "Andy hated me spending time with Jack. My relationship with my brother was apparently a threat to our marriage. I broke off all ties to keep peace."

"Your husband's effort to control you." Matt knew the color of hate. When Catherine's eyes darkened to hunter green and met his, he recognized the look. It was on the tip of his tongue to ask her how her husband died, but Matt held back. A lot of painful memories were buried in her past. He wouldn't try to force her to talk.

"I know," she said. "Maybe we should see what's showing at the theater."

A quick glance at his watch had Matt laughing in surprise. Neither the movie nor the investigation had crossed his mind since she'd grazed his lips with a kiss at six o'clock. "We're too late. It's nine."

"I didn't realize we'd talked so long. Maybe you should take me home."

He didn't respond since it wasn't a question. She'd withdrawn, erected a wall he was sure he couldn't scale. He wouldn't bring up the subject of her family for a while. There was more to learn. Lots more. She had secrets, painful ones. Maybe she'd tell him when she trusted him enough. He had parts of his life he didn't care to relive or discuss, reasons he wouldn't get too close to her or anyone else.

He paid the check and made the obligatory promises to return and to bring Catherine. Maria must've noticed the difference in both their behavior, because she sent him a what-did-you-do look. He lifted one shoulder, kissed her on the cheek, and led Catherine to his pickup. Half the ride home they shared a stiff silence. He'd parked in front of her house when a poke in his ribs brought a quick rush of relief.

"I have trouble talking about the past. I've closed a few doors I don't want opened." Catherine's hand rested on his arm.

"Don't apologize. Sometimes I ask too many questions."

The lines between her eyes relaxed. "Do I get a rain check on the movie?"

"Sure." Matt held out his hand for her key. He unlocked the door, reached in, and flipped on the light. He didn't go inside, now wasn't the time. Instead, he cupped her face in his hands lightly. Not holding too tight, he kissed her. Nice and soft. He lingered, enjoying the softness and taste of her lips. His heart stumbled when she returned the kiss. "Lock the door."

"Thanks for tonight. The restaurant, Antonio and Maria, time with you, everything was wonderful."

The warmth in Catherine's eyes would be what he remembered while he drove home. Something had colored them with hatred earlier, and he'd replaced that look with desire. Rack this evening up as one-hell-of-a-success.

Before turning in, he fed Benedict Arnold. Once again, Matt squatted down and waited until the dog finished eating. Once again, he extended a hand to try to pet him. Once again, he failed.

Chapter Nine

Matt's cell vibrated across the nightstand. He pushed himself to consciousness with great effort. Catherine got the credit for his sound sleep. He'd dozed off with his mind full of pleasant, albeit inappropriate thoughts. Having her in his dreams helped him forget the outside world. For that small respite, he was grateful.

Caller ID read "dispatch," meaning this wasn't a friendly wake-up call.

Less than an hour later, he parked in front of the courthouse and jogged up the steps. Sue, in a prim black dress with a white collar, greeted him.

"They're in your office."

"One of these days you're going to tell me how you manage to be here before me." He made a mental note and filed it. Without fail, the woman stayed one step ahead.

Annie Travers' husband, Ben, and her father, Will Brooking, waited for Matt in his office. After obtaining permission to record their conversation, he identified each person in the room, and tried to calm both men. "It's important you take a deep breath and talk to me with a clear head. You're worried and scared. I get that. But you're no help unless you're under control."

"I understand." Ben nodded.

"What's going on with your wife?"

"She's the night manager at the Dairy Dream and is always home by eleven. Never varies more than fifteen minutes. I called her cell at eleven-thirty. Called again every five minutes. Never got an answer."

Ben might've been in his early thirties, but as he rubbed the back of his neck and grimaced, his eyes looked much older. His thin body stretched over a six-foot frame gave him an Ichabod Crane look. With blond hair, his mustache was barely noticeable until he pulled a corner into his mouth and chewed on it.

"Annie." A mental picture of the young auburn-haired woman formed in Matt's mind. She'd served him lots of hamburgers. "You always wait up?"

"Most nights I'm up grading papers. I teach sixth grade history at Curry Middle School. But yeah, even if I'm done, I wait up. We work different hours." Ben shifted his gaze from Matt to Will and back. "Late at night is our time together."

Matt studied Ben for a second. His eyes were rimmed in red and filled with tears. If he was faking his concern for his wife, he was a damned good actor. "Walk me through her end of shift procedure—if you can."

"She and whoever's working lock the door at ten. The other person cleans up while Annie makes out the night deposit. They always leave together. She goes straight to the night deposit drive-thru at the Republic Bank in Butte Crest. Then she drives home."

Sue stepped in with a pot of coffee and three paper cups. She silently filled each one and then set them in front of the men. She gripped Ben's shoulder before leaving.

"Go on," Matt said.

"At midnight, I called Will to see if Annie had checked in with them." Ben lifted the cup to his mouth with both hands and blew on the hot liquid. Steam rolled up and over his face.

Matt turned to Will who hadn't uttered a word. "That's when you got involved?"

"Yeah. And all this jawing ain't finding my Annie."

Ben flinched at Will's statement. A slight movement the recorder wouldn't pick up, but Matt made a note in his book. There was friction between the two men, maybe because of the "my Annie" reference made by her father.

Will leaned forward. In his mid-fifties, he'd spent years in the field trying to eek a living out of the unforgiving dry land. His weathered, ruddy complexion reflected his hard work. Chapped, rough hands rested on the arms of his chair.

"We couldn't find her," Will said around a wad of dip. "Now it's time you did something about bringing her home."

"You searched for her before reporting her missing?" Matt worked to keep frustration off his face.

"We weren't sure. Not until we found her empty car at the drive-through deposit at the bank." Will stood. His chair wobbled, came close to turning over.

"You found her car?" This was news Matt should've been told first. His jaw muscle ached from gritting his teeth, but he held his temper. He stepped to the door and met Sue on her way in. Her desk sat right outside his office. Nothing got by her ears.

"I've already contacted Jake and Rey. Said you wanted to see them. They'll be in shortly." This time, it was Matt's shoulder she reached up and gripped.

"Always one step ahead of me. Maybe you do deserve detective pay," he said softly before returning to Ben and Will. "You didn't touch anything in or around the car did you?" Matt looked from one man to the other.

"I needed to know if she'd had car trouble, didn't I?"

"Dammit, Will." So much for staying calm. "By trying to start the car, you touched the keys, the steering wheel, and the door handle? What else?"

Will's mistake hit him quick and hard. He sank down on the chair as if someone cut him off at the knees.

"Not the door handle."

"The car door was standing open?" Matt's temples were on the verge of imploding. He pressed a headache back with the heels of his hands when Ben and Will simultaneously nodded.

"I need a photograph of your wife, Ben. Get it to Sue right away."

"I'll bring it by myself."

Matt got the make and model of Annie's vehicle. Rey went to ensure no one else touched or moved the car. Matt asked Sue to call San Antonio for a crime scene unit. Then he sent Ben and Will to check with friends on the off-chance Annie had contacted them.

"Jake, let's make that run between the Dairy Dream to the Republic Bank." They'd lost valuable time by not being called earlier. Now they had a cold trail to follow.

****

"You know the family?" Matt asked Jake during the drive from Curry to Butte Crest.

"They go to our church. Ben's trying to hire on at one of the bigger schools in San Antonio. Pay's better than Curry Middle School."

"I can imagine."

"Annie and Ben are newlyweds."

"Shit."

"Exactly."

Newlyweds. That explained Ben being uncomfortable talking about his and Annie's private time in front of her dad. Sex wouldn't be a topic you'd discuss in front of a new father-in-law. Ben moved further down Matt's list of suspects, but not off. Everybody was subject to scrutiny. Too many times murder led right back to a family member. Matt shook off the thought. For now, he'd assume Annie was alive.

Matt parked and went inside to question the Dairy Dream day shift manager and her team. Annie hadn't mentioned anyone new hanging around, nor had she complained about anybody bothering her. He joined Jake who'd stayed outside to walk the perimeter of the building and lot.

"We can pull fingerprints from inside this squat and gobble if you want. Be a lot, but I'll see to it," Jake said on the way to the bank.

"Squat and gobble?"

"That's what Kaye calls fast food restaurants. Doesn't much care for them."

"Hmm." Matt wasn't touching that one. "Too many people in and out. Don't mess with prints."

"Works for me."

"Where is the bastard hiding these women?"

"Could be anywhere from an old storm cellar to under his bed. We keep turning over rocks, we'll find him."

Annie's car sat inside a circle of yellow tape when Matt and Jake arrived at the bank. Two men were taking pictures. "You recognize either one of those guys?"

"Nope. Let's find out who they are." Jake was unbuckled and out of the cruiser before Matt killed the engine.

He caught up with the shorter Jake, impressed by his impatience. Both relaxed and slowed their pace when the men flashed their ID's from the ME's office.

"Sheriff Matt Ballard. This is Deputy Jake Foley. What have you found?"

The two men introduced themselves. Their hands were covered with latex gloves, neither Dave Foster nor Hector Ruiz offered to shake hands. Foster rocked back and forth on his Reeboks and slid his glasses on top of his head. He handed his camera off to Ruiz, pulled out his notebook, and read.

"We arrived on scene at approximately thirteen- hundred hours and identified ourselves to Deputy Rey Santos. He in turn identified the automobile as belonging to the missing woman. We taped the area around the car—"

"Okay. I get it," Matt interrupted Ruiz. "You've been here twenty minutes, and I'm rushing you. Where's Deputy Santos?"

Ruiz nodded toward the bank. "Inside."

Matt walked a few feet away and punched in Dr. Reinhardt's number. He slapped his phone closed after leaving a message.

"These guys will be here a while." Jake looked up from his notebook and smiled when Matt leaned up against the cruiser.

"Pisses me off Reinhardt only sent two men. It's unacceptable, and he's gonna hear about it. Hell, he had a full complement at Julia's crime scene. And I'm still waiting on DNA and toxicological reports."

"Here's an idea. Why don't I stay here with Rey? Take our own pictures. Then drive over and interview Annie's night shift waitress. You go deal with the ME."

The voice of reason and experience, Jake provided a steady counterbalance to Matt's sometimes-volatile personality. He had earned Matt's trust.

"I picked a hell of a place to do this, but if you'll take the job, I'd be proud to have you accept the position of Deputy Sheriff of Crest County."

Jake raised his eyebrows, pulling his continuous frown into a quizzical expression. "Sort of like a battlefield promotion?"

"Exactly." Matt used Jake's phrase on him.

"I accept." He held his hand out, and his firm grip spoke volumes.

"Good. First, let's check in with Rey. I want to watch the security camera trained on this night drop lane."

Before the front door closed behind them, Bank President Tom Logan in his three piece suit, trim haircut, and pocket full of ballpoint pens pounced like a hungry vulture. Twisting his fingers into knots, he rushed toward them, his face the color of an overripe tomato. Rey leaned against a counter. A snide grin on his face.

"Deputy Santos refuses to have that car moved. It's clogging up the flow of my business."

Matt directed his comment to Rey. "Good call." Rey pushed away, striding toward the exit. "I'll be outside with the techs."

Jake gripped Logan by the elbow and escorted the cigarette-thin man to an office. "Sheriff, Tom's a cooperative fella, aren't you?" Jake's words slid out slow and cold.

Logan collapsed in his desk chair, adjusted his crooked tie, and deflated. Whoosh. He was done. "I've got a job to do."

95 |

"So do we," Matt said. "We need to view your security feed starting at ten-thirty last night. Will that be a problem? If so, we can sit here and wait until I get a warrant."

"No warrant. Right, Tom?" Jake's head swung like a pendulum while he uttered the word no.

Logan fiddled with the buttons and then turned the small monitor around. "I assume you want me to leave."

"Thank you. We can manage," Jake commented. Matt stared at Jake in amazement as he closed the door behind the disgruntled bank manager. "Damn, I made the right decision promoting you. We'll do it again formally when we get back to the office."

"No hurry." Jake smiled.

His expression returned to his deadpan, stoic persona when he sat and pressed the Slow Forward button. The two of them leaned close to the screen, watching in silence. Ben had been right about his wife's schedule. The readout said eleven-fifteen when Annie's car pulled in and stopped. A figure stepped into the shadows, stood at an angle where the camera caught nothing but a hand holding a pistol.

"Stop there." Matt studied the hand in the picture, looking for identifying marks. Seeing none, he nodded. "Gun's a .380. Go ahead."

Annie's eyes flashed wide, and her mouth formed the word "no." She held the night deposit bag out the window and waited. Her expression shifted to confusion right before she pulled her arm back inside and then exited the car. Damn. She stepped out of the frame and never returned. They ran the feed twice more. Annie's kidnapper had avoided the camera.

"She recognized him. Didn't get scared until she spotted the gun." Jake backed the action up and hit pause.

"I'll bet she thought she was being robbed and took the money to him. The bastard knew what he was doing, where to stand and what to say. She trusted him. Didn't she realize he couldn't leave a witness? Not after she saw his face." Matt leaned back in the chair. Pain surged in his temple. "Jake, you'll get a copy?"

"Yep. You go on. I've got this."

Catherine paced and argued with herself. Should she stay or go home? She'd told Matt he'd need a friend after the first woman went missing and now this. She couldn't imagine the pressure he must be under. Her plan had been to have a hot supper waiting for him. She'd basted and basted until the roast withered and fell apart. The once firm potatoes? Mush. The gravy was a light brown paste.

Benedict Arnold stood and trotted to the back door before Catherine heard Matt's pickup. The dog was glad to know Matt was home, too. She leaned back against the kitchen counter and waited.

"Hey." A lame greeting, but seeing him stunned her speechless.

Dark circles and weary blue eyes marred his Michelangelo face. His black hair fell in disarray and looked like he'd raked his fingers through a number of times today. His chiseled jaw and chin were dark with a long day's stubble. With a couple of long strides, he pinned her between him and the counter. He framed her face with his hands, closed his eyes, and lowered his forehead to hers. They stood in silence for a long time, unmoving, their bodies not touching. Fear for the missing woman radiated off him.

His anguish, more than she'd planned for, hit her hard. His dedication and concern, traits she admired, shook her conviction that no man could be trusted. His tenderness, something she'd never had, touched a long-neglected place in her soul.

In that small space of time, where no one else in the world existed, Catherine's heart found hope. Tears she'd promised herself never to shed again, slid unchecked down her cheeks. But these tears weren't because of her pain or grief. She cried because Matt suffered and grieved for the missing woman. She slid her arms around him, stroking his tense muscles.

"Hey, yourself." He leaned back and studied her face. The warmth behind his eyes returned as he wiped away her tears with the pads of his thumbs. "Were those for me?"

She nodded and emotions swirled in her head. Catherine struggled to regain her perspective. "I have to remove no more tears from the *Never* list."

"Why would you hold yourself to such a never?"

"The only thing crying gets you is red eyes."

"Okay, tough guy. Maybe someday you'll trust me enough to explain. Why'd you break a rule for me?"

"The worry for Annie Travers in your eyes broke my heart. I've never known anyone with your compassion and dedication."

"Careful." The corners of his mouth lifted. "You'll be calling me John Wayne again."

"Same soul." She pushed a lock of black hair off his forehead. He caught her wrist in his hand.

"Stop, Catherine. I'm nobody's hero. I failed miserably in that department." He walked to the stove. "What smells good?"

He'd changed the subject. She understood the maneuver. It was probably for the best, because she'd spooked when he grabbed her by the wrist. She needed to put some distance between them. "Dried-out roast. I should've cooked something that could be reheated."

"This'll be great." He lifted the top off the pot, looked inside, and then glanced back over his shoulder. Humor filled his eyes, and the corners of his mouth twitched. "Yum. Looks delicious."

"Yeah. Right."

"Does to me. Let's eat."

To Catherine's surprise, the roast tasted okay. As Matt ate, the circles under his eyes seemed to fade with each bite, but nothing could hide the worry hidden under the surface. She regaled him with small bits of gossip and news. Anything to lighten his spirit. But working at a funeral home offered poor fodder for conversation.

She stacked the dishes in his sink. "You need a dishwasher."

"Too much work involved to install plumbing for one. Besides, until you came along it's been me and Benedict." He walked up behind her. His hands slid around her waist.

Surely, he was joking. "You're saying I'm the first female that's been in your kitchen?"

"Yep. First one inside since I've owned the place."

"You need to get to bed, and I have to go home."

"Stay with me."

He lifted her hair and nuzzled the back of her neck, sending goose bumps across her skin. She tilted her head and relaxed into him, enjoying his low moan. Full body contact with Matt sent her hormones into overdrive. Could she trust her innermost wants and desires to his hands? It was too much control to surrender.

"Matt, I need to go."

He let out a long, slow breath then kissed the top of her head. "Probably be best."

Matt moved back a couple of inches then turned her in place and lowered his forehead to hers. For a quiet minute, they stood exactly the same way they'd started the evening. The urge to comfort him roared through her system. With a sigh, he stepped away, leaving her with an empty feeling inside.

"Thank you for fixing my supper."

Benedict and Matt walked her outside. She placed a kiss on his cheek, rubbed the dog's ears, and then drove away. Her going home was as much for him as for her, she reasoned. Tired and emotional, he didn't know what he wanted. In the middle of an investigation wasn't the time to start an affair. But the yearning in her chest, the desire growing in her lower stomach meant she could feel need. She could desire and be desired.

Catherine dimmed her car lights before she pulled into the driveway to keep from disturbing Emma. Her heart bolted to the back of her throat. A small sack set on her porch. Fear rose up, smashing into her blood stream at high speed. The roast threatened to come up. Was he watching?

Mace in one hand and keys in the other, she ran for the house. She paused only to kick the package inside and lock the door. She turned on every light. Checked the windows and locks. Satisfied the house was secure, she allowed herself to breathe. She pulled her cell out of her purse but couldn't bring herself to call Matt. She'd left him exhausted, with no end in sight to his mounting problems. Pacing, her panic shifted to anger. She wouldn't drag him out of bed because some bastard wanted to have fun by tormenting her. Tomorrow, she'd buy a brighter bulb for the porch and ask Emma to leave her back porch light on. If the jerk came back, he'd think she lived on a runway.

Circling the damn sack like an animal wary of its enemy, curiosity got the best of her. She knelt, caught the corners with her fingertips, and dumped its contents on the floor. A pink diary slid across the rug and lay at her feet. It reminded her of the one she'd had as a kid. She knelt and pushed the tiny button to open it. A picture of a man's torso was inside. On the back he'd signed, "Think of me."

Chapter Ten

"What the hell are you thinking?" Marty shook her head in frustration, sending her long ponytail swishing back and forth. She ripped the pop-top off a can of beer and shoved it across the bar. "You've got to tell the sheriff." Marty left no doubt where she fell on the decision spectrum. She disagreed and voiced her opinion.

"If I told him, what would he do?" Catherine added the beer to her drink tray.

Marty lowered her voice. "Are you armed?"

"Does everybody in Texas automatically think gun when there's trouble?"

"Pretty much. Aren't you scared?"

"Terrified, but not stupid. I'm careful. Being aware is one of my specialties."

"Aware my ass. Careful is a loaded .38 Smith and Wesson."

"No guns."

"Then you should tell the sheriff."

"He's busy. Besides, I haven't seen him since Wednesday night." Catherine arranged her tray by customer order.

"Wait. Wait. Wait. You were with our gorgeous sheriff Wednesday night?" Her eyebrows wiggled up and down. "Tell me more—I need details."

"There's nothing to tell." Catherine hurried away to deliver drink orders.

"You gotta come back sooner or later. I'll be waiting," her boss yelled over the music.

JC was late to work. Catherine hoped when he arrived Marty would shift her attention his direction. Truth was, Marty pressuring for information pleased Catherine. She'd made some good friends in the short time she'd been in Butte Crest. People who cared about her. Dare she hope they'd understand if her story leaked? Could she face the shame?

No newspaper had ever printed the truth, not all of it. They didn't know about her bruised right kidney, Andy's preferred place to punch. He'd hunted her down every time she'd tried to end their marriage. He didn't want her, but he wouldn't let her leave. Andy's family and their lawyer had spun a good story, all lies. Catherine looked like a jealous, vengeful shrew who'd murdered her husband when he'd asked for a divorce. Did she regret not spouting the truth to every rag or TV reporter who'd listen? No. The matter was too personal and private. The horror of sharing every disgusting detail of her marriage with her attorney and again in a courtroom still made her sick to her stomach. She couldn't relive those memories.

A sharp tug on the can in her hand snapped her back.

"You gonna stand there all night or give me my beer?" Jessie jerked the can from Catherine and then waved her fingers. "Now move on. Stop staring at my husband."

Catherine laughed to herself and finished delivering drinks. JC had arrived and looked appropriately contrite until Marty walked away from him. Catherine took a few new drink orders before heading back to the bar. "God, I'm glad you're finally here. Marty can nose around in your personal life."

"She been bitching about me being late?" JC asked. He leaned across the bar and patted Catherine's arm sympathetically.

"Not bitching. But Marty's full of questions tonight."

"I'm not answering her questions." His hazel eyes widened.

"Heads up. She's right behind you." Catherine winked and turned to walk away.

"Hold up." Marty's hand clasped Catherine's arm and held tight. "Now that JC's here, I'm available for romance advice, secret sharing, or you can come right out and tell me. Was it good?"

"Stop." Catherine laughed, unable to hold it back. Heat rushed up her neck, burning her cheeks. "There's nothing to tell."

"Honey, if that's the truth, we do need to talk." Marty handed Catherine's tray to the other weekend waitress. "Take Catherine's tables for a few minutes." Marty sat down on a barstool. Folded her arms across her chest. "Give."

"Give what?" JC wiped the bar down and worked his way closer.

"Our girl and the sheriff are doing the nasty, but I can't get details from her."

"Goddammit, Marty. Get your mind out of the toilet. Give the woman a break." JC scowled and moved on down the bar.

"Really. We're not." Catherine held up her hands in surrender.

"I don't get it." Marty patted the barstool next to her. "Matt is drop-dead, God, I-can't-believe-you- haven't-slept-with-him-yet, gorgeous. A blind man could see the sheriff had the hots for you the first night you worked here. Girl, he all but stuck a sign on his forehead. What's the problem?"

"That's such an exaggeration," Catherine protested. "We're friends."

Marty coughed, sputtered over her swallow of beer. "That's wrong on so-o-o many levels. A fine specimen of a man like him was born to be more than a 'friend.' For you to not have sex with him...the idea hurts my heart."

"Sorry to disappoint, but I don't want more. Sex leads to demands and expectations. The first thing you know, everything goes sour. Trust me. I know." Catherine wished she hadn't spouted off. Marty's expression had sobered. Her chin dropped, and her mouth hung open.

"Oh, honey. If anybody has a negative opinion of relationships, it should be me. But I'm here to tell you, you're crazy if you don't sleep with Matt."

"It's not an opinion. It's a fact." Catherine tapped her watch hinting that the break was over.

"Go back to work, but you and me, we're getting drunk one night and having a long talk. Making love between two grown people, sharing without strings, I'm living proof it can be done."

Catherine made the rounds, checking on her customers. Whenever Marty caught Catherine's eye, Marty would shake her head, making her ponytail flop wildly.

****

Ash Hunter answered on the third ring. His groggy hello followed by a softer more feminine sound confirmed Matt had disturbed something. "Man, you're such a whore-dog. Want to call me later?"

"Hell no. I don't remember the last time you dialed my number. You're not getting away that easy. What's up?"

"Seriously, if you've got a lady with you, and we both know how seldom you have one, I won't keep you."

"Jealousy doesn't become you. Don't make me come to the boonies and kick your ass." Ash's smartass tone shifted to serious. "What's up? How's the head?"

Matt's decision to ask for expert help had been easy. His old partner had an uncanny skill for sniffing out homicide clues. Ash's training in the field far surpassed Matt's or any of his men. Asking for help didn't hurt his pride, he had a murderer to catch.

"The 'boonies' are what I want to talk to you about." Matt skirted the question about his brain-crushing headaches—the ones the shrink had assured him would go away when he dealt with his self-induced stress and misplaced guilt. "I have an offer to make."

"Couldn't be better than the one I got last night."

"Yeah, right." Matt chuckled and envisioned the smirk across his buddy's face. "I need your help."

"Talk to me." In work mode, Ash was possibly the coldest-hearted bastard alive.

"What are the odds of your boss loaning you out on temporary assignment? Could be a few weeks—a couple of months."

"Makes no difference. If he says no, I'll take time off. You need me—I'm there. Is this about the missing woman you mentioned a few weeks back?"

"Yes and no. She's dead. Found propped up on the side of the road naked except for a red bow tied around her neck."

"Sorry to hear it." The rustle in the background said Hunter was out of bed and on his feet. "Keep talking. I gotta fix coffee."

"A second woman went missing five days ago." Matt refused to utter the word serial, but his mind had no qualms about screaming it inside his head.

"She didn't come home after work. No trace of her."

"You think it's the same perp. Don't you?"

"Yeah. I'd bet good money. And we're pounding our heads against a wall. How many times can I interview the same people? Nothing's breaking loose."

"What have you got in mind for me?"

"I'm running out of time. Annie Travers is running out of time. Maybe I overlooked something."

"I don't have to tell you, the chances of finding her alive after this long..."

"I know the odds aren't good."

"You think you've got a serial killer."

"One who kidnaps, rapes, then kills." Matt ran his hands through his hair and tried to block out the picture of Julia Drummond's dead body. Her image haunted him day and night. "You'll understand when you see the crime scene pictures. The poor woman was naked, with her face powdered and lips painted. Ash." Matt paused, swallowed hard. "He glued her eyes open. She looked like a porcelain doll."

"Bastard. Where do you see me fitting in? I don't want a pissing match with your men."

"I have six deputies spread out over almost a thousand square miles with nearly twenty-seven- thousand people to watch over. Two of them are working this case. The rest are spread thin because none of the small towns can support a local police department. The seven of us will welcome your big city expertise."

"Pretty sparse territory you got out there, with people spread out few and far between. You're sounding stressed."

"You need a bigger word. And to answer your earlier question— yes. I've had a couple of killer headaches." Matt pressed the heel of his hand against his temple. "Satisfied?"

"Easy, big fella. I'm on your side."

"That's where I need you to be."

"We just wrapped up a case. Want me to talk to Captain Banks?"

"Leave Banks to me." Matt had a thought he hadn't considered. "You gonna stay at my place?"

"Oh, hell no. Put me in a hotel. Better yet, a corporate apartment. You do have those in the boonies. Don't you? If your budget can't afford it, mine can. Hang on."

Matt listened while Hunter and his lady friend discussed who'd call whom and when. After a few seconds of silence, a door closed.

"Ask the honey in your office to check around. She'll find a place for me."

"I don't have a 'honey' in my office."

"Don't get stingy. I talked to her a few weeks ago. Remember? Thanks to her, I have your cell number."

"You spoke to Sue. She's my right arm. I'll ask her to start looking first thing in the morning."

"Is she single?"

"I appreciate your help." Matt couldn't resist the temptation to have fun with his old partner. He baited his friend by ignoring his question. "If I can ever..."

"Nice try, buddy," Hunter interrupted. "You want my help, don't be ignoring me. I repeat. Is. She. Single?"

"Yes." Matt intentionally huffed out a loud sigh. "But she's not for you."

"Why? She yours?"

"No. Listen to me. This woman will chew you up and spit you out." This conversation was getting better and better. Everything Matt had said was the God's honest truth.

"Hot tempered. I like 'em hot. Talk to me tomorrow after you've spoken to Banks."

A small part of the load eased from Matt's shoulders. He hung up and squatted down in front of Benedict Arnold. The dog stood at a distance and sniffed at the extended hand. "Be that way. If you were nicer to me, I might've taken you with me to see Catherine." He punched buttons on his cell while he held the door open to put the mutt outside. "Join me for lunch?"

****

Catherine pulled into the parking lot, and her jaw dropped. Leaning against the hood of his pickup, wearing jeans and a blue shirt, one booted foot propped on the bumper guard, Matt waited. Hatless, which was unusual, his jet black hair stirred in the breeze and fell across his forehead. He slipped off his sunglasses and smiled. Mesmerized, she bumped into the curb, having failed to press hard enough on the brake pedal.

His fingers were on her door handle by the time she killed the engine, and seconds later, she was in his arms. She'd never have expected him to kiss her in public, but his arms folded her to his chest, and his lips captured hers. She stood on her toes and briefly surrendered.

"There," he said with conviction. "That didn't hurt. Did it?"

"Not at all," she agreed, urging her jumpy stomach to calm down.

"You okay? You almost plowed into the curb."

"I'm great. To quote Marty, 'If it got any better there'd have to be two of me.'"

He frowned and placed his hand on her back again. He glance at her car then back. His behavior struck her as odd.

"What's wrong?"

The corners of his mouth lifted. The smile changed his handsome face to heart stopping beautiful. "Aren't your windows rolled down a tad too low?"

"Not really." Catherine crossed the street. "I leave 'em cracked on purpose." Damn, the detective in him was showing.

"That's further down than cracked. Your car could get stolen." He stepped between her and the door to the café. His gaze pinned her in place. He had cop eyes when he glared. He was goading her, fishing.

"I'm not that lucky."

"How long has your air conditioner been on the fritz?" His brows furrowed.

"Not long." She slid her hand in his and pulled him inside the café. "Aren't you the smart cop? How did you know?"

He rolled his eyes. "It didn't take a genius." He reached behind her, pulling the wet blouse away from her back.

"Eewwww." She scooted away from him and dodged further discussion by becoming engrossed in the menu on the wall. The Pizza Stop was a small order and pick-up-at-the-counter café, but the food was quick and good. Catherine let Matt order their food while she got drinks from the self-serve station. She followed him to a table and sat across from him.

"If we were at Antonio's, Mama would insist you sit next to me." Matt's eyes glistened with mischief while he rubbed the thumb and fingers of his hand together.

"Sitting close is wonderful, but the view's great from over here."

Color rushed up over his sculpted chin to his cheekbones. He bolted from the booth to pick up their lunch. When he returned, his color had returned to normal.

"I didn't mean to make you blush."

"I don't blush. Let's talk about your car."

"Let's not," she mumbled behind a slice of pizza. "I want to know what's wrong with your hands."

Confusion furrowed his brow. "Nothing's wrong with them." He wiggled his fingers to demonstrate.

"Then why do you rub your thumb and fingers together like they've gone numb?"

Matt's gaze shifted from her to his hands and back. For a second he appeared either confused or undecided. Then he rubbed them together and raised one eyebrow in question.

"Yes. Like that." She mimicked his movement.

A sensuous smile spread across his face. This wasn't an ordinary smile. It stripped away her last ounce of resistance—said he had a secret and wasn't about to share—and made the back of her blouse damp again, along with an assortment of other places.

She blinked a couple of times to clear a sudden onset of double vision. "Well?"

He leaned forward and whispered. "I don't know you well enough to answer."

"What does that mean?"

He dismissed her question with a wave of his hand and a couple of gulps of iced tea. "I have a personal question for you. Money's keeping you from having the AC in your car fixed. Right?"

"If you're planning on offering to pay, don't." Their relationship meant a lot to her, but she paid her own way now and was damn proud of it. Being indebted to any man, including Matt, wasn't an option. She hoped they weren't headed for an argument.

"Catherine, I admire how independent you are. Accepting help from a friend isn't a sign of weakness. It's a sign of trust."

"Trust is one thing, money is another. I can't. Won't."

"There weren't any strings attached. Wouldn't keep you from getting a ticket. My help does not come with a price."

"I appreciate the offer. I'll put my car in the shop soon. Until then, well, I've made it this far into the summer." She stretched out her hand. "Friends?"

The second he touched her, a blast of heat shot through her body. He was harder on her than the weather.

"Always."

Catherine kept the topics light for the rest of lunch. Time spent with Matt was limited. She understood why. His mind never strayed far from work. On the way back to her car, she mentally chastised herself for not noticing how tired he looked.

"Why don't I fix your supper tomorrow night?"

"I'm always available for free food."

"Good. Come around seven." She stood on her tiptoes and kissed him, leaning into his solid chest when his hand cupped her chin. She'd never been this brazen. And out in broad daylight.

Maybe Marty was right. Maybe two people could enjoy each other without things getting ugly. Maybe it was time to shorten the *Never* list.

Along with regaining her pride and independence, a bolder, passionate woman had emerged. She liked this version of herself more every day. She pulled up to the stop sign and glanced back over her shoulder. What she'd have given for a camera.

Standing exactly as he'd been when she'd arrived, Matt had leaned against his hood. He was rubbing his fingers and thumb together. It was her turn to smile. She had a mystery of her own to solve.

Yep. He was officially off the *Never* list.

Chapter Eleven

Matt finished off a piece of Sue's apple pie. "You're too good to me. Nobody's ever fed me like this."

He'd mark today down as successful. Minutes ago, he'd finished an open discussion with his small staff. He'd listened to their comments and was satisfied Ash Hunter would be welcomed.

"Not even your mother?" Her expression clearly indicated she doubted him.

"No, ma'am. Not even her."

"Well, she taught you proper manners. Didn't she pass a couple of years back?"

"Yes, ma'am," he repeated. "I moved home when she got sick. The year after, I ran for sheriff."

"Sorry I never met her. She did a good job raising you." Sue's eyes sparkled with pride.

"Did you know my dad?" Texas might be a big state but its politicians were a tight knit group. She'd lived and worked in Crest County too long not to have heard of Drew Ballard from one county over. Yet, she'd never mentioned him. Now that Matt had, he regretted it.

"Knew of him. Heard folks talk, Hotchkiss County lost a good lawman when he died."

"So I've been told."

"Don't remember hearing much about you. I'm guessing you hightailed it to the big city when you were still young."

111 |

"Right after high school."

"Lots of stories out there about him being a ladies' man." Sue cleared her throat. "But I never had first-hand knowledge." She held her hand out for his plate. "Those kinds of rumors would be hard on a young boy. True or not, they'd hurt."

"No need to hedge. They weren't rumors. He was proud of his reputation. I managed to grow up without his help." He turned up his cup for a last swallow of coffee. "So, you think you can find temporary housing for Ash?"

"Don't see why not. I'll call Curry Heights. They'll probably laugh when I ask about a corporate apartment, but I'll pull something together."

He held up a finger to stop her from leaving. "Why don't I give you Ash's number? You can talk directly with him."

"Works for me. I have a friend who lives in the Heights. If I can get him in there, she'll help look out for him."

"He needs somebody to take care of him." Matt held back a satisfied grin until Sue left the office. Ash Hunter would put a move on Sue the minute she got him on the phone. His old buddy was in for a real surprise.

Matt read over his schedule for the day. Reporters from San Antonio and Austin had picked up the story about the second missing woman. He'd agreed to meet with the whole bunch later today. The mayors from Butte Crest and Curry were coming this morning. The forensic information on Julia Drummond, which Dr. Reinhardt had assured him were on a Federal Express truck, hadn't come in the morning delivery. He hated being stuck in the office, but he wasn't leaving until he'd read them. Matt finished his notes on his interviews and carried them to Sue to enter and send copies to Jake and Rey. She rose, followed him to his desk.

He sat and looked up at her. "Did you follow me in here for a reason?" Always ready for a verbal sparring match, her eyes twinkled with mischief.

"I've better things to do than follow you for *no* reason. I got your friend an apartment at Curry Heights. My friend Dotty and I contributed a few pieces of furniture." She held up one small finger to silence him exactly as he'd done to her earlier. "Which you will collect and deliver."

"Thanks. I didn't want him sleeping on my couch."

"Not to worry. He's all set up." She turned to leave, stopping at the last minute. "That was a good thing you did, making Jake your Deputy Sheriff," she commented. "Gained a lot of ground with your men when you promoted him."

"I did what should've already been done." Matt shrugged off Sue's compliment. "Have you told Ash about the apartment?"

"Not yet." She left and returned seconds later with a FedEx package. "I'm calling him now."

Finally. Forensic evidence, Ash Hunter coming to lend a hand, and supper with Catherine...life looked pretty damn good.

Jake would be in soon. Matt intended to send him out for a chat with Marty. Between Jake's easy manner and Marty's talkative nature, he'd get an earful about JC and Julia. Matt would stay and take on the news people. The TV station was interviewing friends and family of both women. Julia and Annie's privacy was about to be laid open for the public to pick apart.

A second discussion with JC? Matt reserved that pleasure for himself.

He moved to the small conference room, closed the door, and then sat down with the victim's board directly in front of him. One pull of the tape and he spread the contents of the package across the table. Matt studied sketches of the crime scene and diagrams of the area surrounding the body. Small details such as how many feet between the highway and the body were included. Copies of pictures taken at the scene and autopsy were clipped together. Pages full of medical and technical terms. He added the pictures to the board next to the ones his men had taken, studied them closely, then settled down to read.

"Come," he answered the light tap on the door, surprised to see over an hour had passed.

Jake pulled a chair out and accepted the pages Matt offered. "This is one of the hardest parts."

"I hear you. Take a look and tell me what you think." Matt let Jake study and absorb. Rey would get a chance and then Ash when he arrived. Matt hoped one of them would find something he'd missed. He pulled the diagrams of the roadside from the stack and spread them out. He and Jake read in silence, each concentrating, looking for that elusive clue.

"So the forensic team and the autopsy came up empty? They found nothing." Jake spit the angry words out, rapid fire for a normally slow talker, like Sue's typing, quick and firm. "Bastard's not leaving anything behind." He pushed his pages across to Matt.

He waited a heartbeat for Jake to relax. "I read the interviews from Tanya's list. Rey's comfortable Mel Hamilton's stayed out of trouble since his eighteen months in Huntsville. Your notes said the same about Danny Mason."

"I've known Danny for years. He was a tough kid. In and out of trouble, but he's kept to himself since he came home. I watched his reaction when I showed up unexpectedly where he worked. Didn't seem to bother him."

"I'm going to do a second interview with Hamilton and Mason." Matt moved quickly to explain. "Nothing against you or Rey, but they're the only two on the list with criminal backgrounds."

"No offense taken. Mel Hamilton's married now. His wife swore he was at home the night Julia went missing. What'd you think about Danny's comment on JC and Julia? I don't remember reading that JC mentioned them dating in your notes."

"A fact he left out. Talk to Marty. See what she knows about JC and Julia."

Jake's smile stopped at his mouth. His eyes told another story, one of dislike for liars. Another reason Matt liked him. Trusted him.

"Son-of-a-bitch lied to me. Now he's gonna explain why. Besides, I need to get out in the field. You and Rey covered a lot of ground last week."

"Didn't learn a damn thing," Jake said. You're not looking at Ben are you?"

"Not particularly, but nobody gets a bye."

"I hear ya. But nothing points to him. Those two kids were putting money back. They wanted to start a family. He's counting on us finding her."

"I'm counting on us, too."

"When's Hunter arriving?"

"I'll bet he's here by the weekend. He's excited about meeting Sue."

Jake stopped in mid-motion. "How old is your friend?"

"Don't know. Thirty-five, maybe. Why?"

"He's interested in Sue?"

"Yep. To hear him tell it, they'll be fast friends." Matt gathered the forensic report and left the conference room with Jake right behind. He stopped when Jake's hand gripped his arm.

"You didn't tell him she was old enough to be his mother? Maybe grandmother?"

Matt frowned and pretended to think for a minute. "Must've slipped my mind."

Jake's face lit up. "Gonna be interesting having you two around."

Sue met them in the hall. "Sheriff, your appointments are in the lobby."

"On my way." He followed her up front.

The mayors wore Matt's patience thin, but he understood their fear. He talked them through the investigation to date. Listed off where they had searched, named the neighborhoods, and covered the questions asked of friends and family. Hell, they'd turned over every rock and looked behind every mesquite tree in the county. Annie had vanished. Like Julia had. The newspaper reporters grilled Matt until he considered assigning all media meetings to his new deputy sheriff. But he wouldn't, not a chance. It was his butt in the sling, and he'd take the abuse.

"You heading out for the day?" Sue looked up from her keyboard and scowled like a principal who'd caught him playing hooky.

"Yes and no. I'm driving out to JC Harper's house. If he lies to me again, he and I may be back. If he convinces me I shouldn't bring him in for questioning, I'll head home from his place."

"Why's that?"

"Why I'm considering bringing him in? Or why I'm going home?" Her question caught him off guard. Sue pried about personal stuff all the time but usually waited to be brought into the loop on police matters.

"He's a good man. JC wouldn't hurt a fly."

"He withheld information when we talked the first time. He conveniently omitted facts that might be important to the investigation. In my book, withholding is the same as lying. A vote of confidence from you carries a lot of weight with me, but this time it won't help."

Sue nodded slightly. "Go get him. Man's got to tell the truth, or he's no good to anybody."

"Pity you're not thirty years younger."

"Why, Sheriff, what would your new girlfriend think?"

"I was thinking of Ash Hunter. He needs a good woman."

****

JC stood in the yard dragging a soaker-hose around the foundation of his house. He turned off the water, picked up his beer, and walked to meet Matt.

"Sheriff." JC drained the bottle and tossed it back toward the porch. "Back so soon? What's up?"

"We need to talk." Matt got out and shook JC's extended hand. "We can sit down here, or we can go to my office. Your call."

"Well, come inside. Too damn hot to stand out in the sun." JC led the way up the sidewalk. "I guess it looked like I was watering the house. I read somewhere if you wet down the base, the foundation was less likely to crack." He pulled a beer from the fridge and held one up to Matt.

"No thanks. This isn't a social call." Matt had listened to JC's idle chatter about the house. But the chitchat was over. "Why didn't you tell me you and Julia dated?"

JC stalled like a sailboat with a broken mainsail. Dead in the water. Speechless. He sat down hard. Matt waited less than a heartbeat, no use giving JC time to gather his thoughts.

"She pissed you off when she dumped you. You decided to teach her a lesson, got carried away, and killed her." Matt concentrated on JC's reactions.

"What?" JC blinked and shook his head. His shaggy brown hair whipped through the air like a dog shaking himself after a hard rain.

Matt had his questions ready. He'd ask them rapid-fire. "What happened? You discover you liked torturing her? Is that why you snatched Annie?" He leaned forward. "Where is she, JC?"

"You're fucking crazy if you think I killed anybody." JC's hazel eyes were wide.

The realization he might be accused of murder had snapped him out of his daze so Matt pushed.

"Here's your chance to set the record straight." Matt kept his tone low and firm. "Start with the fact you dated Julia. Lie to me again and I'll arrest you for impeding a homicide investigation."

"That was a long time ago, man. Past history. She was too young for me. I knew it. She knew it. The whole thing didn't last but a couple of months. I bought her stuff, and she liked getting presents. I think maybe that was all she liked about me."

"Go on."

"That's all, man. I swear. I gave—she took." JC dropped his head into his hands, rocking back and forth on the couch. "You think I'm capable of murder?"

"Might not have if you hadn't lied. Now I don't trust anything you say. Should've told the truth in the beginning."

"Truth is, I didn't kill her. And I damn sure didn't 'snatch' anybody."

JC provided the details of his and Julia's two- month affair. He came across as a man who'd been jilted. He sounded more resigned to the fact than resentful. He defended her morals, insisting he hadn't noticed her hooking up with any of the men at the bar.

"So you could see the dance floor from your work station?"

"Okay. I lied about that. If we're not busy and my head isn't down in the beer cooler, I can see the dance floor. But if the joint's full, I can't see a damn thing for the people sitting at the bar. Besides, then I don't have time."

"Who broke it off?"

"Nobody really. She did, in a roundabout way. She had something else to do. Somewhere she had to be. Always busy when I had the night off. I didn't have to be hit over the head."

"Any arguments at the end?"

JC drained the beer he'd been holding and dropped the bottle to the floor. "No. Like I said we had a few dates. It ended."

"If I need a DNA sample from you, will I need a warrant?" There'd been no useable traces on Julia's body according to the autopsy. The killer had scrubbed the body. Matt paid close attention to JC's reaction.

"Hell no." He grabbed the empty bottle from the floor, spit in it, and held it out to Matt. "Here, take the damn thing. You can get a clear set of prints off the glass, too."

Matt never hesitated. He stuck his ballpoint pen into the open neck and held the bottle sideways to prevent dribbling spit on his hand.

"Got a paper bag?"

****

Danny Mason was one of the two men on the list of Julia's acquaintances from the bar who'd been in prison. His rap sheet indicated he'd been paroled after spending three years in Huntsville for burglary of six residences. His crimes were nonviolent, but prison changed a person. Jake talked to Mason at his job. Matt decided to try the informal approach.

He knocked on the door to apartment 409 but no one answered. He'd turned to leave when the curtain fluttered on 411. He might learn something about Mason from a neighbor, so he knocked.

"Yes?" A female voice asked through the closed door.

"Sheriff Matt Ballard, ma'am. May I ask you a few questions?"

"You got any ID?"

He held his picture identification up to the peephole. Seconds later, he heard tumblers fall, a dead bolt flip followed by the sound of a chain being unhooked, and a silver haired lady stood before him. Her eyes matched the blue jogging suit she wore under a loud yellow apron. She had the epitome of Texas big hair. It looked good on her.

"Come in. Don't stand there letting the cool air out." She smiled and waved him inside. "Don't think I'm senile for asking to see some ID. Just because you're wearing a uniform don't mean I'm opening the door." A nod followed her declaration. "I watch Law and Order. I know all the tricks."

"You can't be too cautious." He suppressed a smile. "I'm glad you checked."

"Follow me. I've got a plate full of homemade cookies fresh out of the oven."

"Yes, ma'am, Ms. Whitley." The aroma of heart and home filled the small apartment.

"Name's Dorothy Whitley. Call me Dotty."

Matt found himself surround by ducks. Ceramic ones of every size and shape decorated her small kitchen. A glass duck's head full of milk and a plate of sugar cookies were placed in front of him. "I actually came to see your neighbor, Danny Mason. I can't seem to catch him at home."

"Sit. Eat," she commanded. "What do you want to see him for?"

"I'm speaking with everyone who knew Julia Drummond."

"I heard about her. That gal on the news said we women should take extra caution when we went out. You say young Danny knew the dead girl?" She pushed his plate closer to him. "Eat your cookies."

"I don't know that he knew her personally, but I need to ask him." Matt ate a cookie and moaned his sincere approval. Dotty rewarded him with a radiant smile.

"He's a loner, doesn't talk much. Goes to work every day over at Millwood's Garage."

"He's a quiet neighbor?"

"Most of the time. Had what I thought was a Super Bowl party that got too loud. I marched right over there and asked him to tone it down. But from what I could see, he was alone." She broke a cookie in half and nibbled on the edge.

"Did he?" Matt pushed his empty plate away.

"Did he what?" She dabbed at the corners of her mouth.

"Tone down the noise?"

"Yes. And right away, too." She leaned across and patted Matt on the shoulder. "He's usually out on Saturday night. Maybe he's on a date. Shouldn't you be?"

Matt chuckled with her and finished off his milk. "As a matter of fact, I should be going. Thanks for the cookies. They were delicious."

Dotty escorted him to the door. "Good luck, son. My money's on you to catch that killer."

"Count on it." He shook her hand. She reminded him of Sue, a sweetheart, and alone. Too bad.

"You watch your back, you hear?" she called out to him as he hurried   down   the   stairs.

Chapter Twelve

Christ, how could he have fallen for that bitch's phony come on? She'd pretended to want him. It had all been a lie. Nothing he hated worse than a liar. He refused to put up with them. It was as fuckin' simple as that.

Mama had lied every time she put him in the closet. Her "little while" had always turned into hours. Hours in the dark. Hours alone while she partied. Hours trying to hold his water. Water his ass. Mama and her guest drank and fucked until his bladder couldn't hold out any longer. He'd invariably pissed his pants. Was she sorry? Hell, no. She'd lied and said it was his fault. Then she'd whipped him with the wire hanger.

Replacing a doll hadn't been a problem. His execution had been perfect. It wasn't his fault the doll was flawed. Anger burned his guts. The buzzing inside his head started when he lost his temper. A few calming breaths, and he was under control. That control was the key to remaining unnoticed. Tonight when he stopped by the trailer to feed her, he'd fuck her one last time, and then he'd kill the bitch.

He'd had the perfect replacement in mind. Catherine was a real beauty. She'd looked him right in the eyes when she'd brought his beer. He recognized that expression. She wanted him bad.

****

"I should head home soon," Matt said

"Yeah, you probably should," Catherine agreed but didn't move. They'd said the same words twice already, but neither seemed to be in a hurry to end the evening. Matt shifted down on the couch, pulling her further on top of him.

"I'm getting possessive about our Monday nights. With our work schedules, this is the only time I have you all to myself. It's a shame. I'd like to take you out somewhere nice." His lips brushed the tip of her nose. "Show off my pretty woman."

"I like it right here." At the moment, she happily rested on his chest, which rose and fell slightly with each breath. The faint scent of aftershave drew her to his chiseled jaw, so she lifted her head and rubbed her cheek against his five o'clock shadow.

"So do I. But San Antonio's less than two hours away. We'd have a nice meal on the River Walk and listen to mariachi bands. I'd ply you with a few margaritas. Maybe then you'd tell me who hurt you."

"Listening to mariachi music might hurt me worse." She squirmed, ready to withdraw, but he held fast.

"You act as if you're not in pain, but it's there—between us."

"It's old news." Her heartbeat picked up, pounding in her ears. Could he feel the thunder in her chest?

"Not to me."

"What about you?" Catherine shifted the subject to him. "How come I know nothing about your past? I told you what brought me to Crest County."

He arched one eyebrow, his way of telling her he knew she'd changed the subject. "I was looking for the same peace I think you're hunting."

"The law is your career, not who you are. Tell me something personal."

"Did I tell you I was married once before?" His fingers smoothed up and down her back, shooting fire to every nerve in her body.

"No. As a matter of fact, you didn't. Why'd you get divorced?" She faked a scowl.

"By mutual agreement."

"One morning you two woke up and decided to put an end to your marriage. Sounds civilized."

"Okay, it was more complicated than that." He idly rolled her hair around one finger while he talked. "Work ate up all of my time, and I left her alone too much. She had an affair and got pregnant. She's happily married and the mother of a baby boy."

"Did you love her?" A blunt question, but Catherine needed to know. The fact he blanched didn't escape her.

"Yeah. In the beginning, we were in love. But I was young, hungry, and determined to make homicide detective. No doubt, I was an insensitive bastard. The fact that I left her sitting at home alone never crossed my mind nor bothered my conscience. The marriage falling apart was my fault."

"It hurt you."

"I'd call it a mixture between anger, hurt, and relief. I threw myself into a new job working undercover. Concentrated on slowing down the flow of drugs coming in through the gulf port."

"And then?" She pushed for more answers. His eyes grew dark, clouded with buried pain. What happened to him during his time undercover? He slid his hand beneath her hair and cradled the back of her neck. He pulled her to him until her mouth was a fraction of an inch from his. She felt his breath on her lips.

"And then—there you were. And you took my breath away. You still do."

Their lips touched, and Catherine's heart melted. Her feelings for him shifted. Lying on top of him gave her a sense of control. A surge of desire flooded her, the blood in her veins burned. She covered his mouth with hers and searched out his tongue. Rising up on her elbows, she greedily devoured his mouth. He responded by matching her fervor. When she pulled away, he gasped out a breath.

"I can't do this friend stuff, Catherine. I want you." His eye color had shifted to midnight blue, his need for her pressed against her skin. "You need to let me up. And let me leave."

She sighed and nodded. "I bagged the leftovers for Benedict Arnold." She hurried to the kitchen on trembling legs and leaned against the counter, her hands pressed against the cool surface. Her insides quaked with desire. The need to make love with Matt was overpowering. An ache like she'd never experienced racked her body and mind. She wanted him to touch places long bereft of tender hands— wanted him to fill the ravenous vacuum in her soul. In his arms, she'd satisfy the hunger. Could she yield this much power to him? Could she take a chance?

She steadied herself and turned. Matt filled the doorway behind her. Raw passion washed across his chiseled features. He was tall, broad shouldered, narrow hipped, and leaving. If she wanted him to stay, she'd have to be the aggressor. She moved a step toward him. He moved one step back.

"I'll call tomorrow." His voice was hoarse, raspy, and thick with desire as he turned to leave.

"Stop," she whispered. His determination to honor his promise propelled her into his arms. Her hands dug into his hair, pulling him down to her. She put her heart into the kiss, but Matt's hands remained at his sides, not touching her. Catherine looked him in the eyes. "Make love to me."

When he leaned down into his usual stance with his forehead touching hers, Catherine knew she'd made the right choice.

"Think about what you're saying. Don't let me pressure you."

"Matt." She pressed a finger to his lips. "Do me a favor?"

He straightened, his eyes clouded with desire. "Just ask."

"Shut up. Make love to me."

His mouth curled up sort of crooked and made her insides go liquid. "Well. Since you asked nicely." He leaned down and gently covered her lips with his. A soft, warm, easy kiss. The beginning of a long sensual journey.

****

Matt's mind whirled. The barriers were coming down. His heart thundered against his rib cage. She trusted him. Trusted him with a part of herself she'd closely guarded. Tonight would be all about her.

Greedy. Hungry. His mouth crushed hers, his tongue slid inside then across her teeth, teasing her. Fisting the back of her shirt in his hands, he pulled her tight against his chest, imagining how her breasts would feel without the thin layers of material separating his flesh from hers. With one quick glance behind, he backed to her bedroom.

She moaned, pressing against him, sparking a firestorm in his blood. Nothing existed but her. He eased her onto the bed. Lying beside her, he ravaged her lips again and again until her hands tore at his clothes. Quickly, they undressed, stopping occasionally to nip or taste a new and previously unseen body part.

"My God, you're a beautiful woman." He ran his hands over her soft skin, touched, kissed, stroked, until she quivered with need. He paused when she stiffened. "Talk to me. What's going through your mind?"

"If I'm not good at this..." She lowered her eyelids. "Don't tell me."

"Don't worry." He drew his fingers down her jaw line. Lifted her chin. "We're in this together. You're gonna be great."

She'd shared another small, private part of herself, a fear Matt was determined to dispel. The bond of trust strengthened. The hesitation in her voice had him itching to kick the crap out of the bastard who'd made her question her sexuality.

She laughed a low, lush sound. "I think so, too."

"I know so." Matt cupped her soft breast in his hand, circled her nipple with his thumb, smiling when it pebbled at his touch. He bent his head, swept across with his tongue, sucked her flesh into his mouth, and feasted on the taste of pure honey. Her back bowed. She cried out with pleasure, sending shock waves through his body. He rose up and crushed her mouth under his. Hard. Demanding. Wanting. They clung to each other, feeding and fueling their mutual need. His hand slid down across her velvety skin and sought out her most private, vulnerable part. This was where she'd learn her sexual power.

She gasped when he slipped a finger inside and then two, pushed and withdrew. When her movements became frantic, and his name rolled off her tongue, he found her center and pressed.

"Matt." Her eyes clenched shut.

"I'm right here," he whispered into her lips. "Come for me."

She bit down on her bottom lip. Her body shook, bucked into his hand. Her lips curled into a smile. She opened her eyes and captured his heart as sure as the warrior takes his prisoner.

"Oh, my God. That was intense." She laughed, the sound filling the room.

Her green eyes shone like emeralds. Matt had only thought his fingers tingled when he touched her. Giving her pleasure sent them into hyper drive.

"And there's an unlimited supply where that came from." He smoothed her hair away from her face, brought his lips to hers, and reveled in her enjoyment. "You were spectacular."

"Hey."

She stretched like a kitten. Arms over her head, her breasts thrust forward, toes pointed. He lost all train of thought, because her seductive, languid movements were the most sensual action he'd ever witnessed. "Hmm?"

"I'm glad we're not friends anymore."

"Me, too." He ran his hands over the creamy flesh of her breasts. Leaned over and flicked his tongue across her still swollen, erect nipples. She gripped his hair and held him in place while he lavished attention on her. Her slender body was sleek, firm, and he tested and tasted every inch of her.

She clawed at him. "More," she gasped. "More."

"Soon." He brushed across her dampness with his thumb, teasing her, before plunging his fingers back inside. Driving her to the edge of surrender, he battled his passion as the pressure built. He fought his need for release until she shivered and trembled with desire. Reason abandoned him and turned to burning hunger. The blood drained from his head. He'd explode soon. "I need you. All of you."

"Yes," she whispered. "Please."

He fumbled with his wallet, retrieved protection, then covered himself. She opened her legs wider, reached down, grasped him, and guided him. She put him at her entrance, offering herself to him.

"Take what you want."

"I want inside you," he murmured. "Look at me."

He pushed. Her body opened, expanding around him. "Feel me buried deep in your body. God, you're wonderful."

Slowly, smoldering green eyes looked down to where their bodies joined. Her gaze slid back up and locked onto his. A weird skip of his heart was pushed from his thoughts.

"No," she said on a gasp. "We're wonderful."

He thrust deeper inside her clutching body. Her mouth formed a silent *oh,* and they began to move in sync. Harder and faster, together, they sped toward ecstasy. Catherine's red hair fell wildly across the bed, and her legs came up to lock around his waist. She met his thrusts with her own.

Crashing waves swamped him, tossing him into the rushing, pulsing darkness. His breath caught. He didn't breathe. Couldn't breathe. She cried out his name, and with one final surge, her body spasmed around him. The sensation was too great, and with a groan of satisfaction, he convulsed inside her.

Doing his best not to crush her under his weight, he collapsed and rested for a moment to catch his breath before rolling to the side, disposing of the condom. He turned back, sated and happy as she snuggled into his open arms. Her chest vibrated against him.

"Are you laughing?"

"Like I won the lottery. You were wonderful."

"No. We were wonderful. You're a giving, sensuous, sexual woman. Never doubt yourself again."

His muscles tightened and instantly blood rushed south when she nuzzled his neck then ran her cheek across the scratchy stubble on his chin. That she had this much power over him surprised him.

"You feel good." She stroked her hand over his hip, leaving a trail of fire.

Matt rolled over on his back and rubbed the fingers and thumb of his right hand together. That tingling sensation seemed to have spread throughout his body. She propped up on one elbow and studied his growing erection. Wrapping her fingers around him, she slid her hand up and down. He expanded with her touch. With eyes full of adventure, she gazed up at him.

"Mind if I explore?"

"Hardly. There are no rules. What we do together, Cat, is up to you. Hold nothing back."

"Then tell me why you do this." She mimicked his fingers and thumb movements.

"Happened the first time my hands touched you. A shock or tingle started at my fingertips and worked up my arm. It's a hell-of-a-lot stronger now."

"I like that reason."

His heart rate shot through the roof when she pushed his arms up over his head, kissed his cheeks, and then worked her way downward. Her lips roved, her tongue tasted with small flicks, traveling across his muscles and tendons as if she were discovering the different textures of his body. What she was really doing was driving him insane with desire.

"You've already broken one rule," she whispered.

"Which one is that?" He slid up on the pillows, clasped his hands behind his head, and studied her while she circled his nipple with her finger. Smiled as it rose to a small hard bud. It was as if she was on a mission of discovery, a kitten with a new ball of twine. He wasn't about to stop her.

"I've never allowed anyone to call me Cat."

"Then I'll only use the nickname in our most private moments. Agreed?" His back went rigid when she licked his nipple. The more she teased and explored the harder he got. Her adventures were killing him, and the tauter his muscles got, the bolder she became. He had to pull his mind back, or he'd lose control.

She straddled him. At last, his aching erection lay beneath her. Slowly, she rocked back and forth against him until Matt hissed through his teeth. "The heat coming off you..."

He fumbled in search of a new condom then handed it to her, silently asking her to slide the protection over him. Her trembling hands touched a place deep inside his heart. The dark, hungry expression on her face when she handed the empty foil package back was pure passion. He gripped her hips and lifted. Filled her, stretched her, impaled her. Then he lay still, wanting her to feel the sensation of fullness, wanting her to take charge, to feel the power of her own sexuality.

"Don't stop."

Her words were heavy, a thick, creamy syrup. His fingers gripped her backside. "You're in complete control. Try your rocking motion again."

She moved forward, eyes widened, her gaze locked on his.

"Now slide back," he whispered, mesmerized by her beautiful face. "Yes. Just like that."

He used his hands and hips to guide her while she rode him, hard and fast. The friction and pressure were instant and blinding. Her head tilted back, red hair swirled in abandonment. She arched into him, tipping her hips to take him deeper, gripping, pulling him closer to the edge. He battled for control.

"So good," she groaned, a sexy, tortured moan. Her enjoyment propelled him on. He'd take everything she could give, and he'd give everything she could take. He tightened his grip, and with powerful thrusts drove in and out, taking her to the outer edge with him. Warmth spread throughout him. Inside her body, he'd fallen into a fire of molten lava. The pressure built until he thought he'd shatter into a million pieces.

She cried out his name, and Matt joined her as the undercurrent pulled them into deep water. He pulled her to him, kissed her deeply, and held her close. Her face was still buried in his chest when she spoke.

"I've never had this much fun. You may have created a monster."

His heart did a funny tug when he realized how completely she'd trusted him tonight. Hopefully, she'd learned she could give him control, and he'd always give it back. That she could take charge and completely abandon herself. Tonight, he'd helped her rediscover and recover her sexuality.

"Even when I was a kid, monsters didn't scare me."

Chapter Thirteen

"Danny Mason is here." Sue stepped inside the office and lowered her voice. "Said you wanted to see him."

"Bring him in. I'll talk to him." The neighbor must've passed the word to Mason.

"Sheriff Ballard." Sue spoke from the doorway before entering and making introductions.

"Come in, Danny." Matt shook the man's hand then waved him to a chair. "Make yourself comfortable." Mason wore grease-stained, dark blue coveralls, and lace-up work boots. Brown hair pulled back in a long braid made him look like a flash back to the sixties.

"My neighbor said you came by to see me."

"Ms. Whitley?"

"Yeah. Nice lady." Mason moved the toothpick in his mouth. "If this is about Julia, I already told Jake everything I know. Which is squat."

"How well did you know her?" Matt got right to the point. He watched for a reaction, a blink or blanch, but saw none. But then Danny Mason knew what Matt wanted before he walked into the office.

"Why're you asking?" Danny slumped down in the chair. "Because of my record," he answered his own question.

"I'm trying to find a killer."

"Well, good luck. Don't look at me. I've kept my nose clean. Ask Jake. He'll tell you."

"Then you won't mind answering my question. How well did you know Julia?" Matt repeated.

"Well enough to have danced with her a few times." Mason lifted a shoulder as if uninterested in the conversation. "I mostly play pool with the guys when I go to the Saddleback."

"Any of them ever show any special interest in Julia?"

"Not that I noticed. Do you shoot pool?"

Matt responded with a nod and let Danny continue.

"Then you know it's hard to pay attention to anything except the position of the balls on the table. That is, if you want to win."

"That's true."

"You gotta watch your opponent, try to figure out his strategy, make your shots, but leave him nothing."

"You're right about that." Matt remembered past games with Ash Hunter. "I've got a friend who's pretty good."

"Bring him out to one of Marty's tournaments. We need the competition." Mason's face lit up with interest, his brown eyes glinted with challenge.

"I might do that. You ever date Julia?"

"Sorry, I didn't mean to get off the subject. No, I didn't."

"Who did?"

"None of the crowd I run with. Except JC. If that's all, I really gotta get back to work."

"Appreciate you stopping by. You think of anything, give me a call." Matt stood and shook Danny's hand.

Matt escorted him out as far as Sue's desk then handed her his notes on the way back to his office. Hard to get a read on Danny. Maybe the follow up talk with Mel Hamilton would be more productive.

Matt kicked back and reread Jake's interview with Mel. He looked for a word, a sentence, something to key on when he went calling.

****

"Catherine, let me help you with that." JC jogged to the rear of her car and finished loading her office supplies. "Storage boxes? You're not moving?"

"Thanks. Just picking up some stuff for the funeral home."

"Did you get your emission system fixed?" JC closed her trunk and then leaned against her car.

At the bar, he wore dress blue jeans, a western shirt, and showy cowboy boots. Women noticed him right away. Today his shaggy hair hadn't been combed. His t-shirt was stained, jeans were dirty, and he wore torn tennis shoes. He looked older and road weary.

"No, and now the air conditioner is on the fritz." Catherine opened her car door. Standing around in front of the office supply wasn't an option. Without rain or a hint of a breeze, the heat literally slammed her in the face when she stepped outside.

"I know a guy who works at a garage. Get you a good deal when you decide to get your car fixed. I can help you out with a ride to work. If you want."

"I might take you up on that." She wiped the sweat forming off her forehead. "What brings you out in this heat?"

He pulled a traffic ticket from his back pocket. "Got to pay a speeding ticket. The sheriff is out to get me."

"You don't believe that. Do you?" Defending any male was a new experience, especially one in law enforcement, but taking up for Matt came easy.

"He thinks I killed Julia." His words tumbled out, desperate sounding. His hazel eyes clouded over with grief. "Didn't come right out and accuse me, but he sent Jake out to Marty's. Pumped her with all kinds of questions."

"JC." Catherine placed her hand on his arm. If she understood anything, it was how being falsely accused of something could hurt. "Marty knows you wouldn't hurt anyone."

"You don't think I could." He raised his head and managed a weak smile. "Do you?" His sad eyes made her wonder if he had any friends he could count on. The kind who stood by him.

"Of course not. And I'm sure Matt...Sheriff Ballard...will clear things up." She wanted to give JC hope but couldn't find the right words.

Catherine drove away thinking about the cost of car repairs. For the last month, she'd spent only the bare minimum, slowly building her stash of moving money. Her heart sank. Moving money. Her insides pitched and rolled. What if Matt got curious about her past? With a push of the button, he had access to her entire life. If he looked, she'd leave Butte Crest sooner than she'd planned. The more she learned about Matt's belief in trust and truth, the more she believed the time to share her secret with him had come and gone. Maybe it would be best if she left before he got too nosy.

Leaving Matt behind would be hard. Her heart grew heavy at the thought.

Monday night they'd made love. She'd cried out when stars exploded behind her eyes, then she'd gathered those stars in her heart when he came, pulsing and throbbing inside her. Hearts pounding, bodies glistening with sweat, they'd collapsed in each other's embrace. He'd snuggled her into his arms, covered them with a sheet, and she'd slept with her head next to his solid chest. She woke the next morning to strong hands caressing her.

Sex with Matt had been beyond all her wildest dreams. She'd never known such cataclysmic orgasms. He'd put her needs first, nurtured her, and helped reawaken her sexuality.

Chill bumps ran over her body, a phenomenon in the middle of such a record heat wave. She allowed herself a satisfied smile. A lot had been accomplished in one night with Matt. For one thing, she'd grown to love the nickname Cat.

As usual, she smiled when The Final Touch Funeral Home sign came into view. Time to stop daydreaming. Matt wasn't looking for a wife, and she wasn't looking for a permanent home. Time to snap out of the sex-induced haze and control her emotions. They weren't star-crossed lovers destined to meet and fulfill each other's dreams. She and Matt were two adults who enjoyed spending time with each other. Exactly as Marty described.

Susan answered the buzzer at the rear door and helped unload the supplies. "I'll give you a key if you want to park back here all the time. Your car will be in the afternoon shade."

Catherine considered the offer and weighed the heat against walking through the back of the funeral home twice a day. Today was her first time to get close to the embalming room. "No thanks. Mr. Abbott doesn't come in my area, and I stay out of his."

"Puleese." Susan's disdain made for an interesting pronunciation of the word. "Steve stopped coming up front because of you."

"Me? What did I do?"

"He'd walk in the room, and you'd run like he was some flesh-eating zombie. The man's already a loner. Since you've been here he's gotten worse."

"You gotta admit he's creepy." Catherine stacked the last box on the two-wheeled cart. "Was I that obvious?"

"Yes. Steve is like family. He and my husband worked together for years."

"In that case, I apologize. I'll park back here and try harder to get to know Steve."

The front door buzzer rang, putting an end to the conversation. Susan always locked up when no one was at the receptionist's desk.

"You go. I'll pull the cart up front." Susan grabbed the handles and deftly rolled the heavy load of supplies up the ramp. "If it's a customer, seat them in my office."

Catherine hurried when the impatient visitor hit the buzzer again. Peering through the glass door, the mailman had his finger poised when Catherine flipped the lock. He pushed the door open then passed her a couple of envelopes and a small box.

"Thanks. I'm running behind today." He turned and jogged back to his Jeep.

Catherine glanced at the package. She tossed the mail on a table and ran into the parking lot waving the box in the air. "Wait," she yelled. "Where did you get this?"

"It was there on the steps when I drove up." He waved and drove off.

Catherine stared at the package with her name printed on it. The urge to throw the damn thing or to stomp it to smithereens was overwhelming. Scanning the horizon, she looked for anyone watching.

"Damn you," she exploded. "Come face me." Who was doing this? Did he hide and watch, hoping for some kind of reaction? Her heart rate shot up, a rocket climbing into the stratosphere. Fury blurred her vision, darkness swirled and closed in, a nightmare she wanted to wake up from but couldn't.

A cool hand touched her arm. She dropped the box, screamed, and whirled around. She delivered a blow to the chest with the heel of her hand.

Steve Abbott stumbled backward, his eyes and mouth open wide. His arms flailed like windmill blades for balance.

Susan rushed down the steps and stepped between them. "What happened?" Her gaze swung from Catherine, crouched and ready to strike again, to Steve who clutched his chest, his face distorted in fear. When he'd gathered his feet under him, he stared at her as if she were crazy.

"She hit me." Steve's lips thinned, and his face went paler than usual. "She was out here yelling at the sky. I ran out to see what was wrong." Steve glared at Catherine, stuffed his hands in his pockets, and turned away. "I won't do it again."

"Wait. Please." Catherine took a tentative step in his direction. God, could things get any worse?

"I'll be in the back if you need me." Steve kept his gaze and comment directed at Susan.

"Steve, I'm sorry." Catherine found herself talking to his back while he went inside.

"You're acting crazy. Are you ill?" Susan put her hand on Catherine's forehead.

"I'm upset, frightened, and furious." Catherine retrieved the box, following Susan to her office. "This wasn't mailed. My name's hand printed on the top."

"Your stalker left this?" Susan's face paled.

"On the front steps. Sneaky bastard must've dropped it off while we were in the back." Catherine's efforts to sound unafraid and flippant came out flat. She stopped. "God, I must sound insane." She plopped the small package on the desk and dusted her hands.

"You're a wreck. I'm calling the sheriff."

"I'm mad as hell and scared of my own shadow, but I'm not a wreck."

Susan pushed Catherine into a side room and onto a beige leather couch. "Sit. Rest. Humor me."

Catherine sat alone in the small area used for family privacy. Whoever left the box had a lot of nerve to deliver it in broad daylight. Who was playing games at her expense? A memory slipped past her guard and an old fear clawed its way to the surface. Being afraid of the dark, afraid to walk to her car in a parking lot, afraid to go to sleep for fear of waking to find a hand on her throat—all those past remembrances sent her heart pounding painfully against her chest. Not again. She lowered her head and closed her eyes.

The wave of pain in her heart was crushing. Time to move on had arrived faster than she wanted. She'd allowed herself to believe she'd found a place to rest for a while. Perhaps it wasn't to be.

****

Matt raced across town, fear eating at his insides, while he pushed the cruiser's speed as high as he dared. Even though Susan had assured him Catherine was okay, he needed to see for himself. He slid into a parking spot and bounded up the steps to the funeral home. Susan met him at the door.

"Catherine?"

"She's in the family room." Susan pointed down the hall.

Matt didn't hesitate. In three strides, he'd opened the door and found Catherine looking like a lost child. He knelt in front of her, pulling her into his arms.

"I knew you'd come," she whispered into his chest.

"Trust me. I'll be there when you need me." Matt leaned back, cupping her face with his hand. "You all right?"

"I'm not as fragile as you might think."

The tremble he heard in her voice spread to a full body shiver. He covered her mouth with his. A warm, you're-all-right-now kiss. He stroked her back until she settled.

"I'm fine."

But she wasn't and he knew it. He buried his face in her hair, his mind a jumble of anger and fear. He wanted her stalker in his grasp so badly his palms burned.

"Well, I'm not. When were you planning on telling me the rest?" Matt reached back and closed the door, never taking his gaze off Catherine.

Her eyes widened. She stared at him. Dammit. He saw fear.

"The rest?"

"What's this about a fourth package? My count is three, unless you kept one from me. Did you?" He swallowed, needing to temper his cop's voice, because her back had stiffened at his tone.

"What if I did? There's nothing you can do. How do you catch an invisible man? Stake out my home? My job? Assign a deputy to follow me around? No? Then what difference does it make?"

"The difference is keeping secrets." He held a finger up to silence her protest. "I understand you can't or won't talk to me about certain parts of your life. But in this case keeping quiet is dangerous." He ran that same finger down her jaw, trying to relax her. "I thought we'd established you could trust me. Secrets can ruin a relationship. Bury it alive. And if I have to explain...we haven't connected like I thought we had."

He sat back on his heels and waited. A myriad of emotions played across her face.

"There's something I need to..."

A knock on the door ended their conversation. Susan stuck her head inside.

"I come bearing food and drink."

"By all means, come in," Catherine said.

"Where's the box?" Matt couldn't work up any interest in food.

"On Susan's desk."

"Let's take a look." He wrapped his arm around Catherine's waist, pleased that she leaned against him as they followed Susan down the hall to the main office.

"There." Catherine pointed. "The mailman's and my fingerprints are on it."

"Anyone else touch it?" His gaze landed on Susan.

"Give me a little credit," she said, setting down the tray of coffee and cookies. "I watch Criminal Minds." She stopped at the door on her way out. "Take all the time you need. I'd better check on Steve."

Matt's eyebrows rose. "What's wrong with Steve?"

****

"I sort of hit him." Catherine's mind replayed the surprised and angry look on Steve's face.

"Sort of? As in you struck him?" Matt's blue eyes shaded with confusion. His hand went to his temple and pressed.

"Do you have a headache?" Catherine tasted a cookie. Vanilla and almond flooded the inside of her mouth. All of a sudden, she was starving.

"Don't change the subject. Did Steve provoke you?"

"No. He surprised me, and I tapped him on his chest. Scared both of us."

"Tapped him? I'd hate for him to file assault charges." Matt snapped on gloves, then carefully removed the paper and box lid. With a low growl, he lay out a pair of pink lace panties and a picture of a tattoo of a woman's lips.

"This is sick and getting sicker by the minute." Catherine's appetite vanished, and she tossed the unfinished cookie in the trash. "He's sending me a message, isn't he?"

"This is his way of being intimate," Matt answered.

His statement hit her with the force of a right cross. Beginning now, she'd look at every man she met with questioning eyes. Until this stopped, she'd have no peace. Her efforts at not giving this stalker the upper hand slipped away. Chills raced up her arms. She paced, scrubbing at the goose bumps with her fingertips.

"I've read stories where these weirdo's get more and more aggressive. Then they turn violent. Is this where he's headed? Maybe it's time I packed up and moved on."

The words had popped out of her mouth. Instantly, she wanted to erase them. She'd slipped back into her old behavior of running when things got the least bit sticky.

The air left the room in a whoosh, silence roared in her ears. She felt his gaze, hot on her skin. Not one sound was made. She used to pretend she was invisible, now she wished for the ability in earnest. It was too late to salvage the moment.

Catherine sank down in the chair and studied her feet. "I didn't mean that."

"Running's a reasonable reaction. But the idea of packing up and leaving, it rolled off your tongue with no effort. I think the thought has crossed your mind before. To be honest, it surprises me."

"That's me, okay? I'm full of surprises." Her joke fell flat. She raised her head and met his gaze. Disappointment, blended with pain, darkened his eyes. Did the thought of losing her hurt? A flutter shot through her heart. She couldn't allow herself to care too much. Moving on wasn't a topic she wanted to consider, but it remained a viable option. "There's not much chance of catching this jerk. Is there?"

"Doesn't mean I won't try. You can help. I need you to think. Anything unusual happen lately? Anyone make you uncomfortable?"

She thought back over the past few days. Took him through her movements and told him about seeing JC. Not a glimmer of a smile crossed his face. "Steve's not mad at me. I don't think. And JC's worried because you believe he's capable of killing someone."

"We're all capable. Some of us control our urges. Others are criminals."

Her heart imploded. She shouldn't have been surprised by his comment. His strong belief in the law made him who he was.

"Other than Vince, anyone paying extra attention to you?"

"Just you." She went back to studying her feet.

"I'll send the box and picture to the lab. What was the third gift?"

"A pink diary and a picture of a man's torso. The picture was signed, 'Think of me.'"

"You should've called. When did you get the damn thing?"

"The night you hunted Julia until late. You were tired. I couldn't disturb you."

"You should've called," he repeated, moving to stand beside her, his hand gripped her shoulder. "You have to be extra careful."

"I am. Every minute of the day. Maybe I need to sleep with the lights on. I'll step up my exercise, concentrate on my self-defense moves. Come to think of it, I'll stop on the way home and pick up some cheap weights. The cans of corn I'm using aren't heavy enough." She clamped her jaw shut to stop her babbling.

Matt slid his hand under her hair and massaged her neck. His fingers found a knot and bore down. "There's one other thing you could do."

"Hmm." Her head lolled forward. She prayed he wouldn't bring up a gun again. "What's that?"

"You could stay at my place."

"You're not serious."

"I'm not?" He continued to apply pressure. His fingers dug deeper until the tension eased.

"I can't." Her nerves did that melting action again when he smiled. She fought to keep from stammering. "Besides, how would that make me safer?"

"Only a limited number of people would know you were there. Plus, there's the bonus of me being around occasionally."

"Thank you for asking, but I can't."

****

Matt opened the door and asked Susan for a paper sack while he considered what he'd done. He'd asked Catherine to move in with him. What if she'd said yes? His libido was doing his thinking for him. She'd been in his thoughts a lot since Monday night. Her raw passion and wide-eyed excitement at rediscovering her own sexuality had dominated his mind. But to ask her to move in?

"Then let me have your air conditioner fixed. At least you could keep your windows rolled up."

"We've talked about this. He's not going to stop because my windows are up. Is he?"

Matt wouldn't lie to her. "No. I don't think so. You should fill out a complaint. All these unwanted gifts should be on record."

"You know about them and that's enough."

Matt bagged the latest gift and kissed his stubborn woman goodbye. Her refusal to file a complaint or walk inside a courthouse bugged the crap out of him.

The idea of googling Catherine sounded better all the time. Her lack   of   trust   hurt   like   hell.

Chapter Fourteen

Matt recognized the sleek, convertible sports car parked in the reserved slot. Questioning ex-con Mel Hamilton had taken longer than expected, causing Matt to miss Ash's arrival.

"When did Ash get here?" Matt asked as Jake descended the steps of the courthouse.

"Over an hour ago." Jake's normally stoic face wore the grin of a kid at a surprise party. "I damn near missed him."

"Was it sweet?"

"Nothing like you expected. He must've figured something was up, because he never missed a step. Grabbed Sue up and hugged her like they were long lost relatives."

"Should've known. It's hard to run a game on him."

"He's set up in the conference room off your office with all the evidence. What'd you think about Hamilton?"

"I don't make him for causing trouble. Mel's trying hard to please his new bride. Why else would he agree to live and work on her daddy's ranch?"

"That woman's reason enough to stay out of trouble." Jake glanced over his shoulder as if afraid someone overheard.

"Where are you headed?" Matt took pity on him and didn't threaten to tell Jake's wife.

"Will Brooking's place. I hear he's taken a leave from work to form his own search party. Says if we can't find Annie, he will. He needs reminding to stay on the right side of the law." Jake pulled the door to his cruiser open, paused, and turned back. "Unless you've got something else in mind."

"You're the Deputy Sheriff. Don't need my approval." Matt waved him off. "Keep me informed." He took the steps two at a time. Ash would have questions.

Sue looked up from her computer and smiled. Sitting on the edge of her desk was a box of chocolates. "You failed to mention Ash is real considerate." She raised the lid and popped a piece of candy in her mouth.

"He's real thoughtful, all right." Matt shook his head while Sue's cheeks turned pink. He handed her the bag containing the panties and picture with instructions. He pushed open the conference room door to find Ash studying the crime scene photos. A frown pulled his eyebrows together. He showed no recognition the door had opened. Damn, Matt had missed him. They'd worked well together, picking up on things the other missed.

"He's a sick bastard." Ash's gaze didn't move from the pictures.

"That, he is. Good to see you made yourself at home." Matt slapped Ash across the back and welcomed the tight grasp of his hand.

"Speaking of home, I'm stealing Sue when she gets a minute. I'll follow her to my new pad, give me a chance to unpack and get ready for my new job." All business, Ash leaned back and flipped the murder-book open. "You've done a good job with the notes. Won't take much to get me up to speed. I may want to double back on some of your interviews."

"Let me know. If I can't take you, one of the deputies will. You met Jake. He and Rey Santos have worked both cases since day one. Sue combined their notes with mine. What you read is up to date."

"Besides the obvious. Did these two women have anything in common?" Ash returned his gaze to Julia Drummond's and Annie Travers's faces.

"One. They both went to the same bar. Julia was a frequent visitor. Being single, she stopped by with one of her girlfriends. Annie went rarely. When she did she was always with her husband.

The Saddleback's the only club of any size for miles. Two of our neighboring counties are dry. This nightspot does big business on the weekends. Have you had a chance to watch the security video from the bank drive-thru window?"

"Not yet. I wanted to read your notes on the first woman before I started on the second. How long's she been missing?"

"Eight days." Matt didn't have to check. Each hour and minute they'd looked for Annie was forever etched in his mind.

"At this point you don't know if that's a good sign or not. What about the first woman? How long before her body was found?"

"Four days. ME estimated she'd been dead twenty-four hours."

"Interesting, these types of crimes usually escalate..." Ash's voice trailed off to a whisper as his mind processed information. "Unless she was taken as a sex slave."

"Then why'd he kill her?"

"Maybe it was part of his game. Could've been an accident."

"Murder's no accident."

"There's a thread that connects these women. We'll find it." Ash's gaze locked on Matt. "You gotta pull back man, stay objective."

"Easy to say."

"But critical to do." Ash finished the long- standing mantra he and Matt had coined years ago.

Matt looked his friend in the eyes. "Did I say welcome? I'm glad you're here."

"Good. Now walk me through the video."

Matt started the film, hoping Ash would pick up on something Matt and his team had missed. Ash watched the f e e d   t w i c e .

"I can't read her lips. The shot is from an angle, and I can't make out the words. Did you look into her finances?"

"Yeah," Matt said. "They weren't too deep in debt. Their house is a rental. Neither car is new and with only a couple grand owed against them. Hell, they'd been saving money to have a kid. I don't think the guy on camera is her husband."

Ash closed the book and straightened the paperwork on the conference table. He used to get pissed if someone on the night shift trashed his desk. Matt would rearrange stuff to hear Ash raise hell. Elena, Matt's partner after he moved to the narcotics squad, had been the opposite. Her work area always looked like a bomb had exploded. She used to joke how her husband had to help keep up with the kids. The same kids who were now growing up without a mother.

Ash stood and studied his handiwork. "That's better. I officially start in the morning, but I wanted to get a feel for what we're up against. Gives me something to think about tonight. I'm having dinner with my new girl and a lady friend of hers. Want to make it a foursome?" Ash tilted his head sideways and waited for a response.

"I've got work to do. Go. Have a good time." Matt made no effort to keep the smile off his face. "I'll see you in the morning." He walked Ash back to Sue's desk and left his gruff, abrasive dispatcher almost purring.

Matt returned to his office. It nagged at him that Will Brooking and some of his buddies were storming through the county searching for Annie. He wasn't opposed to help, but Will was a hothead. A hothead with a missing daughter.

****

He prided himself on staying sober. He'd been pissed and obviously had one beer too many. Too many, unless somebody had painted two extra stripes on the road running out to Mama's trailer. The drive seemed to take forever. But he'd made a decision, and by God, he didn't back down from the tough ones. He'd do it and put the whole damn thing behind him.

Dying would be her own damn fault. Hadn't he been good to her? All that got him was a trashed bathroom. She wanted to wear clothes. She wanted more food. And over and over again, she wanted to go home. Goddamn her, she wanted everything but him.

Mama never tolerated backtalk and crying. She'd whip him until the red streaks were welts. But after...after, she'd hold him in her arms and rock him. Her breasts were soft and sweet. Sometimes she'd let him—no, he wouldn't remember those times.

His head ached, and his heart hurt. Why hadn't she loved him? Why? Worst of all...why did he care?

His tires grabbed and slung gravel against the undercarriage. "What the hell?" His pickup swerved off the road for a second. He cranked the AC up on high, pointed the vents toward his face, and breathed deeply. His mind had cleared by the time he pulled into the driveway.

He might be ready for a new doll. First, he'd let this doll shower and get pretty for him. A ponytail, some makeup, a layer of Mama's red lipstick, and she'd pull him out of this melancholy shit-ditch he was in. He'd tie the bow around her neck himself. For a while, she'd be the doll she was meant to be. One last time. Then he'd end her whining for good.

****

Matt held the door open for Ash, walking past him when he stopped and breathed in the aroma. Mornings at the old-fashioned drugstore smelled of fresh coffee, sizzling bacon, and maple syrup. Lately, it had turned into an unofficial meeting place to discuss the case. He and his detectives were in a mad dash to find Annie before she was killed. Who knew where the bastard would leave her for all the world to see?

Matt led Ash toward the sound of clattering dishes, through the aisles and back to the small café tucked away in the rear. Business was brisk for such a small town. The older male population filled the stools at the counter. The heat had driven them indoors and away from their usual spot on the benches in front of the courthouse. Matt made the obligatory stops to shake hands and answer a few questions. Most were directed at Ash when introduced as the homicide expert from Houston.

While there, Matt planned to ask if anyone remembered JC being around yesterday morning. Matt wanted to know exactly what had been purchased. He'd spent the past hour going over the gifts

Catherine had received. They grabbed the last empty booth. Molly brought brown over-sized mugs filled with steaming coffee without waiting to be asked.

"You boys look hungry this morning." She stood closer to Ash's side of the table, smiled down on him as if the drought had broken, and it was pouring rain.

Ash turned his full attention to Molly. "I'll take the special, scrambled."

"I'm not hungry." Matt choked on his coffee as the scenario unfolded. How Ash captured the woman's heart with nothing more than an appreciative look was unbelievable. She swished her hips at a dizzying speed as she walked away. "You're such a whore-dog. Don't you ever get enough?"

"There's no such thing. And you've been holding out on me." Ash shot a smile in the direction of the now smitten Molly.

"Holding out? Molly's a pretty girl, but there's nothing going on." There could've been. She'd batted her pretty blue eyes at Matt more than once, but there wasn't a spark.

"She's not the one I'm talking about. You get a funny look when you talk about this Catherine woman. I need to know more."

Matt squirmed in the booth. Ash's mind was like the jaws of a pit bull, when he locked down on something he didn't turn loose.

"She's a friend." Matt ignored Ash when he huffed a sound between disgust and disbelief. "And I needed one over the past month or so."

"And..."

"She's damn near perfect." Matt smiled. Fact was she had no flaws on her body.

"So what's not perfect about this mysterious woman?"

"For one thing, she's got a stalker, and yet, refuses to file a complaint. Refuses to walk inside the courthouse or my office."

"Why's that?" Ash leaned forward, his interest piqued.

"Don't know. I haven't pushed the issue."

"When do I get to meet her?"

"Good question. She works two jobs."

"A woman who pays her own bills. I like her already."

"Sure is tempting to dig around in her past. Maybe learn how I can help."

"You could 'help' yourself right out her front door. How pissed you think she's gonna be if she finds out you 'dug around'?"

"I said tempting."

"Listen to an expert. Leave it alone."

Matt bit back a wisecrack but only because breakfast was served.

Ash leaned over the plate Molly put in front of him and stuffed a bite of eggs in his face. "Molly, darling. I think I'm in love."

She leaned down closer to his ear. "I get off at three."

The man was truly an artist with the ladies. Matt took a piece of Ash's toast but put it back when his cell vibrated.

"What's up, Rey?" Matt forced himself to swallow. He closed his eyes and listened to the gruesome facts. Annie Travers had been found. "Be there in twenty."

Ash was already on his feet. He tossed money on the table. "Got a body?"

"Yeah. Annie Travers is in Downey Park. Sonofabitch left her right next to Curry Middle School." Matt an Ash rushed through the store, jumping into the cruiser. "I didn't ask for details, but if she's posed like the last one is, we've got a serial killer on our hands."

Matt radioed Sue to ensure she'd notified Jake and Dr. Reinhardt. Matt had to get a positive ID and secure the crime scene for the forensic team. He feared the children on the way to school might've seen Annie because the buses had driven right past the park. Damn, Annie's husband taught at the school two blocks away. Why did Crest County start school in the middle of August instead of early September? He called Sue back.

"Ben Travers teaches at that school. Get a hold of the principal before Ben hears a body's been found. We have to keep him away from the site." Matt pushed his speed. Siren blaring, he cut the twenty minutes to ten. Annie's mother and father would have to be told. For now, Annie came first. Matt called in three additional deputies to work crowd control. Curry might be a small town but people would congregate quickly.

Matt shut off the siren a couple of blocks prior to arrival in order to lessen the amount of attention drawn to the site. The park was small by big city standards. Six picnic tables were scattered under large oak trees. Under normal circumstances, there'd be shade covering the area, but this summer had been anything but normal. The sun had burned off the majority of the leaves and the swings and slides were too hot to play on by the time school was out. Wood chips had been replaced with plastic pebbles to prevent fires.

A whoosh of air left his lungs when he had to drive to the rear of the park. At least Annie wasn't on the street front. Matt parked and Rey joined them. His crisp uniform shirt and boyish face was quite a contrast to his granite and emotionless expression.

Ash muttered something unintelligible, clipped his badge to his belt, and bailed out of Matt's cruiser. He met and passed Rey with a curt nod.

As Matt walked to the back of Rey's cruiser, dread increased with each step. Rey's rigid posture and cold expression warned Matt, braced him against the horror and indignation Annie had suffered. Naked, arms hanging at her sides, her head slumped to the side. Annie sat, propped against the base of an oak tree. Bare roots ran along the surface of the dry, hard ground, cradling her body like giant arthritic arms. Her hair was pulled back, her face powered a ghastly white, and lips were as bright red as the bow tied around her neck. Her vacant green eyes stared out, not caring how exposed her killer had left her.

"Jesus H. Christ." Ash scrubbed his hands over his eyes. "You fucking never get used it." He moved with Matt to the edge of an unmarked perimeter, one they wouldn't cross for fear of disturbing evidence.

"Same bastard." Matt squatted to his usual position. "Her eyes are too wide open. I'm betting the pervert glued them open."

"Just like Julia Drummond's." Ash's gaze narrowed while he stepped carefully around the perimeter and studied the area. His voice cold and monotone.

Matt marveled at Ash's ability to distance himself from the crime. It was as if he moved to another plane, locking out all exterior sounds and motions. It was how his analytical mind worked. The victim held a place in Ash's soul. Their wound was his, and he'd nurse it until he found justice.

Rey didn't speak until Matt stood and addressed him by name. "Who found her?"

"Clyde Beacon and his son Charlie. They pick up trash through here three times a week. Charlie ran over to grab the barrel and spotted her. Called it in to dispatch right away. I haven't had time to take their statements."

"Jake's here now. He'll handle that for you." Matt moved Rey and Jake to the side and divided up responsibilities.

Jake instructed the fire department where to set up a portable fence to protect the crime scene from being trampled. Matt stationed his officers at strategic points to ward off sightseers and dispatched a couple to canvas all of the homes in the area, maybe somebody noticed a vehicle. Then he escorted the ambulance close to Rey's car. The body would be removed as soon as possible. Confident the integrity of the area would be preserved, he sought out Rey. A flurry of activity was about to explode, and people at the school would soon start noticing.

"Ben Travers?"

Rey shook his head. "Haven't seen him."

"Good. I had him pulled into the principal's office. He knows we need to speak to him, nothing else. I'll go talk to him."

Rey's gaze rose toward the tops of the trees. "Shit. I should've thought about him."

"You've had your hands full." Matt rested his hand on Rey's shoulder. "I wouldn't have done a thing differently."

Matt's deputies were tired and edgy. They'd spent days searching and interviewing. Now they'd backtrack and do it all again. Frustration and anger dug grooves around their mouths and between their eyes. Matt sensed Jake's presence beside him without looking. Steady and strong, Jake would be at Matt's side after everyone else gave up. He turned to face his deputy chief. His pallor matched the rest of the men working this case.

"I'll tell Ben, if you want." Jake's jaw was rigid, but his eyes harbored great pain.

"Not necessary. Comes with my pay grade. How'd your visit with Will go yesterday?"

"Oh, shit. I forgot to tell you. He'd already put together a group to redo our canvassing." Jake expelled a breath of disgust. "We'll have to watch him close. He'll likely go nuts."

"Find out who he recruited. Take over here. Ash's with Annie. Tell him I'll be back."

"Thanks. Annie's mom and dad will be as hard."

"Ben can decide who tells them."

Matt nodded his recognition of Dave Foster and Hector Ruiz when they arrived at the park in the medical examiner's van. A small SUV pulled in right behind. At least Reinhardt had sent a full complement of investigators.

No doubt the autopsy would be alike except for one glaring difference. Julia's hands and ankles had been taped. Her abrasions had been fresh and raw. But Annie only had one angry, red circle on her left ankle, about three inches wide. She'd struggled to free herself. Fought in desperation for eight days.

His system churned while he drove to the school. The pain behind his left eye was sudden and sharp. He blinked rapidly. He pushed against his temple for fear his head might explode and splatter brain matter across the driver's side window. Parked in front of the school, he dry swallowed a couple of ibuprofen and breathed deeply. God, he'd like to catch and kill the murdering sonofabitch with his bare hands.

He wasted no time getting inside the school and to the principal's office. Matt wanted to get Ben behind closed doors to break the news, but he spotted Matt coming down the hall. The door was thrown open, and Ben bolted toward him. Screaming. Screaming. And screaming.

Chapter Fifteen

Matt pulled in at the outer edge of the park and studied the scene in front of him. Christ, he'd been at the school an hour and at least twenty cars now lined the road. The ambulance was gone, and the tension released between his shoulders. Annie's body wouldn't be on display for the horror mongers any longer.

Her husband on the other hand had emptied the classrooms with his grief. Matt's plan of quietly breaking the news to Ben Travers had failed. Children of all ages filled the hallway in fear at the sound of Ben's gut-wrenching wail. The one thing Matt tried to avoid, happened anyway. The students had a front seat to one of their teachers breaking down into hysteria. The staff had their hands full when Matt drove away.

Many a quiet night in his youth Matt had listened as a coyote bayed in search for one of their own. The sound could rip your heart out. Ben Travers had lost his mate, and his grief was the same tortured sound.

Matt squeezed the bridge of his nose. His ex- partner Elena's funeral flashed through his mind like a slide show. Her husband's weeping still resonated in his nightmares. Matt pulled his phone from his hip and called the one person whose voice could lighten his mood.

"Where are you?" Catherine's soft tone eased his tension. The news had spread to the funeral home. "Coming back from telling Ben Travers his wife's dead."

"You okay?"

"Yeah." He was distinctly better hearing the sound of concern in her voice. Matt slowed his pace and allowed himself a few more minutes of peace. Interesting, he thought of her when his mind was crowded with death and misery. Hearing her voice, knowing she cared...and she did care...hell, it kind of scared him. Nevertheless, she was who he needed to talk to.

"How'd you know?" he asked, wanting only to hear her speak.

"Somebody called Susan. I'm sorry, Matt."

"Me, too." Silence hung between them for a minute. "Ash is here. I wanted you to meet him, but now..."

"I understand. Call me when you can."

His respect for Catherine just kept growing. Her tone of voice carried no disappointment. She offered an open invitation, and he appreciated her understanding.

"It might be a couple of days." Damn, her stalker worried him. He wanted to put her in his pocket, keep her close and safe. "Please be careful. Don't turn your back on anybody. Trust no one, regardless of whom."

"I will. I promise. Now go catch this bastard." And he would. For her. For Julia. For Annie.

He disconnected and walked the curved sidewalk back to the crime scene. Jake sat at one of the picnic tables with the two men who'd found Annie. Neither would ever be able to erase the memory, Matt knew. He'd tried. He'd failed.

"How'd it go?" Ash stopped writing and moved with Matt out of the footpath of the forensic team but close enough to see and hear.

"Poor guy wanted to come down here and see for himself. Couldn't believe there hadn't been a mistake. I convinced him to wait, the ME worked wonders with Julia's eyes. He'll do the same for Annie. The principal called a family friend to drive Ben out to his in-laws. Ben can't talk coherently. One look at him and her mama and daddy will know."

"I don't deal well with the bereaved." Ash propped his foot on a picnic bench and brushed at the layer of dust on his shoe. "I'd rather have all four wisdom teeth removed by my ex-wife."

Ash shrugged one shoulder in his "what are you gonna do" way. No doubt to a stranger he came across as dispassionate and unconcerned. They'd be dead wrong.

"Learn anything while I was gone?" Matt asked.

"Jake finished taking pictures, and we talked to the ME's team for a minute. Based on their estimates, she died last night somewhere around midnight. The sick fuck took the time to clean her up before he set her out like yesterday's trash."

"Not like the trash," Matt disagreed. "He leaves her on display where she can be found right away."

"Then he's remorseful or he's taunting you."

"Julia Drummond's autopsy report stated the killer used gloves, at least for the final stages. Assaulted her repeatedly, but used a condom. He's not sorry. He's careful. I have to head back to the office. I'll have press, politicos, and Annie's family to deal with for the rest of the day."

Ash moved away like Matt had a communicable disease. "Leave me here. I'll hitch a ride with Jake or Rey. I've got some questions for the experts." The last word in his sentence spewed enough sarcasm to curdle cream. Ash had already formed a negative opinion of Reinhardt's team.

"Get as much information as you can."

Comfortable the crime scene was in good hands, Matt made his way through the park, touched base with all his deputies and lastly with Jake.

"How's Ben?" Jake removed his hat and wiped sweat from his brow. "Forget that. He's never gonna get over this. How could he?"

"The school nurse wanted to call his doctor, get a Valium or something. But Ben wanted to keep his wits in order to tell Will and Anita."

"We'll hear from Will pretty soon. He's bound to take this hard."

"I expect you're right. When you're finished here, bring Ash and Rey to the office. We'll gather everything and review what we have. We have enough to ask the FBI for a profile. At any rate, I want Sue to get all the notes centralized. We have to read out of the same book."

"You think the FBI will send someone?"

"I'm not going to ask, yet. But they'll give us insight on what makes this bastard tick."

"Amen." Jake handed Matt the camera. "Ask Sue to print these. We'll be along soon."

"Find out from Ruiz when the autopsy's scheduled. And don't forget Ash. I'll never hear the last of it if you do."

Matt made his way back to the street where Sylvia Horning had her microphone stuffed in one of his youngest and greenest deputy's face.

"Deputy Thornton, can you confirm the body found was Annie Travers?"

God bless him, Gary Thornton merely smiled and said no comment.

"Damn," Matt muttered. The local TV station blonde bombshell was exactly what he didn't need. Her cardinal red suit reminded Matt of the bow around Julia and Annie's necks.

"May I quote you?" Sylvia's gaze locked on his. She quickly moved around beside him, putting them both in front of the cameraman.

"No comment." Matt nodded at Thornton, indicating he'd done a good job. The anger in Sylvia's eyes set Matt back a step. She was a professional and should've known she wouldn't get much at this stage of an investigation.

"Kill the camera." She barked the order to the poor schmuck holding the heavy equipment as if she expected him to heel. But when she turned back to Matt she was smiling. Her perfect white teeth reminded Matt of a shark about to angle in for the kill. "Now, Sheriff, my audience would prefer hearing facts from you rather than speculation from me. Rumor has it that the body found was Annie Travers. Is that a true statement?"

"Ms. Horning, a body has been transported to the county morgue in San Antonio pending official identification and notification of the next of kin." Not a bad statement, short, to the point, revealing nothing. Her clenched jaw hinted at her displeasure. "If you'll excuse me, I have to get back to the office."

"Tell the truth, Sheriff. Do we have a serial killer on the loose?"

"It's too soon to make such an assumption."

Her lips vanished into a thin line. "This is my story. I will not be scooped." She carefully enunciated words.

His patience with her was wearing thin. "I'll have a press release with pertinent information from my office soon. Good afternoon."

"You don't want to shut me out." Sylvia stepped between him and the other two men, speaking in a whisper. "This is hot news. And it's mine."

"What's with the anger?" Matt said, keeping his voice low. Sylvia was wrong if she thought pressure would gain her information. "Your reaction is way over the top."

She looked him right in the eyes. "You'll regret blocking me. This story could be picked up by national networks."

Before he made a comment that would get him in a load of trouble, Matt excused himself. He patted Deputy Thornton on the back and made his way to his cruiser.

He drove away with Ms. Horning standing in front of the camera. No doubt she would tell the county how uncooperative their sheriff had been. She took a step forward, lost her footing, and landed butt first into the dried-out shrubbery lining the exterior of the park. He enjoyed her misfortune. But he'd made an enemy. He hoped brushing her off wouldn't come back and bite him someday.

****

Life couldn't get any weirder. No, what was that word? Ironic. Yeah. Life was fuckin' ironic. He smiled and listened to Vince Bradley shout over the noise of the Saddleback's country band.

Yep, poor Ben Travers' wife had been found dead. Yep, her daddy was Will Brooking. Yep, keep nodding politely. There was a nasty rumor she'd been raped. But Vince didn't know the truth. She was a whiny, lying bitch.

Vince paused to catch his breath and resumed yelling. "If you're interested, be at Will Brooking's house Sunday afternoon at three. He's putting together a group of men who give a shit about keeping our women safe."

"Sounds good." It sounded downright hilarious. "What're they gonna do?"

"Don't know, but I'm offering my help. I know what I'd do if some sonofabitch tried to kidnap my Jessie."

"What's that?" The answer was worth leaning forward to hear.

"Cut the bastard's nuts off and feed 'em to him. That's after I kicked his ass." Vince drained his beer can, belched, and adjusted his shirt over his bulging gut.

"Really?" He damn near laughed at the idiot.

"Damn straight. Nobody fucks with my wife." Was that a challenge? He loved a good game.

And sweet Jessie had given the go ahead with her eyes more than once. He knew what she wanted.

He'd picked Catherine to be the new doll. But Vince was too fuckin' cocky. Like he could protect his woman. Might be fun putting him to the test.

"Well?" Vince leaned over and got close.

"Well what?"

"You gonna meet me at Will's or not?" Vince asked.

"Sure thing. I'll do my part."

"Drive past the house and park around back. Will keeps a fridge stocked with beer in the barn." Vince crushed his can and dropped it onto the table.

Catherine walking straight at him caught his attention. Wearing jeans and a yellow blouse, she was showing off her body and her bite-sized tits. Goddamn, she could make his cock hard by smiling at him. But he didn't mind waiting for her. From what he could tell in these dim lights, her eyes were a dead-on match for the original doll. He might keep her alive for a long time.

"You guys ready for another beer?" she asked him and Vince.

"Hell yeah," Vince shouted. "How 'bout you? You ready?"

Fuckin' A, he was ready. He was hard as a rock. But he smiled and said no thanks. She moved on, taking orders, and making her way through the maze of tables.

****

For the third time tonight, Catherine shook off the uncomfortable feeling of being naked. She'd never get used to the men in the bar undressing her with their eyes. Tonight she'd need an extra long shower when she got home. Her grumbling to Marty always fell on deaf ears. Harmless drunks, she'd say and off she'd go, laughing and flirting while raking in the tips. A few more nights like this and Catherine would add working in a bar to the *Never* list.

Quitting the Saddleback sounded better and better. JC always escorted her out and made sure she drove away safely, but what if her car broke down on the way home? That was a real possibility. Catherine mentally counted her savings. Can't give up this job. Not and put her old heap in the shop. Besides, she made more on the weekends in tips than Susan paid for three days.

"You get any last minute orders?" JC removed the empties from her tray and tossed the cans into the recycle bin.

"A few." Catherine passed her list over to him and rested one hip on a stool for a minute. She checked the banjo shaped Miller Lite clock on the wall. In twenty minutes, she'd start clearing tables. If she worked hard, she'd get off her feet for the night in less than an hour.

The band kicked off a waltz, another indication the night was winding down. Marty insisted they play a few slow love songs at the end of the night. She theorized it helped gear down the crowd and made chasing them out easier. Matt popped into her head at the strangest times. Maybe watching the couples sensuously moving in sync with the music reminded her of being in his arms. The rhythm and words made her wish she were.

"Earth to Catherine." JC tapped her on the arm. "Better deliver these and collect your money. It's getting late."

"Sorry. I'll be right back. Maybe we can get out of here early." When she reached for the tray, JC put his hand on hers.

"Want to run into Curry with me after we close? The Righter Truck Stop serves breakfast all night."

"God, no. My feet are killing me. Thanks anyway. I'm going straight home." Catherine had delivered her second order when a thought hit her. JC hadn't mentioned asking Marty or anyone else to go eat. Had he meant the two of them? Alone? He hadn't asked her for a date. Had he? No way. They were friends. He knew that.

She'd finished her last drink delivery and had restocked one beer box when the house lights came up. Marty walked out on the stage to thank the crowd and the band for a successful evening. She did her usual Dolly Parton impression and loudly announced, "Ya'll come back now. Ya hear?"

Catherine started the process of loading her tray with glasses and empty cans, all the while doing her best to ignore the drunks and their comments. Most were jokes. A couple of the guys offered her a night of good loving. She smiled, shook her head no, and said goodnight.

"Let's go home." Marty finally declared the place clean and flipped the master switch sending the colorful beer signs behind the bar into darkness. A lone nightlight lit the path to the door. "Good Lord, three-thirty in the morning and it's hotter than hell," she complained as they walked outside. JC's big red pickup with its oversized tires roared to life first, but as always, he waited. He'd be the last to drive out of the parking lot.

Catherine waved, blinked at the heat inside her car, and hit the gas pedal. She rolled down the driver's side window and let the wind blow.

The driveway was fully illuminated when Catherine got home. Emma never ceased to amaze her, and Catherine loved her more every day. After hearing about the stalker, Emma paid an electrician to string a row of overhead lights from the back of the main house all the way to the front porch of Catherine's place.

Purse over her shoulder, keys in one hand and mace in the other, she wasted no time getting inside. As always, she checked the windows and doors. After she'd performed her safety check, she felt safe enough to relax a little.

Boots off and resting on the bed, she smiled when her cell phone played "Love Me Tender," an old Elvis tune. She'd programmed the special ring tone for Matt.

"Why are you up this late?" she asked in lieu of her usual 'hey.'

"For some reason, I woke and noticed it was four o'clock. I gambled you might be home and still awake." His sleepy, raspy voice rumbled through the night, sexy and inviting.

"I'm inside, safe and sound. Thanks for worrying about me." With all he had going on, he'd thought about her. Hard to keep a guy like him from staking a claim on your heart.

"I wouldn't worry if you were here with me."

"Stop tempting me. You have enough on your mind. I can't imagine how trying today must've been." Catherine punched speaker and set her phone on the bed. She grabbed her robe and stripped off her blouse. The zipper on her jeans was half down when Matt groaned. "What's wrong?" she asked.

"You're undressing, aren't you?"

"How'd you know?"

"I'm a cop. I heard the rustle of clothes. Now I'll never get back to sleep."

"Well, since you're awake."

"I am that." His voice, soft and low, whispered.

"Do you have any experience at phone sex?" Shivers shot through her. Her face heated. God, she'd embarrassed herself. She'd become a sex- craved monster.

"None," he said with a chuckle. "But I'm a fast learner."

"I'm sorry. Selfish and thoughtless. I should take a shower and get to bed. And I'm babbling." She inhaled deeply then pushed the air out in a rush. She'd lost her mind. Completely. "You've got to be up in a couple of hours." He was silent. Had he dozed off? She looked at her cell to check the connection. He hadn't hung up. "Matt? Say something."

"Be there in twenty." The line went dead.

"Yes!" She dropped her cell, grabbed her robe, and raced for the shower.

Chapter Sixteen

"I have to get going."

Matt's sleepy voice barely penetrated the recesses of her mind as she drifted on the edge of slumber. Catherine registered her protest with a groan and reached for his warm body in an effort to keep him close. He brushed her tangled hair off her neck and kissed her softly. She turned over when his weight left the mattress. The plan was to watch him dress, but instead her heart clenched at the sight of the angry scar on his back. She'd wanted to ask him about what had to be a bullet wound but always chickened out. He'd never mentioned being shot. Maybe it was something he couldn't talk about.

He glanced over his shoulder, his blue eyes darkened with desire and sent all reasonable thought skittering under the covers.

"You're looking at me like I'm a smorgasbord and you're starving. Stop licking your lips and go back to sleep," Matt said, reaching for his clothes. "Before I forget I have to go to work."

God, his broad shoulders and narrow hips caused a hungry sensation to spread south. Was she totally insatiable? She pushed herself upright, causing the sheet to fall, uncovering her breasts. Odd, she felt no shame or embarrassment around him. "I'll fix breakfast. You can take time to eat."

His face turned all sexy and soft as his gaze raked across her, blistering her skin with lust. "Get some rest. You've slept about thirty minutes."

"You didn't exactly nap. The least I can do is fix you some coffee." She slid into her robe and tied it on the way to the bathroom.

Matt was dressed except for his bare feet and waiting when she emerged. "Next."

"I left a new toothbrush on the counter for you."

"Did you? Were you planning ahead?"

"No." She rolled her eyes and lied blatantly. "They were buy one get one free."

"Thanks. I didn't think to bring one. I left the house in a bit of a hurry." He kissed her on the forehead and closed the door behind him.

A few minutes later he stepped into the kitchen and sniffed the air. "Something smells good."

"I opened a fresh can of coffee. If you promise to return Emma's cup, you can take it with you."

"Don't expect me to turn down an excuse to come back." He sat at the table and slid on his socks and boots. "If you're out and about early enough, call me. I'll bring Ash and make him buy lunch before you go to work."

"I'd like that. You heard we had two fights at the bar last night?"

"Yeah. Ash and I were still in the office when the calls came in."

"Everybody's jumping at the silliest things. A look or the wrong word and all hell breaks loose."

"I'm afraid it'll only get worse."

"Not to be nosey, but do you have any clues? You know...leads?" She turned and leaned back against the counter.

Sitting in the chair, wearing a black Go Rodeo T-shirt, jeans, and alligator boots, the last thing Matt looked like was a sheriff. Bull rider? You bet. Maybe a cattle rancher. But the one question about the murders changed his demeanor and posture. The shift from sexy, adorable hunk to serious, defender of the public was instantaneous. Catherine was back to licking her lips.

"I wish I could say yes. Truth is every female in the county is in danger. Married or single, it doesn't seem to matter. I believe both women knew this man. Maybe not friends, but they recognized him. He could be the mailman, the guy at the gas station, anybody."

"Even JC?" He'd befriended her, and she hoped Matt's answer was no.

"Maybe." He dragged his hand across the dark stubble on his face. "He had a relationship with Julia Drummond, and he knew Annie."

"You'll catch him. I know it." Her mind flashed on the scar on his back. Should she ask? They'd discussed a few personal issues, but the last thing she wanted was to push him. "Can I ask something that's none of my business?"

"Sure. Coffee's not ready."

"The scar on your back. What happened?" He shifted his gaze away from her, and his back stiffened. She regretted giving into curiosity. "Never mind. I shouldn't have asked."

He turned his head slightly and relaxed his shoulders. "No. It's all right."

"It must've been bad." A chill skated over her arms.

"There's no reason you shouldn't know. Bullet barely missed the aorta. My partner was recognized, blowing our cover. We'd been working on a drug delivery coming in through the port in Houston. Some bastard she'd arrested years earlier got out of prison, and we didn't know he'd rejoined the cartel. They beat us pretty bad, but Elena...being a woman." He stopped talking, rubbed his temple for a minute before continuing. "They raped her while forcing me to watch." His eyes filled with agony coated heavily with hate. "When they finished they shot both of us. Dumped us in amongst some trash and rocks. I lived. She didn't."

"Matt. I'm sorry." She extended her hand. He wrapped his fingers around hers. They sat in silence, the only sound was the laboring sputter of her Mr. Coffee machine. She wanted to say something, to offer comfort. He was tied in knots over the murders and her stalker. Catherine felt inadequate when it came to finding words to sooth him. Pulling away from him to get the coffee was hard to do.

"Coffee's ready." Before she finished pouring, he stood directly behind her.

166 |

"I haven't told that story to many people."

He brushed her hair aside and kissed the side of her neck. She turned into his arms to give him better access.

"Thank you for telling me."

He moved her away from the hot coffeepot. Then as if she weighed nothing, he lifted her onto the countertop. "I worry about you here alone."

"Is that why you came over last night? To check on me?" She spoke into his lips pressing against hers. If this was his way of changing the subject, she was fine with it.

He pulled the tie on her robe loose and pushed it off her shoulders. "No. I came to check on this." He kissed his way down to one breast and tugged the tip into his mouth. "And on this one." He moved to the other side and circled her rigid nipple with his tongue.

"Take me back to bed and do that again." Catherine slid to the edge, but Matt's warm hands on her bare waist held her in position. He stepped closer and pressed his body between her legs.

"Uh-huh. I like you right here." He dropped down to his knees, lifted her legs, and then slipped her thighs over his shoulders. With a devilish smile, he ducked down and stroked his tongue across the soft skin between her legs.

"Good. God," she gasped. Her body involuntarily bucked toward his face. Exquisite sensations rocketed through her blood. Heat exploded from his mouth and shot straight to the top of her head. All rationale left. Slide after slide. Soft. Hard. Invading. He couldn't stop. Not with her this close to heaven. She'd die if he did. A blast of fire built and built until she thought her skin would melt off the bone.

He moved a millimeter back and murmured, "Cat. You taste like honey." His warm breath blew across her hypersensitive flesh.

She wrapped her fingers in his midnight black hair and pulled his mouth back to her burning flesh. He laughed or she thought he did. Whatever he did, the vibration detonated a reaction she'd never felt. Her entire body convulsed, shuddered as if she were having a seizure. If not for Matt's strong hands, she'd have fallen from her perch. Heaving, panting, her body a piece of Silly Putty, she settled back to earth. Oh. God. Had she really pulled his hair? Suddenly, she wished for a place to hide. Finding none, she had no recourse. She laughed a nervous, silly sound.

Matt kissed his way up to her face then gently helped her back into her robe. His strong hands clasped her at the waist and set her feet on the floor. When her knees failed to support her weight, he lifted her onto a chair.

"Hmm." She intended to say thanks but that word didn't come out.

"My pleasure," he said.

Maybe she had said thanks, or maybe he hadn't noticed her acting like a woman whose house had been on fire.

"Coffee?" He calmly poured two cups and placed one in front of her. Holding the other, he sat across the table and smiled. "You should rest a few hours before heading to work tonight."

"Hmm." That was it? She could produce only one single word. Her brain started working again, and she tried to remember another time in her life when she'd been that overwhelmed. She sipped her coffee and watched the most amazing man in the world do the same. Yep. Taking him off the *Never* list ranked right up there with the invention of electricity. It was world changing.

"I wish I didn't have to go. Ash and I are talking with some of the shop owners this morning. Yesterday nobody remembered seeing anything, but sometimes a day later, things come back." He refilled his cup and knelt down in front of her. "Take care of my girl. Watch her back. Okay?"

"Yeah. Okay." She found her legs and followed him to the door. "Sorry, I went off the deep end."

"I'd have been disappointed if you hadn't." He pulled her into his arms, kissed her hard and hot, and then strolled away. He got into his black truck, snapped the seat belt over his black shirt, pushed a lock of gleaming black hair off his forehead, and backed out of the driveway.

Catherine clutched her robe to her chest and watched until he drove out of sight. "God, I love the color black."

****

What a way to start the day. More than Matt's thumb and fingers still tingled. He'd left Catherine speechless, run home for a shower, grabbed a bag of donuts from the bakery and was about to disturb his best friend. Matt pounded on Ash's apartment door while wondering if the smile on his face was permanent.

"It's about time." Ash answered the door fully dressed, ready to leave. "I thought you wanted to get an early start."

"We still can. Relax." Matt pushed past, shoving the sack in Ash's arms. "Eat first. And I need more caffeine." He understood Ash's sense of urgency. They were all going nuts trying to figure out where the killer would strike next.

"Thanks to Sue, I don't have to worry about a lack of sweets."

"Why?" Matt called out from the kitchen. "She's not giving you my apple pie. Is she?"

"Not yet. But thanks for telling me. Her friend Dotty lives in the unit across from me. She brought me cupcakes at eight this morning."

"That's nice." Matt strolled back to the small living room and looked around. Sue and a friend had provided a small brown leather couch, one end table, and a maroon recliner. A small TV sat in one corner. It was better than nothing. Overall, not bad for temporary housing. Matt stretched out in the easy chair.

"Yes, I'll have another cup, thanks," Ash muttered on his way to the small coffee pot. When he returned, he sat across from Matt and studied him in silence for a minute. "What gives?"

"With what?"

"Don't start that shit. You're never this flip or casual. Remember me? You're always wound tight as a gnat's ass. It's always gotta go, balls-to-the-wall with you." He strummed his fingers on his knee. "You didn't go home last night. You dog. Tell me."

"Where do your stupid ideas come from? Eat or do without." Matt's stomach growled. Damn, he was ravenous. Cupcakes, donuts, it didn't matter. His system demanded food, like his body demanded Catherine. He'd had his share of women, before and after his marriage. None had dominated his thoughts and emotions the way she did.

"This woman's turned you into a blithering idiot, and I still haven't met her." Ash snapped his fingers. "You ran a background check. Didn't you?"

"Hell no." He hated that Ash could read him so well. "I got as far as entering her name. Sat there for five minutes watching the cursor blink. Couldn't do it."

"Awww. An honorable man." Ash's mouth curved into a smirk. "Glad you took my advice."

Matt tossed back the last of his coffee. "Screw you. You can be a smartass on the way to the park. I can't sit around waiting on you all day." Matt crumpled the empty sack, tossing the bag in the trash as he headed for the door. "Want to let the top down and go in your car?"

Ash looked at him as if he'd dropped in from outer space. "In this heat? In this dust? She's a high-class, high-dollar automobile. Your pickup is used to it."

Matt pulled out of Ash's apartment complex thinking the tenants were lucky to have covered parking and flashed back on Catherine. Her car sat in the sun. The temperature on the bank across the street read ninety-nine degrees, and it was still before noon. The occasional lawn where the owner watered daily was a visual shock in comparison with the dead and dried grass that surrounded them. Yesterday, the fire department had issued a burn ban and restricted watering. Soon, nothing would be green. Matt was beginning to wonder if they'd ever see a break in the weather.

"I told Catherine you'd buy lunch before she went to work. Give you two a chance to meet." He tried to remember if he'd warned her about Ash. He'd be all over her. Beautiful women were Ash's favorite pastime.

"It's about time. Pick a place close to that drugstore across from your office. We never got around to asking about this JC guy. What did he buy? Or was he following your girlfriend around."

"Can't do it. We'll have to meet her in Butte Crest. We can hit the drugstore in Curry afterward."

"By the time I learn my way around, the case will be solved."

"God. I hope so." Matt parked midway off the block across from where Annie had been found. "You start at one end. I'll take the other. Maybe somebody noticed a car, pickup, anything out of the ordinary."

Matt took the auto parts store and then stopped by the small health food store, learning nothing helpful. He left the last shop with no news and no clues.

Ash waited by the pickup, looking as disappointed as Matt felt.

"I got zilch. Call that woman who keeps you up all night." He snorted a laugh. "I'm hungry."

Matt raised an eyebrow and glared, but didn't faze Ash. "You be nice around Catherine." He got in the pickup, started it, and then called her while ignoring the curious look he was getting from Ash. They agreed to meet at the Dairy Dream in an hour. "We'll have time for you to take a look around where Annie was last seen alive."

"Tell me more about your new honey."

"I've told you enough already. Suffice it to say, I'd appreciate you not slobbering all over her."

Ash stared at Matt for a second before a smile broke across his face. "I'll be damned. You let this one get under your skin."

Matt rolled his eyes. He hadn't let her do any such thing. She was on his mind a lot. The way she responded to his touch, the way her eyes flared with excitement when he entered her, the way she laughed under her breath after she came—all of these things made her important to him. But there was more. They laughed together, and until she came along there hadn't been much humor in his life.

The parking lot at the Dairy Dream overflowed to the church parking lot next door. Was there no end to the thrill seekers? Half of the county must've taken a drive over to see where the dead woman had worked. Matt jerked his phone to his ear and changed lunch plans with Catherine to the Pizza Stop on the square. Again.

"You didn't have your heart set on a burger, did you?" Matt said, heading to the highway.

"I had my heart set on you answering my question." Ash continued to dig for information. "Your silence tells me you're in love."

"I don't intend to dignify that with a response," Matt said. "What'd you learn from your store visits?"

"Nothing. Nobody paid any attention until the cruisers started showing up. However, I came up with a few thoughts and questions last night. You remember last night...while I was alone in my tiny apartment, and you were doing whatever you won't tell me about."

Matt pulled into the parking lot across from the café and backed in, where he could watch for Catherine. He ignored Ash's insinuation, figuring it was best not to egg him on. "I'm listening."

"The first woman went missing for three days, and then she turned up dead. Over two weeks passed before he snatched the second. Why'd he wait?"

"Julia was either a trial run or an accident." Matt thought back to the two weeks between kidnappings. "The first kill might've been unintentional. He decided he liked it, missed the feeling, the thrill. He grabs a second woman, enjoys tormenting her for nine days before killing her."

Ash stared out the window, deep in thought. "Your scenario doesn't compute."

"Then the kill isn't what he's drawn to. It's all about the individual woman." Matt was convinced a third woman would disappear soon.

"He shopped around for two weeks until he found one he liked?"

"Yeah," Matt said.

"Then we need to figure out what about these two women appealed to him."

"Speaking of appealing." Matt pointed to the small blue car with its windows rolled down. Her long wavy hair sparkled like red fire.

"Oh. Hell. Yes. No wonder you didn't want me to meet her." Ash was out of the pickup and moving toward Catherine before she exited her car.

Matt's heart rate skyrocketed. The idea of Ash hitting on Catherine fired Matt's blood like a gladiator going into battle. His best friend wrapped both arms around her and hugged her to his chest.

The word "mine" circled his brain. God. A six-year-old kid had taken up residence in his head. Time to rein in the emotions. He got out and joined them. Catherine extricated herself from Ash's clutches and slid into Matt's arms.

"Hey." She followed her usual greeting by standing on tiptoes for a kiss. His chest ached with pride as he leaned down and claimed his prize.

"Hey, yourself. I see you met Don Juan."

"I did." She turned her gaze to Ash. "He's exactly as you described him."

"Not exactly, I'll wager." Ash pulled her hand into the crook of his arm and escorted her across the street.

As much as it irritated him to see Ash fawn over her, Matt wanted them to be friends. He grudgingly walked behind them.

"Matt failed to tell you I'm a fixer of problems, rescuer of damsels in distress, and an all-around great guy. Didn't he?"

"He might've left out the rescuer part."

Catherine glanced over her shoulder. Her wink was to reassure him, and he returned it with a slight nod. He got the message. When the flirting was over, it would be Matt she'd reach for in the dark.

Chapter Seventeen

One thing for sure, he wasn't waiting two weeks to replace his doll. Last night when Vince went outside to smoke a joint, sweet Jessie had jumped at the chance to flirt. She'd followed him down the hall toward the restrooms. Given him the "fuck me" look before she ducked into the women's toilet. Shit. He'd almost come on the spot. Oh yeah, Jessie wanted him.

And he was going to give her exactly she wanted. In spades.

He'd hung around until Vince and Jessie left and followed them home. This morning he'd returned to their neighborhood, parked down the road, and waited. Sure enough, Jessie drove off in her car alone. He tagged along, stayed out of sight, and followed her to a local grocery store. Interesting, she parked way over to the side of the building. She got out and put on one of those orange vests the employees wore...sweet Jessie had a job. He'd have to be careful, these big-box food marts had cameras trained on the parking lot. It would be better to follow her, pick a safe spot, and bam, she'd be his. It worked the last time. This shit got easier and easier.

Soon Vince would learn he wasn't such as badass after all. He'd cry like a girl at the thought of somebody else fuckin' his old lady.

He'd finally found a doll who wouldn't bitch and lie to him. Excitement buzzed through his system. He and Jessie would party hard. She liked her beer, so he'd stock the fridge tonight.

First, he'd be a good citizen and attend the meeting at Will's place. He needed to know what Will and his little posse were planning. Point them in the direction of a few poor unsuspecting bastards would keep them busy.

Blood raced through his veins when he drove out of the parking lot. The air conditioner ran full blast, but sweat popped out and soaked his shirt under his arms. His cock throbbed against his zipper now that plans were firm and close to being executed. He pointed his pickup toward Will's house.

He shoved his mama's old pistol further under the seat. Pointing the .380 at his last doll had worked great. She'd hopped right into his pickup without a fuss. He'd use it to take Jessie. And why not? She fuckin' wanted him to.

****

Catherine placed the basket on the backseat and closed the door. She didn't mind that the rest of her only day off would be at a dead run. A dinner date with two handsome men required she finish her scullery-maid duties, as she called them, early enough to be dressed by six.

Ash Hunter certainly had made an impression at the Pizza Stop. The women behind the counter had been thoroughly charmed. Ash's blond hair and hazel eyes drew attention to his face. With sharply-honed features, squared jaw and a cleft in his chin, Ash was perfect except for an inch long scar high on his cheekbone. Handsome but not in the same dark, rugged, sexy way Matt was.

She'd had her usual nightmare last night. The dream hadn't held its typical horror, allowing her to wake before the fingers tightened around her throat. A good sign she was putting the past behind her.

She stopped the car and ran up to Emma's front door. Her Monday routine included checking to see if Emma needed anything from town. Catherine called out over the blaring TV after knocking the third time. The door popped open, and she found herself being pulled inside at a run.

"Hurry," Emma insisted. "We're missing the news." She stopped in front of the TV and shushed Catherine, who hadn't said a word.

"Just who is Sheriff Matt Ballard?" The pert blonde-haired woman on the screen leaned forward, her face a portrait of questioning. "And why is he withholding critical information? This reporter believes the public has the right to know if a serial killer lives in our community. Is a mad man murdering the women of our once peaceful county? Your safety could depend on Sheriff Ballard's actions and answers. Yet when I asked our sheriff of less than a year, he refused to give answers." She turned in her chair to watch a film of Matt walking out of the park where Annie Travers was found. When she looked back into the camera, her eyebrows pulled together, giving her a grave expression. "My concerns were brushed aside as if the fear I have for my viewers was unimportant. Be sure to tune in tomorrow. We will learn as the week goes on why you don't have the right to information which might save your life." She lit up the TV with a radiant smile. "This is Sylvia Horning reporting for RBS News at noon."

Emma hit the off button on the remote. Behind the smile of the newswoman was pure unadulterated hate. And she'd declared war on Matt. A tug on Catherine's sleeve pulled her attention away from the blank screen and down into Emma's curious eyes. "You and the sheriff pretty close?"

"Yes, ma'am." No reason to deny their relationship. Emma had watched the driveway like a sentinel on guard duty since the first sign of Catherine's stalker. Matt's pickup had sat outside overnight more than once.

"Well? Is she telling the truth? Do we have a serial killer in the area?" Her grip tightened on Catherine's hand, and fear sparked in Emma's eyes.

"Yes." Catherine had to tell Emma the truth so she'd be careful. "I don't understand why Sylvia Horning is on the attack. She's sensationalizing the murders. Matt's made more than one statement that every woman needs to exercise caution. He wants us to be safe not terrified."

"She insinuated he had secrets about his past he didn't want us to know about."

"We all have secrets, things we want to forget." The last thing Catherine wanted to discuss was the right or wrong of hiding your past. "Please don't judge him by whatever story she cooks up."

"I reckon you're right. You know, if we've got a murderer on the loose, I'm doubly glad I had the lights strung."

"Me, too."

"I did it for both our safety. We girls can't be too careful. I keep a pistol on my nightstand, and you should do the same."

"A gun? I'm surprised at you." Catherine had visions of Grandma Mazur from the Janet Evanovich books. Except Emma might have fewer wrinkles.

"Let me show you." Emma dashed out of the room. She returned waving a weapon nearly as big as she was in the air. "I went to one of those all day classes and got me a license to carry this baby."

"Emma," Catherine gasped. "You'll hurt yourself with that thing."

Emma huffed out a sound of disgust. "I learned to shoot long before you were born."

Catherine checked her watch. "Do you need anything from town?"

"I expected you'd stop. I wrote everything down. Let me get my list."

Catherine tucked the list in her jeans pocket, hugged Emma goodbye, and hurried to the car. Matt probably didn't watch the noon news, but he needed to know he'd picked up his own stalker. She grabbed her cell and punched in his number, but the call went straight to voicemail. The message she left was short and to the point. The laundry still needed to be done, and Catherine wasted no time getting on the road.

****

Matt leaned his head back against the wall in Dr. Reinhardt's office and closed his eyes. "What a mess. This is the first autopsy where I've come close to arresting the victim's father." Damn, Will Brooking's behavior warranted getting hauled to jail.

"How dare he try to push his way into my office. I will not tolerate his kind of behavior in my morgue." Dr. Kurt Reinhardt slapped his open hand on top of his desk, sending a small pencil holder skittering over the edge onto the floor. "If he repeats it, I will press charges."

"He's a man in pain, looking for answers." Matt understood Will was grieving and tried to take his tantrum in stride. He'd certainly pushed the medical examiner's hot button when he'd demanded to hear the gory details.

Dr. Reinhardt stood, picked up his pencils, and replaced them one by one. His office was a study in organization. The stoop in his back appeared to be more pronounced today. Balding, the top of his head turned red when he lost his temper.

Matt changed the conversation back to the subject at hand. "Talk me through your thoughts. Then I'll let you get back to work."

The ME stopped straightening his desk, leaned back, and remained quiet for a minute. "TOD was between midnight and two a.m. Friday morning. Keep in mind that's an estimate. Due to exposure to the elements, I can't pinpoint as accurately as I'd like."

"Sonofabitch left her in the park before daylight. Explains why nobody noticed a vehicle going in or out Friday morning."

"Judging from the contents of her stomach and the condition of her body, she hadn't been eating a lot. Contusions around her ribs and right jaw indicate she was beaten. I found extensive tearing and bruising in the vaginal and anal area. "

"A sex slave. Tethered where she couldn't escape, yet not tended to." Matt's mind whirled with ideas and possibilities. Why starve her? Punishment? "She was strangled."

"That's correct. Only this time the killer was more zealous."

"Zealous? What the hell does that mean?" Matt's nerves snapped.

"Call it what you wish. The strangulation was more brutal with this victim." Reinhardt removed his glasses and pinched the bridge of his nose. "The bruising around her neck was more extensive. Her hyoid bone had been crushed."

"Any idea what kind of tether was around her ankle?"

"Matt, I don't like to guess, but if I had to—"

"Guess," Matt interrupted and insisted.

"Handcuffs. Unlike raw abrasions on the skin left by rope burns, a cuff would leave grooves in the flesh. I'll run some comparison pictures to see if I can find like wounds."

"I can't wait weeks for the autopsy results. You pushed me way out with the first one, but you have to help me out here. I'm sending what I have to the FBI for a profile and would like to follow with your reports."

"You can have everything except the toxicology reports in a couple of days. It's the best I can do." Dr. Reinhardt's mouth closed, his lips drawn to a thin line.

Apparently, that was his last word on the subject.

Matt shook the doc's hand and headed for his cruiser. He turned his cell on to a barrage of beeps and buzzes. He was about to listen to one when a disturbing sight caught his attention. At least a dozen reporters and as many cameras waited at the bottom of the steps. He inhaled deeply and walked to meet them.

"Sheriff. Pat Lawrence with the San Antonio Telegram. Do you have a comment about Sylvia Horning's claim you're deliberately keeping information from the public?"

He laughed at the ridiculousness of the statement. "Deliberately? I don't know what you're talking about. Neither my office nor I keep secrets. I do refuse to share clues or information that might compromise a case with the media."

"Then you're not concerned about the investigation she's launched into your past and your department."

"That's news to me. I'm sure there's been a misunderstanding." Matt shared what he could without divulging too much. The fact that the larger market news agencies had picked up the story of the murders disturbed him. Will Brooking and his crew would stir things up enough without the press making it worse. Matt used all his charm to debunk whatever rumors Sylvia Horning had started.

He chuckled when he checked his messages. He'd been inundated with people trying to forewarn him. The TV reporter was the least of his worries. He needed to get back to the office and enter his notes. As with investigations of this type, one central file became the Bible, holding all the information in one place. Hopefully, at some point everything would come together and the answer would be revealed.

On the trip home, Matt organized his thoughts. Pictures of Julia and Annie were as vivid as though they stood in front of him. White faces, hair slicked back, painted lips, and that hideous red ribbon. Being their bodies were too clean, and the bow had been tied over the bruised neck, indications were this was all done post-mortem. His stomach cramped when he thought about their eyes. They'd haunt him for the rest of his life.

Matt waited until he was closer to radio the dispatcher. He was surprised when Sue answered. She seldom worked this late unless asked. Right away, she ragged on him for not returning her calls, warning him the media had been calling all day. Then she reminded him he hadn't touched base with his deputies since morning.

Irritation simmered right under the surface, but Matt pushed it down deep. Sue's extra gruff mannerism merely indicated fear, the same fear spreading like wildfire across the county. The pounding in his temples set him on the edge. He'd left Houston to get away from death and pain. And failure. The old adage held true, your problems travelled with you. Bow up and handle the situation, his daddy told him one time when a bully had tried to push him around at school. Good advice then and now.

"After quitting time, isn't it?"

"Did I ask for overtime pay?" she fired back.

He smiled to himself, another woman in his life who made him laugh. "You brought me a pie today. Didn't you?"

"What makes you think I'd bring you anything?" The warmth in her voice answered his question.

"You did the last time I went to San Antonio." His stomach rumbled. "You didn't give any to Ash, did you?"

"Course I did, but I saved you some. What kind of name is Ash anyway? Was his mother on fire when he was born?"

"I'd tell you his full name is Ashton Hilton Hunter, but I value my life too much." Sue laughed and Matt relaxed a little.

"I can understand how he'd be upset. Hilton, huh? Any relation to the hotel?"

"If so, he's always denied it."

"How'd the autopsy go?" Her voice softened. "Pretty rough?"

"Worse than rough."

"How far out are you?"

"Pulling in the parking lot."

"Want me to make fresh coffee? Jake and Ash are waiting for you."

"Good idea. We'll be working late. Ask them to meet me in the conference room."

"You got it."

Chapter Eighteen

Matt ended the call with Special Agent Murphy and turned to Ash. He'd sat stone-faced, arms folded across his chest, lips clamped together in a rigid line through the entire conference call. The FBI had agreed to review the documents and film. Sue would overnight the package to their office in Quantico. "Maybe we'll gain some insight from the profile they'll develop." Matt received an eye roll and a look of total disgust from Ash. "What?"

"I had my say before you called the Feds." Ash's gaze went back to the pictures taken by the photographer at the morgue and by Jake at the park.

"Like you're not going to tell me again." Matt believed Ash's miffed profiling abilities were as good as anything the FBI could provide, but the BAU might notice something, hell anything that would help. Matt wasn't too proud to ask for help.

"The sucker is easy to profile," Ash continued his protest. "We need to figure out what set him off. A traumatic experience, a trigger, something sent him off the deep end. He's somebody these women recognized. Hell, man, Annie Travers looked nervous, but not afraid for her life. She got out of her car and went to him. Those two things, the trust and the tragedy, will lead us to him."

Matt agreed. "The tragedy is the stressor and will tell us why he decorated both women to look like porcelain dolls." The clock was ticking. How long did they have before another woman disappeared?

Ash unfolded his arms. He stared in silence, his eyebrows pulled close together. His focus seemed to zone in on Matt's chest. That suited Matt. He had notes to finish. And he wanted to go over what Jake and Rey had added. The longer Ash studied and immersed himself in the case the quicker he'd pick up on something.

Ash reached over and tapped Matt's badge. "You need to look internally."

Matt stopped reading his notes. "For what?" His first chuckle of the day and he needed a good laugh. "You think I killed them."

"Get real. Catherine's got you goofy-eyed. And that's a different conversation we need to have. I'm talking inside your department. Annie fucking trusted the bastard. She'd do that with one of your deputies."

"Your turn to get real." Matt dropped to his lower-octave voice.

Ash did another eye roll. "Don't try your Billy- Bad-Ass tone with me. I've seen your ass. Talk about a traumatic break."

"And exactly how did you pull that off? You have Superman's x-ray vision?"

"After you came out of recovery. How'd you think you got those pink bunny pajama bottoms on?"

"You put those on me?" Matt swallowed a couple of times. Everybody had enjoyed the joke but him. Of course, back then nothing had been funny.

"Me and the pretty blonde nurse. I'll admit she did most of the work."

Sue tapped on the door and entered without waiting. Something was up. She turned on the small TV and sat beside him at the conference table.

"I told you she was a bitch." She lay her hand on Matt's arm.

Sylvia Horning's face filled the screen. "My continuing investigation into Sheriff Ballard and his policies continue on today's show as promised. Through personal resources, I have confirmed the two dead women were killed in the same manner. Both Julia Drummond and Annie Travers were raped and strangled. Their eyes glued open and makeup had been applied to give them a doll-like appearance. Two tragic deaths and yet our sheriff refuses to talk to me. Refuses to inform the public. My question to Sheriff Ballard is this…what is your definition of a serial killer? And how many women must die before you admit you have no clues and no suspects? Here's another question for our not-so- talkative sheriff. Why haven't you asked the Texas Rangers for assistance? This reporter verified Sheriff Ballard has not been in touch with their office." She leaned forward toward the camera. "Anytime the sheriff would like to drop by the station and answer these questions, I'm happy to make myself available. You, my viewers, can rest assured, my investigation into the sheriff and The Green-Eyed Doll killer will be in depth. For now, this is Sylvia Horning, RBS noon news."

Matt turned the TV off and tossed the remote to the side. "So much for Reinhardt and his team keeping their mouths shut."

"You don't know the leak came from his office," Ash commented.

"It sure didn't come from here. My men are under strict orders to keep their comments to themselves." He trusted his deputies. Jake and Rey were loyal and dedicated. "Hell, you'd be wasting time trying to get information out of them.

"I'm not worried about her broadcasts. She can dig all she wants." Matt turned to Sue. "Call the County Record and the Curry Weekly, and ask them to send Steve Evers and Andrea Simpson over for an interview with me. At two today."

"You got it." Sue's eyes flashed her approval, an indication she was as mad as he was.

"You'll piss her off worse than she is now," Ash commented.

No way was Matt running scared from Sylvia Horning. "And my belly will be full when I do. You can buy lunch and explain how Catherine has made me—goofy?"

"You're joking, right? That was me across the booth from you two last night. Remember?"

****

He shoved the trailer door open and stormed out into the darkness. Outside, away from Jessie. Bent over, hands on knees, he filled his lungs with warm night air. He had to stay away from her until he calmed down, else he'd beat the bitch to death. Goddamn her. The hornets stung his brain, setting him on fire from the inside. His hands shook like some fuckin' old woman. He was sick to his stomach with lying women. He'd have been better off going with Will Brooking and his patrol tonight, but Vince being out of pocket made tonight the perfect time to pick up Jessie.

Surrounded by nothing but woods, he let the sound of crickets calm him. This far out you couldn't hear the whine from the big rigs on the highway. This peaceful minute or two would be good for Jessie. She'd be wise to spend time considering her options. She'd be his doll or suffer more punishment.

He couldn't remember the last time he'd been this pissed. A dark laughter bubbled up from deep in his chest. Sure he could. One of Mama's "guests" had tried to play his dirty little game with him. If it had happened years later, it might not have been such a big deal. 'Cause you stay in lockup long enough...you'll stick your dick in a knothole for relief. Back when he was a kid, the idea had made him furious. The feel of his twelve-year-old foot when it connected with the bastard's crotch was still a favorite memory. The sonofabitch was probably still looking for his nuts.

He swiped his hand at the sweat on his neck. It stung. Why were his fingers sticky? He sniffed. Blood? The bitch had scratched him. His ears buzzed. The hornet's rampage worsened. Shit, his mind raced while he paced back and forth down the long driveway.

Maybe he would kill her. He jerked the door open and stormed inside.

He straddled her, leaned down in front of her swollen face, and pulled his shirt away from his neck. "You bitch!" She cried out when his fist crashed into her swollen jaw. "You fuckin' scratched me."

He stood and went to the kitchen, rummaging through the drawers. Finally, he found what he was looking for. When he returned to the bedroom, Jessie was jerking at the cuff around her ankle. A futile exercise that brought a chuckle to the surface. No way could she get loose. Her eyes widened and a scream ripped from her throat when his boot sent her sprawling across the bed.

He sat on her. Pinned her with his knees while she tried in vain to buck him off. She froze stiff when he waved the pliers in front of her. "You won't need those fingernails anymore."

"Please, no." She begged. A river of tears shot from her eyes. "I won't fight anymore. Look, I'm sorry. Fuck me. I want you to. Really."

"You're babbling." His nose flared at the odor coming from her. She stunk with fear, sweat, and piss. Why would he want to fuck somebody who smelled like a pig farm? "Why should I believe you? You haven't done anything but fight me since I picked you up." He wanted to believe because he was horny as hell. His cock ached and balls were ready to explode. After all the trouble she'd caused, she owed him something.

"I'll prove it. Let me show you. You don't have to hurt me again."

He studied her face. Maybe he'd cut her fingernails off with some scissors to prove a point. The fear and submission behind her eyes said he'd won. A light opened in his mind, washed over him, filled him with knowledge. The hornets calmed. He'd found the answer. From now on, he'd establish the doll's role and who was boss right up front. Besides, he wanted her alive long enough to watch Vince suffer knowing somebody was slipping it to his wife.

"First you shower." In the back of his mind, he'd resigned himself; one false move from her, one hint she was lying about cooperating, and he'd kill her.

****

Matt slapped for his cell when it did the vibration dance across his nightstand. The damn thing shot from under his fingers and slid across the floor. Could another woman already be missing?

The warm hand on his back offered no consolation. He'd have to go, but he'd worry about her less when he drove away. She was safely tucked in his bed.

He found the phone and quickly left the room, hoping Catherine could get some sleep. "Who?" he growled.

"This is Valerie Knox, sorry to bother you—"

"Val. Who's missing?" Matt shrugged himself awake, sending the cobwebs to the outer edges of his mind.

"It's not a missing person. There's trouble at the Saddleback. The owner called it in and insisted you be contacted."

His sigh of relief was audible. "Who'd you send?"

"Charles Ray and Ernie."

"Thanks. Let them know I'm coming." His racing heart slowed. What the hell happened? He stepped back into his bedroom to grab his clothes.

"Matt?" Catherine turned on the bedside lamp.

"A fight out at the bar. Marty asked for me specifically." He slid into his jeans, grabbed his socks and boots, and then sat on the side of the bed.

"That's ridiculous," she snapped. "You've been working night and day. When do you get to rest?"

Her protective outburst came at the perfect time. His ego got one hell of a boost from her tirade. A warm hand wrapped around his heart and squeezed. Matt looked over his shoulder at her. Sitting straight up in bed, her wildfire red hair tumbled over shoulders and covered the top her breasts. A dark scowl cast a shadow over her beautiful face, and those fiery green eyes blazed. He couldn't hold back a smile.

"I didn't say anything funny. Did I?" She clamped her teeth together and crossed her arms across her chest.

He leaned over and kissed her downturned lips. "You growl like a mama bear, but look like a Playboy model. Quite a contrast...threw me for a second." He slid his feet into his boots and walked around to her, stepping over his traitorous dog. Whenever Catherine spent the night, that hound slept on the throw rug next to her side of the bed. "I wish I could stay here with you."

He gently lay her down and covered her. Damn, it was hard to leave her warming his sheets. He brushed her tangled hair across the white pillow and captured her lips for a kiss.

"I already miss you." She rolled to her side and dangled her arm over the edge.

Benedict Arnold crawled over and nuzzled her hand. Matt pulled his jaw off his chest, turned out the light, and left with a smile. The dim-witted mutt wasn't completely stupid.

The drive from his house to the Saddleback was a short one. For the first time, he missed the all- night fast-food joints where he could've grabbed a coffee to go. Not only was the gas tank on his pickup low, his personal reservoir was running on empty. When the lights of the bar came into view, he packed away his lack of sleep.

He'd gone without rest a hell of a lot longer than this. When Elena's cover had been blown, and they'd been captured, the bastards kept them both awake for days. After all, what was the fun of torture if she wasn't awake and her partner wasn't watching the horrid scene unfold?

Matt's health improved a lot when Ash told him Elena's killers had fought back when the DEA raided the drug dealer's hideout. The SWAT team wiped them off the face of the planet. Must've been an awesome sight.

Charles Ray Perkins and Ernest Mall probably had things under control. They were two of the most experienced deputies on the force. Matt thought it odd both preferred the late shift. Charles Ray had said most nights were peaceful. Hell, until five weeks ago peace was easy to find in Crest County.

Matt parked and joined Charles Ray, who was shaking his head from side to side like a pendulum. Marty and JC were on the front porch of the Saddleback bending over a prone figure. A quick count told Matt two men sat in the back seats of both cruisers.

"Sorry you had to come out. Marty insisted. She's as big a pain in the ass as the men in the fight."

"Who's lying down?" Matt asked.

"Stevie Covington. They beat him up pretty bad, but he won't allow anyone to call an ambulance." Charles Ray's breath reeked of chewing tobacco. At some point Matt might address his nasty habit, but now wasn't the time. He took a step back to avoid a direct hit when his deputy spoke.

"What the hell happened?" Matt stifled a yawn before he glanced in Marty's direction. He hoped his relationship with Catherine didn't make Marty feel entitled to call him every time something went wrong.

"Stevie's been leaning on Harvey Coleman's daughter pretty hard. Trying to pick her up, take her out on a date, but she don't want anything to do with him. I guess they exchanged words tonight after the pool tournament. She called her daddy, who happens to be on Will Brookings new County Patrol Group."

"What? Jesus, they've named themselves?" That got Matt's eyes open and mind working full speed. "Shit."

"Looks like. You want to talk to them?"

"Not yet. Let them stew. I'll talk to Stevie and Marty first." It was a good decision, because Marty was headed his direction. The way her ponytail swung from side to side, it was a wonder she didn't put somebody's eye out. Matt met her halfway. "Evening, Marty."

"I'm glad you didn't say 'good' evening. There ain't been a damn thing good about tonight. You've got to catch this killer. He's making the men in the county crazy. Feels like I'm running a business sitting on top of a powder keg." She stomped her foot, which made her more comical than intimidating.

With Charles Ray at his side, Matt spent the next hour trying to convince Stevie Covington to press charges and to have stitches in his busted lip.

Four grown men had jumped him in the parking lot and beat the hell out of him. No way would Stevie admit to or testify to such a thing.

When Marty refused to file disturbing the peace charges, Matt's temper flared. He'd been hauled out of a warm bed, and now everyone wanted to wimp out on him. The fear behind her eyes kept him from busting her chops too hard.

"You called me, Marty." He lowered his voice to communicate his displeasure. Will and his boys weren't walking away from this unscathed. "Remember?"

"I'm sorry. I got rattled. And I hate to admit it, scared. But JC ran out and stopped them cold."

"Forget being sorry. If Stevie won't stand up to them, I need you to. I believe you said, 'I want this stopped.' Then step up and help make it happen."

"Can't. They're all my customers. Every last one of them comes in here. They're not bad men. They're scared fathers and husbands."

"Better to lose one regular than four. It's good business, right?" He didn't wait for her response. At three in the morning, he didn't want to hear she felt sorry for the assholes. Matt waved Ernie over and had him take written statements from Stevie, JC, and Marty. Stevie was on his feet and moving around, leaving Matt to believe maybe he didn't need medical attention. His busted lip had bled down the front of his shirt, making him look worse than he was. By morning one eye would be swollen closed.

"Charles Ray, I see Will Brooking and Vince Bradley in your cruiser." Matt stepped back to get a better angle on the two men in Ernie's car, but he'd parked away from the overhead lights. "Who's in Ernie's back seat?"

Matt spent an occasional night riding with the guys on the late shift, but hadn't worked with them since the first murder. He respected Charles Ray in spite of his nicotine breath. His matter of fact way of speech left no doubt as to his opinion. His crooked nose, and the small scar on his chin came from hand- to-hand combat in

Nam. He was a pull-no-punches kind of guy you could count on in a fight despite his years.

"Harvey Coleman and Eric Hadley. You ready for us to haul their asses to lockup?"

"Do it. Neither Marty nor Stevie will press charges. Public intoxication entitles Will and his posse an overnight stay in a cell. The judge can set bail first thing in the morning."

"Cowardly bastards. Will's a Vet. Made me ashamed of him. Grief doesn't excuse his behavior."

Yeah. Matt liked Charles Ray a lot.

****

Catherine woke when Matt's head hit the pillow, and he blew out a long exhale. He rolled over behind her, his warm, solid muscles fit against her body like a glove. She reached back, captured his arm, and pulled it across her body.

"Sorry. I didn't mean to wake you," Matt whispered into her hair.

"I'm glad you're home." She tucked his hand under her breast and smiled into the darkness. His voice, thick and husky with exhaustion, touched her. Lying next to him, feeling his naked body relax, and his breathing level off, she couldn't remember her heart ever being this full.

She snuggled down to get back to sleep, but for some reason Sylvia Horning and today's noon news crossed her mind. Catherine understood better why Matt had been pressing her to be cautious. A shiver raced across her skin. Her eyes were the same color as the two dead women.

She wanted to go straight to the TV station and test her martial arts training.

Despite Ash's efforts at humor, Matt had been tense at supper. He'd never admit it, but Sylvia had said some hurtful things. He didn't deserve her snide remarks. She'd spewed enough venom to bring most grown men to their knees.

Catherine's very own John Wayne, whose muscular chest now rose and fell in a steady rhythm behind her, stood tall and turned a deaf ear.

Chapter Nineteen

Matt stretched out his arm in search of Catherine's warm body, but the sheets were cool on her side of the bed. He rolled over and allowed himself the luxury of breathing in her scent on the pillow. Damn, he might never wash the sucker. He smothered his laugh in the soft cotton. Maybe Ash was right. What was it he'd said? That Matt needed to cool his jets where Catherine was concerned, because he was barreling down that dark and dangerous road called matrimony. Marriage hadn't crossed his mind, but having her in his house to wake up to certainly was nice.

He slipped on a pair of jeans and followed the aroma of coffee to the kitchen. Catherine wore one of his T-shirts and stood with her back to him. Benedict Arnold lay at her feet while she stroked up and down his sorry hide with a bare foot. She reached up to get a cup from the shelf, and the curve of her bare bottom peeked out. The sight sent his blood rushing south. The view was too good not to pause and enjoy. Something funny happened to his heart while he watched her. A nice easy peace settled over him.

Catherine looked over her shoulder and caught him staring at her. "How do you do that?"

He had trouble finding his voice. "Do what?"

"Sneak up on me? I didn't hear you get up."

Matt stepped over the dog that grunted but didn't move. He pulled the hair away from her neck and kissed the soft spot right behind her ear. She chuckled her low sexy rumble but moved away from him right before he turned her.

"Not so fast, cowboy. I'm already a few minutes late. Coffee's ready, I set you a cup down, you're on your own for breakfast."

"If you'd brought a change of clothes, the trip home wouldn't be necessary," he called out as she rushed past him to dress. He fixed her a to-go cup in Emma's mug—the one he'd failed to return—and carried it to her. "You're sure you don't want to shower before you go?"

She finished snapping her bra before she answered. "There's nothing I'd like better. But we wouldn't shower. Would we?"

"Probably not." Matt parked in the chair and watched as she finished dressing. "You had another nightmare. Will you tell me about it?"

"It was nothing."

"You kicked the covers to the floor. Last night's was a rough one."

"Everybody has bad dreams. Don't you need to be going?"

"I'm willing to listen." No response came. "Then I'll head to the jail. Will Brooking and his citizens group are sitting in a cell." He walked her to the car, pulled her in for one more kiss. She grabbed a handful of his hair and devoured his mouth.

"That'll hold me for a while." Her green eyes sparkled in the sunlight.

Matt and the dog stood out of the way while gravel flew from under her tires and a puff of black smoke curled around her taillights.

Damn, he wished she'd let him inside the dark part of her mind, maybe he could help chase her demons away. Some bastard erased her ability to trust. Was her ex a cop? It would explain her fear and refusal to confide in him. He'd have to prove to her not all men were bastards. A feeling of helplessness returned. Last night, all he could do was hold her until the tremors passed.

****

"Comfy?" Matt found Ash sitting at his desk going over paperwork. "Are those the deputy's reports from last night?"

"Yeah. Not much happened after the fight except for a few routine traffic stops. You about ready to let Will and his gang go home?" Ash moved over to the other side of the desk and settled down with a groan.

Matt punched in Jake's number and asked him to arrange for Will and his friends to get in front of the judge. He'd make them pay public intoxication fines and send them home. Matt was surprised none of them had called an attorney.

Ash stood and headed for the conference room, but stopped in the doorway. Matt had known Ash for a long time, and the troubled expression indicated something was on his mind. "What? Spit it out." Matt prepared for another lecture on slowing down with Catherine.

"I want the personnel files on your men. Then I need to know if any of them recently went through a death in the family, a divorce, or bankruptcy, anything traumatic. And I prefer to talk with them individually."

The hair on Matt's arms sizzled as if he stood in an electrical storm. "You're going down the wrong road."

"I might be. You brought me up here and set me on this road. Now let me do my damn job." Ash stuffed his hands in his pockets and didn't blink. "I want to know if any of them had to replace their handcuffs. I'll start with Jake." He spun on his heel and left the room.

Ash's insinuation the killer might be one of Matt's men sent his gut spinning. The cuff theory had already crossed his mind, but he'd dismissed the idea. He spent a few minutes considering the request. His relationship with his men was important. They had to know he trusted them and had their backs. He understood Ash was taking the responsibility of questioning them on his shoulders. Ash could take the brunt of their anger and not have to worry about damaging any long-term relationships. He was, after all, leaving when the case was solved.

Sue brought in the two local newspapers and waited while Matt opened them to the front page. "If Sylvia Horning wasn't furious with you she is now."

"Did you read the articles?"

"I did. They're good. I thought you were as open as you could be. I don't suppose you're in the mood to speak with Doc Reinhardt?"

"I'm in the perfect mood. I asked him to keep a few facts under wraps. The most important one is now part of the killer's nickname. The leak came from his office. I'm sure of it."

She handed Matt a homemade muffin. "Well, he's holding for you."

"Why didn't you say so?"

"Let him sweat. He's bound to know you're P.O.'d."

P.O.'d barely got in the ballpark, but he liked her idea. Let the doc wait. Matt explained Ash's new project to Sue and finished his snack. She'd be the one to furnish the records and files Ash would need. She agreed clearing the department from all suspicion was a good idea. Maybe the men would be as okay with Ash questioning them as she was.

"Put the ME through."

A second later the phone on his desk rang. He wouldn't lose his temper. He'd keep his voice level and breathe normally. Maybe. Nothing he hated worse than a liar or someone he couldn't trust. "Tell me who leaked the information and that you fired said person."

"It was unintentional, I assure you. No harm was meant."

"That's bullshit. Only a handful of people knew my theory about the green eyes. Or the fact the killer left them looking like a made-up doll."

"I'm aware of that, Sheriff Ballard." Reinhardt's tone of voice carried the sound of a defeated politician.

That the doc referred to Matt by his title and not his name told the tale. Pieces fell together. Blood shot to his brain at supersonic speed. The ME had leaked the information. Matt's pulse pounded, roared through his ears like a freight train. Shit, he'd pop a vein if he didn't pull his anger back.

"You helped glamorize the bastard." Silence on the line poured fuel on Matt's already raging temper.

"I'm sorry."

"Sorry? I trusted you. I don't do that lightly." Matt didn't forgive lightly either.

"Sylvia tricked me into believing it was off the record."

"Nothing's off the record with that ambitious bitch. What'd you get out of it doc?" He rubbed his forehead. The blood vessel between his eyes was as big around as his finger, and the headache got worse. "No. Don't tell me." Whether it was money or the sixty-something-year-old fool got a blowjob, Matt didn't want to know.

****

Matt and Jake exchanged glances while Ash wolfed down the noon plate-lunch special. The waitress must've dished the food up herself. The difference between the sizes of the portions hadn't gone unnoticed by Jake. Ash had the lion's share. Matt could've cared less. Still pissed over the leak, the thought of food put a knot in his belly.

Ash looked up, a fork loaded with mashed potatoes a half-inch away from his mouth. "What can I say? She likes me."

"I'll bet he leaves a trail of broken hearts when he goes back to Houston." Jake stirred sugar substitute into his tea and spoke as if Ash weren't sitting in the booth.

"Which is why I'm against Catherine introducing him to Susan King." Matt wasn't in the mood for joking, but he made a lame effort. He hadn't told either man the source of the leak. He'd been too pissed to let Reinhardt explain what happened. Trust and your word, two things Matt expected people to stand behind.

Two cell phones buzzed at the same time. Jake's gaze met Matt's briefly before they both answered. Ash with his uncanny second sense pulled out his wallet, tossed cash on the table, and stood, waiting.

"Bad?" Ash fell in step beside Matt when the call was finished.

"Worse than bad. Jessie Bradley's missing."

"Bradley. Any relation to—?"

"Yeah. Vince. One of the men I locked up last night." Matt finished the sentence as they sprinted out of the building to the courthouse parking lot. "Jake," Matt called over the top of his cruiser. "Call Rey. Have him meet us at the Bradleys'."

Matt flipped on the lights and along with a surge of adrenaline, rolled hot. He cast a glance in Ash's direction, understanding the smile.

"Been a long time since we lit 'em up, partner," Ash commented. "Feels good. Even under these circumstances."

Matt nodded, which sufficed as an answer. He understood completely. The relationship between partners couldn't be compared with normal coworkers. Cops lived and breathed their work, existed in and for that world. In Houston, their only friends had been in law enforcement or one of the many related branches. The camaraderie, the trust, the dependence on each other, formed a bond never to be broken. Not by family. Not by women. Especially not by death.

While on the road, Matt gave Ash a run down on Vince and Jessie to refresh his memory. Ash's ability to capture and retain data made keeping him informed an easy task.

Jake followed Matt and Ash. The two cruisers slid to a stop, and the three men started up the walk. The door flew open and Vince ran straight toward them screaming. Like a flamethrower laying down napalm, his fiery gaze was aimed at Matt.

"You sonofabitch. This is your fault."

Matt spread his feet and braced himself. He grabbed Vince before impact, spun him around, and laid him on the ground with his hands behind his back. The entire thing was one smooth motion and carefully done to not hurt the man.

"Nice," Ash said, grinning like a proud papa. "You didn't forget everything I taught you."

"Vince, control yourself. This isn't about you or me. Don't make me put you back in jail." Matt stood and moved back, allowing Vince to scramble to his feet.

He swiped the back of his hand under his nose. Tears of anger and fear dripped from his eyes. A rough night sleeping off a drunk on a hard bunk coupled with the panic of finding his wife missing had him right on the verge of getting himself into trouble. He didn't know it, but Matt would tolerate a lot under these circumstances. He understood the horror crawling around inside Vince's mind.

"I'll have your badge for this. I wasn't here to know Jessie didn't come home last night. You had me locked up." Vince's voice rose with each syllable, climbing to soprano and ending in a screech. "If the murdering bastard has her—" He turned away, chest heaving and tried to compose himself.

Jake's hand closed around Vince's elbow and together they walked back up the sidewalk. "Let's take this inside. We need a recent picture of Jessie and some information about her." The voice of reason, he might be able to calm Vince enough to talk rationally.

Rey parked his cruiser then joined Ash and spoke directly to Matt. "I'll find out what Jessie drives, then get a BOLO started. I buy groceries at the market where she works. We can drive the route as soon as we know what vehicle we're looking for."

"Let's go inside. Jake's probably got Vince calmed down." Matt considered staying outside. His presence might stir up Vince again, but Matt shrugged off his concern. Jessie's life was more important than Vince's emotions.

With each step Matt took, a small piece of guilt nagged at him. In the dark when he tried to sleep, Jessie's abduction would sneak into his thoughts and he'd wonder. Was it his fault for keeping Vince in jail overnight?

The living room hadn't changed much. Smelly ashtrays still needed emptying. Newspapers and magazines were strewn across the coffee table. Hell, they could've been the same ones from the night he questioned Vince and Jessie about Julia Drummond. The only thing missing was husband and wife.

"Where's Vince?" Ash wrinkled his nose. "Stinks in here." A die hard, reformed smoker, he could be rude when affronted by the stale odor of cigarettes.

"He's getting a recent picture of his wife." Jake stared at the dark screen on the TV. "We missed the noon news." He didn't expand on his announcement.

"I guess we'll have to get an update from Sue. You can bet she watched." Matt had no doubt.

Vince stumbled back into the room holding a wooden frame. His gait was unsteady, but the tears were gone. The blood veins in his eyes rivaled those from old vampire movies. With a whoosh of air, he collapsed into a chair like he'd been on a forty-mile march. He dismantled the frame and held out the snapshot of Jessie to Rey.

"What kind of car does your wife drive?" Rey's voice held a touch of sympathy, pulling Vince's gaze away from the floor.

"A dark blue Focus." Vince's eyes shifted from dazed to that of a wild animal. He sprang to his feet at the sight of Matt. "I gotta call Will and the boys. Get out."

Rey stepped between Vince and the phone on the countertop. "Easy, Vince. We don't know for sure she's been kidnapped."

Vince's lips curled back over clenched teeth. "What the hell are you sayin'?"

"Have you two been having trouble?"

"My wife didn't run off, if that's what you're thinking."

"You and I both know she's left you before." Rey softened his voice. "Last time it was over another woman. Have you been messing around on Jessie again? Maybe she found out?"

"Get. Out." Vince brushed past Rey and grabbed the phone. He punched in a few numbers and stopped, his hands trembled. "You." He glared directly at Matt, hate rolled off his body in waves. "Out."

"Bring the picture, Rey." Jake calmly crossed the room and opened the door.

Matt was the last to leave. He turned to caution Vince about staying on the right side of the law but didn't. The lines of communication between the law and the bereaved husband had been severed. Matters would only get worse if they didn't find Jessie. And soon.

Jake and Rey ran a GPS route to the grocery store then left to try and retrace the drive Jessie might've taken. Before he and Ash headed for the market to question her coworkers, Matt called in a team to canvas her neighborhood. Rob Thornton had made a good impression on Matt the day they'd found Annie's body. He assigned him the responsibilities of coordinating a neighborhood search and interview.

"If she's not dead, she will be soon." Ash spoke when they pulled onto the highway. He'd been silent since they'd arrived at the Bradley's.

"Thanks for pointing out the obvious."

"Just keeping it real."

Ten minutes later Matt pulled in front of the grocery store. Maybe a dozen cars were on the lot. None matched the description of Jessie's.

Jake called with news. Her car was sitting on the side of the road, keys in the ignition, and her purse lay on the seat. No signs of a scuffle, no skid marks, nothing.

Like Julia and Annie, Jessie had vanished.

Chapter Twenty

Catherine had hoped September would bring cooler weather, but she'd also asked Santa to bring her a pony when she was seven. Neither wish had been granted. The bank sign had flashed one-hundred- four degrees when she'd driven past on her way to the Saddleback. August had rolled through Texas with the same vengeance as locusts sweeping across the plains, leaving untold devastation. Spontaneous wildfires ate across the dry, parched pastures devouring homes, horses, and cattle like a ravenous army. Undermanned, volunteer fire fighters abandoned their jobs and families to battle against the hellish heat and wind.

Tonight the Saddleback was hosting a fundraiser for those honorable men and women with a pool tournament and dance to buy additional equipment. Catherine had helped Marty hang flyers all over the county, and working at the bar was off the *Never* list for now.

Catherine glided around the building on a cloud, taking orders and delivering rounds. Her mission? Get back to where a gorgeous hunk and his friend, Ash Hunter, sat on barstools. She understood as Sheriff, Matt couldn't hang out at the Saddleback, but this celebration provided him the opportunity to drop by and say hello. When they arrived, Matt had leaned down and given her a quick kiss. Her heart literally soared when his gaze followed her movements.

His smile—the special one where one side of his scrumptious mouth tilted up higher than the other— pulled her to him. He brushed a wayward strand of her hair back, tucked it behind her ear, and let his fingers lightly trace the line of her jaw. It was a quick motion, probably unnoticed by others. Catherine's world spun away, blurring her vision and hearing for a fleeting moment. Behind his blue eyes was a flicker of unhappiness. She'd noticed it a couple of times tonight but couldn't ask. Not in here. Was he thinking about their relationship? Would he understand when she worked up the courage to tell him the cause of her nightmares? He valued honesty and truth in a person. She'd denied him both.

Oh, God. Matt was talking to her. She had no idea what he'd said. He caught her hand in his when he stood. Ash slapped him on the arm and headed for the men gathered around the pool tables.

"You're leaving?" She hid her disappointment with a smile.

"Yeah. I told Rob Thornton I'd ride patrol with him tonight."

"He's the deputy you told me about?"

"Yeah. Call tomorrow if you're up early enough for company."

"I will. And I promise to be careful."

He tossed her one last look over his shoulder when he reached the exit then disappeared through the door into the darkness. A noise behind her snapped her back. JC was rapping her tray with his knuckles.

"I'm going." She laughed and headed out to collect empties and orders.

She made her way over to where Marty had the tournament brackets spread out across a table. She was setting up the Pairs round of competition. Rey Santos and Ash teamed up as partners in the final match. Catherine had never held a pool cue in her hand, and the players' abilities fascinated her. She stopped and watched when she had a few minutes. At midnight, Marty sent the band on break and announced the final match of the night. Catherine wasn't surprised to hear that Rey and Ash had advanced. Their opponents turned out to be two of the men from the County Patrol Group. A fun night edged toward disaster.

The group had driven back trails, farm roads, and highways, hoping they'd see something. No way could they cover the entire county. Not all fifteen- hundred miles of roads.

Tonight, they were blowing off steam, wisecracking about how inept the sheriff's department had become. Catherine didn't know much about Ash, but Rey came in on the weekend. She'd never seen him get angry, but he had the reputation for having a quick temper. It didn't take Marty long to threaten Harvey and Danny with a forfeit if they didn't shut their mouths.

Catherine relaxed when Ash and Rey won the match. While they argued over who kept the trophy, Marty made the announcement followed by her usual Dolly Parton goodnight. Catherine and JC wasted no time getting the tables cleaned and the chairs stacked while Marty shooed the last of the customers away. Ash stopped by on his way out to say goodbye.

"I'm riding with Rey. You want us to wait outside?"

"No thanks. JC walks us out to the parking lot. He makes sure we're on the road before he drives away."

Ash draped an arm over her shoulder and whispered, "You're sure it's okay? Rey and I are meeting a couple of ladies at the truck stop for breakfast."

"Go. Enjoy. I'm closely watched when I leave."

Marty dabbed the corners of her mouth while Ash walked out of the bar. "Excuse the drool. If I were a few years younger, I'd give that one the ride of his life." She tossed Catherine a rag and joined her wiping down tables. "Let's wrap this night up."

****

He wasn't a last minute kind of guy. He hadn't planned on following Catherine home. It wouldn't do for someone to see him. Forgoing an evening with sweet Jessie was tough, but he'd made the right choice.

Tonight changed everything. JC had been all over her. How many times had he reached across the bar and touched her? He wouldn't allow her to whore around. Mama fucked anybody who'd give her a drink, a dollar, and a good time. No. Hell, no. He wouldn't allow his doll to spread her legs the way Mama did. She should save herself for him.

His hands curled into fists, and he pounded the steering wheel a couple of times. Catherine belonged to him. A dessert you savored a long time, stroking your tongue across the sweetness, and letting the flavor soak in before you wolf it down. Not something you shared.

He'd track Catherine's movements, laying some groundwork for when the time came to kill Jessie. Then he could move on Catherine right away.

Parked behind a row of scraggly trees, he waited. And waited. Soon he'd bust a kidney. He couldn't open the door to piss. The damn overhead light would come on. The windows were down, but sweat ran from every pore. Running the engine was dangerous because somebody might hear. He reached over to start his pickup and leave when Marty, JC, and Catherine came outside. His hand stilled.

That idiot JC stood in the middle of the parking lot as if he was on patrol. Pissing his pants wasn't an option, but when JC yelled, 'Ladies, start your engines' his dick nearly popped a leak. Marty started her car and gave him thumbs up. God, this was too much. They both turned their gaze toward Catherine. Wasn't that too fuckin' sweet. They caravanned for safety. Little did they know, there wasn't a safe place for Catherine. He'd take her when he got ready. Nobody would stop him.

She got inside her car, but a few minutes later popped out. JC hustled to her and sat behind the wheel. Shit, she was having car trouble. Too bad it hadn't happened a few days later and on her way home. His gut slammed into a knot when JC put his hand on her. He fuckin' touched her. Then he walked her to his pickup and opened the door for her.

There was no doubt he had to follow her home. If she let that sleaze ball JC into her bed, they both might die before morning.

The trip out the dark road was hair-raising at best. The only way to remain undetected was to turn off his lights, stay far enough back not to attract attention, and concentrate on the taillights in front of him. He came to a full stop when JC turned down a driveway. Hell, it looked more like a landing strip. He had to see, had to watch. He drove past the house and pulled behind a line of scrub oaks. This was dangerous and stupid, but his doll wasn't a sluts or whore. Catherine had better not let him down.

Lucky for JC, he dropped Catherine off and drove away. She'd redeemed herself. JC hadn't fooled him, acting all chivalrous and shit. Maybe she turned a blind eye to JC's motives, but they were clear as day.

Maybe he should keep an eye on her house. See who visited.

Sweet Jessie expected him. He'd promised to bring her something to eat. No fuckin' way was he going out to the trailer. She'd begged him to lengthen her chain enough that she could reach the kitchen. But he wasn't stupid. He'd have to go through and remove anything she could use as a weapon. No, it was best she only had access to the john. That was enough.

He yawned. Had to go home and get some rest. Missing another shift with the County Patrol wouldn't be smart. Will's schedule paired him with Vince tomorrow night. As an upstanding citizen, he'd be there. They'd drive the streets and back roads keeping a watchful eye on the young women. No one would disappear on his watch. How would he keep from laughing out loud?

Catherine's house went dark. She'd sleep alone tonight. He pictured her naked body sliding into bed, and his cock pushed against the zipper of his jeans. "You want to get inside that, don't you?" He rubbed his crotch. "Soon. For now, we wait. I'll take a leak when I get home then I'll take care of you."

****

"When we finish the dishes, I should be going. I didn't want you to worry when you didn't see my car in the drive." Catherine hadn't intended on staying, but Emma offered lunch.

"I'm glad you told me. You're being stubborn to not take my car. It's old but serviceable." They stood side-by-side while washing and drying the dishes.

"I can't leave you alone with no means of transportation. It wouldn't be safe." Catherine rinsed a plate and passed it to Emma.

"You're a sweet child." She paused, her gaze drifting to the window, and her face softened. "My mother lived in the country all her life without a car. I have everything I need right here."

"Thank you for the offer, but I've already made arrangements to be picked up today and Sunday."

"Then you'll take mine starting Monday. Discussion's over. I insist."

Catherine blinked back tears. Emma's kindness knew no boundaries. The people she'd found in Butte Crest didn't exist in today's world. She must've driven into an old episode of the Twilight Zone.

"You make me miss my mother. She'd have loved you."

"I figured you were alone. Too bad. A person needs family."

"I have a brother, but we've been estranged for years. We talk occasionally but haven't found firm footing, not yet. Too much happened. My fault...not his."

"Guess I'll have to step in and fill that void. If you'll let me."

Emotions flooded Catherine's chest to the point of pain. From out of nowhere, memories of past friends and family who'd turned accusing eyes toward her made her heart ache. The pain hit like a powerful wave, knocking her off her feet. She sat down hard.

Emma quietly refilled their tea glasses and joined her at the table. "Carrying a burden around all by yourself can be mighty daunting. Thank goodness you've found a new home where people love and care about you." She extended both her hands across the table. "You can finally lay it down. Leave it here with me."

Tears flowed from Catherine's eyes. A dam broke in her heart and words poured out, flowing fast like the river after a spring rain. The moment was surreal, as if her spirit hovered above her body while someone else unraveled the past and laid it out for Emma to see. The years of abuse, the cruelty, the belief she had no one and nowhere to go, spewed from her mouth. Bile rose and burned the back of her throat while she explained how she'd fought for her life then ultimately killed her husband.

"Emma, I'm responsible for taking another person's life." Self-recrimination Catherine thought she'd worked through bubbled out on a sob. The taste as bitter as it had been over a year ago.

Emma's delicate hands remained on the table. Still open. Still waiting. She didn't pull them away after learning Catherine's horrible story. Catherine clasped them in hers and squeezed.

"Forgive yourself, child. No one else can do that for you."

Catherine looked into Emma's warm eyes. She showed no sign of blame or disgust. Her expression was understanding and love.

"You're the first person I've ever told. Most of the time I don't have to tell. Somebody recognizes me and calls the local newspaper. I left Oklahoma to get away from the shame."

"You've nothing to be ashamed of. I didn't run from the room screaming and hollering...did I?" Emma released her hands and retrieved a box of tissues. "Tell your story. Tell anybody and everybody who'll listen. Gives folks a chance. They'll surprise you."

"It's hard. I've tried, but I lose my nerve."

"Better they hear it from you instead of on the TV. Sylvia Horning did an awful thing yesterday, telling how the sheriff let his partner get killed. Must've hurt him something powerful."

"I didn't know. Oh, Emma. Something was bothering him last night. You can bet somebody told him." Catherine's lunch soured. Why hadn't she followed him outside? She wanted to run to him and hold him in her arms forever.

"The Horning woman said he failed in Houston and came here to hide. She's a mean-spirited woman, that's what she is."

Catherine's heartbeat jumped when she glanced at the clock on the wall. "I don't believe the time got away from me. I have to run. Marty will be here soon." She hugged Emma close. "Thank you for listening. And for believing in me."

****

Staking out her house was turning into a fuckin' disaster. Things turned for the better when JC called. It seemed he'd told Catherine he could get her a good deal at the garage. Who the fuck did JC think he was promising shit he had no control over?

Nothing had happened except for Catherine running up to the main house. An old woman let her in, and she'd stayed inside for a long time. When she finally came out, she'd hit the ground at a run.

Wasn't long after, Marty pulled into the drive and honked. Catherine, all dressed up in her western clothes ran out and jumped in the car. Soon as they left, he was taking a quick leak and then he'd go straight to the trailer. Jessie would be hungry. He was too. Hungry to have her red lips wrapped around his cock. He'd feed her all right. She'd earn every bite.

He let Marty and Catherine get out of sight before unzipping and taking a pause for the cause. He'd slid behind the wheel when a red pickup came into sight. His fingers squeezed together in fists. JC in his big Dodge Ram and oversized tires. What the fuck was the sonofabitch doing? Did he think Catherine was still here? JC parked on the road and crept around the main house to the back carrying a small package. The sneaky bastard disappeared.

The hornets' nest woke up with a vengeance. The buzzing in his ears grew louder, and his jaw hurt. His mouth tasted like iron. Shit, he'd bit a chunk out of the inside of his cheek.

Ten minutes later JC came back, got in his truck, and drove away. Stupid fucker discovered she wasn't home, but the package was gone. What'd he leave her?

He hiked a good two blocks down the road before cutting through the pasture and coming up behind the small house. Goddammit, the old woman had come out. She was looking around. Had she seen JC? He leaned flat against the back of a rundown barn. He had no excuse for being on the property. What if she caught him? Shit, he'd have to kill her. No way was he explaining what he was doing out here. He could see the top of her head from his vantage point when she walked back down the drive and disappeared into the main house. No reason to turn back now.

The window on the back door revealed nothing except the usual kitchen stuff. A tiny separation in the curtains on the next window told him what he needed to know. JC had been inside. He couldn't have a key. Could he? Why wouldn't he have used the front door?

JC had left her a present. Lying in the middle of her bed was the box with a card on top of it. The hornets' nest exploded. The buzzing grew louder and louder. They wanted out...clawed at the inside of his skull. His fingers curled into fists from the need to smash the glass and take the gift. He closed his eyes and forced the anger to still.

Careful not to leave footprints, he made his way back to his pickup and left.

JC was a dead motherfucker.

Chapter Twenty-One

Catherine ran out the door and into Matt's arms. He staggered backward under the full brunt of her weight. Wrapping her arms around his broad shoulders, she buried her face in his neck. Tears of anger, fear, and frustration flowed unchecked. His strong hands lifted her in his arms as if she weighed no more than a child and carried her back inside.

"Shh," he shushed her softly. "You're okay."

"I'm glad you're here." She wiped her eyes, not caring mascara streaked down her face. He was here, and she could relax a little. "I've cried more in front of you than I've cried in years."

"And that's okay." He turned, still holding her in his arms and zeroed his gaze in on Ash. "You," Matt emphasized the word with a growl. "Can explain what you're doing in my woman's house at four in the morning. Later. For now, I'm damn grateful you were."

She let the words my "woman" roll around in her heart and flow into her veins. His woman. As possessive as it sounded, Matt's definition was different from her dead husband's. She could face anything after that statement.

"Put me down, John." She wriggled from his grasp while ignoring Ash's odd expression. Her nickname for Matt would stay between them like his name for her of Cat. Her hands shook. She laced her fingers through his and led him to the back room.

"The sonofabitch came in your bedroom." Matt's jaw muscles jumped and twitched. He stood by her bed looking at the unopened package. A cold glaze clouded his blue eyes, turning them the color of an angry sea. He spun on Ash. "You checked the windows and doors?"

"Yep. Everything's secure, but a credit card will pop either the front or the back door. The locks in the house are ancient. I'm getting gloves from your truck."

"Box on the floor." Matt pressed his fingers to his temples. He blew out a breath.

"I didn't touch it." Catherine's skin burned with the anger raging through his system. His face, full of hate, brought tears to her eyes. No one had ever been protective of her, never been ready to fight for her. Sweet pain curled around her heart and tightened when he pulled her to him.

"Are you all right?" He lowered his forehead to hers and closed his eyes.

"I am now." In that moment...that singular moment, she dove head first into deep water. Way in over her head. This happiness. This euphoria. She'd be destroyed if his unwavering devotion disappeared.

The snap of latex brought the sheriff back to the job at hand. The swift change in Matt's posture and appearance was startling. He slid on the gloves Ash offered before carefully picking the envelope up from the bed. Ash passed Matt a small knife, and he slit the top in one motion. A picture slid out.

"What is it?" She moved closer with both hands behind her back. The last thing she wanted to do was touch any part of the so-called gift.

"I don't know. Red material?" Matt leaned closer. "Catherine, what does it look like to you?"

"You know what it reminds me of? The brown satin in that Dove's chocolate commercial."

Matt flipped the picture over and read. "I can see you lying on these wearing my present."

"Fucking satin sheets." Ash glanced at Matt. "Oops. Sorry, Catherine."

"No problem." His apology might've been funny another time and place. Right this minute, his words felt appropriate.

"He sealed the envelope. May have been his first mistake."

Matt pulled the top of the small box off, picked up the lacy, white gown by the straps, and laid it across the mattress. His face flushed red. The nerves in his jaw twitched.

"Get that thing off my bed." She literally had to push the words out. "Please." Catherine wanted to take Ash's pocketknife and slash the gown to shreds. Blood rushed to her brain while her heart beat out a rhythm of fear. Try as she might, she couldn't stop her body from trembling. Dammit, she hated being out of control. Take charge of your mind, her martial arts instructor had preached.

"I've got it." Ash carefully stacked the envelope, picture, and nightgown into the small box. "I'll drop this off with the dispatcher on my way home."

"Thanks for the ride. I'm glad you insisted on looking around," she said. Ash pulled her in for a hug.

"Simply a ploy to get inside." His words were joking, but his eyes were deadly serious when he turned to Matt. "Pray the SOB licked the envelope, and he's in the system."

Catherine walked Ash to the door. Drawers slamming sent her rushing to her bedroom. Matt had piled some of her clothes on the bed. "What are you doing?"

"Packing you some stuff. You're coming home with me."

Her jaw dropped. He made no effort to hide his fury. His tone barely covered the rage. Anger seeped from his pores.

"Wait a damn minute." Her things tossed haphazardly sent her reeling. "How dare you order me around?" She stormed across the room and slammed the drawer closed he'd opened. "How dare you come in my bedroom and handle my underwear?"

Matt stared at the fingers that barely escaped being smashed. "You can't stay here alone."

"I told you once before. Don't tell me what to do." The sound of her own screeching voice sounded alien to her. A shrew-like woman had moved in to her body and was screaming. She wanted to pull back, had lost control of all reason. Something pushed her on.

Thank goodness, Matt stepped back. "Where's your car?" His voice was a whisper.

"It broke down. JC had a buddy tow it to a local garage." Nerves simmered and stretched right to the edge. Her car, her finances, two jobs, the unbearable heat, and the stalker had pushed her too far. No one...not even the man she might be in love with would bark orders at her as if she were subservient to him.

His head turned slowly, revealing eyes the color of coal. "When did this happen?"

Catherine picked up a pair of jeans and straightened them out. She made an effort to keep her voice calm. "Friday night."

"Why didn't you call me?" His jaw muscle twitched, and his lips barely moved.

"Because I worked things out for myself. That's what I do. I take care of my own problems." She knew that statement was a lie. She couldn't keep the stalker out of her own home. But the point of backing down had passed.

Matt closed his eyes and rubbed the bridge of his nose. She could feel the heat coming off him. See him rein in his emotions. Without another word, he stormed out.

Catherine stomped into the bathroom and closed the door. She couldn't jerk her clothes off fast enough. She stepped into the shower and stood while the water ran full blast. She scrubbed because her skin felt dirty. Her hair and body reeked of cigarette smoke. Then she scrubbed again. Tears of anger, fear, and frustration mingled with the warm torrent sluicing across her exhausted frame. Why had she snapped at Matt? Why hadn't she stopped him? His fury wasn't directed at her. Great, now she could add guilt to the mix of emotions racing through her nervous system.

She pulled her nightshirt from the hook on the door and slipped it on before running a comb through her hair. When she opened the door, an unfamiliar noise stopped her. Now what? The house was dark except for the glow from the outside lights and her bedroom.

215 |

Again. That sound. Could it be a soft snore? Tiptoeing down the hall, she peered around the corner, and her heart imploded. Wadded up into a ball on the small loveseat, Matt slept twisted as a pretzel. His boots and gun lay within reach.

She crept in and sat in the chair directly in front of him. The light array Emma had installed outside streamed through the white curtains and across his face. Strong legs ran up to narrow hips and waist. The peaks and valleys of his muscles couldn't be masked by jeans and a T-shirt. He made her mouth water. God, he was beautiful. Catherine leaned her head back and closed her eyes. Her protector was the last thing she remembered until his strong arms lifted her from the chair. Broad shoulders supported her head and a musky, masculine scent drifted into her senses. She snuggled against Matt's warm neck while he carried her to her bed.

****

Matt bit back a groan as he tried stretching the kinks from his back. Catherine's loveseat wasn't built for someone his size. A glance at his watch said he was already behind on the day. He eased down the hall far enough to see Catherine had kicked her covers to the floor. Doing his best to be quiet, he pulled the blanket over her tempting body. Catherine opened her eyes and smiled a sexy, sleepy "come here" grin.

"Don't leave. I don't want to sleep in this bed alone tonight."

"It's not night, it's eleven Sunday morning." He stood over her, itching to jerk that blanket back off her. "You need to rest."

"But I'm not tired." She flipped the covers back and patted the bed. "If you're not in a hurry."

She wiggled out of her sleep-shirt and tossed it at him. Matt shed his clothes before she changed her mind. She'd forgiven his macho outburst from last night. He was right, she shouldn't stay here, but his anger at her stalker and fear for her was no excuse for his behavior. He crawled in and pulled her to him, covering her mouth with his. He'd apologize with his tongue, his kiss, and his hands, but first he'd tell her.

"I'm sorry I jumped on you last night." He nibbled across her shoulders while he spoke. "My mouth overloaded my brain. You're right, I can't order you around."

"Let's accept each other's apology and forget what happened. Thank you for sleeping on the couch."

"That damn thing's not a couch. Sleeping on it should be on your *Never* list." His fingers rolled her nipple through them, and her moan sent waves of lust through him. He kissed her breasts and feasted on her tender flesh.

"Come here."

She pulled him on top of her and with one quick motion seated him right in her glorious sweet spot. Her hips rose up in an open invitation, which he took. Pushing himself deep in her warmth.

"Oh. My. God. I could stay in here, inside where you're warm and wet." He slid his hands under her hips, lifted, and pushed himself deeper. There was no place on earth he belonged any more than buried in her. His soul opened with each thrust as they set a slow pace. Eyes locked on each other, they fell into a rhythm of give and take. Ebb and flow. He wanted her emerald green eyes to darken with passion, her dark auburn eyelashes to flutter with surrender, and her mouth to speak his name with release.

Matt Ballard was in love.

"Matt," she gasped. Her eyes wide, she ground her hips into him.

"Come for me, Cat. Let go." She clenched and released around him, milked him until, unable to hold on any longer, he emptied himself with a roar. He reached down for one more kiss before he rolled to her side.

"Before I leave, let's walk down and ask Emma if she noticed anything unusual after you left yesterday. First, how about some coffee? Then you can tell me how Ash managed to be here with you last night. I'd hate to lose another partner." Instantly he wanted that wisecrack back. He could've bitten his tongue off. How could he joke about the death of a partner? His mistakes with Elena flooded his mind.

"Matt, what is it? What's wrong?" Her face radiated concern.

"Nothing, forget it." Damn, he wished he could disappear. Catherine was smart, and she'd picked up on his change of mood. The sun rose to the perfect spot and cast a gold path across her face. He could lay there and look into her beautiful eyes forever. He had many things he wanted to tell her, share with her. Could it be the universe had forgiven him?

"Please don't shut me out."

"I'll fix coffee." He rolled away from her penetrating gaze, rose, and grabbed his jeans on the way to the kitchen. She'd looked at him through childlike eyes. Innocent and pure. He was everything but that.

The sound of the bathroom door closing let him know she'd followed him out of bed. A few minutes later, she joined him in the kitchen. Jesus, she knocked his breath right out of his lungs. Without makeup, she'd managed to look like she hadn't been awake most of the night. She'd pulled her red hair back with a head band and let her wild curls hang around her shoulders. She'd definitely been working out, and a pair of shorts showcased long, well- defined legs. A yellow top with narrow straps made the freckles on her chest and nose more noticeable. Damn, he wanted to kiss every one of them.

"Your toothbrush is still in the holder."

She smelled of minty mouthwash and soap when she kissed his cheek. They'd only made love a few minutes ago, but he instantly hardened. Her eyes searched his face, and he pushed his lusty thoughts away. He poured a cup from the unfinished pot and carried his fix of caffeine with him. By the time he'd washed up and brushed his teeth, he'd made a decision. If he wanted her to trust him, maybe, he should try trusting her. She deserved to know the truth about her imaginary hero, John Wayne.

Catherine had moved to the living room and was stretched out exactly where he'd slept. She looked a lot more comfortable on the love seat than he'd been. She sat up and started speaking the minute he sat across from her.

"Ash was at the bar last night, seems he's good at the pool table. He asked why my car wasn't in the parking lot. I told him about my car trouble. Marty and JC had agreed to shuttle me back and forth for the rest of the weekend. JC was my ride home. Ash offered to let JC go on, it was late, and I said yes. I'm glad, Matt. Because he insisted on coming inside to check my doors and windows. He was here when I found the box. He told me to call you right away."

"I'm glad he was here, too."

"Were you jealous? Just a little? " She lifted an eyebrow.

"Me? Of Ash? You've gotta be kidding." He didn't know why he denied it. She rolled her eyes and hit him with a grin. She read him way too easy.

"When you mentioned losing another partner, the pain in your voice and eyes broke my heart. You'll never make me believe you were responsible."

All the air left his lungs. She believed her statement to be true. "I lived. She didn't."

"I'm sure you know about survivor guilt. But, explain to me how it was your fault that you didn't die?"

"I should've kept my edge. Kept my focus better. I couldn't have prevented her being recognized but might've avoided capture if my head had been in the game. Our personal feelings had gotten all screwed up. We'd stayed under too long. The lines between reality and make-believe blurred. Sometimes you start believing the lies you're living."

"I don't understand."

She moved from the loveseat and sat on the floor in front of him. Her hands rested on his knees, warmth ran straight to his heart.

"I know you don't. We lived as husband and wife for two years. Did everything within the gang together. Went months without the opportunity to come out of the role. We had no one but each other to talk to. Somehow we—" He looked away, couldn't bring himself to finish the sentence.

She rose to her knees and cupped his face in her hands. "You fell in love."

Her gentle voice pulled his gaze to hers. Compassion lit her face, a glow radiated from her alabaster skin. No recrimination or condemnation, only understanding shined from clear green eyes. Through her, he'd found the strength to trust. Trust her with the truth.

"No. Elena loved her husband." He swallowed the lump jammed into the back of his throat. He closed his eyes and drew strength from the woman whose compassion filled his heart. "We had sex. We were in Mexico. Hadn't slept for days trying to broker a deal that would put us inside the main cartel. Exhausted, nerves about to explode, we had sex. Pure and simple, blowing-off-steam sex. It was a hundred percent my fault. Afterward things were awkward between us. After we crossed the border to Texas, our relationship didn't improve. Both of us were confused and confounded. I'll always wonder if our personal guilt let the edge dull, let our senses weaken."

"You were discovered right after you came back?"

"Yes. As lead investigator, I'd made up my mind to have her pulled out. I could've made up some excuse. She'd have been furious, but the infidelity ate at her. Changed her. Obviously, I never got the chance to send her home."

"Matt, you turned to each other to keep your humanity alive. The affection and warmth you shared with her wasn't wrong. The touch of another caring human being probably saved both your sanity. Sex was a lifeline for you and Elena."

Catherine rose onto her knees, slid between his thighs, and her arms wrapped around him. Her fingers dug into his muscles and held tightly.

"I don't know about all that. She's dead and I'm not. That's what I know." Pressed close enough he felt her heart beat against his chest. Somehow, the rhythms synchronized. Two hearts beat as one. The tingle in his hands grew stronger and stronger. This beautiful, loving woman looked at him...looked deep inside. With all his mistakes and fuckups, she'd found something redeeming. Maybe she was right. Maybe he could move on. Maybe he'd take her hand in his and make a life for them...hell, he was sure of it.

"My offer stands. Until this stalker's caught, I'd like you to stay at my place." He nipped her bottom lip with his teeth. "Who knows, you might like it and want to move in. That way I can drive you around until your car's fixed."

"Emma has graciously loaned me her car until mine's ready. It wouldn't be right for me to move off and leave her." A gleam lit her eyes. "But you could stay here."

"You're sure?" He eyed the loveseat with disdain. "I wouldn't have to sleep on that torture chamber, would I?"

"I kind of like having you in my bed. Besides, you put it on the *Never* list." She stood and pulled him to his feet. "But, Marty will be here soon. I won't have time to talk with Emma, if we don't get going." She jogged into her bedroom and came back wearing sandals. She held a foot up for inspection. "Remember these?"

He could remember every sensuous curve of her naked body, the small mole just south of her navel, the scent she wore...but shoes...not so much. "I'll be in a world of hurt if I say no. Right?"

She tilted her head sideways and frowned. "You should remember the first time we met. I talked you out of giving me a ticket."

The memory of her wildfire hair shimmering in the sunlight came flooding back. "You mean the day you tried to knock me down?"

"I did not! You made me get back in my car."

"You called me John Wayne."

"Exactly." She beamed a smile at him. "Well, I needed a John Wayne or Prince Charming to come into my life."

"John was definitely the better choice."

"Why's that?"

"Because I might've arrested you for assault if you'd called me Prince."

Chapter Twenty-Two

Catherine's spirit soared. Matt's opening up to her meant a great deal. They held hands all the way to Emma's back porch.

Emma answered the door with a huge smile, wrapped her arm around Catherine's waist, and led them to the kitchen table. The bond she felt with the older woman helped fill the empty space losing her mother had caused. They worked as a team, one cut slices of cake and the other poured glasses of milk. Matt didn't hesitate to dig in.

"Good," he said around a bite.

"Glad you like it." Emma beamed. "I was about to walk back to see you. Somebody came on the property yesterday after you left."

Matt swallowed, leaning forward in his chair. "Did you get a close look?"

"No. Checked out both houses. Saw some boot prints behind the storage shed. Weren't there yesterday."

"You shouldn't have gone outside. If it happens again, call my office. We'll send a car out. Don't take unnecessary chances."

Catherine could tell by Emma's expression he'd wasted his breath.

"I didn't. By the time I got my pistol from the nightstand, hid the darn thing in my apron pocket, and went to take a peek, he was gone." Her eyes narrowed, and her mouth formed a grim line. "Don't look at me like that, Sheriff. I've got a license, and don't you think for a minute I won't protect my property."

"I believe you. Emma, I have to advise you against pulling a gun on an intruder. You could've been hurt or killed. Did you see or hear a vehicle?"

She frowned and thought for a second. "No, but someone drove by. They didn't stop, and I didn't go check."

"Speaking of safety, we came to tell you our news." Catherine pulled her chair closer to his and sat. "Matt's staying with me for a while."

Matt opened his mouth but then closed it. Catherine would remember to tell him later it was nice to see his cheeks turn pink for a change.

"Great. Between the two of us, we'll protect Catherine from this Tom-fool stalker. I'll be right back." Emma scurried away, her arms flapped as if perhaps the motion helped propel her forward

"She worries me a little," Matt said keeping his voice low.

"Why? She's harmless."

"That's not how I'd describe her...a pistol- packing granny is a scary thought."

Emma beamed with pride when she came back and handed him a key. "Here you go."

"Why, thank you, Miss Emma." He stuffed the key in his pocket. "I better run. Work's waiting."

"I'll walk you out." Catherine stood on her tip- toes, waiting for a quick kiss, laughing at the widening of his eyes.

"I'll see you around closing time."

She waited until Matt was out of sight to blurt out her secret to Emma. "I think I'm in love with him. Good Lord. Did those words come from my mouth?"

"I know you are."

"Really? Oh, wise Obi-Wan Kenobi, tell me how you came to this conclusion."

"I'm old...not blind. There's an unspoken communication, a look two people exchange when they trust each other completely. His eyes shout it. You followed my advice and told him then?"

"No. I didn't." Catherine ran to the window to watch while his truck pulled down the driveway. He honked, and the engine accelerated as he drove away. Tears sprang to her eyes when she felt Emma's hand rest lightly on her arm.

"Child, the man loves you. I thought for sure he knew."

"I couldn't take the chance of losing him. He's dealing with a lot. Not catching this killer is eating him alive. And then the stalker pops up again. Right now, I can't add to the load Matt's already carrying on his shoulders."

Catherine left Emma's and slowly walked back to her place. The tendons in her back tensed and tightened with each step. The stalker had invaded her life on such a personal level her fear had turned to pure unadulterated hate. Was he the killer? Was she his next victim? She didn't feel safe anywhere except in Matt's arms, but he couldn't be there all the time. She had to be able to take care of herself. Her stomach roiled against the coffee and cake she'd eaten. Food of any flavor sounded revolting.

Thankfully, she had enough time to exercise. She increased her reps, doubled her aerobics, and moved to the heavier dumbbells she'd bought at Wal-Mart. Sweat poured and muscles screamed, but she pressed on. In the limited space of her living room, she worked on her kicks, spins, and punches.

Catherine removed a small wooden box from the top of her closet. The story of her tormented past, the court documents, doctor's deposition, and a few nasty news articles resided inside. Odd, how the thick stack of paperwork, which represented all those wasted years, weighed so lightly in her hands.

It wasn't in Matt's personality to snoop, but she couldn't have him stumble across her past without previous explanation. Catherine ran back to Emma and pressed the box in her hands. Then she went home.

Home to a mess. Dishes needed washed, bedcovers needed picked up off the floor. God, how did things get so screwed up? Before she showered and dressed for work, Catherine went into a cleaning frenzy. Crazy thoughts ran through her mind while she worked. One minute she was sure she loved Matt, and the next she'd panic and contemplate moving on. No, she wouldn't run. Fear would not rule her life.

By the time Marty honked, Catherine had control of her emotions. Again.

****

Catherine cleaned the last table and turned to find Matt walking toward her. The blood in her veins double-clutched and shifted from calm to rapid. Did pleasure show on her face? "You're right on time. I'm not quite finished."

"I can help. Show me what to do." He leaned down and kissed her cheek hello.

She and Matt stacked the chairs and worked their way around the bar.

"I wish I could tell you to take Catherine home. But JC not showing up put me in a bind." Marty loaded another flat of beer into the cooler, slamming one can after another hard enough the metal rack reverberated in protest.

"No problem. Did he call?"

"Hell, no. And he's not answering his phone. I'll wring his scrawny neck for leaving me and Catherine high and dry."

"Did you send somebody out to check on him?"

"No. He's pulled this once before. Disappeared on me for a couple of weeks. Drinking and mourning the loss of some girlfriend." Marty halted her movement, the flat of beer suspended in midair. Her eyebrows shot toward the ceiling. "You think I should've?"

"It might be a good idea to send a car. I'll call Charles Ray." He pulled his phone from his hip and dialed. "Hold on a second." He covered the mouthpiece. "I need JC's address."

"I've got it." Marty grabbed her bag from behind the counter and rummaged through a purse the size of Idaho. She handed an open address book to Matt. "On the bottom of the page."

Marty hadn't seemed concerned about JC not coming to work. At the same time, Catherine trusted Matt's instincts and training. He certainly appeared worried, and a nagging doubt formed. She pushed her thoughts aside and concentrated on finishing her work. Within minutes, Matt hung up and finished the chairs.

"We'll call if we learn anything." Matt and

Catherine waited while Marty locked the building. "Good. Don't disturb me if he's passed out drunk. I'm tired and pissed. Going home and getting some shut-eye."

Marty's abrasive tone of voice didn't fool anybody. She was worried now that Matt had Charles Ray checking on JC.

"Ready to go home?" He held her door then went around to the driver's side without waiting for an answer.

Home? Together? Everything had happened fast. There hadn't been much discussion about him moving in with her. She'd suggested Matt stay with her, and he'd said yes. He'd moved in this afternoon after she went to work. She hadn't completely figured out what that meant. Were they a couple? Or was he her bodyguard? Either way Matt was sleeping in her bed.

Catherine turned and stared at his beautiful profile. Breathed in his masculine scent. Matt in her bed every night. Matt in her bed every morning. Matt making love to her whenever they wanted. He'd shown her the way back to passion, and she couldn't get enough of him. Fire shot through her. Desire flared and swept across her like a coastal wave. Moisture pooled between her legs.

"Hey." His hand gripped her knee. "It's been a while since you spaced out on me. Where'd you go?"

Thank God for the darkness. Catherine had no idea they were already on the road. No doubt, she was blushing. "You sure you want to know?"

"Let me have it."

"I was thinking of all the things we'll do now you're putting your boots next to my bed."

"Don't forget the kitchen." His laugh, a low, sexy, rumbling growl filled the cab of the pickup. "I definitely want a repeat of the counter. You tasted like honey. Sweet honey."

Lust flashed through her body like wildfire. Her nipples pebbled and pushed against the lace of her bra. Anticipation throbbed between her legs. He made love to her with his words. The memory of her losing her mind while his raven head was buried between her thighs heightened her already electrified nervous system.

"Matt?"

His gaze left the road for a second and blistered her skin. "Hmm?"

"Do you have to drive like an old lady?"

"We're almost home, Cat." The word was a mere whisper.

She cried out in frustration when his cell buzzed. Not now. Not tonight. She didn't work tomorrow, and she planned on sending a tired sheriff to the office Monday morning. She held her breath and listened to his half of the conversation.

"Thanks for the callback, Charles Ray. Yeah. Leave it on my desk." He ended the call and slid the phone into its clip.

"JC sleeping one off?" She sighed audibly in relief.

"Don't know. His pickup's nowhere in sight, and there were no signs of trouble. Not much we can do at this point."

Emma's outside light array came into view. They were on a back road with no traffic. Catherine unhooked her seatbelt and slid across next to Matt. She leaned up and pulled his earlobe into her mouth.

"You're breaking the law, lady."

He sucked in a breath when she slipped her hands between his legs.

"So arrest me, Sheriff."

****

"Jesus H. Christ. At least make an effort to wipe the silly grin off your face." Ash made a disgusted sounding huff and went back to reading the weekend reports lying on Matt's desk.

"Remind me again why I had Sue fix you a work area." Matt eased himself into his chair and propped the heels of his boots on his desk. Something he normally wouldn't have done.

"So you got Catherine all squared away? Must have, I didn't hear from you yesterday." Ash passed the file over.

"I'm staying at her place until we catch her stalker. The bastard breaking into her house was the final affront. She's filing charges." He watched for a blink or reaction to his moving in with Catherine, but Ash showed neither surprise nor disapproval.

"Good. Looks like she's beginning to trust you. What about JC?"

"Marty said he's disappeared before. I'll call her today. Let her know we checked on him."

"Sue's typing a couple of interviews I conducted with your team. Are you aware she had to purchase new handcuffs for Rey Santos a couple of months ago?"

Matt blew out a sigh and tried to remember. "No. She doesn't report every expenditure. What are you trying to say?"

"Nothing. I'm telling you what I learned. Jake's so damn clean he should sound like a squeegee when he walks. His alibis were easy to check. Did you know he coaches both his boys' summer hardball teams?"

"I didn't." For some reason Ash knowing the intimate details of Jake's life irritated Matt. Maybe he wasn't as close to his men as he thought.

"Well, he does. And Rey? He's the original whore-dog. Women follow him around like his dick's made of solid gold. I can't imagine him having to kidnap one. Not when the few good looking ones out here in the boonies are willing to give it to him."

"So is he a suspect because he lost his handcuffs or because his dick's bigger than yours?"

"Very funny. You should feel good they all checked out clean." Ash stood and strolled out of Matt's office.

Ash leaving was a good thing, because folders covered Matt's desk, his callback stand ran over, and two mayors had scheduled meetings with him later today.

Sue tried to keep him organized. A file rack sat on the front left corner of his workspace. Each slot held a different colored folder.

Each color held its own significance. Matt had finally memorized which was which. Blue, the color of her eyes, and being a color of leisure meant read when you have a chance. Green indicated money and held performance reviews, renewals, or expenditures of some nature. Yellow, he'd refused the original pink one, meant this is getting old and needs your attention soon. Red, would never be placed in the rack because that would be hand delivered, meant handle immediately.

Movement in the doorway brought his attention up from signing the approval on an outrageously high electricity bill.

All Sue's grin needed was a yellow feather sticking out of her mouth. "Ms. McCoy would like to see you."

"Catherine's here? She really came." He pushed back from his desk. Damn, he was proud of her. Whatever her hang-up was, she'd put it behind her and climbed those steps alone. "Where?"

"At my desk." She wiggled her eyebrows then winked at him. "Want me to show her in?"

"Yeah, it's business. Is Jake in his office?" This must've been hard for Catherine. Somewhere, somehow, the legal system had let her down. He hoped to change her opinion.

Sue's back straightened and her cheeks flushed. "I'm sorry, Sheriff. I'll get him right away."

"Sue." He stopped her with his tone of voice. "There's nothing to apologize for. Catherine's here to file charges on the stalker."

"I shouldn't be joking and running my mouth about things none of my concern."

Matt stood, went to Sue, and draped his arm over her shoulder. "Please don't change. Your sense of humor is why we love you around here."

Relieved eyes looked up at him. "You're trying to butter me up so I'll bake you another apple pie." She huffed a sound of disgust and ambled out.

"Duh," he called out after her.

Catherine stepped inside his door with the reluctance of a child headed for the principal's office.

Work be damned, he pulled her into his arms and held her for a second. Maybe the hug was more for him than her, because he breathed deeply and moaned. Her hair smelled like some exotic flower, and if he ever figured out the name, he was ordering her a bouquet of them. Her slender body molded against his briefly before the muscles in her back tightened.

"I'm proud of you. We'll make this as quick and painless as possible."

"Easy boss, you make it sound like we're about to execute her." Jake stepped around Matt to the small table and held a chair for Catherine. "With your complaint and the evidence you've given us, we'll make a good case when we catch this guy."

"I hope so." She squirmed in the chair. "Can we get this over with? Today's my only day off. I've got tons to do."

Matt remained silent while Jake took her statement. The different emotions playing across her face while she retold her shock and horror as each item got more personal sent Matt's anger meter spinning. His nerve endings burned with the desire to pummel the sonofabitch to oblivion. He'd gladly leave his gun and badge in the drawer for a good street fight with the bastard.

Catherine finished her written statement, signed the complaint, and leaned back in her chair with a whoosh of air. "Done." She handed Jake's pen back. "Now, all you need is the guy to come forward and confess."

Always the patient one, Jake either ignored her sarcasm or didn't take the bait. "Yes, ma'am." He slid the form and statement into a folder before standing. "My missus and I want to have you two over for a backyard cookout, but time for socializing has been slim to none lately."

"I understand. Until JC shows up, getting a day off on the weekend might be impossible for me."

Matt marveled at her stamina. How could she not be exhausted? She worked nonstop, dealt with the stalker, constantly worried about her car, and now had a coworker missing. Not to mention the fact neither of them slept much last night. Yet when she stood to leave, she looked like she'd spent the weekend at a spa instead of an emotional rollercoaster.

Catherine brushed past him on her way to the door. Her nearness set off an involuntary chain reaction in his body. Instantly blood surged and rushed through his veins. He had to consciously pull his hands back and make himself not touch her. Shit. He was at work. He had to step away from the situation, analyze what was happening to him. How the hell would he pull that trick off when he'd moved in with her yesterday? He'd lost his edge once. Was the same thing happening again?

"I'll walk her out, Jake."

"Okay." Jake grasped her hand and pumped it up and down. Tan and weathered, his big paw made hers look smaller. "Thanks for coming in."

"Nice man," she commented after Jake left the room. "Come on, Matt. You've got to see my new ride."

Matt couldn't resist gripping her shoulder in a silent 'atta girl.' He paused at the top of the steps. "Have I told you how proud I am of you for coming in today?"

"You did. We erased another *Never* off the list, but don't expect me to pop in and out." She stopped half way and looked up at him. "What?"

He closed the distance between them and stood looking down at her. "Law enforcement let you down in a big way. Will you tell me how?"

"You don't want to hear all that, and I don't have time."

"Sure I do." His hand caught hers, and they walked to the bottom of the steps. "He abused you, and the law didn't stop him. Right?"

He thought for a second she would run. Her gaze shifted everywhere but at him. Her chest rose and fell rapidly. He'd hit a hot button, and she was sorting through her fight or flight response. Did she expect him to defend a police department that hadn't stood up for her?

"Right."

She'd pushed the word out as if it caused great pain. The honesty closed the last gap in Matt's feelings for her. He wanted to pull her into his arms and hold her. But he didn't want her to feel like he was restraining her.

"I'm sorry, Catherine. Sorry for every woman who didn't get the help she needed. I'm especially sorry we let you down. It sets my gut on fire to think anybody put a hand on you and got away with it."

Her breathing slowed, and her gaze rested on his face. "He didn't. We've got to have a serious talk. And soon." She placed her hand on his chest over his heart. "Thank you for apologizing. You proved my theory about your soul, John Wayne. Now come see my new ride. Emma talked me into using her car."

She jogged across the parking lot and stopped next to a white four door Lincoln Continental Town Coupe. Polished to a high sheen the big, long, luxurious car swallowed its parking space.

"How do you like me now?" she announced with a Vanna White wave of her arms. "Best part? The air-conditioner will freeze your buns off."

"Outstanding." Matt moved around the antique car, trailing his fingers across the metal. "This must be a—"

"Nineteen seventy-nine." Ash said from behind Matt. "This baby is worth a fortune." He lovingly ran his hand across the hood. "Hello, beautiful." He glanced up. "Oh. Hello, Catherine."

"Don't tell me it's worth a lot of money. I'm already scared to drive it. No way can I parallel park." She unlocked and swung the heavy door open. "Emma's kept it in mint condition. Has it serviced regularly but seldom drives it anywhere."

Matt leaned over and studied the information on the windshield. "Plates and inspection are up to date. You're good to go."

"First stop is to check on my car. Before they fix whatever's wrong, I want a price."

232 |

Matt held up one finger. "Regardless of what it costs, have your AC repaired." He ignored the don't- tell-me-what-to-do look she sent him.

Ash pulled himself away from inspecting the interior. "Want me to go with you?"

"Thanks anyway. The mechanic is a friend of JC's, but I want details before they work on my car."

Chapter Twenty-Three

The day seemed to drag on forever. Concentrating was damn near impossible. His mind wandered. Fuckin' nerves wouldn't let him eat. And then he'd downed coffee all morning, which made it worse. Now acid from his gut rose to the back of his throat and burned. Maybe he should go home. *No, keep your head and leave at the regular time.* Tonight would be a big night.

Keeping his doll chained was a snap, but figuring out a way to keep JC subdued had been tricky. He'd ground up enough of Mama's tranquilizers to knock a horse out. What if it had been too much and the stupid fucker died? Wouldn't that be a kick in the ass?

Taking JC had been easy. The fool would lend a hand to anybody who asked. JC had followed him out the highway like a lamb to slaughter. He was probably uncomfortable trussed up like a chicken with a hood over his head, but that was too damn bad.

Not killing him had been hard. The original plan to beat the stupid sonofabitch to death in his bed with a bat was a sweet one. But the hornets had settled, and like a miracle, a new plan came out of the blue. JC would be the main player in the scenario that was about to unfold.

"You working today? Or standing around staring into space?" the boss griped.

"Ease up, man. I finished replacing the alternator." How sweet was it? He was working on his next doll's car.

****

"Stand up and let me check for you," Sue said from the doorway.

"Check what?" Matt swallowed the last of his cold coffee. Humor danced in her eyes. She was up to something.

"I figured the mayors chewed most of your ass clean off." She did her usual eyebrow wiggle. "Want me to check for you?"

"Your heart couldn't stand it."

"Both looked pretty upset when they stormed by me."

"They felt compelled to repeat the concerns of their constituents. What you got there?" He reached for the thick envelope in Sue's hand.

"Afternoon delivery. From the FBI."

"Already? It's barely been a week."

"They're obviously not as busy as you." She stopped at the door. "You want me to send Ash or Jake in?"

He considered her question for a full heartbeat. "Not yet."

Sue nodded and closed the door behind her.

Matt read the profile and reviews of similar cases the BAU team provided. The Special Agent in Charge had included a personal letter, making himself available for phone conferences and extended the use of any resource his division had to offer.

The feds concurred with Matt's original opinion. The common eye color, gluing the eyes open, along with the bow around the neck, indicated the killer targeted a particular look. He could be replacing someone he lost recently. A wife or lover who'd been taken from him through divorce, death, or separation. When his victim disappointed or didn't live up to expectations, he killed and started his hunt again.

Matt headed down the hall to the small conference room where Ash and Jake had set up shop. Six weeks ago, the room was barren except for the table, chairs, and a blank white board. Now a bustling city about to overflow had been born. The murder-book and phone sat in the middle of the conference table surrounded by stacks of files, disks, notes, a coffee pot, and at least a dozen markers. The board had 'before' pictures of two healthy and alive women on one end. A picture of Jessie—because she was considered missing—was taped to the other. In the middle were the 'after' snapshots of two green- eyed women who stared out into space. Together they waited for justice.

Matt handed the package to Jake then kicked back in his chair. "I'm going home in a few minutes to catch a few hours sleep. This killer works under the cover of darkness, which means I'm working the late shift for a while."

"Adding another patrol car to nights is a good idea. But I'll do it," Jake said without a hint of displeasure at changing his hours.

"No. You have a family. I don't. There's no reason I can't work the—" Matt stopped in mid- sentence. He'd moved his stuff to Catherine's house. Shit. He should've insisted she stay at his place. Insisted? With Catherine, insisting was the equivalent of a matador waving his red cape at a bull.

"The answer is obvious," Ash chimed in. "I'll do it."

"You can't. I'm sure you've noticed we don't have street lamps and all night gas stations at every corner for you to stop and get directions. You'd get out there and get lost."

"And you'd be worried about me." Ash laid his hand over his heart. "I'm touched."

"No, I'd be short one patrol car, because my men would be out hunting you."

"Let's do this," Jake said. "I'll take weeknights. You work the weekend shift."

"Works for me." Matt stared at the closed door for a second before turning to Ash. Apparently, the discussion was over.

Ash shifted in his chair. "You'll be on patrol while Catherine's at work. I'll hang out at the Saddleback and keep an eye on her from inside."

"How thoughtful of you," Matt said on his way out of the room.

"Want to see the front page?" Sue caught his attention with a wave. "You made the headlines."

"More good news." He snapped the paper open. Sure enough, the County Record had a picture of him looking down at someone from the top of the courthouse steps. In the bottom corner of the shot, Catherine faced him with a big smile. Matt leaned a hip on Sue's desk and read the article on the front page. "I see the newspaper decided to join Sylvia Horning in questioning my ability as sheriff."

"The paper is repeating the same crap she said on the noon news."

Sue's disgusted tone left little doubt she was displeased with the article. The pat of her hand on his back made reading about his ineptitude easier. "She said I left Houston because I couldn't cut it? Out loud?" His jaw tightened.

"She mostly insinuates and suggests. She's too smart to outright accuse you or make firm statements. She's hashed the failure of your undercover operation in Houston until no one knows the real story. I hate to admit it, but maybe you should let her interview you. Put a stop to the rumors."

He dropped the paper on her desk. "She'll stop when I catch the killer. As will the rest of the media."

****

Steam clouded the bathroom mirror. Catherine wasn't sure if the hot water or the incredible sex she and Matt had during their shower caused the fog. She leaned across the counter to rub a spot dry with her towel. The handsome reflection behind her sent her heart into freefall. Having Matt all to herself Monday night had been wonderful. Sex, a quiet supper, and more sex. A woman couldn't ask for anything more.

She'd planned on having a long truthful talk with him. She'd rehearsed in her head all day. The belief he'd listen to her and not judge gave her courage. Her good intentions had fallen by the wayside when he'd carried her to bed and made slow, leisurely love to her. His incredible mouth had driven her to the brink of insanity then gently pushed her over the edge.

Strong hands slid up her back to her shoulders. He wouldn't find any knots or tension in her muscles. If she were more relaxed, her already weak legs would fold up like venetian blinds. "God. You're beautiful." Matt's voice was thick and husky. "You wanted to talk to me last night." He turned her around and kissed her lightly. "But I sidetracked us."

"We sidetracked each other."

"A couple of times." His gaze slid across her chest, down to the red tuft of hair between her legs, and back up to her face. He ran one finger down her belly. "I can do two things at once. Can you talk and come?"

"No," she said on a chuckle. "And I don't want to be rushed when we talk."

"Sounds serious." One hand closed over her nipple, and his lips pulled the other into his mouth.

"We'll talk at supper tonight."

He swept her into his arms, carried her to the kitchen, and sat down. He lifted her, swung her around in one motion, and held her above his erection. Catherine seated herself, burying him deep inside.

A faint buzzing disrupted her attention. She tried to block out the distraction, but the sound was relentless. Matt's cell was about to bounce off her nightstand.

Sighing, she kissed his forehead. "Your phone's vibrating. It might be important."

Deep blue eyes filled with passion shifted to serious mode. His crooked smile evaporated, and his mouth turned down at the corners in disappointment. "You make me a better sheriff."

Her cell rang out her favorite Elvis tune. Something important had happened. Catherine reluctantly stood and stepped back. "If mine's ringing this early, they're hunting you." She rushed back, grabbed both phones, answered hers as she handed Matt his. "Hello," she said.

Ash launched into an apology.

She interrupted. "He's on his cell. Do you want to hold?"

"No. He's probably talking to Rey. He'll bring Matt up to speed. Tell him I'll meet him at the courthouse."

"Okay." She was speaking to dead air.

Ash was a different man when things were all business. His persona changed like Matt's when he received news of a crime. Stoic, rigid, and all cop. Her heart broke at the pain in his eyes.

Matt disconnected. His expression was the picture of doom. She asked if Jessie had been found. He nodded his head before heading for the bedroom. She repeated the message from Ash while they dressed.

The sight of Matt in uniform sliding his gun in place sent shivers of pride over her body. His belief in right and wrong was strong. His face was heavy with the strain of losing another person he'd sworn to protect. A narrowed gaze filled with tornadoes and dark thunderheads met hers. His face was that of a stone cold hunter.

"Matt." She went to him, stood toe to toe, and cupped his face in her hands. He hadn't shaved and stubble scratched the inside of her palms as she held him. He lowered his forehead to hers, inhaled and exhaled a couple of times, before kissing the tip of her nose.

"They found Jessie leaning against an old Civil War marker out on county road thirteen fifty-seven. I don't know what time I'll be back tonight."

"Go. I'll be careful. And I'll put Emma on high alert." Her heart clenched when he managed a slight smile.

She watched from the porch as he covered his jet-back hair with his hat and then slid behind the wheel of the jet-black pickup. He'd backed to the end of the driveway when he stopped. He drove forward, put the gearshift in park, and stared at her for a long minute.

Barefoot and curious, she stepped off the tiny porch. Matt got out and in ground-covering strides came to her. He put his hands under her arms, lifted her to eye level, and let her dangle for a second. Laser blue eyes seemed to probe deep into her soul. He put her down. The hunter's gaze tempered with softness melted her heart.

"I think I'm in love with you." Without waiting for a response, he spun on his heel and left.

****

Matt parked the cruiser. He and Ash walked to where Jessie's body had been propped upright against the cement base of the marker.

"Jesus H. Christ," Ash muttered. "It's a fucking wonder she was ever found. Who puts a historical monument in the middle of nowhere?" Ash said to Rey Santos, who was waiting at the scene.

"It wasn't 'nowhere' a hundred years ago, " Rey answered. " Old man Forrester came out to hay his cattle. With the drought, there's no pasture to graze, only thing they're eating is what he feeds them. Otherwise, it might've been days," Rey answered.

"We'll be here a while." Matt carefully moved around the scene. "Sue contacted the ME's office for me and then lined up a deputy to lead the forensic team out here."

"Not much for them to do," Rey commented. "They won't find useable tracks or footprints on this hard red clay." The murders had pushed his frustration level to high.

Matt squatted then rolled back on his boot heels. He studied the body. He was aware of Rey taking pictures and Ash moving around with his notepad in hand, but he tuned out all external sights and sounds. Jessie deserved his full, undivided attention, exactly like Julia and Annie.

Like the two previous victims, Jessie's hair had been pulled back in a ponytail. Her face appeared to be heavily powdered with a color much lighter than her natural tone. No amount of makeup could hide the purple bruises covering her face. Whoever this bastard was, he liked that crimson lipstick, because Jessie's lips were smeared with the stuff. Why the red ribbon around the neck? Matt stood and walked behind the body. No doubt, he'd find the same kind of raw streaks on her as Julia and Annie.

Ash joined him. "Jessie wasn't whipped like the first two."

"Doesn't appear to be as many welts across her back and legs," Matt agreed.

"That bastard used her face for a punching bag. My guess is she fought back, and he lost his temper. Why else would he change his pattern?"

"You're right. It's something different every time. He's unsure or is still perfecting his methods." Matt ran the earlier cases through his mind. "She must've initially put up a fight, and he beat the shit out of her. Then she tried to play his game. Jessie was street savvy, smart enough to know the more she protested the worse the situation would get."

Ash pointed his pen at Jessie's hand. "Check out her fingernails."

"Yeah. I'll bet she scratched the bastard, and he cut off her fingernails. With any luck, she left us his DNA. We'll have every deputy watch for anybody with scratches."

Ash circled the perimeter a second time. He'd pace and think. Walk and study. Commit the scene to memory. While Ash leaned against the hood of Rey's car and worked on his notes, Matt retrieved the sheet Dr. Reinhardt had given him after he'd completed Annie's autopsy.

"I'm going back to town and break the news to Vince," Matt said while he covered the body. "No need making him wait."

"Not alone." Ash's expression left no room for argument.

****

The wait for the ME's men turned into an endurance test. Matt and Ash returned from a grueling hour with Vince to find Matt's small team still working by themselves.

"How's Vince?" Rey crossed the short distance to Matt.

"Not good," Matt answered. "Luckily, he wasn't alone. You guys find anything?"

"Nothing but flies."

Rey fell in step with Ash when Matt peeled off and circled the scene to speak to the rest of his team. The sun beat down on the red clay road and bounced back, sending ripples of heat across the horizon. Cattle fought off the heat and buzzing flies by swatting at them with their tails while bunched under scrub oak trees, which provided no real shade.

Ash hadn't been out in the sun long before he complained that his extra-long appendage couldn't be used to fight flies. Decency forced him to tolerate the irritating pests all day. It was a claim Matt and Rey exchanged glances over and chose to ignore.

The high wind sandblasted exposed skin. By the time the forensic crew drove away with the body, Ash was threatening to kill one of the rancher's steers and cook the damn thing for supper.

"I'd like you to tell me how you managed to survive the day and not look like shit." Ash glared at Rey and then finished the bottle of water one of the forensic team had provided.

"It's in the genes. The heat doesn't bother me." Rey didn't look like he'd crossed the Sahara on foot. Ash looked like he'd tried and failed. Matt knew when to keep his mouth shut.

Chapter Twenty-Four

JC was still alive. Groggy, but alive. Shit, he'd talked nonstop since the trailer door opened. Thankfully, safely tucked away in Mama's closet, his ramblings were muffled.

Apparently, men were no different from women, because they all asked the same question. Why are you doing this? Over and over again.

He restrained himself from opening the door and kicking the shit out of JC to shut him up. The plan was working, and now wasn't the time to fuck things up. He slid on a pair of gloves, grabbed JC's feet, and pulled him into the living room. Answering his questions would be fun, and since he'd be dead shortly, the bag could come off.

JC blinked repeatedly. Inside that closet was dark and must've been pitch black with the bag over his head.

"What happened?" JC shook his head like a dog.

"You were kidnapped." That was as honest an answer as he could give.

"I don't get it. If this is a joke, it's not funny."

"I'm not laughing am I?" Interesting how calm he felt now the time to kill JC had come. He'd jumped at every sound all day long, like somebody might read his mind. The jitters were gone, probably because his plan was perfect.

"The fun's over." JC huffed out through clenched teeth. "Untie me. Right now."

"Stop struggling. You can't have rope burns." He spoke in a calm, level tone but pulled the pistol and pointed it at JC's head. The slime ball needed to know the seriousness of the situation.

"I what? Untie me, goddammit. I gotta piss."

He flipped open his pocket knife and sliced the rope, freeing JC's feet while keeping the gun steady. "Get up and listen closely. You walk down that hall and take a leak. Remember, I'll be watching. You fuckin' flinch, and I'll put a bullet in your head."

JC's legs wobbled as he got his feet under him and stumbled to the john. He turned and held his hands out. "I can't do this with my hands tied."

Fuck. He studied a minute, could JC maneuver all the steps without help? Holding his dick for him wasn't an option, but he didn't want piss all over the trailer either. "Sit down on the floor."

"What?"

"Are you deaf? Sit down." He went to the kitchen and returned with a knife. "When I cut the rope you roll over on your belly. Understand?"

"Why?"

The cold steel of the .380 against JC's temple silenced any argument. "Ready?" JC obeyed instructions, his eyes darted around looking for an escape route.

"Now what?" JC asked from his down-facing position.

"Crawl in the bathroom and sit on the toilet. Remember I'm watching. If you want to die sitting on the toilet, make the wrong move."

None of this was in the plan, and the time wasted ate into his schedule. He had to get things moving before the whole thing turned into a cluster- fuck. He wound up seeing a lot more of JC's anatomy than he wanted before JC finally zipped his jeans and crawled back into the hall. Belly down, he held his hands over his head and retied them. The extra precautions were necessary. JC wasn't stupid. He'd do his best to find an opening and break free. *Not happening.*

Catherine had better appreciate everything he was doing for her.

"We're taking a ride." He forced JC into his pickup.

The rest of the night had been planned carefully. Obeying the speed limits, he drove out to the site where he'd left Julia Drummond and parked. It was a bit of a drive from the trailer, not too bad of a hike back, all he had to do was cut through a few pastures.

"Get out." He stood back and waited.

JC gulped the night air while his gaze sorted out his location. The stench of nervous sweat had filled the air inside the pickup. His jaw twitched. "You crazy motherfucker, when I get my hands on you, you'll think twice before you pull shit like this again."

The point of the gun shoved hard against JC's spine drove home who was in charge. The stupid bastard still thought this was some kind of a joke.

"Sit at the base of the sign post."

"Why are you doing this? I've never done anything to you," JC whined, as if it would do any good.

"You brought this on yourself. You should've left Catherine alone."

"What?" His eyes bugged, the pale moonlight glinted off the fear. "I didn't mean any harm. I'd never hurt her. Come on, we can talk this over."

"You picked the wrong woman." His index finger tightened on the trigger. "Catherine is mine." A single pop and it was done.

JC slumped to the side. Shit, the report of the .380 in the night air was louder than he'd expected. His heart raced and the hornets roared louder. He pushed the buzzing to the recesses of his mind. This was a busy highway during the daytime, and time was of the essence. He had to follow the schedule.

He ran the plan through his mind, and his body followed the commands. Not to worry. He had everything under control. He retrieved Julia's blouse from the pickup and slid it under JC's hands. He untied the knot around his wrists, then slowly pulled the rope free. Holding the soft piece of silk to his nose, he breathed deeply— remembering his first doll—then he shook it hard into the wind. He tucked the blouse in JC's left hand. The gun went in JC's right hand.

The sheriff would find articles of clothing from Annie and Jessie inside JC's pickup. The cab and steering wheel were wiped down. Now, all he had to do was disappear into the night.

He'd grown up hunting in this area and knew to skirt around the thickets. As he walked, he replayed tonight's events through his mind. Would the sheriff buy it? At first blush, hell yes, everybody would believe for a few days. And that's all the time he'd need.

****

Matt drove under the glare of the lights and up the driveway Catherine referred to as the runway. He stepped out of his pickup and crossed the walk into her open arms.

"You shouldn't have waited up." He leaned down and buried his face in the tumble of wild, red curls. She smelled of vanilla and home. "Damn, I'm glad you did."

She led him inside by the hand. Again, the thought hit him that he'd follow her anywhere if it meant she'd put her arms around him one more time.

"Have you eaten?"

Matt had to think about the question. "Yeah. Ash went after burgers. I probably smell like onions."

She stood on her toes and kissed him. Ran her tongue across her lips. "Nope. Coffee."

"I'm sorry—"

"Don't be. I like coffee."

"I said I'd be here. With you. To make you feel safe. I failed."

She waved him off with a flick of her wrist. "Please. I don't expect you to be here every minute of the day and night. Come to bed. You need to rest."

One of the many things he liked about her was she never pressed him...never made demands. She accepted him. Understood the requirements of the job. She waited until he was ready. Tonight he was especially grateful, because there were no words for the frustration and the anger eating away at him.

He kissed her lightly. A quick peck, a small taste of her soft lips, anything more, and he'd forget he smelled worse than a man on a ten-day-drunk. He knocked at exhaustion's door, reaching the point of bone weary. Yet his need to make love to her, to hear her cry out his name threatened his resolve to get some rest.

"I'm hitting the shower. I expect you to be asleep when I get out. I'm not the only one who gets up early."

"Yes, sir." She saluted and swished her way down the hall.

Matt stripped off his badge, watch, and gun then emptied his pockets on the kitchen table. He made a beeline to the bathroom and shed his grimy uniform, which he'd sweat through several times today. Once in the shower, he put both hands against the wall while hot water sluiced across the back of his head rinsing some of the grit and stench of the day off.

Once again, the killer had left no visible clues. Matt's hopes rested on Jessie's fingernails. He prayed the ME might find skin under them. The forensic people had bagged her hands, and the ME would scrape for DNA samples during autopsy. Obtaining DNA results took months and then only produced a suspect if the bastard was in the system.

He laughed when he caught a glimpse of himself in the mirror. The junkie's living around the shipyards in Houston weren't any grosser. He rubbed his hand down his cheek. This was way past stubble, and the circles under his eyes matched the color of the hair on his face. When he finished shaving, he moved quietly down the hall into the bedroom. At last, his body hit the cool sheets, and Matt breathed out a sigh when his head sunk into the pillow. Catherine turned toward him, rested her hand over his heart, and rubbed a small circle. Her touch steadied his world, calmed his ragged nerves, and soothed the pain in his temples. The rumbling volcano of need woke, and he reached for her.

Wordlessly, she slid on top and took him inside.

****

Catherine pulled on her robe and peeked out the window to her front porch. Ash with his cold eyes and gritted teeth could only mean bad news. The pounding on the front door hadn't fazed him. She pulled the door open, blocking entrance with her body.

"Is he up?" Ash asked, stepping closer.

Matt looked rough last night, but not compared to Ash today. His disheveled hair and sunburn made him appear gaunt and harsh. Her heart physically hurt at the thought of waking Matt. He'd promised to protect the public—well, who protected him? She would if necessary.

"Shh," Catherine whispered. "No. He's not. I didn't disturb him." She balled her hands into fists and glared at Ash. "He's exhausted. Can't you give him a few hours to himself?"

His gaze narrowed, impatience flitted across his face. He studied her for a minute and then closed his eyes. When he looked at her again, he appeared to be better composed. In fact, he sort of smiled. He might as well, because he hadn't frightened her one bit. She was ready to fight to get Matt some rest.

"I'm glad you want to take care of him. Let me assure you, he wants to hear the news. Now go disturb his beauty sleep." He cocked his head at an angle, waiting.

Damn she hated to yield. Ash had something important to tell Matt, and she had no right to refuse. She stepped back, allowing Ash inside. He surprised her by walking past her into her kitchen, where he began opening cabinet doors.

"Make yourself at home," she whispered.

"Catherine. Somebody died last night—"

"I'm aware Jessie's body was found."

For the second time, he narrowed his gaze and glared at her. He opened his mouth then snapped it shut. What was he not saying?

"Say it," she challenged him.

"JC was found dead this morning."

His razor sharp words stabbed through her chest walls and sucked the oxygen from her lungs. Her mind refused to register his words. He couldn't possibly be right. JC dead? She walked to the cabinet, pulled out the coffee canister, and handed it to Ash. Moving on autopilot, she went to wake Matt.

She knelt by the bed and kissed his closed eyelids. Her heart squeezed and tears found their way to the surface. Unchecked they ran down her cheeks. "Matt. Wake up." Her hands trembled when she shook his shoulder and called his name again. "Matt."

His eyes snapped open. "What's wrong?"

"Ash is waiting for you in the kitchen." She couldn't force additional words from her mouth, not without breaking down. How could JC be gone?

Matt was up and on the side of the bed so fast she lost balance, and he grabbed her arms to steady her. Fully awake, he pulled her chin up higher so he could see her face.

"Tears?" He brushed her wet cheeks with his thumbs while icy blue eyes searched hers. "Ash made you cry?"

"Something's happened. I'll let him tell you." She pulled away from him, held her emotions in check, and returned to the kitchen while Matt dressed. Ash had started the coffee pot and sat waiting.

"I'm sorry if I leaned on you too hard. Matt would expect me to come get him."

Ash's tone hit her raw nerves like an acid wash. "If you'd leaned too hard, you'd know it. Matt's dressing."

"I know this death is a big shock."

"Who's dead?" Matt filled the doorway. Hair disheveled and half dressed, his presence commanded attention.

"JC Harper was found dead a couple of hours ago." Ash's tone was blunt and to the point. Flat without emotion.

Matt's gaze shifted to her. His hand caressed her shoulder. "You want us to take this outside?"

"No. I'd like to listen."

"I don't see why not." Matt pulled a chair out for her and then turned his attention to Ash. "What do you know so far?"

"I haven't seen for myself. I'm told it's an apparent suicide. Rey caught the call, said to tell you the body was at the drop site where Julia was found."

Matt scrubbed his hand through his hair. "Let's get out there."

"There's more." Ash shifted his gaze directly at her then back to Matt. "According to Jake, JC may have been our killer."

Catherine blinked back the tears. "I don't believe it. JC wouldn't hurt anyone."

"We're all capable of murder...given the right circumstances." Ash stood and started opening cabinet doors again.

"No," she argued. "He was too sincere when we talked."

"You talked about the killings?" Matt asked.

"I told you. The day the package was left at the funeral home. JC and I talked when I was in town. He was sick to think you could possibly believe he would kill anybody."

"He had items of women's clothing in his pickup." Ash poured three cups of coffee and passed one to her and Matt.

"I'll meet you at the office." Matt blew on his steaming coffee, turned, and left Ash with Catherine.

"Did he tell me to get lost?" Ash sat his untouched cup down.

"Sounded like it." She made an effort to smile. She closed the door behind Ash. Numbness seeped through her limbs. Putting one foot in front of the other, she joined Matt in her bedroom. He'd moved at record speed and was fully dressed. Catherine went to her closet and stood staring. He pulled her to his chest and tried to soothe her. She couldn't relax because given the opportunity, she'd fall apart. To prevent that from happening she retreated inward. She was an old hand at handling grief and pain on her own.

"Will you be all right?" His eyes searched across her face, no doubt looking for reassurance.

"No problem. Go. I've got to get to work myself." She mindlessly grabbed a pair of slacks and blouse.

He kissed her on the tip of her nose, and then he was gone. She sagged down on the bed and dropped her head in her hands. With so much happening, there was never a good time to tell him about her past.

She pulled herself together, dressed for work, and went out to Emma's old Lincoln. With a twist of the key, the car hummed like it was brand new. When the air conditioning instantly cooled the inside air, Catherine drove away not missing her old Ford one bit.

By the time she parked in the rear of the funeral home, she'd made progress at sorting out the news. That was until a name flashed through her mind. Marty. Had anyone called Marty?

Chapter Twenty-Five

"I understand the body is male. You have an ID?" Reporter Steve Evers stood between Matt and the crime scene. "Any comments?"

"One. Move." Matt's glare sent the County Recorder reporter to the side of the road.

"And stay behind the yellow tape unless you want to write your column from jail," Ash called out. He returned to his solitary inspection.

Matt went directly to where Dave Foster and Hector Ruiz stood over JC's body. Matt hated to be late, but Jake and Rey had things under control. The perimeter had been secured, and extra deputies kept a watchful eye on the gathering crowd.

"Foster. Ruiz." Matt spoke to the forensic experts. "I appreciate you getting here so fast."

"Sheriff," Ruiz acknowledged Matt's arrival. "Dr. Reinhardt is in route. Dave called him after we found evidence that might connect the dead guy to the recent homicides. He's staying on top of the doll murders."

"He's on top of something," Ash commented when he passed behind the group.

Matt caught Ash's reference to the ME leaking information to Sylvia Horning. He and Ash exchanged knowing glances, but he didn't speak. He didn't care how Sylvia wormed the information out of Reinhardt. Forgiving the breach of trust wasn't on the horizon.

Matt squatted and studied the body. A chill stirred the hair on his arms in spite of the sweat cascading down his back. A bullet had entered JC's right temple and exited the left side taking brain matter and bone with it. Matt pulled in a lungful of air when a question popped into his mind. Was there any significance that JC's hazel eyes were damn close to being green?

"No note? Confession?" Matt asked.

"Nada. It's never that easy." Ruiz looked up from bagging JC's hands.

"What'd you find tying him to the murdered women?"

"There's a silk blouse in his hand," Foster supplied the answer.

"So? It's too early to make such a broad statement." Matt needed a lot more proof.

Rey moved to Matt's side. "There's another blouse and a pair of women's panties in the glove compartment. All different sizes."

"Shit." Ash looked up from taking notes. "I liked the sonofabitch."

"I've known him for years. Easy going, everybody's friend. He'd give you the shirt off his back." Jake spoke for the first time. Disappointment mingled with anger in his eyes. He blew out a sigh. "I'd have trusted him with my sister."

Matt didn't know what to say. Trust was a fragile thing to him. Jake would have to work past his disillusionment. "You about finished here?" he asked Ash. "I want to take a look inside JC's house."

"Let's ride." Ash strode to Matt's cruiser without saying goodbye to anyone.

"Jake, when you and Rey wrap things up here, let Ruiz and Foster follow you to JC's. We'll meet you there." Matt wanted a look around before anyone else. Something nagged at him. Like Ruiz had said, life wasn't this easy. A couple of articles of clothing didn't sew this case up for Matt.

The television news van and the ME's car arrived at the same time Matt started the cruiser. The sixty-something-year-old Reinhardt exited his vehicle and hurried toward the young blonde reporter. Not much about JC's death would be kept from the press.

"What's eating you?" Ash asked after they got out on the highway. He pulled the sun visor down, opened the mirror, poking at his sunburned skin with his finger.

"I told you to wear a hat."

"So you did. What's eating you?" Ash repeated the question.

"I wasn't ignoring you. I don't have an answer to give you."

"Talk it out. Like we used to. No wisecracks if I get melancholy about days gone by."

"You have a permanent badge here with me whenever you want one." Matt reminded him.

"I was thinking more along the lines of you returning to civilization. After you get married, Catherine might be happier in the big city."

"When did we quit discussing the case and start talking about my personal life?"

"You started it by mothering me over my sunburn."

Matt would miss the camaraderie if the case was over and Ash went back to Houston. Crest County was home for Matt, and he hadn't given any thought as to how Catherine felt about the area. Maybe he should. But marriage? That was a whole other ball game.

Matt kicked off the brainstorming with a question. "Let's say, for the sake of argument, JC killed all three women. He was careful not to leave one shred of evidence. Nothing. He was super cautious. Then he up and kills himself. Why?"

"I think I'm supposed to say he felt guilty, but I'm still having trouble believing JC killed anybody."

"And wasn't it considerate of him to off himself in the same place he left the first body. A location every person in the county read about. If that weren't enough, he provided us lots of clues. A couple of blouses and a pair of panties happened to be with him."

"Sounds too convenient."

"We'd have been blind fools not to put two and two together." Matt parked in front of JC's house. The trellis was bare. Obviously, the scraggly roses Matt noticed a month ago had perished in the dry heat.

Matt and Ash put on gloves as they exited the car. Ash walked the length of the porch and disappeared around back.

Matt tried the door and found it locked as expected. JC's house was like Catherine's, old and easy to get into. A good shoulder push would do it.

He froze. Somebody was inside the house. He stepped back, unsnapped his holster, his hand automatically resting on his Glock. A figure appeared, and the door opened.

"Shit, Ash. I could've shot you." Matt rubbed his hand across his face.

"Then you'd have to take care of me. You know...payback."

Matt did know. Ash was joking, but Matt would never forget the physical therapy sessions with Ash egging him on, challenging him to do more. "Maybe I will shoot you next time. I wouldn't mind getting to call you sissy, wimp, and your favorite...pussy boy."

Ash grimaced. "Did I call you a wimp? I'm sorry, man."

The two men worked in unison. Sparsely furnished, the living room hadn't changed since Matt's last visit. Neither noticed anything of interest. Ash took off toward the bedrooms, and Matt went to the kitchen. He was staring at beer, milk and something that might be green bologna when Ash exploded with a stream of cuss words.

"Sonofabitch." Ash's expletive echoed down the hallway. "Come take a look at this."

Matt walked into the bedroom and then stumbled backward a step. Adrenaline pumped through him at supersonic speed. Bile rose up in the back of his throat and for a second, rage blinded his vision. Never in a million years would he have thought JC capable of this. The bastard had been right under his nose all the time. He removed his hat, dragging his fingers through his hair.

A shrine to Catherine filled one wall. Snapshots of her in different locations, wearing different outfits were tacked side-by-side and on top of the other. Matt forced his hands to remain at his sides when what he wanted to do was rip them to shreds. A digital camera sat on a small table, accompanied by a neat stack of snapshots. Matt spread them with the finger of a gloved hand. They were pictures of male body parts. No doubt to go with future gifts. Bile filled the back of his throat. He wanted ten minutes alone with this bastard alive. Matt pulled himself out of the gathering fog.

"There's a box of clothes here on the floor." Ash had knelt down on one knee, half in, and half out of the closet. "Odds and ends. And they're not his."

Matt looked over Ash's shoulder at the assortment of women's wear. "The forensic techs can take them to the lab. I want pictures to show the families of the murder victims. If they ID them—"

Rey calling Matt's name pulled his attention to the front porch. "Come on, Ash. Let's get out of here.

Give these guys some space." Maybe it was an excuse, Matt didn't care. He needed fresh air. JC's bedroom was closing in on him.

Jake and Rey waited in the front yard with Foster and Ruiz until Matt brought him up to speed on what he and Ash had found inside the house. Foster shifted his collections kit to the other shoulder and inched toward the house, eager to get to work.

"We'll get you the clothes as soon as they're processed," Foster said. "No need making the families drive to San Antonio."

"I want to know everything about JC, all his secrets. If he was the killer, he had a hiding place. I have to find it."

"You got it." Foster and Ruiz headed inside the house.

Ruiz turned back to Matt. "Dr. Reinhardt went back to San Antonio with the body. Said to tell you Jessie Bradley's autopsy will be as scheduled. He's got a couple ahead of JC, couldn't give you a date on him."

"Hell, he performs more than one a day, doesn't he?" Matt's patience with the good doctor was thin. If he had time to talk to the press, he had time to work on JC.

"Sorry. He's got a double homicide on the slab. The mayor of San Antonio's all over us wanting results." Ruiz raised his hands in surrender. "I'm telling you what the man said."

****

"Another reason to not work in the boonies," Ash announced after he bid goodbye to his new lady friend in the drugstore.

"What's that?" Matt paid the tab for lunch. The coffee shop had become one of Ash's favorite hangouts. There was more involved here than larger portions. Matt didn't question the frequency of their visits, because the eye contact and body language between Ash and the waitress told enough.

"Small town equals low priority. The mayor of San Antonio gets what he wants before you small town boys."

"Small town equals less crime. Until recently." Matt responded to the eye roll he had no doubt Ash had given him. "I'm going to lean on Reinhardt. I need a firm ruling on cause of death for JC."

"You haven't told Catherine what we found at his house. She should know."

"I'm going now. If you need me, I'll be at the funeral home." Matt stopped after they crossed the street. No need in climbing the stairs to his office.

"I thought you might. Remind her she's introducing me to her friend. Susan? Yeah. Susan."

"You're such a whore-dog." Matt laughed as he crossed the parking lot to his cruiser.

The drive allowed him to gather his thoughts. He welcomed the quiet time. It helped to rewind and move through the day again in his mind. Begin at the beginning, his old Chief would've said. Clichéd? Maybe. But it worked.

That he'd interviewed JC twice ate at Matt's insides. Been in the man's living room for Christ's sake. The man had come across as sincere and shocked when Matt insinuated JC might've killed Julia. The two had dated some time back, not recently. A "long time ago" was JC's timeframe. Shit, he did mention giving her stuff. What was it he'd said? "I bought her stuff, and she liked it. I think maybe that was all she liked about me." Was he covertly admitting he stalked her? When he discovered she only cared about the presents, did he get angry enough to kill her? If so, why'd he wait so long? What set him off?

Matt and his deputies had questioned the families and friends of the three victims, asked more than once if the women had received gifts or been stalked. Tomorrow he'd ask them again.

The pieces of this puzzle wouldn't come together, but he wasn't finished. Later he'd get back to all the unanswered questions.

****

Catherine backed out of the supply closet to find Susan standing behind her. Catherine clapped her hand over her chest. "You startled me."

"At least you didn't go all Kung Fu on me."

"True. I shouldn't let my guard down."

"The sheriff's waiting for you in my office." Susan caught Catherine's hand and squeezed.

"Now you're scaring me. What else has happened?"

"Don't know. He said he had business with you." Catherine allowed herself to be led down the hall. She'd told Susan first thing this morning about JC's body being found. After all, the funeral home would probably be his next stop after the autopsy. The irony of the name Final Touch struck Catherine. How silly of her not to get it before.

Regardless of why he was here, her heart fluttered at the sight of Matt standing in the doorway of the office. His official stance and stern sheriff's face, sent the message that this was serious. He removed his hat and swiped the back of his hand across the ridge where the sweatband rode. His lopsided grin stole its way to the surface and made him more handsome.

"Hey."

"I'll be out here if you need something," Susan announced, then disappeared into the break room.

"Susan." Matt's voice was in the sheriff's mode. "Nobody knows for sure if JC killed anyone. That investigation's ongoing."

"Folks are saying guilt got the best of JC. I've known him off and on all my life. Hard to believe he went wrong." Susan paused. "I'll give you two some privacy."

"What's wrong?" Catherine hated to think or ask that out loud, but lately when he stopped by the funeral home, it wasn't for pleasure.

"Come sit down."

Something deep inside Catherine stirred when Matt closed the door. Stomach acid churned as nerves reacted to the unknown. She perched on the edge of a chair. He sat in front of her, their knees touching.

"What's wrong?"

"JC was your stalker."

Matt delivered the announcement with the skill of a surgeon. Quick and clean. Catherine's brain didn't register his meaning for a second.

"No." She wasn't disputing his word so much as she didn't want to hear them. JC was a friend. He was Marty's friend. She couldn't believe underneath that good-old-boy facade a heinous killer and demented stalker had been hiding.

"We found irrefutable evidence when we searched his house." Matt knelt in front of her and held her hands in his. "There's no doubt he was the stalker."

Disappointment morphed to disgust. Anger ignited every neuron, and every synapse in her brain fired like an overheated circuit board. Her skin felt the buzz of an electrical storm. Her thoughts ran in different directions. How could she have been so blind? What had she missed? She'd gotten into JC's pickup and ridden away with him.

"Breathe, honey. Breathe."

His voice touched her somewhere deep in her soul. Life refocused. His hand cupped her cheek, and his touch calmed the raging seas.

She did as he instructed and let some of the pent up air out of her lungs. "Did you call me 'honey'?"

"I don't know, did I?"

"You did. It's the first time you've called me by a nickname."

"Not really." One corner of his smile rose higher. "Occasionally, I call you Cat."

"Yes, you do." The tension in her shoulders relaxed. He was doing a great job of calming her. "Only in private."

"True. Are you all right now?"

"Yeah. Shocked. Madder than hell. Yeah, I'm fine."

"How's Marty?" he asked.

"Brokenhearted. She can't wrap her mind around the fact JC was a murderer or that he committed suicide. Telling her he was the stalker will crush her."

"If he was the killer, she'll survive. She'll be less trusting for a while. Who won't be?"

Matt's joints snapped and cracked when he stood. They shared a laugh at the noise. She didn't know about him, but it was the first bit of humor she'd found all day.

"If?" she asked.

"Just continue to exercise caution, and keep your guard up."

"Why? And why aren't you relieved this is over?" Catherine could've kicked herself for not noticing his apprehension sooner. As hard as he tried to appear calm, every tendon and muscle stood out rigid as an iron rail.

"I'm not convinced of anything other than the stalking is over. Too many unanswered questions surround JC's suicide. I can't officially call the murder cases closed. Not yet."

"The news is all over town."

"Catherine, this is confidential and stays in this room. We think Jessie scratched her killer. He cut off her fingernails, but the ME managed to find enough skin under her nails to get us a definitive answer."

"Did JC have any scratches?" She loosened the too-tight clip in her hair.

"No." Strong hands gripped her arms. "Don't jump to conclusions. Like I said, we think the killer was scratched."

"Thank you for trusting me."

"Of course. Pay attention to your surroundings. As I said, JC was the stalker. You deserved to know the truth right away."

In that one sentence, Matt reaffirmed his code of honor. His words "You deserve the truth right away" burned straight through her heart. She had to tell him.

His cell buzzed and the moment was gone. When he hung up, he stood, returning his chair to its original spot. "We're taking search dogs into the woods behind JC's house. If he had a hideout where he kept his victims, I've got to find it."

"You'll be home later?"

"I don't know. Until we find all the answers, things will be chaotic." He pushed a lock of hair behind her ear and kissed the tip of her nose. "Be safe."

Chapter Twenty-Six

Catherine pressed her breast deeper into his warm hand. She stretched and wiggled backward. Anything to get closer to the strength and power Matt's body radiated. "You should've let me know when you got home."

He pulled her hair away and kissed the soft spot behind her ear, a sensual spot sure to stir and tantalize her. "You needed a good night's rest."

"I did for a fact." There'd been no nightmares, no lights on the driveway, and no jumping at every noise. Renewed and refreshed, she rolled over on her back and studied his face. "You needed sleep as badly if not worse than I did. Why are you awake?"

"I wanted to connect the dots before we had to get out of bed." He straddled her. Keeping his weight on his arms, he kissed her forehead, then the tip of her nose. His tongue touched repeatedly in a pattern down to her neck.

She lifted her hips to help when he pulled her shirt off. "What dots?"

"The little tan ones...all over your body." His tongue flicked out and touched a freckle on her chest, then touched another before pausing to torment and nibble her nipple with his teeth. He tossed the covers to the floor. "And you have lots of them. Each one more fascinating than the other."

His raspy, sexy words coupled with the hungry flicks and licks sent desire coursing throughout her body. He pulled her breast into his mouth, leaving a needy, ridged peak when he continued his search.

"There's one." His gaze feasted, warming her skin. "Yes. There appears to be a string of them. Let's see where they lead me." A kiss here. A lick there. He shouldered her legs apart and worked his way down. Teasing her toward insanity. With one long stroke, he brushed across the cleft at the juncture of her thighs.

"I don't think you'll find a freckle there." She choked out the words trying to retain a semblance of sanity, yet hoping against hope he wouldn't be discouraged by not finding one.

"That's what you think." His slid his hands under her hips, raised her as if she weighed nothing, and plunged his glorious tongue inside her.

She cried out from sheer pleasure. She wanted time to stop and allow this sensation to go on forever. When he pressed his thumb into her flesh above his mouth, she completely lost control of her mind and body. Tremors shot through her, stars exploded behind her eyes, and she grasped his silky hair in her hands until her breathing slowed.

With gentle kisses, he worked his way back to her face. She wanted more. Catherine grasped his rigid erection and guided him to her. Eyes the color of midnight locked with hers as he joined their bodies and sank deep into her. Again and again. Her hips rose higher as the thrusts became frenzied. Harder. Faster. Deeper. She surprised herself as desire reignited. The fullness of him and the friction sent a new passion pouring through her body and soul. They moved as one, frantically searching for the end. Or was it the beginning? Together they found the threshold and exploded in a series of simultaneous, exquisite eruptions.

He kept the bulk of his weight on his arms while they both gasped for air. Then the buzzing started.

"Damn. I forgot to shut the alarm off." He shifted over and hit the button.

Catherine couldn't remember the last time she wanted to stay in bed, to be lazy and enjoy the day with another person. "You noticed Emma turned the runway lights off?"

"I did. I'm glad you both felt safe without them."

"I feel safe inside my little house." She laughed when he narrowed his gaze to slits. "And I'm watching my back."

"Good." His face relaxed, making him more handsome than ever. "I'm sorry I didn't call last night. We tried to search the thicket for a cabin. Between the mesquite trees, scrub oaks and undergrowth, there are some places we couldn't get through without shredding our arms and legs."

"If there's one out there, you'll find it."

"Thanks. Your vote of confidence means a lot." His lips touched hers, tender and gentle. "I'd better shower and get to the office. I've scheduled press conferences at ten-thirty. The press is trying to call this case closed. It's my responsibility to tell them the truth. Hell, I may give Sylvia Horning a personal interview."

"No time for breakfast?" She stood and slid on his T-shirt, one she'd taken over as her own.

He hit her with his lopsided smile, and her cheeks heated before he spoke a word.

"I had breakfast."

"Not much protein there." She dashed out of the room to the sound of his laughter. She'd come a long way, made friends with her sexuality, but could still be embarrassed by a sexy smile or an intimate phrase.

Catherine smoothed her hand over his T-shirt. She had to tell him about Andy. Tonight. There never seemed to be the perfect time.

The coffee was half-perked, but she poured him a cup, and handed it to him when he headed for the door. "You're beautiful in uniform. The camera will love you."

"Speaking of cameras. We made the front page. Did you see it?"

"No. When was this?" she asked, following him out onto the porch. Her stomach rolled and pitched. She didn't like the idea of her picture in the newspaper even if her past wasn't hot news anymore. It had been a big deal in Tulsa.

"I don't know. Yesterday? The day before? My days and nights have run together. We were in front of the courthouse. You were showing me Emma's Lincoln."

He pulled her close, wrapped his strong arms around her, and breathed deeply. When he stepped back, he dropped his forehead down to hers. "So help me. I'm coming in early tonight."

Catherine loved his routine where he leaned down for one last touch. She placed her hand on his chest and rubbed in a circle. His heart beat, strong and steady. For her. She believed there was a life here for the two of them. Her body filled with light. Her heart filled with peace and tranquility. Her soul filled with love for this man standing in front of her.

Catherine went up on her tiptoes, as tall as she could stand. Back straight, shoulders squared, she looked directly into his eyes. "I'm in love with you, too." She planted a quick kiss on his stunned face and then ran back in the house.

****

Matt stole a moment to enjoy the view from his office windows. The wind had picked up and gusts to forty miles an hour tossed dry leaves through the air like confetti. The weatherman's prediction a storm might blow through in the next couple of days gave Matt hope for a break in the heat.

"Be sure to smile for the camera. When they film the made-for-TV movie, they'll want the real deal for the part of the sheriff."

Matt read between the lines. He didn't need to see Ash's face to know his friend was looking toward Houston. Small town life would never appeal to him for long.

"If you think you're leaving, think again." Matt turned and joined Ash, who'd made himself at home with a piece of Sue's apple pie.

"Why not? Waiting around for Catherine to introduce me to this friend isn't a good reason to keep me on the payroll."

"We've got too many unanswered questions."

"You've got plenty of help." Ash pointed his fork at Rey, who nodded slightly as he walked past Matt's open door. "Although, I would still like to know why he doesn't look like shit. He spent all day in the sun yesterday and tromped through the woods with us last night."

Matt tried not to laugh at the pitiful sight before him. Weeks would pass before Ash's sunburn would heal, and the scratches on his arms looked downright painful. This morning Sue smeared some kind of ointment on him. Now his skin was not only red, it had a sickly shine. "You look like you had a fight with a wildcat and lost. I told you to wear long sleeves."

"Don't want to hear it." Ash waved his fork, sprinkling crust on the floor. "Not if you want me to stay."

"It's not in your DNA to leave before the autopsy results on Jessie and JC are back. Besides, you can't go back until you heal. You'd be too embarrassed to go work."

"Speaking of DNA, give your FBI guy a call. His letter offered help...well, have the ME's office send him some of the scrapings from under Jessie's fingernails. The feds can move stuff through the system faster than Reinhardt can. Hell, I'll have gray hair if we wait on him."

"True. I'll contact him after the press conference. Then we dig deeper. Prove or disprove JC had a sex den."

"Can't argue with that. He's the only suspect we have."

"Press room is filling up." Sue not only brought pie today, she'd worn a light blue skirted suit with a white ruffled blouse as opposed to her usual dress.

"You look nice today." Matt rethought his compliment when her eyes widened in question. "Not that you don't look beautiful every day.

"Nice recovery." She straightened her jacket with a snap of her wrists. "A friend suggested I'd mourned my husband long enough."

"The color matches your eyes," Ash interjected. "How long were you in mourning?"

"Nearly eighteen years." Never missing a beat, she turned to Matt. "Sylvia Horning is early. Insists she needs to share something with you."

"Good pie." Ash swallowed the last crumb. "Maybe Ms. Horning wants to make nice." He handed his empty plate to Sue. "Matt, if you're planning on staying in the boonies, a vendetta with the media is pointless."

"Show her in." No way was he doing this alone. "You." He pointed at Ash. "Stay. I'm not talking to her without a witness. The next thing you'll hear is how I harassed her." Matt drew a line in the air with his finger from Ash back to the chair. "Sit."

Minutes later the TV reporter glided into his office with a glint in her eyes and a false smile plastered across her face. She'd pulled her blond hair back in a severe knot. Dressed for success, she wore a navy blue corporate-cut suit. She set her briefcase on the small conference table and turned her on-air persona on Ash.

"Sylvia Horning, RBS news."

The air in Matt's office electrified, every hair on his body rose slightly and vibrated.

"Ash Hunter, best friend."

Ash's don't-fuck-with-me-tone and flat smile was a warning. He'd picked up on the negative energy in the room, too.

"Have a seat, Ms. Horning. You have something for me." Matt kept his voice friendly.

"Thank you for seeing me." She wiggled her too- tight-skirted ass down to a chair and pulled the case onto her lap. "I won't be attending the press conference. Since the mystery has solved itself, there's not much of a story. I might do something personal later. You know...a who was JC Harper retrospective."

"The case isn't closed. We haven't proven JC killed anybody. You had something to discuss?" Matt hadn't missed the drumming of her fingers on the aluminum briefcase. Had she uncovered something about JC's past everyone had missed? Something else to make him look inept?

Her smirk drove his curiosity further. She removed a small camcorder, flipped the viewer open, and then sat it on his desk with the screen facing him. Ash stood and moved around behind Matt's desk.

"I wanted to give you the opportunity to comment on my breaking news before I ran the story. You're aware I've been delving into your personal life. Doing a 'What makes the sheriff tick' series."

"I am. Sorry there was no big secret for you to uncover." His blood turned cold when she locked her gaze on his.

"There's always a secret. You have to look hard enough. When you and your girlfriend made the front page of the County Reporter...I did just that. I looked." She kept her eyes trained on him when she pushed the small button on the camera.

A newscaster he'd never seen before stood in front of what appeared to be a courthouse. Blonde like Ms. Horning, she wore the same type suit Horning wore today.

She shoved her microphone in front of a middle- aged couple. "Mr. Randall. How do you feel about the Grand Jury's decision not to prosecute?"

"It's a travesty of justice. She murdered our son." The gray-haired man's jaw clenched and released. Hate oozed from him as he spoke. "Andrew was a good man. A respectable member of the community. He wanted to divorce his insanely jealous wife." He folded the sobbing woman against his chest. "She killed him in cold blood."

Matt had seen enough. If Sylvia was making a point, she needed to make it quickly. So far, her tape held nothing of interest. Then someone off screen shouted, "There she is."

The reporters turned away from the couple. Like stampeding cattle, the media rushed the other direction. The camera panned the area and came to rest on a redheaded woman. She ran down the steps, pushing her way to a waiting taxi. She turned and looked in the direction of the horde for a fleeting second before disappearing into the cab.

The click of the camcorder snapping closed pulled Matt from the blackness surrounding him. He looked into Sylvia Horning's smiling face, unable to process a single word.

Ash moved between Matt and the reporter. "You vicious bitch. Get the fuck out of here before I throw your ass down the courthouse steps."

"Without a comment as to why our sheriff is living with a killer? No wonder he couldn't catch the Green-Eyed Doll murderer. He hides them from the public."

"Take your camera and leave." Matt forced himself to say.

"Keep it." She delivered one last smug curve of her lips. "My compliments."

Ash followed the newscaster out, closing the door behind him.

Matt opened the viewer and stared at the blank screen. This had to be a mistake, a cruel joke. He leaned closer, pushed Rewind, and then Play. He hit Stop when the crowd turned away from the couple and set the speed of the camera on slow motion.

He swallowed hard when the woman who'd made him believe in life and love appeared. Her wildfire hair glistened in the sunlight. Long legs carried her down the steps and into a cab. Matt ran the segment again and again.

His vision darkened...tunneled. A tightness spread across his chest. He'd shared his darkest secrets and professed his growing love to a stranger. A stranger who'd made a complete fool of him. His blood boiled and raged through his veins straight to his head.

He forced his eyes away from the nightmare on the screen. Matt pressed the heels of his hands to his temples and mashed. Someone knocked on the door, prompting him to close the camera and put it in his desk drawer. "Come."

Ash opened the door a fraction. His face a blank page, he'd shifted to protect mode. "I'm canceling the press conference."

"No fucking way. I'll be right there." Matt wouldn't duck and run. He had a job to do. He wasn't going to Catherine and demand she explain herself. Why should he? There was no acceptable explanation. She'd betrayed his trust. Lied about herself. Not only to the outside world...to him.

"You don't have to do this."

"Yes. I do." Matt's steady voice belied the turmoil raging inside.

Ash stepped inside and pulled the door closed, allowing Matt time to mentally pull himself together. The press conference was about three dead women and their families. They deserved him to stand for them.

He forced his hands to unclench. Swallowed the bitter bile hovering at the back of his throat and stood. His personal problems would wait. He closed his eyes, felt her soft caress on his face. A treacherous touch and a heart full of lies and deceit.

"Matt."

Ash stood between Matt and the door. Ash reached out and gripped his arm. The touch of another human being chilled his blood. He needed no man's pity. "Leave it alone."

Sue waited for Matt outside the conference room. "I served coffee, but they're getting restless. You better get in there."

"I'm going. After the press conference, I'll be out of the office for the rest of the day."

"Good, because you look worse than Ash."

Chapter Twenty-Seven

Catherine had successfully pushed her fear aside today and scratched another item off the *Never* list. She'd straightened her shoulders, walked to the back of the funeral home, and spent the afternoon helping Steve Abbott. They'd inventoried, categorized, and labeled his supplies, while she'd vanquished her abnormal fear of the mortician and his work area.

Tonight, she'd scratch the most important *Never* from the list. She'd share her past with Matt. Expose her most hidden of secrets. Her stomach had jumped and squirmed all day. Seeing his pickup parked in front of her house, a calm confidence came over her. Dredging up the years of abuse and describing how she'd killed her husband in self-defense would be hard. If she could trust anyone with the truth, it was Matt.

Tomorrow would be the first day of her new life. Catherine parked Emma's Lincoln in her garage for the last time. Her own car would be ready in the morning. Her savings would take a hit, but she'd pay for the repairs with her own money. She pulled the door open and rushed inside to Matt.

"Hey," she called. When he didn't answer, she walked into the kitchen. Matt stood with his back to her. The key Emma had given him lay on the table. A foreboding chill lodged in her heart. "Hey," she repeated.

He turned, and his face explained everything. A gasp rushed from her mouth.

He glared at her with eyes cold as a great white shark. Arms folded across his chest, the tendons in his neck bulged. Catherine's heart went into freefall. His chiseled jaw was set in a hard line, and one corner of his mouth twitched.

He knew.

Inside her body, every muscle liquefied. She groped for something to hang onto. She stumbled to the chair and gripped the back. "Matt. Say something."

"'Say' what, Catherine?" He advanced one menacing step.

He spit her name out with such venom she flinched as if he'd struck her.

"'Say' you're a liar? ' Say' I watched a news video today in which you were the star attraction?" He flicked his wrist as if shooing away something disgusting. "Why don't I 'say' what I came to? Goodbye."

"Wait. Please." She held her hand out to stop him. Her throat constricted. Mouth went dry. She swallowed and forced a whisper. "I tried to tell you."

"Did you? You didn't try too hard. You didn't grab me by the shoulders the first time we made love and insist I listen to you. You didn't run out to my pickup this morning to tell me, 'I love you, too. Oh, and by the way, I killed my husband,' so don't try now."

"I'm sorry," she choked out the only words in her heart.

He brushed past her and out the door unable or unwilling to respond to her.

Catherine closed her eyes and pictured him getting into his shiny black truck and driving out of her life forever. She clamped her hands over her mouth when a loud sob of unfathomable pain gushed from deep inside. She didn't run after him. How could she? Tears poured from her eyes. From her heart. From her soul.

She staggered to the bathroom with seconds to spare before collapsing on the tile floor and emptying the contents of her churning stomach in the toilet. Afraid to stand, she pushed herself upright into a corner, placed her back against the wall, and waited for the revulsion to hit again.

Catherine had spent plenty of time on the floor in years past, her spirit broken and confidence shaken, but she'd never felt such a loss. This pain was much greater than any beating she'd endured. This was her fault. Her willingness to lie, and her refusal to deal with the past had brought on this disaster. Her refusal to stand up for the truth had cost her the most important thing in her life. Matt's love.

A light tap on the front door forced Catherine off the bathroom floor. Had Matt returned? Was he willing to listen? The outline of Emma's small frame on the other side of the glass brought mixed emotions. Catherine didn't feel social. She opened the door prepared to brush Emma off, instead found herself gathered into a soft, loving hug. How could Emma have known she needed somebody?

Without speaking, Emma moved them to the couch where she cradled Catherine in her arms and let her weep. Her hand slid back and forth across Catherine's back, soothing and comforting.

"You were right. I should've spoken up. He never should've been blindsided this way," Catherine whispered.

"After that story ran on television, I worried a mite. Then he showed up here and loaded his stuff. His actions told the tale."

"Yeah. I broke his trust. Lied to him." Catherine had no trouble remembering his exact words.

"That Horning witch, she got curious who the sheriff was spending his time with instead of looking for a serial killer. She did some investigating and turned up the video, which she aired today." Emma's lips thinned to narrow line. "She spun an ugly story. Left out the fact you fought for your life."

Catherine leaned forward, dropping her head in her hands. "God, it's worse than I thought."

"I called the station manager. Gave him an earful." Emma stood and jammed both balled up hands in the pocket of her housedress. "He's responsible for that woman telling half-truths. They ought to be ashamed that she's on the payroll. And let me tell you, I intend to see what I can do about her."

Catherine's bottom lip trembled. Emma's caring touched a place in her heart. "Thank you for standing up for me."

"You're welcome. So what's the plan?"

"There's nothing I can do. He won't listen."

"That's an excuse to give up and run. You love Matt? Stand and fight."

While Emma talked, an idea formed in Catherine's mind. "Maybe I can help him before I leave. I'll set the record straight."

"I wish you'd rethink moving on. Don't give up on your dreams."

Catherine's promise to eat something was the only reason Emma went home. The idea of food made Catherine's stomach cramp. She crawled in on Matt's side of the bed, burying her face in his pillow. His scent surrounded her. She closed her eyes. Not to think, not to regret, not to remember. To plan.

She couldn't allow Matt to suffer for her lies. Tomorrow after Emma drove her to town to pick up her car, Catherine would go to the television station and then to the newspaper offices. Somebody would listen to her side of the story. She'd make them hear the truth. She'd explain that she'd kept the truth from him. Maybe she could stop the people of his county from holding him responsible for her mistakes. She'd broken Matt's trust and lost him. The least she could do was try to save his reputation.

****

The growl of Ash's sports car rumbling down the driveway brought mumbled cuss words from Matt. The barn was his refuge, a place to be quiet, so he ignored the banging up at the house and Ash's persistent shouts. Avoiding him was impossible, and within minutes, Ash followed Benedict Arnold into the barn.

"Smart dog. I asked him where the idiot was, and damned if he didn't lead me right to you."

"You like him? Take him to Houston with you." Matt smeared more leather wax onto his rag and continued polishing one of the saddles sitting on sawhorses.

Ash sat a six-pack on the ground, pulled the tabs off two beers, and placed one in front of Matt. "How are things?"

He leveled a gaze at Ash that would've sent a normal person a message. Knowing his bull-headed friend would ignore it, Matt added, "Don't fucking start with me."

"Is it your intention to rub the design off the skirt of that saddle?"

"It's mine. Bought and paid for."

"Yes, sir, if that's the case, it does belong to you. And I see you bought two." Ash walked over, swung a leg over the other sawhorse, and eased down on the second saddle. "The seat is a mite small on this one, must be for a woman." He wiggled his butt a few times, hopped off, and studied the construction. "What'll you do with it now?"

"You can have the damn thing, if you'll take it and the dog, and leave me the hell alone."

"You bought this for Catherine. Right?"

Matt whipped his head around at the sound of her name. His gut was on fire, life in shambles, and he desperately wanted to punch somebody. Ash was dangerously close to becoming the prefect target.

"Now you're my shrink? You want me to talk about my problems? Well, fuck off."

Ash ran his hand down the suede seat and across the padded rise on the front of the saddle made especially for a female rider. Matt had driven to San Antonio and handpicked this one for Catherine. Sparks shot to his brain when Ash's big paw rubbed back and forth. A pang of jealousy knifed through Matt straight to his belly.

"I'll bet you've been shopping for two horses."

"Ash," Matt ground out the words. "You go too far."

"The man I know wouldn't do this for an ordinary woman. That same man made plans. Long term plans. Probably bought two horses." Apparently impervious to the fact he was close to getting his ass kicked, Ash continued speaking. "When are they being delivered?"

Matt answered without thinking. "Sunday."

"Bingo! No man does all this for a woman...unless he's in love with her."

Ash's words hit their target like a sniper's bullet. Hard, fast, and piercing. Matt threw the can of leather wax across the barn. He flexed his fingers, closed them tight, then quickly released the tension. No way could he swing at Ash, not after all they'd been through.

Matt backed up, relaxed his knees, and slid down the wall. "I knew before I opened my mouth that you leaving me alone was out of the question."

"If I thought you'd do the right thing, I would." Ash brought Matt his beer and joined him on the ground. "You're sitting in the middle of a shit-storm. Lots of people watch TV, some watch Sylvia Horning. After you left, Sue couldn't keep up with the phone calls. People demanded answers. Some wanted your badge. Interesting enough, most of them supported you. They're pissed at Horning's underhanded methods."

"I could care less what the public is saying. Let them talk. If they want my badge, they'll have to hold a special election. I'm not leaving."

"Good to know. Now, how will you fix your real problem?"

Matt leaned his head back and banged the wall a couple of times. "There's no other problem. I handled that this afternoon. End of story. I expect you to be at work in the morning. I'm driving to San Antonio tomorrow for Jessie's autopsy, and then I'll head to the office. You and Rey can hunt for JC's hidden cabin."

"Not so fast. If my deductive powers serve me well, and they're superior, you screwed up royally with Catherine. You better get over your pride before it's all you have to keep you warm." Ash opened himself another beer.

"You don't know what happened between me and Catherine this afternoon."

"Duh." Ash huffed out his irritating disgusted noise before he continued. "You're here with me and not at her place."

"Stop right there. She had over six weeks to tell me she'd killed her husband. I asked her what caused the nightmares and why she moved from one town to the next. She had plenty of chances. It was too much fun playing the sheriff for a fool. I not only acted like an idiot in private, I did it out in public."

"I thought you didn't care what people thought. Did you at least ask her why?"

"Hell, I don't think she's a cold-blooded murderer. It didn't me take long to figure out somebody had mistreated Catherine. She should have told me. Trusted me. Instead when I asked her questions, she sidestepped the issue." He shook his head in disgust. "She lied to me."

Ash stood and tossed his two empty cans into the trash barrel. "Okay. You win. She lied. Kept a secret. You fell in love with who she is, not who she used to be. I never thought I'd say this, you're a fool if you let this one get away."

Matt stared into the eyes of the friend who'd been there for him so many times. He'd never seen pity in Ash's gaze. Tonight, sympathy tinged with disappointment radiated from his face.

"Keep the dog." Ash's tone brimmed with anger. "You need a friend."

Ash's words fell heavy on Matt. "You don't understand. I told her things I've never told you." He dropped his head in his hands. "Spilled my guts to her. Trusted her. Too bad the feeling wasn't mutual." The silence was deafening. Now of all times, Ash had nothing to say? When Matt looked up he was alone. A few minutes later the fancy sports car roared off into the night.

Matt straightened up the barn and headed to the house. The small sliver of a moon surrounded by millions of stars offered no answers when he stopped and looked up for help.

"Come on, Benedict." He patted his leg, and the traitorous dog followed him in the house.

He'd told Catherine the day they met he didn't like being played. And that's exactly what she'd done, played him for a fool. Could he go on with his life and be happy without her? Did he want to? She'd looked inside him, looked deep under all the layers of bullshit and saw the man he was and still fell in love with him.

Surrendering to fatigue, he went to his bedroom, undressed, and lay flat of his back across the mattress. There in the silence, in the total darkness of night, memories of Catherine slammed into him in giant tidal waves. Her scent, vanilla. Her wild, unruly long hair, silken wildfire. Her laughter, sunshine. Her taste, pure honey.

His imagination brought her back to him. Her hand slid across his chest and rested over his heart. The pressure weighed him down. He cursed and flipped over on his belly, one arm dangled over the side of the bed. A soft, damp nose nuzzled the palm of his hand. A warm tongue licked his fingers. The dog that for months wouldn't let Matt touch him— the same mutt that fell in love with Catherine at first sight, Benedict Arnold—had come to offer comfort.

Chapter Twenty-Eight

"I wish you'd let me fill your car with gas or pay for having it serviced." Catherine thanked Emma for her generosity. She prayed Emma would stop talking about Matt.

"Nonsense. I'm glad I could help." She glanced at Catherine, her eyebrows pulled together over her driving glasses. "I wish you'd let me come with you to the newspapers and especially that blasted TV station."

"I have to do this by myself. I've caused Matt a lot of trouble he doesn't deserve." Catherine blinked her eyes rapidly.

Putting "no more tears" back on her *Never* list was an important step today. Showing weakness in front of Sylvia Horning would get the same reaction as throwing chum in a shark tank.

Emma parked in front of the garage and turned to Catherine. "So your mind is made up?"

"Yes, ma'am. I have to try to get the truth out to the public. Then I'll come home and start packing."

"I wish you wouldn't leave."

Catherine studied the crease in her linen slacks to keep from facing Emma. "He'll be much better off with me out of the picture. People will forget quicker if I'm not around as a reminder."

"When and where will you go?"

"I'll work this weekend. The tips from the bar will help restock my travel funds." She covered Emma's hand with hers. "But you're not getting rid of me. I love you, and I promise to stay in touch."

The disbelief in Emma's eyes made the lump in Catherine's throat too large to continue. She opened the car door before leaning across and kissing Emma's cheek.

"I'll see you back at the house after my soul- baring interviews."

Catherine settled the strap to her purse over her shoulder and went into the garage office to pay the repair bill. Her hand shook when she handed over the money. Her old car had better run like new. The woman in the office led her outside where the mechanic walked over and opened her car door.

She recognized him from the Saddleback. He was the friend JC had recommended to fix her car, but she decided not to mention JC's death. "Danny, isn't it?"

"Yes, ma'am. The car's ready to go, and the AC's also working fine."

"Thank you. I'm leaving in a few days. I need it to be dependable." She patted the top of her car then slid into the comfortable feeling of an old friend.

Catherine pulled out onto the street and mentally rehearsed what she'd say to that bitch at the TV station. The main thing would be to keep her temper in check. Catherine wanted to tell Sylvia how much damage and pain her news story had caused, but that wasn't today's mission. There was a story to be told, and if the media would listen, maybe the rest of the people would too.

Catherine yawned and fought back exhaustion. The nightmares had returned with a vengeance last night. The confusing mess of horrible images made rest impossible. She slammed on her brakes barely stopping at a red light. Her reaction time seemed to move in slow motion. Yet when her cell rang, she jumped. "Hello."

"This is Danny from the garage. I think my wallet fell out when I test drove your car. I can't find it here at the shop."

"Let me pull over and check." Catherine stopped on the shoulder of the road and felt around on the seat. She opened the door, stepped out, finding nothing. She told Danny to hold, and then she set her phone down. Catherine squatted beside the car and ran her hand under the seat. Sure enough, she pulled a man's billfold out in her hand. She grabbed the phone. "Danny. I found it. I'll bring it back to the garage."

"I'll take it."

She jumped and whirled, striking at the sound of a male voice standing right behind her. Danny stood just out of reach. She clapped her hand over her heart and gasped for breath. "Damn. I could've hurt you. How'd you know where I was?"

He slid a gun from his pocket and aimed it at her. "I followed you. Turn the phone off and toss it on the seat."

"Danny. No." Catherine jerked her head to the side looking for an escape route or someone to shout out to. He pointed the gun at her heart.

"Goddammit. Don't ruin this." His chest heaved, and he leaned close to her face. "Don't you dare. Understand?"

She nodded. His eyes were glassy, and his hand trembled. "Now what?

"Get in my pickup." His hand wrapped around her arm in a bruising grip. He pulled her to the driver's side, opened the door, and then shoved her in. "Over there. Get on the floor."

Catherine's pulse hammered, but she did as instructed, anything to put distance between them. She folded her knees up to fit in the small space. With the gun aimed between her eyes, he drove away. Random thoughts rushed through her mind.

Did anyone see what happened? Had they called the sheriff's office? If they had, Matt would come. No matter how angry he was with her. Matt would come.

"Talk to me, Danny. What's going on? Please don't get yourself into trouble. Somebody might have seen us. The sheriff is probably on the way. Pull over and let me out. No hard feelings. Okay?" A compulsion to speak, to reason with him had taken over. "Stop right here before it's too late."

"Shut up," he screamed. "That cocksucker isn't smart enough to find his dick in the dark. He don't scare me none. Keep talking and I'll drop by and pay a visit to that old bitch you seem to be so crazy about. How long's it been you think since she's had a good fuck?"

Fear for Emma rocketed through her nervous system. Catherine fought to control her bladder. She pulled her panic inside. She'd learned while in the woman's shelter how to diffuse or at least slow down a temper tantrum. Her martial arts training taught her how to remain calm and defend herself. At the first opportunity, she'd put those to the test.

His gun hand shook. Sweat ran down his neck. The inside of the truck was sweltering.

"You forced me to move too fast. Made me change plans. After that news story broke, getting you alone was gonna be impossible. You're a big time celebrity now everybody knows you killed your husband. Let me say, you won't get that chance with me. You've been a naughty doll."

"If I did something to upset you...." Her words trailed off. Mouth went dry. One word stopped her cold. Doll.

"Oh. You finally catching up? Well, I don't have time to explain. I've got to get back to work. Can't have the boss start wondering about me. You and me gonna get a few things straight later tonight."

Danny shot her a look, eyes flat, his lips turned down into a snarl. She clamped a hand over her mouth to keep from throwing up. The blood rushed from her head, and she struggled to hang on to the light. She refused to blackout. The way to survive was to stay alert and pay attention to everything. Learn as much as possible. A quick glance at her watch said they'd been driving for twenty minutes. Which direction? Where to?

The odors in the cab of his truck nauseated her. The smell of fear and hate coupled with the raw heat from the sun beating down on the pickup pitched her stomach into turmoil. She gagged.

"Don't you puke in my truck."

"I'm cooking down here. My clothes are stuck to my body. If you don't turn the air on, I might not be able to control myself."

"Put your hands under your ass." He waved the pistol at her.

"What?"

"Sit on your hands or sweat. Your choice."

After Catherine managed to wiggle her hands far enough under her to satisfy him, he held the gun and fiddled with the air conditioner buttons at the same time. She held her breath. How easy it would be for him to accidently squeeze the trigger. The air came on full blast, but she couldn't feel much from her position. Danny had the vents pointed straight at his face. He stretched his neck and the blood ran from her head. Scratches. Dear God.

When the pickup left the pavement, Catherine paid close attention. The road was filled with potholes. A few minutes later, Danny stopped and let out a big sigh.

"We're home. Safe and sound."

The change in him sent ice crystals spiraling up Catherine's spine. He'd morphed in front of her eyes from an angry, desperate lunatic to an excited child.

He turned the engine off and ran around to her side. "Easy getting out. Let me help." He slid his sweaty hands under her arms and pulled her to her feet. "It's not much, but it's private."

Catherine scanned the outside of the mobile home and its surroundings. She couldn't see the road from where she stood. He'd isolated her somewhere deep in a heavily wooded area. No—in a thicket. Matt's words came to mind. He and his men tried to search a thicket on JC's property. JC and Danny couldn't have been partners. Could they? Was Matt searching this area? Hope rose and soared through her heart.

"Go in the house, Catherine. You're looking for a way out. Believe me when I tell you there isn't one. You can scream your lungs out. Ain't nobody gonna hear." The glint behind his eyes turned icy. "So forget escape."

He held her hand and led her in the house. "You'll be happy here with me. You made it clear you wanted me. Out here it's just the two of us."

He shoved her down on a bed and jerked one of her shoes off. She watched in horror while he snapped a handcuff around her ankle. The metal bit into her skin, but she refused to cry out.

"I've got to get back to work. Bathroom's right there. Make use of it as you see fit."

Danny hurried to the kitchen and a few minutes later returned with a Dairy Dream cup containing a drink poured over ice. "In case you get thirsty before I get back. This'll have to tide you over."

Without another word, he left. Catherine squeezed her eyes shut, breathing deeply for a second. Images of what could happen when Danny returned flashed through her mind. Grasping onto a thread of reason, she refused to believe it was her time to die.

She looked around the bedroom. A small chest of drawers was wedged into one corner, a closet with mirrored sliding glass doors, and the bed filled the space. Three women had been raped and murdered. Had those women died on the mattress where she now sat?

"Shit." Catherine jumped and ran. The small chain attached to the handcuff tangled around her foot and sent her crashing to the floor face first. She scrambled backward into the hall, unable to wrench her gaze away. The bedroom was a death chamber. A tremor rocked her body, and what felt like millions of ants stung under her skin.

Now wasn't the time to lose control. She pulled herself together and inspected the cuff around her ankle, ignoring the bruise already forming. She tugged at the chain, stood, and followed it back to its origin. The damn thing ran under the bed and through a small hole in the floor. It had to be anchored to something underneath the trailer.

Catherine pushed herself to her feet and walked the length of her tether. She could make it to the bathroom sink and toilet. Fully aware the other women had probably done the same, she methodically conducted a search for anything to use as a weapon or a way to unlock the cuff. The places she couldn't walk to, she scanned carefully.

She tested the drink Danny left for her. It tasted like stale, bitter iced tea, but at least it was cold and wet. Before the second swallow, a memory of something she'd seen on the kitchen counter blasted into her mind. She retraced her steps down the hall and studied the kitchen counter. A medicine bottle and capsules lay on the counter. A few of them had been pulled apart.

"You should've put those up before you left to get back to work. Got in a hurry, didn't you?" Careful not to let the ice fall in the toilet, she poured out the liquid contents of the drink. The cup with the ice was laid on its side next to the deathbed. Catherine sat on the floor and planned her escape. She'd be ready when Danny returned.

****

Ash looked up from reading the report from Jessie's autopsy. "If she scratched JC, they had to have been under his clothes."

"Reinhardt sent everything he dug out from under her fingernails to the feds. Now we wait. Too bad she didn't gouge an eye out, make him easier to ID."

Matt's eyelids felt like raw sandpaper every time he blinked. No sleep for him last night. He and the dog had tried to sort out how their life had gotten so messed up. Benedict had stuck to Matt's side, rubbing his head against Matt at every opportunity. He'd picked up on Matt's pain, and they'd connected through their mutual loss.

"Old buddy, you need to get some rest. You look like crap."

"Don't mother me," Matt growled.

Ash had his mouth open when the conference room door opened, and Jake stepped inside. "You have an emergency call." He nodded at the phone on the conference room table. "Line one. It's Emma Williamson."

Matt punched the button and had Emma on the speaker before Jake finished his sentence. "Matt here. What's up?"

"It's Catherine. She hasn't come back, and I'm getting worried. She should've already dressed for work and gone to the Saddleback."

"Come back from where?" Matt asked.

"The newspaper offices and TV station. She went to set the record straight."

"How early? What record?" Matt stood, and the hair on his arms rose with him.

"I drove her to town so she could pick up her car around eight this morning. Her first stop should've been before nine. Catherine was determined to tell her side of the story and make it clear you had no knowledge of her past. Then she was coming home, and..." Emma paused.

"Go on." Matt shoved his cell across to Ash. "Call Catherine," he whispered. Without hesitation, Ash scrolled through to a number and pushed Call.

"She was coming home to start packing."

"Emma, listen carefully. Get a pen and write down my cell. If you see her pull in the driveway or contacts you, call me. You said she was driving her car again?"

"Yes. I don't know her license plate number."

"I'll get it." Matt's mind jumped from thought to thought. Ash laid the cell down and shook his head. "Emma, I promise, you'll hear as soon as I know something." Matt disconnected.

Jake stood in the doorway, listening, his face was somber. "I checked with Marty while you were on the phone. She hasn't talked to Catherine. Marty had called, got voicemail."

"Thanks. You're always two steps ahead of me." Matt combed his hands through his hair and pushed back the gnawing in his gut.

Ash and Jake stood shoulder-to-shoulder in front of his desk. Matt tried to convince himself that with his dedicated men on his side they'd find her. "Let's try to locate her car and her phone."

"Matt," Jake said in his calm and steady voice. "I'll get a BOLO and a GPS trace on the cell started right away. You have to let me take point. You're too close."

"I can't. If she's done something crazy, it's my fault." Matt leaned back in his chair and tried to catch his breath.

"You think she could've gotten in and out without Emma seeing her?" Ash theorized. "Maybe she wanted to avoid a tearful goodbye. She might already be gone."

"I need to know." He pushed away and started for the door. Matt had to be sure she wasn't in trouble. Had he driven her out of town? Given the way he'd behaved, he wouldn't blame her for leaving.

Ash followed with hunched shoulders and hands stuffed into his pockets. Matt read the signs of worry on his old partner.

Matt stopped at Sue's desk on the way out. "Tell Jake to fill you in. He can call or radio me with any information he comes up with." He ignored the questions in her eyes. There wasn't time to explain.

Jake radioed Matt before they reached Catherine's house. They'd located her car. He spun the cruiser around and headed for the address. It was a few blocks away from the courthouse and a mile from the garage where her car had been repaired. He sent a deputy to the garage with instructions to talk to everyone there who'd spoken to her. Had she seemed upset? Mentioned leaving town?

"Sonofabitch. The motherfucker has her." Matt slapped the hood of her car. "I knew JC wasn't the killer."

"You're no good to us if you lose it."

"Don't treat me like I'm some ordinary husband who doesn't know jack-shit. The murdering bastard has her." The words sliced him wide open, the truth made him bleed inside. "Her car's empty, her cell and purse left behind. It's the same damn MO." The sharp pain in Matt's chest was rivaled only by the flood of fear racing through his veins.

He snatched his vibrating cell off his hip and hope flared. Emma was calling. "Did Catherine call?" "No. There's something you should see. I'd like you to come to my house."

"Emma." Matt tried to put her off.

"No, Sheriff," she interrupted. "This is important."

Chapter Twenty-Nine

Emma ran out the front door to Matt. "Did you find her?" Her face was pale, her eyes wide with hope.

"Not yet." He stepped out and walked to meet Emma, keeping his tone reassuring as possible. "What did you want me to see?"

Ash joined them. "May we take a look in the little house while we're here?"

"If it will help." Her hand fluttered in the direction of the main house. "The extra key's on a nail by the back door. I'll get it."

Ash was already moving. "Let me." He sprinted up on the back porch and into Emma's home.

"You wanted to show me something." Matt drew her attention back to him. She was frustrated and scared, and he tried to be patient.

Ash burst out of her back door. "Got it."

"Go with him," Emma said. "I'll bring it to you." Matt wanted to argue, but instead he went with Ash.

Matt walked past Catherine's bathroom. "Shit," he hissed. His fear rocketed to terror. Pain slashed through his gut, a scalpel slicing away at hope. Her makeup, hair dryer, everything, reminded him of how stupid he'd been. He had to find her.

"Sheriff?" Emma called from the front porch. Matt turned on his heel and went to Emma, who held a small wooden box in her hands. She handed it to him then backed away. Indecision played across her face.

"I hope I'm doing the right thing. She left this with me for safekeeping. She was afraid you'd find it before she had a chance to tell you, but now things are out in the open. It's my opinion that you need to read this."

Matt fought back his need to rejoin the search for Catherine. Emma believed this information was important, so he sat on the love seat and opened the box.

He picked up the document on top and read a physician's sworn statement regarding the abuse of Catherine Marie McCoy Andrews. Cracked ribs. Multiple times treated for bruised kidneys. Contusions, all carefully placed where no one would see. The night she shot and killed her husband, she had choke marks on her neck. She'd almost died.

The weight of the world slowly pressed him further and further down. He studied the sworn statement from a women's shelter in Tulsa where she'd sought refuge, and then found a job before moving to her own place. Tears for her suffering threatened, causing him to close his eyes and concentrate.

How could he have been so bull-headed?

He was vaguely aware of Ash sitting down, clamping a strong hand on Matt's shoulder. He forced himself to continue reading. Ash handed him an arrest warrant for Catherine and a couple of news stories in direct contradiction to the doctor's deposition. On the bottom of the pile, Matt found a document from the Oklahoma Grand Jury finding Catherine killed her estranged husband in self-defense.

"She'd made it out, found a job, and started a new life. This crazy bastard hunted her down and tried to kill her." Ash's voice dropped as he spoke, filled with compassion.

"My God. What she went through." Matt threw the papers back into the box. "I had no doubt if she took his life she had no other choice. But hell no, I wouldn't listen. For a second time in her life, a man, and the law let her down. One tried to kill her and the other ran her out of her home into a killer's arms." He searched Ash's face for answers or hope and found neither.

"I'm sorry, man," Ash said, his tone troubled. Matt jerked his vibrating cell to his ear. "Talk."

"We've got something," Jake said, excitement riding high in his voice. "The deputy I sent to the garage talked to the owner. He remembered Catherine picking up her car but didn't notice her acting weird or nervous. She paid her bill and left. Here's the kicker, Danny Mason left right after she did. He came back a couple of hours later, but wasn't worth a shit for the rest of the day. Matt, he has scratches on his neck."

Matt ran for the cruiser, Ash at his side. "Sonofabitch. We've got him."

"I sent a car, he's not at home," Jake continued.

"Search his apartment. Ash and I are on our way."

"I've already called the judge and got a verbal on a warrant. Rey will meet us there."

Matt disconnected. "Goddammit. I should've dug deeper into Danny Mason."

"Didn't you do a follow up after Jake talked to him?"

"Yeah. I talked to him and Mel Hamilton. Both checked out clean."

"You had no way of knowing. Stop kicking yourself in the ass."

Matt called Sue and updated her quickly. "I want to know everything about this bastard. If he has Catherine, we have to figure out where. Fast."

****

A door slam sent Catherine's brain whirring. The time had come to fight back. She wouldn't die peacefully. She wanted to live, to make things right for Matt. No way was she giving up. She loved him, and that knowledge strengthened her. She would escape. Catherine grudgingly lay down on the disgusting bed and draped her arm to look as if the cup had fallen from her hand, and the ice had melted where it landed.

She'd prayed Danny would return while it was daylight, but it was dark inside the trailer. Adrenaline pumped through her veins, and her heart beat too fast. She was awake and alert. He had to believe she was still drugged or her plan would fail. She slowed her breathing and forced her eyes closed.

The light came on down the hall and footsteps came closer. Her insides were on fire, but she lay still as death.

"Wake up."

When Catherine felt Danny's hand on her rib cage, she bit down on the inside of her mouth to suppress a scream. He shook her, and she feigned a groggy look by batting her eyes rapidly before slowly looking up at the face looming over her. "I'm awake." She purposely slurred her words. "What happened?"

"It's time you learned the house rules." He grasped her shoulders tightly and shook hard.

Tremors shot through her body, and she couldn't control the twitching. She had to convince him to take the cuff off her ankle. Then she'd escape or he would kill her, but he wouldn't rape her. Not while she was alive. No more surrendering her self- respect. No more submitting to humiliation. These were numbers one and two on the *Never* list.

"Rules?" she said with a slight slur.

An odd noise startled her, pulled her gaze to him. Danny slapped himself on the leg with a piece of wire. Smack. Smack.

"What the fuck's wrong with you? That shit should've worn off by now." He pulled her upright. "Get up and go wash your face. Snap out of it, or you'll get a taste of Mama's hanger."

She stood and found wobbling her knees didn't have to be faked. He pushed her toward the bathroom, and she meekly followed his instructions. Catherine struggled against the blood boiling through her veins. The urge to panic competed with the knowledge she had to remain calm when she stumbled back into the hall. Controlling her fear was more difficult than she'd imagined.

His gaze raked across her body and settled on her breasts. His hand covered her left breast and squeezed hard. She sucked in a gasp of air from the pain. Tears filled her eyes, and his lips curved upward. His eyes and his mouth screamed satisfaction that he'd hurt her. This was the look of a lunatic. One she was all too familiar with. He wanted her to be terrified.

"Don't hurt me. Tell me the rules." The words jarred old memories. She'd delivered them with a remembered sincerity.

The blow to the side of her head came so fast and unexpectedly she cried out with surprise and pain. Her ear rang from the percussion and stars swirled in the blackness in front of her eyes. He followed with a stinging smack of the wire across her thigh.

"Rule one. You're here to please me. You don't tell me what to do."

Danny went to the kitchen and opened a cabinet. He removed a red ribbon and a tube of lipstick, placing them on the counter. Next came a pair of scissors. His erection bulged, straining against his jeans as he massaged himself.

Catherine's blood rushed to her brain, and she fought back the scream rising in her throat.

"I'm going to cut you out of those clothes." He waggled the scissors in his hand.

"I'll take them off for you." She attempted a lopsided smile, trying to look subservient. .

His lip curled, and he advanced a step toward her. "Have you decided to be nice to me?"

"I'll do exactly what you say." She intentionally rubbed her thigh to show him her pain.

"You behave and we'll have some fun."

"Okay. Let's have some fun." She rubbed her hand across her eyes, staggered, bracing against the wall for support. She had to make him believe the drug still had a strong hold on her.

He lay the scissors down then reached behind his back and pulled the gun from his belt. Escape would be easy if she could get her hands on the pistol, but he wasn't stupid. She had to catch him off guard, but he pushed her backward until she fell on the bed. He pointed the gun at her, pulled a small key out of his pocket, and then tossed it on the mattress.

"Unlock the cuff and then strip. Do it right, or I'll punish you. Got it?" He followed with a smack of the wire on his own leg.

She nodded her understanding but deliberately fumbled with the handcuff, stopping once to rub her face and push her hair out of her eyes. Catherine removed the one remaining shoe she wore then pushed herself up on her knees and unzipped her wrinkled slacks. She stole a glance at Danny. His free hand busily stroked the front of his pants. The gun pointed in her direction, but his gaze and attention were between her legs. She stood up, and then hooked her thumbs in the sides and wiggled out of her pants.

Catherine welcomed the surge of adrenaline rocketing through her system. The stronger the flow the more physical power she'd have.

With one leg, she kicked the slacks at Danny's head. Then she launched herself using the mattress as a springboard. The heel of her hand missed his nose, but her body slammed solidly into him. Pain shot through her shoulder when they hit the floor. The gun flew out of his hand, and she focused on its path as it skittered out of reach. When the pistol slid to a stop, she scrambled for it, but Danny recovered quickly and grabbed her foot. She kicked hard and pulled herself away. All she needed was a few more inches, when she felt the grip under her hand there was no hesitation. Catherine rolled and fired. The pistol jumped in her hands, the recoil vibrated up her arm, and the noise bounced off the walls of the trailer.

Danny fell backward. He struggled to his feet, and one hand went to the wound in his chest. His eyes went wide and wild when he screamed with fury. "You bitch. I'll kill you." His face contorted into pure evil.

He staggered toward her, grabbed at her arm, knocking the gun out of her hand. Catherine struck out with her foot. The force of the blow sent a sharp pain up her leg when she connected with his right kneecap. He howled and stumbled sideways, giving her needed seconds to reach the door first. She ran outside and down the long, dirt driveway into the darkness. Barefoot, wearing nothing but a cotton blouse, a bra and panties, she hurled herself forward blindly.

The night was silent except for her heart pounding and labored breathing. She couldn't slow down. He could be right behind her. At the end of the driveway, confusion hit her. Which way to safety? She scanned the horizon, found nothing but darkness. No lights or nearby homes to seek shelter.

The sliver of a moon offered no help, and dark eerie clouds covered most of the stars.

Danny's pickup roared to life forcing her to make a decision. Catherine stepped onto the road and felt the warm pavement under her bare feet. Relief washed over her, a paved road meant civilization. Which direction? With no time to debate, she turned left and ran as fast as she could. What seemed like seconds later, the screech of tires warned her. She stole a quick glance over her shoulder. Shit! He'd chosen the same direction she had, and his headlights were coming up behind her. Fast. She couldn't continue down the middle of the road. He was gaining ground. She had no choice but to cut across the ditch and run headlong into the woods.

The sound of his engine dying and the door slamming sent a warning. He was coming for her. She ran with all her strength, fighting the urge to look back.

"You crazy bitch. I'll kill you. It's you, me, and the rattlesnakes."

She never broke stride, plunging deeper into the dark trees, which were nearly impassable. Given a choice between Danny and rattlers, the snakes won hands down. Damn, if she'd only managed to get to the gun.

Danny coughed a couple of times. He'd followed her into the ticket, but it was impossible to tell exactly which direction the sound came from. Fear rocketed through her blood. She couldn't go back, and she couldn't see to go forward. Using her hands to feel her way, she pressed on. Thorns jammed into her feet. She tripped and fell to her knees in the underbrush. The flesh on her legs and arms ripped and Catherine failed to stifle her moan. Had her gasp told Danny where to find her? She gritted her teeth, got up, and pressed deeper into the darkness. Getting caught meant sure death, and she was not ready to die.

Oppressive heat stole her breath. Not a hint of a breeze found its way to give relief. Catherine tried to swallow, but her mouth and throat were parched and dry. Blood trickled down from where the undergrowth and mesquite thorns cut her flesh. Sweat covered her body. Every scratch burned from the salt. A tree limb snagged and pulled at her hair, but she didn't stop. She jerked the knot of hair loose and bit back the urge to cry out in pain. Leaves crackled and snapped with her every step, the sound echoed like gunshots.

How far had she travelled? In which direction? Mosquitoes and flies flocked to her drying blood, sweat, and the smell of fear. Still, she moved forward. Or did she? In this darkness, for all she knew, she'd been stumbling around in circles for hours.

The dry, barren trees looked like arms reaching out to grab her. None large enough to offer protection, they were mere outlines. She stopped and listened. The sounds surrounded her, seemingly from every direction. Unwilling to take chances, she kept moving until she stumbled onto what appeared to be a clearing. Catherine knelt down at the base of a tree and listened for the dull roar of car or truck engines. Nothing but the background music of crickets and the constant buzzing of bugs broke the silence. She remained in her position for what seemed like hours, jumping at each rustle of the leaves and readying herself for a fight. Pain in her knees forced her to rise occasionally, but here was where she would take a stand.

****

"Jesus Christ. How could we not have known about Danny's mother?" Matt tightened his grip on the steering wheel and pressed his foot on the gas pedal, praying this lead would pan out.

"Just be glad Sue remembered." Ash slammed his seat buckle home. "Sounded like Danny and his mama had been estranged for years."

"If Catherine is…" Matt couldn't force himself to say the word, "it will be my fault." The words had burned their way from inside his soul. A miserable failure, he couldn't protect, much less find, the woman he loved. The woman who'd be safe if he hadn't been such an ass.

"Don't start. Just concentrate on keeping this white tornado you're driving on the road," Ash grumbled.

They followed Jake and Rey because nobody knew the back roads better than those two. Jake turned off the main highway and headed out the farm-to-market. Matt radioed them to kill the lights and run silent.

His heart jack-hammered against his ribcage, reminding him that without Catherine, it had no reason to keep beating. The lead car slowed and a minute later, turned down a dirt driveway.

A trailer-house finally came into view. The night was pitch black except for the light shining through the open front door. Bile that had settled in the back of Matt's throat rose higher. His muscles tightened, ready to fight as he brought the cruiser to a stop. He jumped out, Ash at his heels. Matt held up a finger to silence his deputies.

Glock in hand, he quietly stepped through the doorway. His heart landed at his feet at the sight of blood smeared across the linoleum floor. A string of drops ended at the tip of his boot. Matt opened his mouth, but no words would come. Whose blood was he looking at? Please, God. Not Catherine's. Careful where he put his feet, he moved through the house.

Smells of urine, stale beer, and death assaulted his senses.

"You don't know it's Catherine's." Ash stood close, his tone a futile attempt to comfort.

"But it could be." Matt's throat closed, making it difficult to speak. Ash squeezed Matt's shoulder. He pulled away. The last thing he needed was sympathy.

"The place is empty." Matt called out to his deputies when he and Ash finished their search.

"We found a blood trail."

Matt hurried to where Jake pointed his flashlight in the driveway. The hard dirt provided the perfect path to follow for a few feet. Frustration exploded in Matt's head, he jerked his hat off, and swiped at the sweat on his forehead with his arm. He reached deep inside, clinging to the belief that she was alive. Maybe she was in pain, somewhere needing attention, needing him.

A search of the immediate area left Matt more baffled and frustrated than before. He had to assume Danny and Catherine had left in a vehicle. But which direction. Where to?

"We'll split up. Jake, you and Rey backtrack the way we came in. Ash and I'll go South."

Matt gave instructions, and Ash started the cruiser, waiting. Less than half a mile up the road, they spotted a pickup parked on the shoulder. Waves of dread spread through Matt's system.

"If that bastard has hurt Catherine, I'll kill him with my bare hands."

"Beating him to death is an option." Ash shined his light over the dried weeds.

Matt pointed his flashlight at the ground, working in tandem with Ash. A blood trail led straight into the roughest, darkest part of the thicket.

"Call Jake. I want a search party in these woods," Matt said. Battling back the fear and panic trying to claw its way to the surface, he pushed forward, ignoring the vines and thorns grabbing at his limbs. About a hundred feet in, Danny Mason lay sprawled in the weeds. A hole in his chest, his lifeless eyes staring into the dark.

"Catherine," Matt called out. Louder and louder each time. She had to be alive, maybe wounded, needing him to find her. Where was she? He couldn't lose her.

****

A sob rose up from Catherine's chest when the sky turned a golden hue. Slowly, minute by minute, the darkness receded as shards of orange and pink accompanied the rising of the sun and the no-where- but-Texas blue sky. Tears flowed unchecked at the sheer beauty of the birth of a new dawn and perhaps a chance to live. More than anything, she wanted the opportunity to make things right with Matt. No more running. For a life with him, she'd stay and fight.

She jumped to her feet at the sound of a bell in the distance. Fear moved her behind the skinny tree and away from the clearing. The clanging came closer and closer. A Holstein cow followed by two that looked identical walked right in front of her, completely oblivious to her plight. An old-fashioned cowbell hanging from a collar around the lead cow's neck rang a steady rhythm. Their udders were full and hung inches from the ground. Didn't matter if they were milked by hand or machine, human beings would be waiting for this small herd.

Catherine's hand flew to her mouth, and her lips trembled under her fingers. She was at the edge of somebody's pasture. But whose? Should she follow the small herd? Fear and hope warred in her heart. Should she walk into the open? Danny could be anywhere. Waiting. Watching.

Her mind and body rejected the thought of stepping out of her protected area where no trees or bushes provided a place to hide. Her insides rolled. If he was hiding in the shadows, she'd be an easy target. Would she feel the bullet? She had no doubt if Danny got the chance, he'd kill her. She'd be stripped bare without the thicket to hide her.

She had to make a decision, because the cows weren't waiting for her. Their mission was to go home. She couldn't let them get out of sight. Catherine gathered her courage and ran into the meadow. No sound followed. No gunfire. Only the bell, getting further away. She cried and laughed, ignoring the pain in her feet. She rushed to catch up. She had the same goal in mind as the little Holstein herd.

She gasped out a sob of relief when a white farmhouse loomed in the distance. This wasn't Danny's trailer. Adrenaline pumped renewed energy into her veins, and with a final burst of energy, she ran toward the silver haired woman who'd walked outside to the gate where the cows gathered.

"Pat," the woman screamed at the top of her lungs when Catherine came staggering toward her.

"Help me," Catherine shouted, waving her arms in the air to show she was unarmed and harmless. A man ran from a small barn with a rifle pointed right at her belly.

"Stop right there," he commanded.

"Please." Catherine tried to speak, but thirst scratched at the back of her throat, and her voice came out a whisper. She extended her arms, begging.

"I'll shoot you graveyard dead if you take another step," he yelled.

He studied Catherine from a distance while the sky darkened and dark clouds gathered overhead.

The wind stirred, blowing a hot breeze across her face. Catherine looked down at herself. Half-naked, filthy, bloody arms, legs, and feet and no doubt wild, tangled hair, she had to look like a mad woman.

"Get in the house and call the sheriff," he shouted to the woman. "You." He braced the rifle against his shoulder. "You stay right where you are." Catherine crumpled to the ground and curled into a ball, suddenly aware of how near naked she was. The tears she'd fought since Danny forced her into his pickup flowed freely. The silence she'd held herself to was broken by the sound of relieved sobs.

The farmer had uttered the one word she needed to hear. "Sheriff." He might not forgive her, but Matt would save her, because that's what he did. It's who he was. John Wayne would come.

****

Matt rushed past the old man and his wife straight to the body on the other side of the fence. He prayed as he ran. Before he cleared the gate, the red hair spread across the dry grass pulled a cry from him.

"Catherine!" he yelled, running while his heart shredded to slivers with each step. He threw his hat on the ground, fell to his knees, and pressed his face down next to hers.

"Catherine," he whispered, swallowing back the tears begging to escape. He laid his hand on her back. "You're safe."

She jerked away, slapping and kicking at his hands. Wild green eyes filled with unknown horrors searched his face. Her lips quivered as recognition skittered across her face. With the cry of a wounded animal, she scrambled toward him, her hands clawing him to her.

He pulled her onto his lap, shielded her with his arms, and rocked her as if she were a child. "Thank God, you're alive."

Matt's heart ached while her body trembled and shuddered. Pressing kisses across her forehead, he winced at the cuts, scratches, and bruises on her arms and legs. Her feet were torn and raw. "You're safe now. It's all over."

She sat up, eyes wide, and scanned the horizon, pointing her finger in the direction of the thicket. "No. He's out there. Danny. It was Danny, and he's hunting me."

"No, he's not."

"You don't know," she protested. "You don't understand."

"Listen to me, Cat. We identified Danny as the killer last night."

She hiccupped a breath and studied Matt's face. Had his nickname for her registered? Eased her fears?

"You've been searching for me?"

"Lots of folks hunted all night. Sue remembered Danny's mother had died and thought of her mobile home out in the woods." Catherine shuddered in his arms, her body shaking violently at the mention of the trailer. "We found his pickup on the side of the road and followed a trail of blood into the thicket. Did you shoot him?"

"Yes." She frowned.

"I'm so proud of you." Matt hugged her tighter. What she'd endured, he didn't know. But he'd spend the rest of his life making sure this brave woman never suffered again. If she'd let him.

A drop of rain fell and then another. Within a blink of an eye, the sky opened up and poured. As predicted, the drought had come to an end. He and Catherine looked to the sky at the dark thunderhead. She closed her beautiful green eyes, leaned her head back, and let the rain wash over her face.

Ash squatted beside them in the downpour as if this were any ordinary day. He smiled and pulled a patch of grass from Catherine's wet hair. "How would you like to ride to town in an ambulance?"

"I wouldn't. I'm fine now." She opened her eyes and studied Matt's face. "I knew you'd save me."

"No, honey. Danny's dead. You saved yourself." He removed his rain-soaked shirt and laid it over her chest when she tried to cover her bra with her shredded blouse. Pulling her closer, he let her rest until the EMTs made their way out to them.

"I've killed two men," she said on a sob. Her head buried against his shoulder.

"Both justifiable." He tipped her chin up, bracketed her face with his hands, and then kissed her. "Remember when I told you I loved you? I meant it. And if you'll forgive me, I'll prove it."

"I love you, too."

She tried to stand, but her legs wobbled like a newborn foal. When she reached out to him for support, the fear he'd been holding back broke to the surface. Matt waved off the EMTs and scooped her into his arms. She pressed her face into his neck, placed her hand over his heart, and rubbed in a small circle. He thanked the torrential downpour for hiding the tears he couldn't manage to hold back.

"You walked this far, I'll carry you the rest of the way."

Chapter Thirty

"I might as well have gone to the hospital," Catherine complained when Matt arrived to relieve Emma.

"Thanks for babysitting. I'll take over from here."

Emma leaned over and kissed Catherine on the cheek. "She's all yours, Matt. And she's not a good patient."

Catherine eavesdropped while Matt walked Emma to the door and discussed the healing of her feet like they were about to launch a space shuttle. Two weeks had passed, and Catherine was ready to get on with life. If she had to repeat her ordeal one more time, she'd scream. The nightmares would never go away if she didn't put the episode behind her.

The truth about her life was out for the free world to form their personal judgments. That Matt read the documents in her secret box hadn't troubled her, but he'd been beating himself up long enough for the judicial system's failure to protect her.

She'd had two brushes with death and came out a winner both times. Life couldn't deal her any blows she couldn't overcome, not as long as Matt loved her. And he'd spent the past two weeks telling her just how much.

"Shame on you for picking on such a sweet old woman."

Catherine's breath caught at the sight of him standing in the doorway. His lean, muscular body looked as if an artist sculpted it from granite, and luckily the same guy had carved his face. His broad shoulders, which she was convinced could carry any load, and lopsided grin which melted her with a glance, jetted her hormones south at record speeds.

"Sweet? She's a drill sergeant in disguise. She insisted I lie down and rest." Catherine patted the side of the bed. "But since I'm here..."

Matt stuffed his hands in his pockets and leaned back against the chest of drawers.

"I can't come over there. We have to talk."

"That's all we've done. Police reports and news stories have worn me out. I've purged my soul and my past to God and country. I have no more secrets to tell." She patted the bed again, amazed at how brazen she'd become. "And if you forgive me—"

"You're not the one who needs forgiveness," he interrupted. "I turned my back on you when you needed me. Will you ever be able to trust me completely?"

His incredibly blue eyes, so serious and so concerned drew her to him. She scooted to the edge of the mattress and held his steady gaze.

"I never stopped trusting you. But we've both learned valuable lessons about honesty between two people in love."

"So if I proposed, would you say yes?" His lips quirked up in a grin, and her heart rate hit the superhighway.

"I have one question before I can answer."

His face grew serious, and his eyes never left her face. "By all means, ask away."

"What would John Wayne do?"

"Nothing, he's dead." His eyebrows dipped into a scowl. "I'm being serious."

"So am I." She glared back at him.

He stood quietly for a minute. "You mean right now...if he was standing here instead of me?"

"Right now."

Matt pushed himself upright. His eyes sparkled with intrigue. "Can you wear boots?"

"I'm sure I can. Why?"

"Get dressed."

＊＊＊＊

He was taking one hell of a gamble to see if his idea would work. Was he supposed to channel the Duke to know what she wanted him to say? His insides were jumping, and his mind raced from thought to thought.

Matt had ushered her to the pickup. The fact she'd limped hadn't escaped him. Her feet hadn't healed completely. Had her heart? Only one way to find out.

He drove around the back way to his place. The short trip lasted an eternity because he felt her eyes bearing down on him all the way. He parked, walked around to her, and scooped her into his arms. He carried her to a chair in the house. "Wait here until I come to get you."

"I can walk, silly." She demonstrated by walking to the door and letting Benedict Arnold inside. "What am I waiting on?"

Matt leaned down, and Benedict stuck his muzzle in his hand. He absentmindedly scratched behind his ears.

Her gaze dropped, followed by her jaw.

"What?"

"Oh. My. God. He likes you."

"When I thought I'd lost you, he sensed my pain. Been at my heels ever since." Matt waved Catherine to a kitchen chair. "Remember, wait here. Don't come outside," Matt instructed in his firmest voice. "Promise me."

"Oka-ay." She arched one eyebrow, a smile playing at the corners of her lips. "I'm waiting."

Heart pounding, nerves racing, with Benedict at his side, Matt ran to the barn. Thirty minutes later, he glanced down at the dog. "It's now or never."

He stepped into the saddle, rode up the driveway, and called Catherine outside.

Eyes wide, jaw hanging lax. Priceless would describe her expression. But when he handed her the reins to the second horse, tears welled and ran down her cheeks.

"Oh, hell." Matt slid off his new bay gelding, wrapping Catherine in his arms. "You think I'm nuts. I'll put them back in the barn."

"This is your answer to my question?" She smiled up at him and brushed away her tears.

"Well, hell. Wouldn't John Wayne have put you on a horse and then ridden into the sunset with you at his side."

She stood on her tiptoes and covered his lips with hers. "That's exactly what he would've done."

The kiss sealed the deal as far as Matt was concerned. Anything else would be incidental, nothing they couldn't overcome together.

"What do you think? Want to give him a try?" Matt offered her the reins a second time.

"What's his name?"

Matt couldn't help himself. "Horse."

"You can't *not* give him a name." Her words mingled with her laughter.

"You're right. His official name's Poco Red Dawn."

Without his help, she swung into the saddle. "God. That's a mouthful."

"Yeah. It's Red for short."

"Red. I like it."

With a stab of her heels, she and Red ran toward the back pasture. Matt mounted and hurried to catch her.

Catherine slowed, leaned forward, and patted the big gelding on his neck. "I love him. And you."

Riding side-by-side, Matt turned and asked one last question. "I'd like Ash to be the best man at our wedding. You okay with that?"

"As long as you're there, I'm happy." Catherine kicked her horse in the flank, and the red gelding lunged forward. The wildfire-haired woman raced across his pasture on her sorrel horse, her face turned into the wind. She ran free. He'd gladly spend the rest of his life trying to keep up with her.

Also By Jerrie Alexander

Romantic Suspense
The Green-Eyed Doll
The Last Execution
Hell or High Water
Cold Day in Hell
No Chance in Hell
No Greater Hell
A Helluva Holiday
Till Justice is Served
Till the Dead Speak
Someone To Watch Over Me
Flirting With Fate
Skyway to Hell – coming soon

Contemporary Erotic Romance
Come Hard
Come Hot
Come Together
Come Undone

Meet Jerrie

A career in logistics offered me the opportunity to travel to many beautiful locations in America, and I revisit them in her romantic suspense novels.

I write romantic suspense and contemporary erotic romance with alpha males and kick-ass women who weave their way through life's obstacles to emerge stronger because of, and on occasion in spite of, their love for each other. I like to put my characters in difficult positions, make them suffer, and if they're strong enough, they live happily ever after.

My books are written as standalone with no cliffhangers.

www.ingramcontent.com/pod-product-compliance
Lightning Source LLC
Chambersburg PA
CBHW051410170626
46809CB00006B/2095